By the same author

Another Life

Oh, Sister

Oh, Sister

JODIE CHAPMAN

MICHAEL JOSEPH

PENGUIN MICHAEL JOSEPH

UK | USA | Canada | Ireland | Australia
India | New Zealand | South Africa

Penguin Michael Joseph is part of the Penguin Random House group of companies
whose addresses can be found at global.penguinrandomhouse.com

First published 2023
002

Set in 12/14.75pt Bembo Book MT Std
Typeset by Jouve (UK), Milton Keynes
Printed and bound in Great Britain by Clays Ltd, Elcograf S.p.A.

The authorized representative in the EEA is Penguin Random House Ireland,
Morrison Chambers, 32 Nassau Street, Dublin D02 YH68

A CIP catalogue record for this book is available from the British Library

HARDBACK ISBN: 978–0–241–45695–8
OPEN MARKET ISBN: 978–0–241–45696–5

www.greenpenguin.co.uk

For Sarah, my sister

Out of respect for my mother, I have changed the name of the religion.
Out of respect for myself, I have written this book.

A woman is always accompanied – except when quite alone, and perhaps even then – by her own image of herself. While she is walking across a room or weeping at the death of her father, she cannot avoid envisaging herself walking or weeping. From earliest childhood, she is taught and persuaded to survey herself continually. She has to survey everything she is and everything she does, because how she appears to others and particularly how she appears to men is of crucial importance, for it is normally thought of as the success of her life.

– John Berger, *Ways of Seeing*

The first feminist gesture is to say: 'OK, they're looking at me. But I'm looking at them.' The act of deciding to look, of deciding that the world is not defined by how people see me, but how I see them.

– Agnès Varda, *Filming Desire: A Journey Through Women's Film*, 2000, distributed by Women Make Movies, directed by Marie Mandy

Paradise

Brothers and sisters, I'd like you to join me in a little game.

Perhaps *exercise* is a better word. It's one that you know well, that you have played many times before. Get yourselves comfortable and close your eyes.

Imagine that Armageddon is over. The great day of our heavenly Father has come, and you are waking up in the new world. Can you hear the birds singing? They too are praising our Almighty God. In the air is the heavy scent of flowers and fruit ripening on the branch. Perhaps the bees are buzzing, woozy as they feast on nectar. Paradise. Can you feel it, brothers?

That limp you had – gone. The problems with your sight – vanished. The wheelchair you relied on and the medication you took daily – those have been thrown away. Your body is now perfect.

Fast-forward a year. You have staked out your land, a patch of earth to call your own. We don't need fences, gates or barbed wire in this world. We trust our neighbours. We no longer lock our doors like we once did. And as for our homes? Well, brothers . . . Imagine the home you will have created for your family. Built by your own hands. No mortgage to pay off; it is simply all yours.

Now imagine you are sitting in your garden, enjoying the fruits of your labour. Your wife has laid out a lunch of the finest foods. Can you imagine, sisters, the meals you will make with the food you have grown? No more trips to the supermarket, no more having to budget to feed your family. God will provide, and every meal will be a banquet.

As you break bread, you laugh and make plans for the day. You no longer live for the weekend. Every day is the weekend. Look about you. You have never been so happy. There is almost nothing more you could need.

But our Father has one more gift.

What's that? The squeak of the garden gate. It is faint, the sound, but you hear it. Look. Someone is there in the doorway.

We all have a different *someone*. Perhaps it is your mother or father, whom you've not seen in many years. Their skin is young again. Or your wife or husband, whom you nursed when they fell sick, and whom you promised to welcome back in Paradise. Or perhaps it's your little boy or girl, the one you have thought of every day since they fell asleep in death. Brothers and sisters, you promised you would be there when they woke, and there you are.

Now that they have returned, you can live together in peace forever. Just as the scriptures said.

Open your eyes. You are back from that world and once more in this one. Life is grey. When you leave here today, you will return to homes where the bank may own a bigger chunk than you, where your landlord is demanding rent which you are struggling to pay.

Brothers and sisters, my love goes out to you. We know what to do in times like these, don't we? *Pray.* Our heavenly Father knows what we endure, and He has promised us a new world to keep us going. So do *this* every day. Carve out five minutes – perhaps on the bus, or between doors on the ministry, or before you drift off to sleep each night – when you can close your eyes and imagine the Paradise earth that awaits us.

Call it an *exercise*, because it keeps us fighting fit. It keeps hope front and centre in our minds, so that we do not allow ourselves to become distracted in this time of the end. Death is not for us. We keep focused, determined not to be blown off course, and continue to run the race. Brothers, the time is near.

Keep your eyes on the prize.

– Excerpt from a talk by Brother Diaz,
a Disciple of the Last Days

You will know the truth, and the truth will set you free.

— John 8:32

PART ONE

Half a Heart
Zelda

'Has someone come with you for support today?'

Zelda doesn't hear the question. She is distracted by a shaft of light coming through the window that shines a perfect square on the blue rubber floor. Dust dances in the stale office air.

The nurse looks up from her clipboard. 'Is there someone waiting outside? A friend, a family member?'

'No,' Zelda says, folding her arms. 'That's okay, right? I'm only seven weeks, so thought I could just pop the pill and go.'

The nurse smiles, flicking the biro between her fingers. 'So I'm assuming the answer to the question of whether this is your first termination is "no"?'

She says it kindly, and Zelda wants to laugh. She remembers this woman from the last time, and, when she walked in and saw a familiar face, she felt a twinge of comfort. But the nurse has no memory of her. Zelda wonders how many women with electric-red hair dressed in men's clothes come to the clinic and whether she is really that easy to forget.

'Third time a charm,' says Zelda.

The nurse writes on the clipboard, her face free of judgement. She wears half a heart on a chain around her neck, and Zelda remembers her own, which her friend Leila gave to her at the turn of the millennium, soon after they left school. Zelda wonders who possesses the other half of the nurse's heart. She can hardly remember Leila now.

Outside, there is early-morning traffic, the sound of a truck reversing, people chatting in the street. The trees that line the pavement have yet to bloom, but the buds are there, waiting. Zelda lets the

3

door swing shut and pauses to light a cigarette. She pulls up her jacket collar against the breeze as she leans against a wall to smoke. A nearby radio talks of an impending snowstorm. *The Beast from the East.* Zelda turns her face towards the sun.

The pills are tucked into her pocket to take when she gets home. She hopes she still has enough whisky left to help knock them back. The cramps feel better when the edges are fuzzy, whatever the nurses say.

A passing woman gives her a filthy look. Maybe it's the cigarette, or the abortion-clinic backdrop. Zelda stares the woman out.

The sweet scent of cinnamon hangs in the air as she starts down the street. The reason for her heightened sense of smell does not escape her, and she decides to buy the thickest, flakiest pastry in an attempt to forget that, right now, her body is not entirely her own. She can hardly remember a time when it was.

Zelda is taking a bite when she turns the corner and sees them. She stops. There they are, up ahead, a trolley stand of brochures on the pavement, two women standing nearby with regulation smiles and knee-length skirts. She doesn't recognize them – she usually goes to a clinic in a different town – but they look like all the others. The banner on the trolley screams LIFE WITHOUT END – WHEN?

She starts to choke and steps back around the corner, pressing herself to the wall. She is too dizzy to notice her velvet jacket snagging on the brickwork.

A nearby alley gives shelter. Zelda has an overwhelming urge to be sick, and so she is, all down the side of a bright blue dumpster. Her vomit seeps on to the ground.

'Fuck's sake,' she says to the floor. 'All these years on and you still let them get to you.'

Blank Page
Jen

Jen dashes into the department store to escape the driving rain. Running is beyond her. She forgot to say goodbye to her feet before they disappeared, before new parts of her took over. Her cheeks, her thighs, her chest, her stomach. All blooming with water and life.

She picks up a leaflet to fan her face. Winter is cold inside the store, but sweat still creeps from her pores. She strips her layers as she walks to the back.

She has spent hours here. Wandering between aisles of cots and baths, and clothing that looks miniature. The volume of paraphernalia is overwhelming. Pete nearly gave up after an hour spent trying to collapse the buggy. What clichés we are, Jen had thought as she watched him. He loses his temper with inanimate objects, and I just want someone to massage my feet.

Jen often lingers, waiting for another mum-to-be. She pretends to smell lotions as she studies the women who look and move just like her. How they rest their hand on their stomach. How Breton stripes stretch over skin. She feels a kinship with these women. All her friends have had their babies, and have forgotten the feel of Braxton Hicks, the acidic twinge of midnight heartburn, how it feels to climb into bed with thighs and torso slick with oil. Here, in these aisles, the women are living the same things as her.

She waits a while, and eventually two young women turn down the aisle in her direction, holding hands and stopping every now and again to pick something up. A pot, a picture frame, a pair of nail scissors. Jen tries not to watch. But she cannot look away from their hands, the way their fingers tangle. The sight is equal parts foreign and familiar.

They give her a brief glance as they pass. Blonde and brunette.

Jen tries to get a look at their stomachs, but the blonde wears a loose dress and the brunette's oversized denim jacket is done up. She cannot work out which is the mother, if indeed either is, and she frowns. Make it obvious, she thinks. I want to know. But their stomachs give no clue, and neither do their faces. She cannot tell if their cheeks are fuller than normal, because she doesn't know what their normal is.

Jen follows them as they move out of the aisle. They walk down the middle towards the door, before stopping by Make-up to embrace. The blonde kisses the brunette. It is a goodbye kiss. Anyone can tell. She strokes her girlfriend's cheek, whispers, then walks out. The brunette watches her go, and, after a long moment, she climbs the stairs to the café.

The queue at the till takes forever. Jen taps her feet. She gives her armpits a discreet sniff then steals quick sprays of bottled scent. When she has paid, she finds her feet moving towards the stairs and taking them two at a time. So much for not being able to run. She pauses at the top, fighting for breath, feeling the writhing weight inside.

'Are you okay, dear?' an old lady asks, touching her shoulder.

Jen nods, putting her energy into convincing the woman she is fine. She pulls away with a sweet smile and goes towards the café.

The brunette sits in the corner with a full cup of coffee. She looks out of the window, and Jen stares as she waits in line. The woman is a little younger than her, late twenties perhaps. Dark curls frame her face, and she looks lost as she stares out across the street.

Jen sits down at the adjacent table, taking out a pen and the baby journal she bought. The brunette looks at her briefly, then sighs and turns away.

Jen takes her time with her herbal tea, stirring the bag in the pot, drawing comfort from the steam. Nothing like a hot drink, she thinks, and is reminded of her mother.

She spills the first sip on her stomach. Her sigh catches the attention of the woman, who looks down at Jen's bump and smiles. 'Oops.'

'You'd think I'd have learnt,' says Jen. 'The number of tops I've ruined. I'm too far away from the cup.'

6

The woman smiles again but with sadness. She turns away, and in this moment, Jen wants nothing more than to know her story. 'Not long until I can have caffeine again,' Jen says, pointing to the coffee.

The woman gives a polite nod. 'Any day now?'

'Ten weeks. I can't wait to meet him.'

'Congratulations.'

Jen touches her belly in response, and the woman glances at the rhythm of her strokes. She watches Jen's hand for a moment, then her eyes drift up to Jen's face. Oh, Jen thinks. There is a stab of recognition, perhaps even yearning, in the woman's face, and Jen wonders if it's also in her own. All she knows for sure is blushing skin.

'I have to go,' says the brunette, rising.

'But your coffee?' Jen feels a rising panic, not wanting her to leave.

The woman looks down at the untouched cup, as if surprised by its presence. 'Never mind,' she says. 'I didn't want it anyway.'

Jen opens her mouth, but no words come out. Instead, she gulps her tea and watches the woman move away. When she disappears completely, Jen sighs and turns to the first page of the journal. *Final Days of Pregnancy*.

She looks towards the staircase, then down at the blank page.

Newer Model

Isobel

26th March

Took the car for its first MOT. It passed (obviously) but perhaps now is the time to trade it in for a newer model. Spoke to Steven about going to the forecourt at the weekend, but he didn't reply. In strange mood so I made his favourite chicken pie. Tried ordering groceries online, but the red peppers they delivered were green! Never again. Sunny and warm today.

27th March

Toni came for coffee. She didn't comment on the new sofa, even though I saw her eyeing it. Her new haircut is much too short – she looks like a springer spaniel. I'm glad I don't have curly hair, as it always looks so manic. Must be hell for upkeep. Went to the meeting. Cloudy and cool.

28th March

Spoke to Patrick and tried Cassandra, but no answer as usual. More time for her friends than her own mother. The trees we planted still look small and sickly. It must be several years now. Steven says the soil is likely full of rubble left from the original build. I said we should have it excavated and returfed, but he isn't keen. I suppose the lawn itself is fine. Doesn't so much matter what's underneath. Steven took the youngsters from the congregation bowling. More cloud.

29th March

Booked night away for our anniversary in October. Haven't told Steven. Tried a new cookbook that Jude recommended, and the recipe called for ten spices! Honestly, the carrots tasted *foreign*. I wonder if she cooks it for Patrick. He liked his food plain as a child. Can't imagine he's changed that much. Warm today.

30th March

Steven left. Rain.

Ballad

Jen

A couple of years ago, on their fifteenth wedding anniversary, Jen and Pete went to Margate for the day. They asked some friends if they wanted to come along, but everyone had kids by then and was tied up. Jen was secretly glad. She wanted to celebrate with beers on the beach, perhaps dinner at an oyster bar, not by being lifeguard for other people's children or eating at a family-friendly chain. She wouldn't have felt like that if she and Pete had had kids. But they didn't, and so she did.

They went to the beach first, before it was busy. The air was thick, the sky cloudless, and they read magazines and lay in the sun. Pete bought cans from the craft-beer shop, and they drank and listened to the conversations of other people. Occasionally Pete read something aloud, not bothering to notice that she was deep into reading herself. Jen was glad of the sunglasses hiding her face. She wondered if there was anyone on that beach as lonely as her.

They took a walk around the shops. There was a vintage-furniture place at the top of town, and Jen peered through the glass at the Scandinavian wood. She pointed to an armchair, and Pete cocked his head to one side as he strained to read the price. He snorted. I'd like to buy something, though, she said. To remember the day. He shrugged. On the way back down, she stopped and bought a new oven-glove.

At dinnertime, they were turned away from the oyster bar. They should have booked, said the huffy waitress. It was Saturday, after all.

On the drive home, Pete said between mouthfuls of French fries, 'Do you think we should get you tested?'

'For what?' she said, although she already knew.

'All I'm saying is it's been two years and nothing.'

Jen looked out at the flat, barren landscape. Telegraph poles flew by, blurring into one. 'How are you so sure it's me that's the problem?'

Pete sighed. 'Don't take it that way. I just assume they start with the woman.'

She didn't answer.

'I heard female fertility drops off a cliff at thirty-five, so maybe we shouldn't leave it much longer.' He reached across and put a hand on her leg. 'What do you think? Shall we just get things checked out?'

Jen turned on the stereo and scrolled through her music. She pressed 'play', and the synths and drums of an eighties ballad started up around them. Lyrics of silence and heartbreak. Pete took his hand away.

'What are you trying to do?' he said. 'Make me cry?'

The stench of fast food turned her stomach. 'I put music on because you always want music on when driving. Not the right choice, then? Did I still get it wrong?'

He pursed his lips. 'I was only making a joke.'

Jen slid her palms between her bare legs and the cheap uphol-stery. 'So was I.'

Still driving, Pete took out his phone and changed the song to the croon of an old country singer, exactly the music he knows she hates. An old man sitting round a campfire, singing of a woman he once saw get on a bus. His honky-tonk voice crackled with regret.

When did this happen, Jen thought, as the world passed by her window. When did we stop listening to songs about what we'd do, and start listening to songs about what we never did?

When it ended, he played it again.

Skin to Skin

Jen

You can do it, a voice says inside, and then her body screams to push. One hour, two hours, three hours. Nobody counts. But still, the minutes pass.

For the rest of her life, Jen could describe in perfect detail the room in which she birthed Jacob into the world. Not that she would. In a story like this, nobody wants to hear about the run of clerestory windows along one wall, the dry squeak of the door whenever a midwife entered, the swing-arm wall lights without any bulbs, the other empty beds. But she'd have the detail ready in case. How it felt like a funeral. Pete by her side, crying. A midwife rubbing her back. In fact, all the midwives with their sympathy, their sucked-in lips, their *come on, Jen*s dripping with softness, not urgency.

There is no urgency.

They know how this will go, just as she has known for days that the spare room would stay one. Days that passed as years. But she is a liar if she denies there is a part of her that hopes.

The midwives are tender. They are. Still, Jen wants them rushing. She wants contingency plans, the best doctors, a code red. When she feels Jacob finally leave her body, a midwife takes his sparrow form in her hands and walks carefully to the table behind the curtain, where the rest gather round as if to observe a lesson.

'Is he breathing?' she hears herself say into the coolness of the pillow.

The silence is deafening.

Pete is stuck beside her, his hand clamping shut his mouth. I should've had Mum here, thinks Jen.

When Jacob is placed in her arms, the midwife peels back Jen's top so he can rest against her heart. Skin to skin. There will be no talk of trying to get him to feed. When the midwives speak, their words are thick with finality.

'Are you sure he is dead, though? Are you absolutely sure?' Her voice is drugged and slow.

Fight for him.

Pete sobs, and Jen looks down at her son.

A shock of red hair gives way to a forehead, eyebrows and a nose that morphs perfectly into his cheeks. She is struck by the beauty of his fingers. The delicate nature of his toes. Here is a face that was woven in secret. She wonders about the colour of his eyes, and her urge splits in two. She doesn't want to disturb him, for look, he is clearly at peace, and yet. Shake him. Wake him. Peel back those lids. How could something be wrong, when the appearance is so perfect, so right?

He is beautiful, but still, and now she sees he has no hope.

She is jealous at first and does not want to hand him over. She is convinced their hearts are in rhythm. Jacob's fingers curl around her thumb, and Jen is sure he is tensing his grip, as if his brain knows she is someone to hold tight to. Pete talks, but she doesn't hear. Her eyes are paparazzi cameras, taking shots with every blink. She doesn't want to think of time, or the lack of it, and yet it is all she can do.

'Can I hold him?' Pete's voice cuts in.

Without a word, she passes him over. They are alone now, the midwives having left to tend to babies who will not leave the ward in a box. The ones who will gurgle, punch-drunk on milk, whose mothers feast sleepily on tea and toast. Jen wonders if they're the only couple who entered the ward today without a car seat.

The midwife who rubbed her back comes in. She shuffles her feet a while, then opens the squeaking door to leave. Funny how the world is still going on out there, thinks Jen.

Jacob looks tiny in Pete's skinny arms, cradled like a bag of carrots. Pete is jigging him, and she says *Stop, you'll hurt him* without realizing. She looks up at Pete's face to see he is crying. The rocking is his body losing control. A seething hatred shoots through her core. It is sudden, this feeling, irrational even. If she examined the emotion, it would frighten her, but how dare he be the first to break.

'No,' Jen says. She cannot look at another person's sadness. 'Give him back. He needs my heart.'

He is returned to her, and there he will stay. She strokes his red, matted curls. The fold of his ear is soft against her lips. He is wrapped in a hospital blanket, scratchy from overwashing, its texture that of a sun-bleached towel. I'm sorry, my darling, she thinks. I should have brought you cashmere.

The door opens again. Another check. Pete waves and then a stranger's hand on her shoulder.

Jen's mind is filled with violence. Bright, raging televisions of emotion with her strapped to a chair, unable to look away. As his body cools, she sees now that her life will consist of two parts: the before, the after.

Is this really how the world ends? Without warning. Without knowledge of a final breath. We should know when it is coming, she thinks, that last drink of air, of amniotic fluid, so that we pay attention. And what would that do? She pulls the blanket tight. What good is attention? He would still be dead.

The midwife checks her watch and gently squeezes Jen's shoulder. 'I'll let you be for a while.' Another squeak of the door.

They don't know what to do with themselves. Pete is still standing, but now his hands are on his hips and he looks about as if searching for a lost shoe. He would make a good village idiot, thinks Jen. She wants him gone, out of the room, so it's just her and Jacob. She had him all to herself for nine months. His kicks were hers. She is not ready to share him, or give him away.

What seems like minutes later, the midwife returns with a colleague. *Already?*

'Should we pass him to you?' Pete says.

We.

In another life, Jen has loved Pete's politeness. The way he chats with baristas and shop assistants, how he thanks the waiter each time a piece of cutlery is placed on the table, so that within the space of ten seconds he has expressed his gratitude multiple times. It is a quality she has always found adorable. But now, a few moments after their dead son is born, she knows he is thinking of how to endear himself to the midwives, so that they will leave the room and think *What a nice man.* He wants to hurry this along for the midwives' sake. So they'll like him. Their time is what matters to him right now.

Jen drops her hands as Jacob leaves her arms for the final time. She watches the midwife drift away and disappear behind the curtain. Perhaps they place him in a box, thinks Jen, and then she no longer wants to think.

The other midwife is talking, but the words are heavy and slow. She feels a pinpricking all over her skin and imagines the microscopic holes as craters filling with sweat. Now everything is on fast-forward, and she is falling. Her head is thrown back, and she is moving side to side, so that each cheek feels the coarseness of the pillow. As her vision starts to right itself, she sees a midwife in front of her, silently shouting. Pete is pulling at her hand. The other midwife comes out from behind the curtain, her arms now empty. Where is he, Jen wants to scream. She hears the words echo in her ears – perhaps she really did shout. Her eyes detach from her head and float up into the corner of the room, assuming the role of a surveillance camera. There she is, on the bed, her face a horror film. She watches a midwife throw back the cover and push up her gown, to reveal red paint all over her legs. The other runs to the door and pulls a long cord. Jen's eyes begin to lose interest. She looks towards the corner where Jacob is, the only section of the room screened off from view. She considers pushing herself over, then almost scoffs at the suggestion. She left her arms and legs down there on the bed. There is nothing to push. But I have to get him back, she says. I have to see him again. Is he in a box? Or has the woman left him on the bed? He might fall – why is nobody watching him? She wills herself to move from the corner, to float above the action that is taking place on the hospital floor. If she wants it enough, it will happen.

She is so absorbed in what could be that she doesn't notice what is. The flood of people entering the room.

I am coming, my darling. I may be only a pair of eyes, but this means I can see. You wait there. I am coming for you. You'll wake up and this will all have been a bad dream.

That's when they start rushing.

This Ends Tonight

Zelda

Zelda pushes open the pub door and steps inside. The lighting is low and soft, perfect for first impressions. Faces turn to look, but they hardly register now.

She was the one to choose the pub, a sixteenth-century inn with panelled walls and taxidermied animal heads over the inglenook fireplace. Its acoustics are well-tuned for a first date.

This week's one is at the bar, shoulders slouched over a whisky. Zelda hangs back as she judges the reality. His hair is blonder than his picture, but that youthful glow is all his.

He jumps up as she walks over, a smile breaking across his cheeks, his eyes steady on her face. 'Zelda, right? Here, take my stool. I'll grab another.'

Zelda watches, amused, as he goes off in search of a seat. The bar is busy and the first woman says no, she isn't just resting her bag but saving it for someone, so he tries a guy who isn't even sitting on a stool but casually looping his foot around its leg. The man puts a protective hand on the seat, and Zelda's date walks back towards her, his hands up in surrender. 'No room at the inn.'

Zelda laughs, then realizes she can't remember his name. She takes out her phone and flicks through to their conversation.

'Better offer?' says Will.

'Not for tonight,' she says, slipping her phone into her bag.

Will laughs. His body faces forward, his elbows on the bar, but he turns his face towards her.

'Good choice on the drink,' says Zelda. 'Makes a change.'

'From . . .'

She shrugs. 'A pint of wife beater. Something that makes you belch a lot. No, wait' – she clicks her fingers – 'craft-beer man, right? If it hasn't been fermented in some New England shack, it's too commercial for your palate.'

Will nods as he scratches his chin. 'Are we that easy to peg?'

'Oh, you know. Do this a while and you become a bit of an expert.'

He raises an eyebrow over his whisky. 'How long you been doing it?'

'Clearly longer than you.' She waves at the bartender.

'Sorry,' says Will, straightening up and patting his jacket in search of his wallet. 'What would you like?'

'It's okay, I'll get it.'

'No, I insist.'

'No. *I* insist.'

They widen their eyes at each other.

'Ah,' says Will. 'I see.'

'What?'

Will shakes his head, smiling, and Zelda notices his strong Roman nose. She is often attracted to the features most people see as flaws. Big noses make her giddy.

She orders a spiced rum and Coke.

'A Cuban for the lady?' The bartender winks.

'Please, my good sir. And he'll take another . . .' She gestures to Will.

'Scotch'll do it,' he says, holding up the empty tumbler.

Zelda pays, and they chink glasses, watching each other take a sip. 'So go on,' she says. 'You had me all figured out?'

Will shakes his head. 'I'm not going there. The night's only just begun.'

'You think it's going to be a long one? Interesting.'

A waitress comes over with a couple of menus and smiles at them both. 'Dinner? We've just had a cancellation, and there's a spare table out back.'

Zelda is about to say no when Will gestures for the menu. 'How about it?' he says. 'Can you hack my company for two hours?'

She looks down at her watch, bringing it closer to make out the vintage dial. A first date is always a drink – that way there's no pressure and they can leave at the end and need never see each other again, without having wasted much money or conversation. Is she up for the next step already? *Maybe if you're paying*, she says in her head, but then she did just do her whole feminist bit.

'We'll take it,' Will says to the waitress as he picks up Zelda's jacket and their drinks. He glances over his shoulder and winks. 'Come on. At least this way I get a seat!'

She sighs as she stands and flicks her hair. Big noses and cock-sure taking-charge are vices she can't seem to kick. She'll try to change tomorrow.

Ten minutes into their meal and Zelda wonders if she had him all wrong. He actually asks her questions – where she grew up, what's her work, what's her pleasure – and he isn't content with the mono-syllabic answers she throws back. 'Wedding photographer?' he says. 'You must have some stories to tell.' Zelda shrugs and takes a mouthful of food. Usually she spends the hour or so of a date sorting through to-do lists in her head, or trying to remember the name of the celebrity he reminds her of, anything to while away the time until they go back to his. But Will doesn't seem interested in talking about how he sees the world. His eyes and attention are fixed on her. They are staring right now in anticipation of an answer to a question she forgot to hear.

'I don't know,' she says, automatically.

'You don't know where you live?'

'Oh . . .' She coughs into her napkin and runs a hand through her hair. 'Just outside of town. I'm a country girl.'

'I can see you rolling around in a hayloft.'

Zelda licks her fork. 'My turn now for questions.'

He pretends to bow as he shovels roast potatoes on to his plate.

'How old are you, really?'

His spoon hovers, mid-air. 'What do you mean?' He clears his throat. 'I'm twenty-nine?'

'Bullshit.'

Will shuffles in his seat, one eyebrow rising in a frown as he tries not to laugh. 'Why don't you think I'm twenty-nine?'

'It's obvious,' says Zelda, sipping wine as she takes in his face. 'There's a brightness to you. You're not jaded.'

He stares at her.

She stares back.

'I'm twenty-six,' he says at last.

The waitress appears at their table to top up their glasses, and the trickling sound of wine amplifies their silence. She takes her cue and leaves without asking how they're enjoying their food.

'Twenty-four,' Will says. 'But that's it. Promise.'

'God's sake.'

Will screws up his face. 'Too young? How old are you, really?'

'Thirty-four and I've got no problem with thirty-four.'

'You think I'm a knob now, don't you?'

Zelda pours the wine and doesn't reply. She couldn't care less about his lying – this ends tonight, whatever his birth certificate says – but there is something delicious in gaining the upper hand.

'I thought if I put my real age, you wouldn't be interested.'

Zelda picks up her wine. 'Why are *you* interested?'

He frowns. 'You're kidding, right?'

'I thought men wanted their females young.' The tannins burn her tongue.

'Maybe some do, but then maybe I'm not like anything you've had before.'

'Oh, *please*.'

'I've always liked older women. They know what they want.'

'Do they?' Zelda stares at his nose and imagines running her teeth over its tip, pressing herself into his flesh. 'Yes, I suppose they do.'

She looks at her watch. Almost ten. She needs more wine if the buzz is to kick in when she needs it. 'You're not a virgin, are you?' she says, pouring another glass.

Crimson floods his face. 'No. Are you?'

She laughs into her drink. 'We're not telling each other our numbers. This is a first date, remember.'

The waitress reappears to ask if they'd like the dessert menu, but Zelda is too quick for him. 'Just the bill,' she says, downing the wine and licking the dregs from her lips.

Outside, they slip on their jackets. March is only just starting, the nippy air lingering on their skin. Zelda grabs a fistful of Will's shirt and pulls him forward. It is a good kiss.

'I'd prefer your place to mine,' she whispers. 'You don't live with your mum, do you?'

He gives a soft laugh and runs a hand over his head. 'Yeah, not sure. First date, remember?'

'You what?' she says, jabbing a finger into his chest.

Will rubs his hand against his lips. 'I've, er, got a really early start.'

Zelda steps back, open-mouthed. 'Did you really just say that?'

'I'm not saying I'm not interested,' he says, stepping forward and putting his arms around her waist. 'I changed my age, didn't I?'

'Right . . .'

He goes to speak, but kisses her instead. It's a long, slow kiss, the kind to get lost in. The kind Zelda dreamt of when she was just getting started in life. An ambulance screams past, some drunks float by, but there is nothing in their spheres but each other.

'You kiss great for a teenage boy,' Zelda says, coming up for air.

'I love middle-aged women.'

She play-slaps him with her bag.

Will smiles, his eyes searching her face. 'I'll walk you to a cab.'

'Ah,' she says, pulling back. She knows this code. 'Lead the way.'

He takes her hand and they start down the street, looking like any other couple. It's quiet for a Friday, and they have to walk further into town for a taxi. Will looks at her, now and then. Brief glances with a smile.

Zelda stares at the buildings as they walk. Why did she never leave this town, with its bland boxy design and its memories on every corner? This town that looks like every other, where the people look the same. She feels a sudden ache for a life she hasn't lived.

As they are about to turn into the high street, Zelda gives up waiting and pulls him into an alley. It's a dead end, and the orange streetlight throws a dim glow over the shadows.

'What are you doing?' says Will, laughing as she leads him in.

Zelda takes his mouth roughly with her own. Her palms are spread flat against the grimy brickwork, penning him in, then she feels down his body to where he is hard under his jeans. 'I've got something if you need it,' she says between kisses.

'Got what?' His voice is breathless. This only makes her rub him harder.

'You know.' She guides his hand under her top, moulding it around her chest. 'Come on, don't be a dick tease.'

And then it clicks what she's saying, and Will nudges her away. 'Wait –'

'What the hell?' She pulls her top down and steps back.

Will stands there, clearly turned on, hands running back and forth through his hair. He gives a hard exhale, as if he's been holding all his breath.

Zelda shows him a picture on her phone. 'This you? The guy with one picture showing his torso with no description underneath?'

'So?'

'So you just want to screw, yeah?'

'What are you on about?'

Zelda rolls her eyes and gives a bored sigh. 'Everyone knows that one picture and no description means you're here for a good time. Look' – she scrolls through and brings up her own profile picture of her leaning forward into the camera – 'Tits and teeth. One picture. No words. Just here for a good time.'

Will puts a hand to his mouth. 'I did not know that.'

'Bloody amateurs,' says Zelda, stepping away and tidying her hair.

He shakes his head and kicks a wheelie bin. 'God, this tech. They make it so complicated. How am I to know? I don't do selfies and can't describe myself without sounding like an idiot. I thought one picture looked humble, like I wasn't arrogant; instead I look like a slag.'

'Cheers.'

'I'm not saying that. You can do whatever the hell you want, and, Zelda, let's be honest, I'd love to go there . . . but that's not all I want.'

'Oh, come on.' She has heard the lines a thousand times before from different faces.

'You don't want to get to know me?'

'I've only just met you!'

'Yet you want to sleep with me.'

'And you don't?'

'Yeah. I do.'

Zelda throws up her hands.

'Look, I tried one-night stands. A few times at uni.' He stuffs his hands in his pockets and shakes his head. 'They just leave me cold.'

'You're sweet,' says Zelda, doing up her jacket.

'And you don't like sweet.' He gives a quiet laugh and looks down. 'Doesn't it make you feel lonely, though?'

She stares at him. Friends tell her it's mad, the way she deals with men, but in madness lies sanity. Keep expectations low and never be disappointed.

But there is something in the way he runs a hand through his hair, how the strands he brushes away fall straight back down. There is something in the way he sticks out his tongue when nervous, so its tip almost touches his cheek. There is something in the way he looks at her. Like he sees all the parts she keeps hidden.

There is something.

She draws herself up straight. 'I'm never lonely,' she says. 'Besides, what's the point in wasting time getting to know each other, only to discover we're not sexually compatible? May as well work that out first.'

Now he is watching her. His smile says he has her licked and knows everything she doesn't say.

A flash of rage in her stomach. Who is this kid, hardly done with puberty, who thinks he can just stroll inside and kick down walls? Now he is walking towards her, biting his lip in the way he has been doing all night. She balls her hands into fists.

He is a foot away, and she can feel his warm breath.

He says it again. 'Doesn't it make you feel lonely?'

'What?'

'Not giving a damn.'

'I'm never lonely,' she says again. 'There's always someone new to swipe.'

He pretends to flinch, then tuts a few times and shakes his head. It reminds her of someone she'd rather forget.

'Bye, then,' she says, not moving.

He comes closer. 'Bye.'

She is whispering now. 'Why does swapping bodily fluids have to be this holy grail? Telling you the deep, dark things, letting you in there' – she taps the side of her head – 'that's sacred. It's not just for anyone.'

They stare as they listen to the sounds of the street.

He moves his head in, slowly, giving her time to push him away. She doesn't. Their mouths fit like gloves, their spit mingles together, and Zelda tastes a dry patch of skin on Will's lip. It chafes her own. Her body starts to soften.

'See,' she whispers, 'just live a little. It's not so hard.' Her hand travels down, taking control again. 'Hang on . . . ding-dong, I was wrong.'

He laughs in her ear, his breathing uneven. She can tell he is unsure.

'If we do,' he says, 'will you still call me tomorrow?' Their noses touch.

Zelda closes her eyes. 'Sure.'

And so he lets her fuck him. Or him her. It isn't clear. It is clouded with doubt and certainty, never completely dark but never light either. The murky glow hides their fingers, but there is clarity when their eyes meet, when they watch the other's face contort, and, instead of rushing like men always do with Zelda, he breaks off the rhythm in places just to stop and kiss her and hold her face. The air is loud with their mouths and throats, the occasional shout from the street, as they make a moment for themselves of themselves in a filthy alley off the main drag of the town.

★

He walks her to a taxi, holding her hand, proud to be with her. Zelda keeps trying to pull away, but he only tightens his grip.

When he asks for her number, Zelda gives him the one with a different final digit. He won't call it. They never do, not after she's performed the whole show.

But then he puts the phone to his ear and his eyes don't leave her face.

'What are you doing?' she asks in a panic.

'Calling you.'

'But it's on silent.'

'So pick up.' His voice is calm.

Zelda freezes, half in the cab, unsure of what to do.

'Hello?' he says, still looking at her. 'Is that Zelda?' A pause. 'I'm sorry. I must have the wrong number.' He hangs up.

'Oh,' she says. 'That's strange. Let me look.' She cranes her neck towards the screen. 'Final digit should be a five, not a three. You must have misheard.'

He tries again, this time with a smile. 'Check your phone,' he says, jokey-strict.

She fumbles with her clutch bag and takes out her phone, waving it at him. 'Hello? Yes, this is Zelda. Now can you please let her go?'

Will pockets his phone and nods. 'Better.'

'You're a persistent bastard.'

'It's my best quality.'

'I really need to go,' she says, making no move to pull away.

'So we got the sexual compatibility sorted.' Will leans in and gives her a final kiss. 'Now I'm looking forward to talking' – he taps the side of her head – 'and getting in there.'

Zelda wakes in a huddle on her bed. A sea of exhaustion hit her in the taxi, and it was all she could do to pay and stumble out without falling asleep. She doesn't remember making it through the door, but here she is, still dressed in last night's clothes. The crumpled dress is marked from the alley. Her fingers stroke the stains.

Eventually, Zelda leans down to find her phone. A missed call from an unknown number and a voicemail. She shields her eyes from the sun as she waits for it to play.

'Hey. Just wanted to check you got in okay. The driver didn't look like a creep, but you never know. Anyway, text, or even call . . . Let me know you're all right. I, uh, had a really good time tonight, Zelda. Something tells me I should play hard to get, but . . . yeah. Not up for games. Call me.'

Zelda frowns and stares at the phone.

She plays it again, dancing with the idea of him. Will in her bed. Tangled fingers. Swimming with him in a lake. Raising glasses in celebration at a foreign café table. Together on the sofa, dressed in old pyjamas and watching a film. Him cooking. His face the first thing she sees when she wakes.

She deletes the message.

He was right. He should have played hard to get.

Your Own House

Isobel

It rained all day, and Isobel scrubbed the kitchen from top to bottom. She secretly loved days like this, when ministry was cancelled and she could delight in the scent of bleach. Steven always went on about hiring a cleaner, but why pay someone to do what she loved? Besides, no one else could do it how she wanted. *Maybe your standards are too high*, Steven said. And what if they were? What was so wrong with excellence?

She made Steven's packed lunch before he left for work and then spent two hours baking cakes. There was a workday at the Worship Hall the next morning – weeding, deep cleaning, painting over any marks on the walls. The brothers always appreciated a slice of something sweet, and she liked to think her fruitcake had become a workday tradition, something they would miss if it wasn't there. Toni's effort was always inappropriate – frosted and sticky and requiring cutlery. *It's not a competition*, Steven said once, when she complained on the journey home. *Besides, I thought hers tasted very good.*

She put a costume drama on the TV and watched while she cleaned the kettle. Just buy a water filter, Cassandra said years ago when she walked in to find her mother scouring off the scale. But then I wouldn't get to clean it, Isobel replied. Cassandra threw up her hands and left the room.

The surfaces were gleaming when Steven returned. She'd made a lasagne for dinner and told him about her day as she dished up. The car showroom rang again to ask if they wanted to visit. Had he given the matter any thought? Toni called to ask them to dinner the following weekend, and Isobel checked the calendar and said yes. Oh, and did he remember that ridiculous woman down the road, the one who clad her post-war bungalow in painted shiplap so it looks brand new, despite everyone knowing that underneath it was plain old breeze-block . . . Well, someone in the Neighbourhood Watch had asked online whereabouts she lived and she replied: the lovely house on the corner. When Steven didn't respond, she waved the spoon at him and said, 'Well?'

He looked up. 'What's wrong with that?'

Isobel's mouth dropped open. 'You can't describe your *own* house as *lovely*.'

Steven pushed his hands against the table and scraped back his chair. He stayed seated, his eyes fixed on the floor, and Isobel wondered if he'd dropped something. Outside, the rain pounded the patio.

'I'm leaving you, Isobel.'

Three-piece Suite

Jen

'They're here.'

Jen sits on the edge of the bed, her feet half pushed into her slippers. She watches Pete pace the short length of their bedroom. 'Why did you answer the phone?'

'I assumed Steven wanted to discuss the game. We won three–nil. How was I to know he meant something else?'

Jen looks down at the floor, where dust balls gather. Three weeks since she almost died and Pete hasn't once touched the hoover. 'Well, I won't see them.'

'Bit late when they're in the living room.'

Through the window, the trees stretch tall towards the flat, grey sky. It is early March and the leaves must now be budding, but Jen narrows her eyes to hide the detail, to make the branches bare. She cannot take the sight of new life.

'I didn't invite them,' she says.

'Well, it's you they've come to see. I can't turf them out. They've given up a Saturday to come over –'

'How kind.'

Pete stops pacing and looks at her, his lanky shadow stretching the full height of the nineties-wallpapered walls. 'Don't be like that.'

'You're defending them now?'

'If you didn't want to see them, you should have said.'

Jen closes her eyes. She wants darkness. 'When did you give me the chance? You invited them over without asking, so *you* tell them to leave.'

Pete comes over to sit on the bed. He takes her hand. Jen knows he is trying a different tack, and she has an urge to pull back and slap him.

'Listen,' he says, stroking her wrist like she's a child. 'Think of all the texts and meals the sisters have dropped us. We've felt their love, haven't we? That's why they've come. To show love.'

Jen looks at his face. It is milky and thin, and she knows he hasn't been sleeping. But Jen knows the worry is not for their son. It is fear of the repercussions, from what will come of the conversation to take place in their living room. Sitting on their faded three-piece suite, they are to pass biscuits and tea and hope for absolution.

'Pete,' she says. 'There are three of them. You know what that means.'

He looks scared. 'But how would they know? No, no. Impossible.'

Now it is Jen who reaches out. 'Think about it. *Three*.'

He sighs. 'Well, then, can't you just say you're sorry?'

She catches sight of herself in the mirror. The weeks have stripped years from her face. Her skin looks sallow, its colour bleeding into the blondeness of her hair. She will have to put on mascara before she sees them. Blusher too.

'We've had this conversation,' she says, her voice flat.

'But don't you see how easy this is? Just say you're sorry. That's all. You wish you hadn't said yes and that'll be the end of it.'

'But I'm not sorry.'

Pete turns to her. 'Surely there's a tiny part inside that wishes it hadn't happened? Just focus on that. That small twinge of regret.'

Jen stares at a patch of mould in the corner where the paper peels from the wall. She had asked Pete for years to redecorate. She'd bought four rolls of patterned wallpaper and propped them up beside the wardrobe. But their weekends were busy preaching the end of the world, and renovations on a rented house didn't seem as important. Several years on, the walls are the same. Shabby. Neglected. The rolls still stand in the corner, the print out of fashion now.

'It would be a lie,' she says. 'Are you asking me to lie?'

'Goddamnit, Jen,' Pete says, jumping up. 'Just *say* it. Two words. A slap on the wrist and it's over. Who cares if it isn't the whole truth? Pray for forgiveness later. This is my life you're ruining too.'

Jen has never heard Pete swear. She's surprised to realize this doesn't shock her, but confirms a knowledge she has always felt deep inside. '*Your* life?'

They are sitting on the three-piece suite, as expected. Three men in suits, all in varying stages of middle to advanced age, identical in whiteness of skin, receding hairlines, grey Bibles on their knees. They perch on the edge of the sofa, as if this is a quick visit or they've come to deliver bad news.

'Jen,' says Brother Bill Norris, leaping up and waving to her to take his place. He moves to the other side of the coffee table, where Pete has placed two hard-backed dining chairs to complete the circle.

Jen sinks into the sofa, checking her robe to ensure it is not too tight or too loose. All at once, she feels underdressed and a stranger in her own home. Brother Steven Forge sits to her right, leaning back with his legs splayed open. He smiles his megawatt grin and rests his hand on her shoulder. Jen wants to bite off his fingers and spit them out on the rug.

'How are you, Jen?' he asks in a warm voice.

'Fine,' she replies, as she has throughout the weeks. She says nothing of the milk that weighs her down with no one to drink it, left to seep through her clothes. The chilled cabbage leaves in her bra to relieve the pain. And what of her heart? Left to rot. No vegetable for that one.

'You're looking well,' says Brother Norris, nudging Pete. 'Her cheeks . . . they look ruddy. I hope this one's doing a good job of nursemaid.'

Jen looks at the floor beneath the coffee table. More dust. Are you serious, she thinks. He knew they were coming and yet didn't lift a finger. Her ears burn as she imagines them going home and telling their wives of the state of her house. 'I'm sorry,' she says, sitting forward. 'I should get you some tea.'

'I'll put the kettle on,' Pete says, jumping up to demonstrate his helpfulness. 'How does everyone take it?'

While they wait for him to return, the brothers ask if Jen enjoyed the meals their wives dropped off. Yes, she replies. Isobel's chilli was exquisite, she tells Steven. They are so grateful. Yes, she can tell from their waistlines that their wives are exceptional cooks. Now if someone could rustle up her baby, because that's her only craving. Everything else tastes like mud. Please leave her house.

Only a few of these thoughts she says out loud.

Pete returns with the tea and a half-eaten packet of biscuits. Jen wills him to find a plate on which to decant them before they are passed around, but his eyes are only for the men.

'We really appreciate you taking the time to come over,' he says, sitting down.

'Of course, Pete,' says Brother Norris, taking a biscuit. 'This is what our organization is about, coming to the aid of those who need —'

A hand shoots out from Jen's left, Brother Connell sitting in the armchair. 'Perhaps we should begin with prayer?'

Bill Norris swallows his mouthful of tea and leans forward to put down his cup. He clears his chastened throat. 'Sorry, Les. Running away with myself there.'

Brother Connell turns to Jen and pats her hand. His other palm — she stares at its wrinkled and hairy back — rests on his leather Bible. 'It's a good idea to get our Father's blessing on these matters.'

Jen's instinct is to pull away, but she has learnt to fight it. She counts the seconds until he lets her go. Then he bows his head.

'Dear heavenly Father, we come before you now as your servants at this especially difficult time for Pete and Jennifer . . .'

Jen has never liked Leslie Connell. There are brothers who love the sound of their own voices, and, as overseer of the congregation, his own booms the loudest. His prayers go on until everyone falls asleep; his preferred seat is always reserved; it is he who calls the shots. Now, as he prays in her living room for God's blessing, Jen notices a sovereign ring on his finger. She stifles a laugh at this feminine touch.

The prayer finally ends, and the men dunk biscuits in their tea.

Jen watches the clock. The cabbage leaves sit warm against her flesh, and the Bibles have yet to open.

Finally, Brother Connell looks at Pete and says, 'It's come to our attention that, while in hospital, Jen suffered a haemorrhage and lost a great deal of blood. Is that right?'

Jen swallows and looks at Pete. Everyone knows about Jacob, but they have taken care to keep the rest private.

'Where did you hear that?' she says.

Brother Connell smiles. 'Is that right?'

Pete shifts in his chair.

'Before I say anything' – *I'd like a lawyer* – 'I'd be interested to know your source.'

Brother Norris gives a warm laugh. 'It's okay, Jen. We're just trying to establish the facts.'

'So am I,' she says in as sweet a voice as she can muster. 'Have you, by any chance, been speaking to Sister Boyd?'

The brothers look at Les Connell, who watches Jen with interest. Clearly he has underestimated this petite, quiet sister, with her hand always ready to answer and her modest, sensible shoes.

'Sister Boyd is a midwife at the hospital?' He frames it as a question. His eyes do not leave her face.

'Aren't nurses required to keep patient details confidential?'

'Jen,' says Steven. 'No need to be guarded. The scriptures say the elders are there to give comfort, and that's all we want. To comfort you and Pete.'

'You are both much loved friends and members of our hall,' says Brother Norris. 'Help us help you.'

Pete leans forward and covers his face with his hands. He lets out a long sigh, as if he is the one being interrogated. 'Maybe we should tell them the truth.'

Jen almost laughs. She sits on her fingers to stop herself throwing hot tea in his face. Didn't this happen to her? Wasn't she the one who nearly died? Why does everyone else decide the words she should speak?

'I haemorrhaged,' she says. 'Straight after I delivered my dead baby.'

Bill Norris looks away, and Jen remembers that he and Toni lost a baby a decade before. Then you know, she thinks. Or Toni does.

'That must have been very difficult,' Steven says to Pete.

'Did you accept a blood transfusion?' asks Brother Connell.

The room is silent.

'Yes,' says Jen. 'I lost a lot of blood. I have no memory other than them taking Jacob. Pete says they took me to the emergency room and gave me a transfusion.'

The brothers turn to Pete. He sits with his arms folded and his legs out, knees knocking against the coffee table. His turn.

'They wouldn't let me in,' he says, and his voice breaks. 'I told them *no blood*, that we were Disciples, but they said she'd die without it, so . . . I didn't fight them.' His skin burns. 'I'm sorry. It was the heat of the moment and I-I . . .' He's almost sobbing, and Brother Norris puts a hand on his shoulder.

You're sorry, Jen says inside. You're sorry for saving my life. She stares at his shaking body, the way he can summon the tears. A stranger would think this romantic. How he must love her, they'd say. Jen bites her lip to suppress a smile. Somehow, in this dangerous and terrifying room, her body wants to laugh.

'What confuses me is the hospital going against Jen's wishes,' says Steven. 'The Advance Directive in her notes would have clearly said NO BLOOD, so it shouldn't matter what you tell them, Pete. They cannot override an adult patient's wishes.'

Pete catches Jen's eye, and she has a flashback to their honeymoon, how in the early days they really did try.

'That would all depend,' says Brother Connell, 'on whether Jen gave them a copy of the Advance Directive.'

She feels naked as they turn to look.

'I did not,' she says finally.

'Didn't you receive it?' Steven scratches his head. 'I'm sure I ordered the pack when you found out you were expecting. All the forms were in there.'

'No, I got it. But I chose not to give the form to the doctor.' Her truth gushes out like lost blood.

34

There is a longer silence, broken by the cat meowing outside the door. Nobody moves.

'But why, Jen?' says Brother Norris.

'I don't think it's right to ban blood transfusions.' Mutiny tastes strange on her meek, submissive tongue.

Steven clears his throat. 'But the scriptures clearly state that consuming blood is detestable to God.'

'I didn't consume blood.'

'Jen, you took it into your body.'

Stop saying my name. 'That's not the same. The scriptures only describe *eating* blood as unacceptable.' She knows she is on dangerous ground. There are shifting sands and she cannot see them.

It is Brother Connell's turn to speak. 'Of course, the Bible cannot condemn transfusions, as they didn't exist when the books were written. But the principle is very clear that we should *abstain* from blood.'

'But if there's a blanket ban on blood, a baby shouldn't drink breastmilk, because it's made of white blood cells from the mother. And if we literally abstain from everything blood-related, we shouldn't allow it to be taken *from* us via blood tests. But we do.'

'Jen,' says Brother Connell. 'Have you been reading information from outside the organization?'

Pete's eyes burn through her as she says, 'I'm able to think for myself.'

The silence is heavy as the men look at each other and frown.

'If this is life and death, the scriptures must be black and white. No room for doubt.' Jen takes a deep breath as the reality of what she is saying hits her. 'They are not black and white here, and so it should be a personal decision.'

A mournful wail from the cat.

Jen's arms press against her waist as the milk floods in. Here is her body taunting her with life when all she has birthed is death. Her breasts are hard rocks that weigh her down. She wants to hug them. She wants to sink into sleep.

Brother Norris reaches across the table to put his hand on hers, and she knows his tears are real.

'Jen,' he says, his voice almost breaking, 'we are here for you. Hold tight to your faith in the Resurrection, when our Father will bring back your boy. Just a little while longer.'

Jen closes her eyes. She believes in the Resurrection over everything else. It is what keeps her going. 'I know you would leave it if I said I was sorry, but it would be a lie. And a lie means losing my hope of seeing Jacob.'

'So you are not sorry?' says Pete.

She looks up. He is a hundred miles from her now.

'If blood is the symbol of life, how can the symbol be more important than what it represents?' She will sob if she looks at their faces. 'I'm glad I'm alive. Frankly, it amazes me that you all think I should be dead.'

Silence. Even the cat has gone away.

Brother Connell lays down his Bible and puts his fingers to pursed lips. 'You understand what this means? What will happen?'

They stand on the shore as she waves from the sea.

Cheap Soap
Isobel

Several years ago

The roses are bold against the blue sky on the day of the party. They are the colour of blood, and the petals' edges are sharp and picture-perfect. The white picket fence still smells of fresh paint.

Isobel spent yesterday prepping the garden. Not many weeds had sprouted since the Friday before, but still, she got down on her knees and ripped them out. She made sure to wear her widest straw hat. It wouldn't do to catch the sun.

'Have you got the ice?' she asks Steven, as they pass in the hall.

He doesn't look at her. 'Just going.'

'We need at least ten bags. Perhaps get fifteen, just in case.' She checks her watch. 'It is quite late.'

'Better late than melted,' he mutters, going out the door.

Earlier that morning, she had laid his clothes out on the bed — the linen shirt and tailored shorts he wore one evening in the Bahamas the previous year. Isobel had glanced at him across the dinner table, his face lit by the sunset, and thought how handsome he looked, all these years on. She was debating whether to tell him when his fist hammered down on the table as his team scored on his phone.

'Right,' he said, when he came into the bedroom and saw the outfit, freshly pressed. He stood in the doorway and stared at the clothes for a while, then turned and went downstairs.

Half an hour before the guests are due, Isobel is refilling the soap when he comes down in a different outfit.

'Oh,' she says, straightening up. 'I thought –'

'I'm not a child, Isobel.'

She spills the soap. It runs down the side of the bottle, forming a sticky pool on the china sink. She'd forgotten to order more in time, so instead she had Steven pick up a cheap supermarket tub to decant into the heavy glass bottle whose label says mandarin and Sicilian bergamot.

Toni is the first to arrive, in bright pink lipstick to mark the men's cheeks. Steven looks uneasy as she skims the edge of his mouth. He takes the corkscrew from the drawer and hands it to her – 'I know this is what you want' – and ducks away from her playful slap.

'Really,' she says, half to herself, leaning against the kitchen island and touching her hair. 'That man . . . Your husband . . .'

Isobel is mixing the dressing into the salad. 'Here,' she says, and stabs the tongs into the leaves. 'Take this out, would you?' She hands her friend the bowl.

The party takes place outside. The bar is set up on the other side of the pool, past the outdoor kitchen and shepherd's hut, which are sure to draw attention. When people arrive through the side gate, Steven hands them a drink and Isobel offers a canapé. The couples split up as they always do, the men huddling by the bar as the women move nearer the kitchen. There are squeals as they embrace. Everyone knows everyone. At its fullest, there must be over a hundred people gathered in the back garden of Steven and Isobel Forge's executive detached home. Their stories, their anecdotes, their conversations are all of each other. Nothing exists outside of this world. Years have been spent in the same company, catching up at weekly meetings at the Worship Hall, celebrating at weddings, consoling at funerals, falling out over the littlest things. Playground friendships. Strong, but with taped-up cuts.

Isobel reloads a silver platter with canapés and checks her reflection in the oven door before going out.

Brother Connell is the first to lean in, and he frowns in pleasure as he tastes and swallows. 'Exquisite, Isobel. You must give Eileen the recipe.'

Isobel almost shivers as she recalls the mushroom pie his wife made when they went for dinner at the Connells'. She can still taste the raw pastry, wet on her tongue. 'I'm sure Eileen makes wonderful canapés, Les.'

He gives a sad shake of his head and takes two more.

Isobel weaves through the crowd, smiling and nodding as she extends the tray. Faces turn towards her, their eyes widening as they scoop up pastries with quick licks of their fingers, before closing the gap and continuing their conversations.

Steven holds fort at the bar, ensuring the wine never runs dry. A small fortune is spent each year on their parties. Very special friends are invited to camp overnight, and the host will ensure no guest leaves without a bottle. Isobel has heard their parties talked of, how invitations are greedily sought. Steven puffed out his chest when she told him. A slight nod as he acknowledged his worth.

Isobel catches snippets of talk as she moves among her guests.

'That *dress*, Toni. Divine.'

'New-builds are a nightmare. They look nice on the outside, but dig deeper and . . .'

'It *says* mandarin and Sicilian bergamot, but . . .'

'Did you hear about . . .'

'He still looks good, though.'

'Oh, no, I don't like pastry.'

'Must cost a packet, heating that. Look, there's even a hot-tub –'
'*Shh!*'

Someone drops a glass, and there is a momentary silence as a hundred faces turn to look. Isobel parks the tray on a table and grabs the dustpan and brush from the bar. She rushes forward, her face red as she fixes her smile. *It's fine, it's fine* is her mantra on repeat. She bends her knees to clear up. Her hand slightly shakes as she rests it on the offender's arm. As she once read in a magazine, the good hostess laughs it off.

The broken glass tinkles as it slides into the bin.

Isobel retrieves her tray and takes a deep breath before continuing around the lawn. The voices grow distant as her cheeks begin to hurt. Summer is high in the sky, and she has to shield her eyes with her hand to find shade. Sunshine smothers the garden. Steven's laughter sings over the crowd.

This is Home, she tells herself. This is my home. These people are my home.

Seventeen

Jen

Seventeen years ago

Jen stopped desiring her husband almost immediately after their wedding.

She grew rainforests on her legs, long tangles that she'd stroke while watching crap TV, the pleasure almost mindless as she soothed her skin. Then she would look down and be struck with equal jolts of thrill and revulsion. There was a constant battle between her carnal lust at the sight of her natural state and the pictures she absorbed daily of women overjoyed by their hair-free bodies. Adverts of faceless women shaving already-bare legs or hands pouring blue liquid on to a sanitary towel. Hair and blood were too offensive even to contemplate.

Then Pete would grumble and she'd shave it off. This is what it is to be Woman, she'd think. There are always two opinions on how to be, and it's never clear which way she should go.

On the morning of her wedding, Jen's dad came to her room in his best suit and kissed her forehead. They stood there, father and daughter, admiring what they saw in the mirror.

She looked beautiful, he said. Like a princess. Then he took her hand, turned to her and said, 'You leave this house for the final time. After today, if you have a row, do not come here. He is your husband and you now belong with him.'

Jen smiled and nodded, in love with the romance of being given away by the father she adored to the boy she would marry. She saw the love in his eyes. There it was, it existed. She was so taken with the weight of the moment, the graveness of her father's voice, the way he fought back tears. Her marrying Pete made him proud. Relief overwhelmed her.

Never mind that she was six months shy of her eighteenth birthday, that technically she was still just a girl. This was everything she had been raised to want.

The day passed in a blur.

Pete's dad gave the sermon before their vows. He stood on the platform and held up two cups to the audience. 'This is a mug,' he said of the first. 'It's strong, solid, it takes a lot to break a mug like this. That's you, Pete.' Everyone laughed. 'Now this' – he held up the other cup – 'is fine bone china. It's what the Apostle Peter called *the weaker vessel*. The woman. Beautiful, delicate, to be handled with care. She is easily broken.'

Her uncle Roger took the photos. He posed her and Pete together, telling them how close they should be and what to do with their hands. When it was time for the group shots, he put Jen and Pete in place, then called out, 'Who do you want, Rich?' to her dad.

After the fifteenth line-up with family and her parents' friends, Jen was about to request a shot when Pete said, 'Can this be over? My face hurts from smiling.'

She bit her lip and nodded.

Great-aunts kissed her cheeks, exclaiming how she'd grown, and second cousins said how jealous they were that she'd already passed her driving test. She felt all of her seventeen years. When she caught sight of herself in the mirror of the village-hall toilets at the reception, she almost recoiled in surprise. Oh, it's me, she thought, touching her veil. I thought I saw a ghost.

During the meal, Pete sneaked her some wine under the table.

When they left the reception not long after the dinner, she tried to ignore the knowing raised eyebrows, the awkward hug with her dad before she climbed in the car. The night hid her blush.

At home, Pete carried her over the threshold. They had waited twelve months for the moment when they could tear off each other's clothes, and they did it with all the awkwardness of teenagers.

Her first time took place in the bed where all her other times would happen in future. There were already bills on the mat, energy companies to call, the beginnings of a full laundry basket. By the time she would turn the age when she became herself, she had already taken the name of another.

Mrs Musgrove at seventeen. But that was okay. She was happy.

When Pete came for the first time inside of her, she cried out in pain as he called out in pleasure. Are you okay, he asked afterwards, splayed out on the bed. Did it hurt? A bit, she replied. A lot. Sorry, he'd said, and given her a tender kiss. We'll go slower next time.

By the time of their honeymoon two days later, they were screwing like pros. The height difference evened out when horizontal, and they'd found the ideal positioning for Pete's giraffe legs. Going abroad was too complicated – being under eighteen, her parents had already had to give consent for her marriage and she couldn't bear to ask permission for her honeymoon too – so they chose a hotel on the Cornish coast that was affordable on window-cleaner wages. They may as well have stayed home and pocketed the money for all the sights they saw. One night, they staggered downhill to a restaurant off the pier, walking like cowboys and laughing until they cried. I'm so sore, said Pete. Shh, said Jen, clamping a hand over his mouth. Someone will hear.

She let him do whatever he wanted. Ever since she was small and would dress up with her sister in their mum's clothes and heels, her life had been pointing her in this direction. The seventeen years had been the picking up of a rifle and aiming it, and now she had made the kill. What would follow were love and babies, just as it had for nearly every woman she knew. This would happen if she gave herself completely. This was what she was meant to do.

A few days into their honeymoon, Pete came out of the shower, wrapped himself in a robe and fell back on to the bed.

'Was it close this time? Did you feel anywhere close?'

Jen pulled the cover up tightly and shook her head.

He drummed his fingers on the back of his hand. 'Hmm. Odd.'

'Maybe . . . I don't know . . .'

'What?'

'Maybe you could . . .' Jen stroked the duvet. 'If you, um, touched me down there for a while . . . That may help.'

Pete frowned. 'I do touch you down there.'

Only when we're taking care of *you*, she thinks. 'Maybe you could spend a bit longer? It just probably takes a little more work than it does for a man.'

'Are you saying something's off with my technique?'

She paused. 'No.'

'Because I don't think *that's* the problem.' He gave a slight snort. 'This is quite common, you know.'

Jen raised her eyebrows, waiting for him to finish.

'Most women struggle to orgasm. It's just a fact.'

'Yeah, I'm not sure that's it,' she said, remembering the countless nights before their wedding when she rubbed herself against a pillow. 'I really think that if we took the time, it would happen.'

We're just young, she told herself. It will come. Fairytales put the wedding at the end, as if, after the vows, everything will be perfect. But of course that's not real. No, let's accept we're still learning here. It will happen. It must.

That evening, Pete wasn't in the mood. They had dinner in the hotel restaurant, pushing food around their plates, taking turns to stare out of the window. Jen sat with a smile and answered the waiter's questions with the right degree of pep.

The next night, Pete paid a little more attention. The spill of the full moon through the curtain lit up his face, and Jen watched him grimace while attempting a rhythm. After a few excruciating minutes, in which she heard the neighbouring guests return and discuss plans for the next day, she told him to enter her and timed her pleasure to coincide with his. She hated herself as she gasped in fake wonder, but found it was easier to lie with her eyes closed. To not look at his face.

When he'd finished, he rolled off and took a smug stroll to the bathroom. Jen covered her face with her hands. He'd made an effort like she'd asked. She had to give him something. Hadn't she been raised to believe there was greater happiness in giving?

So why did she now feel so empty inside.

When they arrived home, their new lives began. Pete drove off in his van each morning, a long ladder strapped to the roof, and Jen went back to work in the clothing store in town. She spent Tuesdays and Thursdays on the ministry, knocking on people's doors to find lives to save. She dressed smartly on these days. A knee-length skirt, a sensible coat, her thermos filled with tea. Each afternoon she arrived home at exactly 6 p.m. and prepared their dinner, which they ate on their laps in front of the television. She phoned her mum some nights, or they did Bible study, and then there were the two midweek meetings at the Worship Hall. When the sixth of September came around, it went unmarked, as the Disciples command, and Jen forgot she had even turned eighteen until she saw the date on the TV guide when they sat down to eat.

She was officially an adult.

Lightshade

Jen

Six months after their honeymoon, Pete accompanied Jen to the doctor. They sat in the GP's office, and she smiled and asked the problem. I'm never in the mood, Jen said with burnt cheeks. We got married in the summer and I was into it at first, but then a switch went off inside and I don't know how to turn it on again. I should be wanting it all the time at this age, shouldn't I? What's happened to me?

The GP had asked questions, throwing curious glances at Pete. It's perfectly normal, she replied. Hormones are tricky things. They don't always behave how we'd like. You'll figure it out.

They went home and continued their lives as before. When Pete began to touch her, Jen stared at the ceiling and heard the lie sing from her throat. She knew the exact pattern of the lightshade, had counted the number of squares on the fabric in both English and French, and could predict where the shadows would fall depending on the strength of the moon that night.

Her desire never came back.

Gas and Air
Isobel

Thirty-three years ago

She always wondered why her parents named her Isobel. Dereks and Patricias called their female offspring Susan, Jackie or Deborah. Normal names that didn't draw attention.

She could sense it when she met people. They'd hear her name and do a double-take, as if there was an arrogance to the name being claimed by someone so generic. Brown hair, brown eyes, nothing of consequence. This was how she saw herself. You don't look like an Isobel, they'd say, their eyes moving up and down. I know, she'd reply in her head. I'm more of a Carol or a Julie. Face in the crowd. She got used to disappointing people before they even knew her.

But the spelling of her name was apt. The lack of an *elle* on paper removed any trace of softness. She was relieved to have the *o* instead of the *a* – *Is-a-bel(l)! Imagine!* Some girls at school once tried to shorten it to 'Izzy' or 'Bel', and she had recoiled in disgust.

When she started courting Steven, she was twenty-two and already a spinster. Her friends were married by nineteen, and she became someone to pat on the arm and say *sorry* to whenever they talked of their happy, newly-wed lives. They would cock their heads and say *You'll find someone, I know it* and she'd reply *I don't care, really* when the truth was she was terrified.

But then, one day, Steven moved into the hall, fresh from heart-break up north. As the only singles in the group, they gravitated towards each other and did the recommended thing of getting acquainted at public gatherings – barbecues, the cinema with friends, and beach trips where they could view the other's half-naked body in the name of wholesome recreation. Isobel spent a small fortune on a two-piece, knowing full well that a scrap of nylon that leaves little to the imagination was not an area in which to scrimp. She knew she had a good body and his eyes on her skin left her breathless. It was worth every one of the five thousand pennies.

Their first kiss was her first ever. From the moment she presented her mouth to his, her mind was racing through their future.

Her married friends quit with their sympathy. At meetings, their eyes tracked Steven as he passed the roving mic around the hall. They sat beside their beige, boring husbands, and, for the first time in her life, Isobel was the subject of envy. How could this hand-some, amusing deacon just fall into Isobel Abbott's lap? Their jealousy fired her blood. *How's that for left on the shelf?*

He was two years younger, but Isobel didn't care. 'It's better that way,' said a friend. 'Everyone knows women mature quicker than men.' She frowned as she realized the reality was the opposite of the point she was making.

About six months into their relationship, word came that the girl who broke Steven's heart had come crawling back and Isobel drove to his rented flat to quietly ask what was happening. His response was cagey, and she stepped through his front door and jammed a finger into his chest. 'I have waited this long,' she said, through grit-ted teeth. 'You end this and everyone will know what a scoundrel you are. Your reputation will be ruined.'

Four months later, they married.

Life was hard at first. Steven was a window-cleaner, and Isobel's job at the bank brought a respectable but modest wage. They made enough to pay the rent on their little terraced house, and Isobel grew vegetables and learnt how to make a whole chicken last three meals. Sometimes she wondered if that was when they had been happiest, in the days when they'd had almost nothing.

When her parents died two years after their wedding, they used the inheritance to buy a house and start a cleaning business. Steven wanted to down tools and oversee a team, and Isobel's money made that happen. She was more than happy to do it. After all, the Bible described them as one flesh and Steven as her head. Who better to trust than the one who'd made a public vow to cherish her?

Cassandra arrived the following year.

The birth was long and arduous, Isobel almost unconscious throughout. When the pain relief wore off, a warm bundle was placed in her drowsy arms and declared her daughter.

Isobel had always taken pride in her pragmatism, her ability to know exactly what to do. Motherhood defeated her. Her body took months to recover – much to Steven's frustration – and her mind was a hot, gluey mess. When Cassandra screamed in the Moses basket, Isobel leant her forehead against the wall and cried for her mother.

She began to imagine they had given her the wrong baby.

'There was a mix-up at the hospital,' she said to Steven, once when he returned from work. 'Look at her. She's nothing like me. Someone else has our baby.' Her voice was high and dry.

'Don't be ridiculous, Isobel,' he sighed. 'She's the spitting image of you. Everyone says so.' He grumbled when he went into the kitchen and found she hadn't made dinner.

Two years after Cassandra, Isobel was pregnant again. 'So much for being careful,' she said, as she buried the test in the bathroom bin. She stared at herself in the mirror before going down to make his least-favourite dinner.

But this time was different. Almost from the moment she discovered Patrick inside her, Isobel felt an unknown peace. She rejoiced in her changing body, bought floaty maternity clothes and braided little plaits in her hair. The testosterone took her over, but she forbade Steven from entering her in their usual position. She had to protect the new life within her, and so she turned over and, for once, let him take her on her knees.

This new feeling of motherhood infiltrated her dealings with Cassandra too. She sat in the garden and laughed as Cassandra spun herself in circles. Nothing her daughter did upset her, and Isobel was surprised by the woman she could be. Is this what motherhood is meant to be like, she wondered. Or is this unusual too?

Her mind was present for his birth. She made sure of it. Gas and

49

air took her through, and, when his writhing body was placed against hers, Isobel knew just how to be. She kissed his hair. She felt a great swell of tenderness within her.

This must be how it feels to fall in love, she thought.

Patrick was her second chance. Cassandra's first few months were lost to her, her daughter a story whose opening lines were rubbed out. Isobel would spend her life trying to catch up with her first-born, searching for those feelings that should have been there at the beginning, as if their discovery would unlock the mystery of Cassandra.

But Patrick's story was clear from the start. The love she felt took no effort or prayer, but came as heat from fire. She didn't move from the sofa that first fortnight, savouring the bliss of his body against her chest. This will pass, she thought. I must make the most of the present.

Isobel thanked her heavenly Father almost hourly for the gift of Patrick. *You knew exactly what I needed*. She was so consumed with thanks for her son that she forgot to offer any for her daughter.

Cassandra was placed in preschool as soon as possible. Isobel would grip her hand as they waited for the doors to open. Other children cried and clung on to their parents for comfort, but Cassandra pulled free and ran straight in without looking back. Isobel laughed at comments from other mothers on her child's eagerness. She took credit for Cassandra, reinventing their distance as some deliberate attempt on her part to produce a capable daughter.

She'd walk back to the car, relieved finally to be alone with her son.

Once, she was driving home when they almost careered off into a ditch. He was eighteen months old at the time, and the rhythm of the car had sent him to sleep. Isobel turned briefly and saw how his full cheeks rippled as the car went over bumps in the road. My beautiful boy, she thought, and looked again to watch them wobble. She often did this, staring at him for longer than she should. But, one day, she looked for a second too long, and the car swerved as it struck a pothole. She screamed and righted the wheel, then waved at the car behind that was beeping. Her heart pounded, her mind playing through the worst-case scenario – Patrick thrown from the car and lying dead several feet from her. The idea of this made her sob. And yet . . . was it possible to love someone so much that you'd be prepared to risk their death for one more look at their face?

When people asked if she'd have any more, Isobel shook her head and said, 'No, no. One of each. That will do,' when the truth was she'd have thousands. She wanted to fall in love again and again.

Patrick fell ill with chicken pox when he was five years old. Huge welts sprang up all over his body, and she bathed him in oat milk and dabbed chamomile on his skin. At night she slept beside him in his bed and put her hand on his heart. It fired so fast that her first instinct was to snatch her hand away. *This is life*, said the beat. *The entire existence of the thing you love most is out of your control.* It still hammered after the scabs faded, so she took her son to the doctor, who examined him and declared it perfectly normal. 'Some hearts beat quicker than others,' he said. 'We're all different, Mrs Forge.' And then he waved her out.

Nothing good can come from that, she said to herself about Patrick's beating heart. Nothing good at all.

There was too much life within him.

Cassandra confounded her.

She would point at scaly fruit in the supermarket and start to scream, refusing to calm down until Isobel marched her out. The ends of steel pipes on the back of trucks also set her off. She would beg Isobel to overtake, insisting the sight made her teeth hurt. What rubbish, Isobel would reply.

She often took hours to eat her toast. Isobel, a stickler about leaving food, would not allow her children to be wasteful. Think of those African children, she said. We have been given this beautiful food to enjoy and we cannot squander it. Cassandra sat in silence. Her eyes stared off into space. Three hours later, she picked up the cold, stale toast as if it had just been set down and ate every last crumb. Isobel watched, helpless. Even when Cassandra hadn't got her own way, it still felt like she'd won.

One day in summer, when Cassandra was six, Isobel caught her stamping on ants. She watched her daughter remove her sock and shoe before pressing her foot down on the flagstone, then lifting her foot to examine the dead ants on her skin. Isobel threw open the window and scolded her. *A life is a life.* When they had friends over the following weekend, Steven manned the barbecue. Cassandra stared at the blackened meat on the grill, and during a lull in conversation said, 'I thought a life was a life?'

It didn't help that Cassandra always took sides with her dad. They were in a pact against her, whispering together. At times it felt like their family was comprised of two teams, her and Patrick versus Steven and Cassandra. That's fine, thought Isobel. As long as she kept Patrick, she didn't care what the rest of them did.

But then once, when Cassandra was seven and Patrick almost five, Isobel listened from the other room as her son asked his sister, 'What does *outnumbered* mean?' They were playing with toy figures and re-enacting a battle they'd seen on TV.

'It means you lost,' said Cassandra.

Isobel was about to clarify this when it dawned on her that her two children were forming a relationship that was theirs alone. She was not invited. Isobel, an only child, realized for the first time that Patrick would form bonds with people other than herself.

She took two aspirin and went to bed.

Making a Scene

Jen

'Jennifer Musgrove is no longer a Disciple of the Last Days.'

The suspended ceiling stretches low over the congregation, the grey polystyrene tiles occasionally interrupted by a square of artificial light. The windowless hall is the quartered shape of an octagon, with the chairs fanning out in three directions from the platform.

Jen was a child when the brothers spent a weekend putting up the structure. She and Lina had made cakes with the other sisters, and their job was to satisfy the men's hunger and thirst. It was proof of our Father's blessing, they said, that the halls were constructed so quickly. A team of a hundred brothers worked all day and night, the work of their hands offered for free. One brother made a time-lapse video of the build, and, when Jen watched it afterwards, she thought how everyone looked like scurrying ants.

Today is the first of April, and the hall is silent.

Brother Connell steps back down. The brother on stage continues his talk, but the audience are lost to him now. They are whispering, nudging, trying to make sense of it. How could this be? The minister wife of a deacon? What a juicy bone to gnaw on the journey home.

Jen sits in her usual seat. She hadn't wanted to come, but Pete said it would demonstrate the right attitude if she showed up to hear her fate. A prisoner hearing a guilty verdict will have a greater chance of early parole if he is silent and doesn't shout at the gallery, Pete said. So this is jail, thought Jen.

She stares at the white fluorescent lights until they blind her.

The worst sight of all is her parents in front. Her father's shoulders slumped, her mum's hand covering her face. They knew it was coming, but nothing could soften the shock. Their little girl.

'But . . . why?' her mum had wailed when Jen had gone to their house to tell them. 'Can't you just say you're sorry?'

'Mum, you know why.' She doesn't want this, she says, but she can't pretend.

Her mother cuts her off. 'There must be a part of you that wishes you hadn't taken blood. Focus on that.'

Jen was lost. Hadn't they taught her to tell the truth? Hadn't they drummed into her that God was always watching? Doubt began to roll like fog as she wondered if she were missing something obvious. Something everyone got but her.

'Dad, *you* must see why I can't lie?'

He stood in silence, his finger against his mouth, where he always placed it when lost in thought. Finally, he looked at her. 'Which elders were on your jury?'

'It was more informal. They came to the house. Bill Norris, Steven Forge and Les Connell.'

His finger flew towards his wife. 'Ha! There we go. Les Connell has always had it in for me.' He slapped his leg as if he'd solved the case.

Angela shook her head. 'But you can appeal it? Richard, surely she can appeal?'

The smugness disappeared. He stared at his daughter, his face draining of colour.

'There is no appeal,' said Jen.

'What?' Her mum blinked back tears.

Jen wanted to shake her. How could her mother not know the rules? She listened as her father explained how taking blood isn't a disfellowshipping offence. It's classed as disassociation, and therefore there is no appeal procedure because Jen is the one taking the action of leaving the congregation. It is not the elders forcing her out. It is Jen.

Jen had already forgotten her own naivety. How she hadn't known the rules herself before this week.

'So that's it?' said her mum.

'They said they would consider reinstatement in six months,

perhaps,' said Jen, trying not to notice the changed way her father looked at her. 'They'll review then, if I'm attending all meetings and showing signs of repentance.' She will do her time.

'Six months is usually the minimum,' he said, looking down at his hands.

'But . . . how can this be? Richard, surely you can have a word.'

Her father stared at her mother, and Jen remembered the evenings he spent at the hall, sitting on juries and deciding the fates of other sons and daughters. 'And how would it look,' he said, 'if I can dish it out but not take it back?'

Angela looked from her husband to her daughter. 'So that's it. Everyone's to know. How can I walk into the hall after this? A daughter of mine taking blood?'

They were embarrassed by her. Oh, God, Jen thought. Oh, *God*.

'Nobody will know the reason, Angela.' Her father's tone was impatient. 'That part isn't public.'

Jen curled her hands into fists behind her back. Didn't Jesus stand up for truth? Didn't he take the unpopular road, go against the accepted teaching of his day? Was she not to be a footstep follower of Christ?

'Tell everyone if you like,' she said. 'Tell all your friends. I'm not ashamed. I stood up for my conscience, and –'

'Oh, Jennifer, enough with the self-righteousness. I think we know a thing or two about truth, or is the student cleverer than the teacher?' The words spat from her mother's mouth, then a hand gripped her throat. She turned to the mirror and smoothed her hair. The movements were slow and deliberate as she examined her reflection and repinned a fallen tendril. 'Have you told Lina?' Her voice was smooth with control.

Jen watched her. 'I thought I'd come to you.'

'This will break your sister's heart.' Her mother's manicured fingers wiped away the discarded beginnings of tears.

As she stood in the hallway of her childhood home, her mother's gestures reminded her of the day a phone-call announced the death of Jen's grandad. He'd been killed in an accident abroad. On receiving the news, Jen's grandmother, staying with them at the time, screamed and tore her dress before collapsing in a heap on the floor. Angela held her mother's arms and said, 'That's hardly going to help matters, Mum. Ripping your beautiful dress.'

A ruined piece of clothing cost more than grief. Making a scene was worse than feeling.

Twenty-six years on, she stood in that hallway and noticed how small everything looked. It reminded her of *Alice in Wonderland*, her favourite childhood film, when Alice visits the White Rabbit's house and eats the biscuit that makes her grow. Her arms push through the windows, her legs shoot through the doors. She can no longer fit inside.

Jen stared about her. The rectangular desk in the hallway that held the telephone directories and paperwork, the bookcases crammed with Bible publications that stretched to the ceiling, the family photographs in neat, orderly lines.

Looking at it now, it was all so woefully small.

Jen and Pete leave as soon as the meeting is over. The moment the brother says *Amen* – before everyone has put down their songbooks and turned to look – they pick up their bags and hurry out. A few brothers put a hand on Pete's shoulder as he goes by, brief smiles exchanged, but nobody does this to Jen. As she passes a group of sisters in the foyer, she keeps her eyes down but senses that they step back. The tips of her ears burn. She knows the rules, and, yet, it surprises her. These women, her friends, the ones who cooked and baked and cried when Jacob left her a month ago. These women turn away.

Lina is standing at the door, holding her youngest. 'Aunty Jen!' says her niece and lunges towards her, but her mother tightens her grip.

Jen catches her sister's eye and opens her mouth, but her voice is gone now. It will not return until the elders allow it, and not a word will be said to her until then. Even her family will look in the other direction.

Lina's husband hugs Pete, as if he is the one hurting.

It has been days since her milk last rushed. The cabbage leaves have gone from the shopping list, and her old bras are beginning to fit just fine. After weeks of praying for the pain to stop, she now longs for its tremors. A distraction from knowing that the milk came and went. Jacob came and went. Life, went.

Her body is starting to mend as deeper wounds crack open.

She is not ready for him to belong to *last month*. How can he be her past, when he will forever be her present and future? How can time continue to tick, her body heal from its bruises, when her mind lies trapped in a hospital bed?

Jen glances at her niece, at her sister's full arms, then down at the emptiness of her own. Because it isn't just words she needs.

Nobody will touch her either.

Crushed Silk

Zelda

Zelda has just picked up her sewing when her phone buzzes. She ignores it at first, her head lowered towards the cloth. This jacket has taken six weeks, and she is so close to the end. The dusky pink linen feels cool under her fingers as she nips the needle through its weave. This time, she has chosen a pattern of large suns or eyes, depending on the person looking. Crushed gold silk for the orbs within circles of red spidery thread. They will blind or hypnotize if you stare too long.

This is her happy place: lying here on her bed in a patch of sun, the sight of blooming roses through the circular window, her skill bringing something to life. This didn't exist until I made it, she thinks. The cloth would still be uncut, the thread lonely on the spool, the surveillant suns forever trapped in the darkness of her imagination. It has taken years of practice to get this good. All those lost shreds of fabric she embroidered at the beginning, when her fingers were strangers to the needle. None of those scraps were wasted. Each time she makes something with her own hands, it is a reminder of how life gets it wrong until it gets it right.

The phone hums five times in quick succession, and Zelda knows who it is without looking. The latest one never drafts a complete message before sending – his style is a stream of consciousness so her phone never stops. Zelda knows it's a trick, a calling card, a way of getting attention. It works.

She picks up her phone. *Hey, sexy. Hot out there today. Send me something so I can think of you.* She rests against the bed and sighs. She is so close to finishing the jacket. All that is left is to stitch together the pieces of pink.

Zelda pulls up her top and turns on the camera.

The best angles come naturally now. These too she has practised, discarding unflattering poses and bad light to the *Recently Deleted*. She splays her hair across the pillow and turns to almost spill from her bra. A finger between her teeth. Click. She flicks through and opens the best photo in another app, where she smooths and retouches her skin. Freckles, be gone. Perhaps spill some more. A few clicks and her flaws are hidden, her strongest assets enhanced. Send.

Seconds later: *Bloody hell, yes.* And then the usual masturbation commentary.

She hasn't met this one yet. A swipe and chat, followed by pictures exchanged. She couldn't give a damn about them, really. With their tattoos and slick, waxed bodies, they all look the same. But the idea of them wanting her, their attention captured by *typing* . . . it gives power that is all for herself.

Will has called twice since their date. The first time it rang, she stared at his name and the reflection of her terrified face. It went to voicemail, and he left a message on the second try. *Hey. You said you'd call . . . I won't wait around like a sad sack, so consider this me making a move. We had a great time, didn't we? Zelda, I can't get you out of my head.*

She hadn't called back, but she saved the message and on some evenings played it on repeat. She'd liked it when he held her face with his hands. But what more did he want? His razor in her bathroom, joint bills, to kiss her skin at midnight?

Some pieces stay broken.

Amaretto

Isobel

'As you can see, it's a very cosy space. Perfect for one of those love-seats that are so fashionable now. You know the ones? They come in the most wonderful shades of velvet. It would up the cosy-factor even more. And these floor-to-ceiling windows dividing the lounge and kitchen allow the light to flood through. I know today is over-cast, but just wait for the sun.

'And through the glass door into the kitchen . . . Now, as soon as I saw this, it reminded me of those little Parisian apartments where painters and artists live. You've seen the films? Look how the light pours through these skylights. I know the cupboards may not be flashy, but who really needs all those bells and whistles? This is what I call "rustic chic". So romantic. And these pantry shelves above the worktop are very trendy these days – we get a lot of requests for details like these.

'You'll know from the particulars that the sleeping area is on the mezzanine and accessed via these – also wonderfully rustic – wooden stairs. Again, just look at those black metal skylights – this really is the benefit of a loft apartment. Don't they look straight out of Paris? You wouldn't get this in a typical flat. Yes, this really is something special.'

Isobel wipes a finger along the top of a door frame as the woman prattles on. She's able to decipher the agent's words spieling from her neon mouth. Cosy means *small*. Rustic for *filthy*. Parisian instead of *squalor*. A loveseat, really . . . Whatever would she do with a loveseat?

The agent flicks through her notes. 'It's a rental for one, right?'

Isobel glances at the woman in her ill-fitting trouser suit and stilettos she can hardly walk in. Her eyes fix on the flash of gold on the agent's left hand. 'For now,' she says, in the overly posh voice she sometimes assumes. 'My husband is abroad, you see, on business. But I imagine it won't be long until he returns, and then we'll get something bigger.'

'Oh,' she says, frowning. 'It's just this is a long-term let, so a year minimum.'

Isobel smiles as if the woman doesn't understand. 'It's fine. A year is fine.'

There are people who would make something of this space. Isobel can see it would have a kind of charm, for those who throw down sisal rugs and houseplants and strangle the air with incense. Cassandra would know what to do, and a memory appears of her daughter's feather collection stuck to her bedroom wall, despite Isobel's protestations (the paint! the fleas!). But this is very much not Isobel's sort of place, and sisal is so hard on bare feet.

'I'll take it,' she says, barely concealing a sigh.

She has never been inside the sixties box of a building that sits on the busiest road in town. Isobel wears an old coat for the occasion, a navy macintosh with a generous hood. There is no rain, apart from the relentless pour of cars behind her, filled with people who may turn her into a tasty little titbit at dinner – 'You'll never guess who I saw going into the Job Centre,' they'll say, as they pass their husbands the gravy. 'Isobel Forge!' She shudders and pulls down her hood. The knowledge that she would do the same only scares her more. She knows what would be said.

She hurries by the youths smoking outside in hope of making it in without comment, but they don't even notice her pass.

When her number is called, Isobel crosses the ocean of eighties carpet and sits down at the desk of a woman who is tapping away at a keyboard. 'Be with you in a sec,' she says, not taking her eyes off the screen. Isobel glances at an open can of Dr Pepper and back at the woman, whose shirt buttons almost pop at her chest. Figures, she thinks. How does she fit into that chair?

'So how can I help you?' The woman's voice is forced and high-pitched, as if she has delivered this line too many times today.

Isobel huffs. Surely the reason for her visit is obvious. 'I need a job.' The words make her blush.

'Well, that's what we're here for,' the woman sings, and her name badge – KARA – shakes as she laughs. 'Let's start with your experience. Have you got your CV?'

Isobel unzips a plastic folder and takes out a sheet of A4 paper. It wasn't hard to keep to one page.

Kara sips from the can as she takes in Isobel's professional life. 'Ooh, that's nice,' she says, examining the label. 'Amaretto. I've not tried this flavour before. Think it's my new favourite.' She continues to read. 'So . . . it says your last job was in a bank in the late' – she pauses – '1980s?' She says the full decade, as if to emphasize that Isobel belongs in the past.

All she can hear is the woman smacking her lips. 'Yes, but I've done book-keeping since then for my husband's company.'

'Right, but your last customer-facing job was in 1988?'

Isobel bristles. 'I also answer the telephone and manage appointments. It's a cleaning business, so I take care of clients whilst my husband organizes the labour. Or . . . I *did* take care of clients, but a year ago he took someone else on, and . . . well, she's handled it since.' She looks down.

'Hmm,' says Kara, frowning as she scans the rest. 'It's just that customer-facing experience is necessary unless you want factory work or cleaning or shelf-stacking. Which I'm not sure is up your alley.'

'I spent a number of years at the bank. Perhaps it was rather a long time ago, but customers haven't really changed, have they?'

'See, now that's the determination we want to project in an interview. Turn your weakness into a positive.' Kara's smile fades. 'Only, most employers do prefer a fuller history of customer service before we send candidates for an interview. And looking at this . . .' She chews her lip.

'I also regularly knock on people's doors and speak face to face.'

Kara looks up. 'Oh, really? Sales catalogues?'

Isobel gives a polite laugh. 'No, teaching the Bible. I'm a full-time minister so I spend a hundred hours a month in the ministry.'

Kara looks confused so she rephrases. 'I knock on people's doors and offer them free Bible studies.'

'Ah . . .' She leans in. 'Are you a Last Dayers?'

Isobel gives a strained smile. She hates the slang term, used only by worldly people. 'I'm a Disciple of the Last Days, if that's what you mean.'

Kara's eyes widen. 'Oh, wow. My best mate at school was one of those. She couldn't celebrate *anything*. I felt so sorry for her.' She looks down at the CV. 'But I don't see any of that here. The door-knocking thing.'

'Well, it wouldn't be. It's not employment, as such.'

'You don't get paid for it?'

'No,' says Isobel, frowning. 'We share the message because it's God's command. Who would we charge? God?'

Kara glances at the screen. 'Okay, so I may have something. You drive, yeah? It's for a receptionist at a dental surgery on the outskirts of town. Full time, Monday to Friday with the occasional Saturday, and the pay is . . .'

'Full time? Oh, is there nothing part time? Three days a week?'

Kara laughs. 'No hope unless you want the jobs I mentioned. This vacancy only came up today and will probably be gone by tomorrow. Cushy jobs are rare.'

Isobel grips the edge of the seat. A full-time job means giving up ministering, her vocation for the past twenty years. More failure. But she thinks of the flat and remembers that the balance in her account after the rental deposit will hardly last her a month. A supermarket job where everyone will see her is the alternative. 'Full time's fine.'

'Let me put in a call and see if they want to schedule an interview.'

Isobel sits upright as Kara sells her to a stranger. *Well-presented. Experience with the public, a while since any employed work but a lot of informal customer-facing since.* Isobel quite enjoys listening to Kara, and she warms to the girl despite her continuing to sip her drink throughout.

'This afternoon?' Kara says, looking at Isobel. 'In an hour? Yes, that should be fine. Lovely. Let me know afterwards. Byeee.' She replaces the receiver and stifles a belch. 'Now, let's get that experience typed up on your CV. The computers are over there. Maybe don't say anything about the Last Dayers – put charity? – up to you, obviously, but you may find it better to say Christian. Some people aren't very broad-minded.'

She tries Patrick first. It rings and rings. No answer. She tries again.
'Hello?'
'Oh. Hello, Jude. I wondered if I may speak with Patrick, please.'
A sigh and then, 'Hi, Isobel. I'll just get him for you. Everything all right?'
'Yes. Everything's fine. Thank you.'
'Okay. Well, just a sec.' There's a thud as the phone is put down.
As she waits, Isobel looks at the cardboard boxes in the hallway, the words scrawled on the side. Steven, Isobel, Cassandra, Patrick, Tip. If love is measured by cardboard, Tip is the favourite child.
'Mum?' His voice is a tonic.
'Hello, darling. How are you?'
'Just sitting down for dinner, actually. You okay?'
'Oh. What's Jude cooked? Shall I let you go?'
'No, it was my turn tonight. Baked potato, salad and beans. It's okay, I can chat for a minute.' There's the sound of him pulling up a chair.
Isobel clears her throat. 'Is a jacket potato substantial enough? I imagine it's exhausting fitting windows all day. The least you can expect is a decent meal to come home to.'
'Well, Jude works too, Mum. It's not fair to expect her to make dinner every night, and, besides, I'm quite happy with that. It leaves room for pudding, doesn't it?'
Isobel doesn't reply. She'd been surprised when Patrick started courting Jude, and even more when he'd got engaged. Still, Steven had liked her, and she had always trusted his judgement. She had comforted herself with the knowledge that the Japanese have good traditional values and therefore her only son would be well looked

after. But Steven had shown he was not to be trusted, and his betrayal now only validates Isobel's initial dislike of her daughter-in-law. It doesn't matter how often Patrick tells her that Jude was born here, that only one parent is Japanese, that she's been to Japan only once. The jacket potato clinches it. She'd been misled.

'How was your day?' says Patrick.

'Oh, I found a flat and a job. Nothing important. I'll let you get back to Jude and your baked potato.'

'What? Mum, that's brilliant. Tell me.'

After some persuasion, Isobel relays the details. She starts in a fortnight at the surgery and the salary is decent with acceptable hours. The flat will be free next week. It's just about big enough for a shrew, but then that's the situation his father has left her in.

'You know you can stay in the house?' says Patrick. 'He can't kick you out, even if the house *is* solely in his name. You have rights. I said I'd help you get this sorted.'

'No,' she says, staring at the boxes. 'I don't want to live here any more. It's too big anyway. What would I do with five bedrooms?'

'At least stay until it sells?'

'And have strangers trotting through my house every weekend? Opening the wardrobes to see only one set of clothes? I have got some pride, Patrick.'

'But, Mum . . .' He goes quiet. 'He's the one who's done this to you. The only person who should be feeling shame is him, wherever he is now.'

'Yes, well, it would be nice if feelings followed logic.' The oven-timer says that her supermarket chilli is done. She's already laid out one placemat. 'Now go back to your dinner before it's cold. Jude won't want to eat alone.'

'But Mum –'

'Go.' She puts down the receiver before he hears her start to cry.

Keyser Soze

Jen

Jen hardly hears his phone when it goes the first time, her hands deep in suds. Pete made a fry-up for lunch. His choice. Their agreement is that if one person cooks, the other clears, but during the week it is usually her doing both. He likes to cook at weekends, usually dishes that take several pans or bowls, and Jen's arms always ache from scouring off the remnants flicked all over the wall.

At the weekend, after they've been out on ministry or to the meeting, they take off their Sunday best and have a few hours to themselves before heading to someone's house for an evening of games or a group quiz. Or, this is what they used to do. In the month since Jen's disassociation, everyone has played without them. Pete could still go, but for the past fortnight he has been strangely clingy and not left her side. Jen is no longer allowed on the ministry, but Pete makes her wait in the car while he knocks on doors. She sits and reads the Bible while the rest of the group pretend she isn't there. It shows the right attitude, Pete reminds her when she says she'd rather stay home. As always, she turns to stare out of the window.

Leaving does not even occur to her. This is how her world has always been. A sin is committed, discipline doled out, and the sun continues to set. Where would she go? How would she survive? The questions are unasked because they cannot be imagined.

The radio switches song, and Pete's phone dings on the counter.

Jen stops scrubbing and scratches her heel with her foot. She didn't change from her ministry clothes before lunch and regrets it now. The feel of her tights against crumbs on the kitchen floor disgusts her. There is no better time of day than when she sits on her bed and peels the nylon skin from her legs. When she washes them each week in the bathroom sink, she slings them over the shower rail to dry along with her bras. They hang as floaty wisps of fabric, feminine and weak with their tendency to ladder. She hates the damn things. But the Disciples' ban on women wearing trousers at meetings or on the ministry leaves her with no choice. She has never understood why they enforce the scriptures so literally on those occasions, yet fail to do so when a sister wears them in regular life. Surely if God hates it on Monday, then he still hates it on Tuesday? She just shrugs these thoughts away.

When his phone buzzes twice, Jen huffs and leans across to look. She takes care to ensure her gloved hands drip over the draining board. There are three messages from a name she doesn't know. 'Pete, phone,' she calls, but the rattle of the pipes says he's in the shower.

Jen's favourite song comes on, and she starts to dance while scrubbing an oven-tray. His phone hums again. She groans, dropping the tray, then wipes her gloves so she won't spill puddles. She goes to switch the phone to silent, but the screen lights up again. This time, the message has come through a different app, and displays in its entirety on the locked screen: *I know you said to leave you alone but don't think you can have your way, then bugger off. We need to talk.*

The name on the screen is 'Keyser Soze'. She stares at the message, and it repeats in the voice of an angry woman. Female. Definitely female.

Jen puts down the phone and returns to the sink. She is balancing the clean oven-tray on the draining board when Pete walks in.

'Who's Keyser Soze?' she asks, her voice calm. She has no idea of the correct pronunciation.

The room is silent. Pete picks up his phone and clears his throat. Guilty. Jen imagines the sweat gathering on his lip, his fingers raking his thinning hair.

'Oh,' he says. 'Just a customer.'

She should throw an arm out and launch the pots on to the floor, the way they do in a sex scene. The noise would be immense. Jen almost laughs at how much it would delight her, but then there are neighbours to consider.

She asks, 'Do you think I'm stupid?'

'Mmm?'

She strips off the gloves. 'Come on, Pete. You can do better than that.'

'I didn't say anything because . . . well, obvious reasons.'

Jen turns and leans back against the cold metal sink. 'Obvious meaning bullshit?'

Pete looks at her. He has never heard her swear, and she takes pleasure in his surprise, as if he is noticing her for the first time. 'It's not bullshit,' he says. 'Obvious as in I knew you'd overreact.'

'So why does it say *don't think you can have your way, then bugger off*? That doesn't have a particularly innocent ring.'

He swallows. 'It's not what you think.'

'Well, perhaps we'll let the elders decide. They're pretty good at that.' She walks across the kitchen and picks up her phone.

'Jen,' he says, laughing and changing tack. 'You've no proof of anything.'

'Maybe I took a photo of the message. Maybe I could send it to Les Connell right now and see what he thinks.' This isn't a lie. She said *maybe*.

Pete's hand flies out. 'Okay, I'll tell you.'

She folds her arms and feels the sun stream in through the glass window, suffocating her legs in heat. The urge to rip off her tights is overwhelming.

'She *is* a customer,' he says. 'That part is true.'

'How honest.'

'I'm trying to tell you the truth here.'

'*Truth?*' Jen wants to burn this place down. 'Didn't *I* tell the truth? Didn't you tell me to lie to make your life easier?'

He takes a deep breath and looks down at where the lino peels away from the floor. 'It happened at the end of last summer, then a few times since.'

'How many?'

'Ten?'

'Ten?' Jen grips the edge of the counter. 'How did this happen, exactly? I mean, you're up a ladder cleaning windows – how does that lead to adultery?'

Pete shuts his eyes. 'You really want to know this? Won't it just hurt you more?'

Jen shakes her head, confused. She is unsure how much more hurt she can be, knowing that, when she was pregnant, he was bedding someone else. That even when her body was changing to accommodate their future, he carried on. He hasn't earned the right to be concerned about hurt. 'I would like to know who I've been married to for seventeen years.'

Pete straightens up. 'All right. I was cleaning the upstairs windows and she came in the bedroom and started undressing.'

Jen bursts out laughing. 'Wait, what?'

'Yeah, I know,' he says, almost relieved. 'Crazy, right? I looked away, but, as I started down the ladder, she came over to me, then carried on stripping.'

Jen's mouth hangs open.

'I couldn't move, and I don't know what came over me – Jen, I was in some kind of trance – but I went inside, and . . .' She knows how the story ends.

Jen clasps her hands as if praying and rests them against her forehead. She has spent her marriage fighting urges and unclean thoughts, while he has been in thrall to his own. 'Well, this is fantasy jackpot, right?' She looks at him. 'Lucky boy. Ticked that off your bucket list.'

'Jen, I'm sorry, I –'

'Did you charge her?'

'Eh?'

'For the windows. Did you charge her?'

'Don't be ridiculous,' he says, quietly. 'Of course not.'

'So not only did you shag a customer but you also took money from the wages.' Jen nods as if in agreement. 'Excellent.'

'Like I said, it was like she bewitched me.'

Jen hugs herself to stop laughing. 'So it's all her fault? She *seduced* you?'

A fly disrupts the silence, buzzing above their heads. Its body thrashes against the window – again and again and again – before moving to the corner. Jen stares at the fly, transfixed by its mundane presence in the room where her marriage is dissolving.

She remembers their wedding sermon, Pete's dad likening his strength to a solid mug, with her as fine bone china. Beautiful, delicate, easily broken. Jen still remembers how it felt to push Jacob from her body. How the swell of his form bore down through her centre until she screamed his arrival to the world. Her, *the weaker vessel*. Now here was Pete, the strong one, unable to control his own body. His dad was right. He was a mug.

She is still laughing, and the sight of this makes Pete clench his fists.

'You've never wanted me. I could tell at the start of our marriage, all those years ago, something in you shut down.'

'Don't put this on me,' she hisses. 'You had me whenever you wanted. I never refused you. Not once. I was what a wife is meant to be.'

He stares at her. 'You think this is all about sex? About *taking* you?' His hands soften. 'When did you last reach out? Hug me, or . . .' He shakes his head. 'I need more, Jen.'

'I've just given birth to your baby, Pete. I nearly died.' The enormity of the words hits her like a wave, but she doesn't faint. Instead she reaches down and tears off her tights, and her fingers continue ripping. Her skirt, her blouse, flung across the vinyl floor, and then she is standing there in the middle of their rented kitchen in nothing more than her underwear.

They stare at each other. The sounds of the outside world float through the glass.

'You're the only person I'm allowed to talk to,' says Jen. 'And then this.'

70

Younger Blood

Isobel

Isobel tried to get Jude on side when Patrick got married. She knew the balance of power had shifted.

'Can't you get him to cut his hair?' she said once, reaching up to brush Patrick's fringe from his eyes. 'Not have it so mop-like?'

Jude watched her fuss and smiled. 'I can't tell him how to look, Isobel. That's up to him.'

Pert and indifferent, that was Jude. *Jude*. What a name. Short for Judith, which had a sort of sophistication. But Jude? No.

Despite her reservations, Isobel tried to foster friendship with her daughter-in-law. In her mind was the Irish saying *A son is a son till he takes him a wife, a daughter is a daughter all of her life*. I can't lose him, she thought. What will I have left if Jude drives him away? And so she tried playing ball.

'Are you being naughty today?' Isobel said, when Jude took a slice of Victoria sponge from the buffet table at a party. She nudged Jude's arm with a wink.

Jude paused with her fork mid-air, unsure how to reply. 'I'm just eating cake,' she said. 'Should I be watching my weight, then?' She looked down at her body. 'Funny how people never say that to men.'

Of course, Jude was one of those feminists. Isobel had been horrified when Patrick told her they didn't practise the headship arrangement in their house.

'But it's a command from the Bible,' said Isobel. 'The husband is head of his wife. It's not optional.'

Patrick shrugged. 'Well, we don't practise slavery despite the scriptures telling slaves to respect their masters. Jude and I think the same about the headship principle.'

Isobel stared at him, open-mouthed.

Or when Jude and Patrick had been discussing their future plans to have children. 'Is your plan to be a working mum?' she said to Jude, who replied, 'I don't know,' before turning to Patrick to ask, 'Is your plan to be a working dad?'

You go ahead and try to have it all, my dear, thought Isobel. See how tired it makes you.

When Steven left, everyone rallied round. They dropped by for coffee or sent cards or texts. After the meeting, sisters rushed over to cock their heads or pat her arm, just as they did when she was still single at twenty-two. The déjà vu made her dizzy.

Nobody brought her meals, though. Of course, Isobel was a brilliant cook. Still, nothing prepared her for the loneliness of cooking for one, or the knowledge that, if *she* had left, every sister would have knocked on Steven's door with a casserole. He was always the more popular one.

Toni would definitely have dropped off a dish. With her wild blonde hair and warm laugh that always drew attention, she and Isobel were polar opposites. If Isobel's hand held a Bible, Toni's was rarely without a glass of white wine. She was married to Bill Norris, an elder whose talks sent the congregation to sleep, and it was well known they had separate bedrooms. Toni loved flirting with Steven, and at first it bothered Isobel, but, when she asked Steven if he found her attractive, he laughed and said, 'Don't be ridiculous. She's old enough to be my mother.'

She'd frowned. Toni was the same age as her.

Isobel began calling her 'that little bitch' as soon as Steven took Amber on. *Sorry, Father.* Not out loud, of course. Just when Amber rang deep into the evening and Steven always took the call in his study. Or if he arrived an hour late home from work to a stone-cold dinner and she asked, 'Well, couldn't you call?' and he said he'd lost track of time showing Amber how to use the software. That little bitch. *Sorry, Father.*

Isobel had protested when he said he was hiring someone to take over her role.

'But I've always done it,' she said, pouring gravy on his potatoes. 'Why would you need anyone else?'

He sighed. 'It would be good to bring in some younger blood. We need to diversify. I'd like to send someone out to pitch to the bigger companies, and . . . don't take this the wrong way, Isobel, but you're more suited to a background role.'

She said nothing, but overdid his gravy.

It's not that she was overly suspicious. Amber looked younger than her age, with a tiny frame and a face full of freckles, and she didn't dress in an especially provocative way or drip with sexuality. She was like a child. Her physique was nothing like Isobel's, not even when Isobel herself was in her teens.

When he disappeared with Amber to the South of France, what shocked Isobel the most was not that he was leaving her for his eighteen-year-old little bitch, but that he was turning his back on God. How could someone go from being an elder to throwing away his eternal life? In her head, she prayed for the strength to forgive, and implored her God to return her husband to the truth.

In her heart, she wished him a long, painful death.

Another Daughter

Jen

1995

She stares at the shelf before glancing at the open door to the hall-way. The house is quiet. Her mother is at the supermarket, her father in the garage, Lina is listening to music in her room.

Now or never.

Jen clears a stack of books from a footstool and positions it by the bookcase. With frequent checks of the door, she steps up in her socks and takes the book from the top shelf. Her fingers slide over the tex-tured hardback cover. The title's gold-embossed letters catch the light.

She is never alone in her father's study. The dark heavy furniture and moss-coloured walls speak of a masculinity that is closed to her. Sunshine never reaches this north-facing room.

Her heart rate quickens as she looks through the pages. The words themselves make little sense to her twelve-year-old brain. It is the very idea of the book in her hands that excites her. She im-agines herself telling Alice tomorrow how she strode into her father's study and simply picked it up.

'Jennifer?'

The book falls from her hands as she sees her dad in the doorway. His body language suggests he has been there a while.

Time stretches as he comes over and bends to pick up the book. He looks at the cover, then up at her face.

'I slammed a door out in the hall and heard a crash in here, so I came in and the book was on the floor.' She is surprised by how eas-ily the lie falls out.

Her father leans the book against his chest as he looks down at her socked feet on the stool, then up at her face.

'I was in the middle of putting it back, because I know this book is just for you . . .' She rubs her sweaty hands on her jeans.

He watches her.

She was meant to have been a boy, her mother said once. After Lina, her father had hoped for a son. There is never any question in her mind of his love, but sometimes she imagines his reaction when he knew it was another daughter. The disappointment on his face.

Jen wills herself to stop blushing and frowns as her father holds out the book.

'Take it,' he says.

She doesn't move.

'Take it.'

She cups her hands and he lays it on top. It is ceremonial in feel. Jen is unsure of what to do.

'Open the book,' he says.

Jen goes to speak, but stops herself. This feels like a trick question and perhaps requires a trick answer.

'You want to open it, don't you?' His voice is smooth.

She shrugs, this feeling the safest option, but a glance at his face says to pick a side. Jen shakes her head.

'Why not?'

'Because it's only for men.'

A flicker of a frown. 'For *elders*,' he says.

Who are all men, she thinks.

'Do I need to put a lock on this room, Jennifer?' he asks, glancing at the door, then back at her.

She slowly shakes her head. 'I was just picking it up,' she whispers.

He nods at the shelf, and Jen reaches up to slide the book back in its original place. She avoids his eye as she climbs down and replaces the books on the stool.

Did you know the elders have a handbook, her friend Alice told her after the midweek meeting. It says how to deal with ones who step out of line. How to work out if they're actually sorry. Only elders are allowed to read it. Do you think your dad has one? Can you get it?

As Jen runs from the room, she sees the way her father looks at her. The disappointment on his face.

Z

Jen

'Room to rent, eh?'

Jen turns to see two figures at the front silhouetted against the shop window. She squints and makes out the figure of a woman in a wide-brimmed hat. The old man behind the counter is holding an index card, frowning as he reads. Jen moves the tins of baked beans into the crook of her arm as she grabs a loaf of bread.

'Yeah, but listen, Max, no oddballs,' says the woman, her voice muffled by an unlit cigarette between her lips. 'If anyone asks for details and you think they look crackpot, don't give them over.'

The shopkeeper pins the card to the shelf behind him and waves her away. 'Over and out. Be off with you.'

'Cheers, darl,' calls the woman, and the bell dings again as she goes out.

Jen drops the supplies on the counter and cranes her head to look out as the woman climbs into a beat-up Volvo, flings down her hat and shakes out her red hair. The car speeds off as the man rings up the items.

The card is written in thick black pen. ROOM TO RENT IN THE VILLAGE. NO PETS, NO WEIRDOS, PREFERABLY FEMALE, and then a monthly rent that Jen could afford if she begs her boss for extra hours. As she pays, Jen memorizes the name – Z – and number, and saves them in her phone as soon as she's left. She doesn't ask the man for the details. Would he judge her as crackpot? She can't bring herself to risk another person turning away.

The elders decided that a slap on the wrist was sufficient.

Jen was folding clothes when Pete returned from the Worship Hall to tell her. He stood by his side of the bed and summarized the jury's findings. They accepted his repentance, his deep hurt at having turned his back on God, his regret at bringing shame on the congregation. It's a private reprimand, he said. No announcement to the congregation, no curtailing of his freedoms, no taking his voice away. His life would continue as normal.

Jen listened as she folded. She had been making two neat piles of clothes – his and hers – to tidy away into drawers. This was what she had always done. But now she stared at Pete's mouth and no longer heard what he said.

They didn't once ask for her opinion. Those three men didn't once call to check if she'd forgiven him. How could the transfusion that saved her be worse than a husband who repeatedly cheats on his pregnant wife? And yet his sin is nothing compared with hers.

As Pete talked, Jen remembered that he'd seen his dad the previous day. He would have been coached. His dad is an elder and has the handbook – he would have told his only son what to say.

Somehow she knew this would happen. Of course this was how it would go.

A gear shifted inside her. She left his clothing on the bed and put away only her own.

She dials the number from the safety of her car, but hangs up when it rings. The idea of living with a stranger would have been unthinkable two months ago. She spends an unknown length of time staring out of the window, thinking of Pete and that house, the life she has lived up to now.

'Hello?'

'Hi,' says Jen. 'I'm calling about a room. Is this' – she pauses – 'Zed?'

'Zee,' says the voice, its tone suggesting Jen has failed the first test. 'Zelda. And, blimey, that was fast.'

'Oh, sorry. Z. Yes, I was in the shop and heard you say there was a room to rent, so . . . could I come and take a look?'

'Now?'

Jen looks at the clock. Pete isn't due home for an hour, maybe later if he's fingering a customer. 'Only if that suits you? I could do later in the week if that's b—'

'Ah, what the hell. You're in the village? I'll give you directions.'

Jen made the decision to leave while her hands were still in the suds. Despite the humiliation, an internal voice said *This is what you've been waiting for.* A whisper at first, now it is a clashing cymbal whenever she enters a room. Sorry, Father, she thinks each time and raises her eyes to the ceiling, and she is, but that doesn't stop the colour flooding back to her cheeks.

Even if Pete had beaten her, according to the Bible, she would still stay his wife. But pumping himself into another means all bets are off.

Since his confession, Jen has taken to going for random drives in the car. It suits her, not bumping into friends and watching them ignore her. She is safe there. She can put on the angriest music and scream, and nobody hears. She can meander around the villages as they wake from winter, pretending the picture-perfect cottages are hers.

Sometimes Jen buys a coffee from the drive-thru and parks up in the sunshine. She keeps the windows rolled up so the sun will penetrate the glass and burn through her jeans. It feels dangerous, like she might catch fire. She rests her head back and closes her eyes.

Jacob.

Jen pulls up outside a small wooden bungalow, sitting alone on a narrow country lane. The tall trees on either side of the house are heavy with green. Pink blossom lies scattered throughout the front lawn, shaken to the ground by yesterday's hard winds.

Jen steps out. The road is quiet, a dead end leading to a timber yard. Across the road are fields stretching to the horizon, their borders peppered with the occasional tree. The grass is bathed in sunshine. She is struck by the difference in geography, how a simple, quiet road can separate a forest from a prairie.

Z said to go in through the side gate, and so she does, closing it behind her. The habit of closing gates is automatic, ingrained by years of ministering. Jen doesn't consider herself a salesperson – she brings the gift of life – but she knows she is scrutinized more than the message. The little things are important – not treading on lawns and remembering to shut the gate. Net curtains are prone to movement. How things appear are how things are taken.

The path veers left away from the main house and into a thicket. Here, the boughs bend to create a canopy and fairytale shade. The path is a curled ribbon of baked earth, formed from years of being stepped on.

There is a distant glow up ahead. With every step, the light gets brighter, until Jen reaches the end in a blaze of sunshine. She gasps. Here, in a clearing in the woods, is Paradise.

A tin tabernacle stands tall and proud in the centre, its blue-green corrugated-metal walls coated in rust. The square structure with its pitched roof looks like a child's drawing. Tall, red portal doors form an entrance, and their gold, ornate hinges glint in the sun. Above is a large window with small panes of stained glass. Rising to the left of the doors is a narrow bell tower, with a large nailed cross painted the same blue-green shade as the walls.

Jen takes a step back at the sight of the cross. All her life she has been taught that crosses are wrong, a deceptive twist of scripture.

But, oh, the building is beautiful, and the gardens around magnificent. They are great, rambling things, tended by hands yet allowed to swell and cascade with life. It is early June and the roses are in bloom. Peach, apricot, red, pink and white – the hues dance together to create a whole new colour. There are hydrangeas, sweet peas, peonies and entire carpets of wildflowers.

Jen compares the scene with her mother's manicured garden, which flowers only in regimented drills. Daffodils in March, tulips in May, clipped topiary round the clock. Plants may sprout but only by invitation, and there is nothing unexpected. Weeds are ripped out before they even have the chance to begin. Here, Jen imagines a thick web of underground weeds, their heads left to burst and seed and make every year a surprise.

She steps forward.

An image comes to mind of her with Jacob on her hip, him leaning in to inhale the scent. He has thick red curls and a laugh that goes straight through her. This is how it will be in Paradise. This is how it will be if she keeps telling the truth.

Jen has never pictured such beauty. She forgets the painted cross.

A hinge creaks, and the woman from the shop appears in the doorway. Hair the colour of fire, bare legs, a patchwork house coat. She leans against the door with her arms folded and stares at Jen.

Z, short for Zelda.

Jen looks closer. She knows this woman, or the girl she used to be. She has laughed with her, shared food with her, spent nights talking crushes and life and all those silly, important things.

She was Alice Kay then.

PART TWO

Coke

Jen and Alice

Jen still remembers meeting Alice.

Her family had been invited to a barbecue held to welcome them into the hall, Jen's dad having fallen out with the elders in their previous congregation.

One of Jen's favourite things about her faith was being part of *a worldwide brotherhood*, the idea that you could rock up in any town with a Worship Hall and be welcomed with open arms. There is a safety and comfort in meeting strangers who think exactly like you. There's no need to dig deep, to ask how they define right and wrong, to know if a person is honest. The label of 'Disciple' means the work is already done. It's like finding a Coke in the middle of the desert. You trust the brand on the outside and don't question the taste of the liquid.

Jen's dad would test this theory by taking them to the meeting wherever they went on holiday. While Lina and Jen would have preferred to spend their only Sunday off at the beach, he insisted they pack their best clothes so they could visit the local hall. And the theory proved true each time. Wherever they went, the brothers and sisters crowded around, showering them with love. Aren't we lucky, girls, their father would say on the way back to their villa. Isn't this proof of God's love? It was like discovering home on the other side of the world.

And so when Jen and her family walked through a stranger's gate for a barbecue, people they'd never met came over to hug them. Lina quickly made small talk with the other fifteen-year-olds and was led away to their corner of the garden. Jen waited awkwardly as the crowd dispersed and she realized no one was coming forth to claim her.

A middle-aged woman in a floral dress was standing by the back door. 'Alice,' she called over her shoulder, not taking her eyes off Jen. 'Come here and meet Jenny. She looks about your age.'

There were huffs from the kitchen and then a girl pushed past the woman and stepped out on to the patio. She wore a floppy hat with a red flower stitched on the front brim, jeans and a crochet waistcoat over a t-shirt. A silver mood ring on her finger. Her mouth chewed fast, and she ate another crisp as she eyed Jen up and down.

'Jenny, is it?'

Jen shuffled her feet. 'Most people call me Jen, but you can call me Jenny if you like.'

The girl frowned. 'Well, which is it? I'm not going to call you something you're not.'

'Jen, then, I guess.'

'Well, Jen-then-I-guess, I'm Alice. Hungry? They still haven't bloody cooked anything, but there are crisps in there.' She jerked her head towards the back door.

Jen started to shrug but stopped herself. She followed Alice into the kitchen, where platters of food sat covered in clingfilm. On the wall was a Bible calendar, exactly like the one in her kitchen at home.

'Here,' said Alice, ripping open a multipack and throwing a bag to Jen, who caught it and looked unsure.

'Are we meant to be eating these? It's just' – she craned her head to see her dad – 'if it's close to dinner, maybe I should wait for the prayer.'

Alice stopped eating. 'Blimey, no wonder my mum wants us to be friends. Nothing gets past you. It's fine, open it.'

As Jen debated whether to listen to her conscience or her new and only friend, a man's voice sounded behind them.

'What are we up to, girls? Not causing mischief, I hope.'

His voice was friendly, like his face, which looked roughly the same age as Jen's dad's. He wore a loudly printed shirt, and his skin bore the colour of a recent holiday. As he bent down to take a beer from the fridge, Jen noticed how tight his shorts were, as if keen to show off his trim physique.

'You're new to the hall, right?' he said to Jen, angling the bottle against the worktop and striking the lid off with his palm. He leant his elbow on the top of the fridge.

'Yes,' said Jen, blushing at how this thirty-something man spoke like she was an adult. 'I'm Jen. My parents are out there with my sister, Lina.'

'Cool,' he said, smiling. 'Well, I'm Steven and it's a pleasure to have you. I'm sure Alice will be a good partner-in-crime, but let me know if you have any problems because she does like to spout rubbish.'

'Get lost, would you?' said Alice, throwing a crisp in his direction and flicking her brown hair. Her face said she was far from offended.

Steven winked and went out through the back door.

'That was . . . weird,' said Jen.

Alice stared at her mood ring. 'Look, it's gone purple.'

'What does that mean?'

'Passion.'

Jen wrinkled her nose and nodded at the door. 'Is he always like that?'

'Ah, that's just Steven. He's the only fun elder.'

'Elder?' Jen said, almost choking.

Alice nodded. 'You wouldn't think it, right? He's so nice and always arranging stuff, like ice-skating or bowling. He's the resident DJ if there's ever a party. Wife's a cow, though. I feel sorry for him, being married to her.'

'What's so bad about her?'

'She's a right snob. Thinks she's better than everyone because she buys her food from Marks and Spencer. Oh, crap, this is her now.'

Alice stuffed the last crisp into her mouth and threw the empty bag in the bin as a stern-looking woman came in from the garden. She wore a floaty monochrome dress and beige sandals, and eyed them both suspiciously as she picked up the open bag of crisps.

'I think these are meant to be put into a bowl, not eaten individually,' she said to no one in particular, then turned and walked out.

Alice raised her eyebrows at Jen. 'See? Cow.'

They were eleven then, or nearly. Only a month separated them in age, but the way it fell – Alice in August, Jen in September – meant they were in separate years at school. Alice would start at the local girls' school after the holidays, with Jen following a year later.

Their friendship formed thick and fast. At meetings, Alice and her mother usually sat in the row behind Jen, and Alice would slip her notes through the gaps in the chairs. *Turn to page 1,642 in your Bible and read the first subheading. Say it quickly.* Jen flicked to the page and read as instructed: *Animals are Souls.* Jen snorted and got a sharp *Shh* from her mother. Alice would write about the dullness of the brother giving the talk, or gush at length about the attractiveness of boys in the hall. Jen made sure to rip up the rude ones.

Angela did not like Alice. As soon as she heard that Alice's father was not in the truth, Jen's mum took steps to limit their friendship. She knew girls like that, she said to her daughter. You have to watch yourself. Once she was sorting out Jen's meeting bag and found one of Alice's notes, and Jen had to explain why a brother was described as *a pasty Ribena berry*, or a lad's bum called *peachy* with *down, tiger* in brackets.

Jen knew Alice was all talk. Her bravado concealed the chip on her shoulder about having a worldly dad, something she sensed was a mark against her, her family not wholly clean. 'I know your mum doesn't like me,' she said once to Jen. 'That's not true,' Jen fired back, but her blush revealed more. 'It's okay,' said Alice. 'It's not your fault your mum's a bitch. Just like it's not my fault my dad doesn't believe it.' Her adoration for him was without limit.

Jen was never allowed to go to Alice's house. She had never even seen it. She kept making excuses at first, until one day Alice stopped asking. She knew. Jen was sure of it. They enacted an unspoken rebellion by writing all over Jen's bedroom walls and hiding it with posters. Their scribbles were silly cartoons and quotes from TV shows, but something about taking permanent ink to mortgaged walls felt revolutionary.

They saw *Titanic* ten times at the cinema, throwing popcorn at the screen whenever Rose's mum appeared and Alice gripped Jen's arm when Leo slipped beneath the water. Doomed love invaded their subconscious. They slid hands down fogged windows until they nailed the slick.

The summer they turned thirteen, they had their first proper row. They were walking in the fields near Jen's house when Jen said she'd love to get a tattoo.

'What?' said Alice, stopping. 'You can't do that. It goes against the Bible.'

'Oh, I probably won't, but I'd love to. Maybe.'

'Well, I think it's disgusting even to want one. If God can read your heart and you want something He hates, it's not going to go well for you, is it?' Alice marched back to the house and called her mum to come get her.

The strangeness of it all was that their responses were entirely uncharacteristic, as if that day they'd been raised up into the air and switched around. Jen had no interest in tattoos, but she thought she'd try it on, just for a minute. Alice's notebook, however, teemed with ideas.

Alice got baptized soon after. People gave her cards and gifts, and everyone hugged and congratulated her on the most important event of her life. She was now dedicated to God. Jen took a photo of Alice standing with her mum, her hair still dripping wet from the pool, her mum's arm wrapped tightly around her. They both cried happy tears.

Something changed in Alice, soon after. A light went out. Her moods became darker, her behaviour manic.

It started with shoplifting. In the make-up section of Boots, Jen pointed out a blue eyeshadow she liked. When they left the shop and went further down the road, Alice pressed the palette into Jen's palm. Jen's mouth dropped open. She began to protest. Don't be stupid, said Alice, walking off. You said you wanted it, so I got it for you. You can't take it back now.

One afternoon, Jen glanced up from where they lay on her bed and screamed, 'The size of that spider!' She pressed herself against the opposite wall.

Alice stayed where she was, craning her head to look. 'It's tiny,' she said, turning back to the TV. 'It's more scared of us, anyway.'

'Well, you're not the one who has to sleep here. And I won't be able to sleep, knowing that could crawl over me if it wanted.'

Alice stared at the spider. Her mouth hardened. 'You want me to get rid of it?'

Jen nodded, her eyes not leaving its thick body. 'I'll get a glass and envelope,' she said, but Alice was already standing on the bed, her hands slowly reaching upwards. Jen noticed her bare midriff, how her friend's body was morphing from straightness to curves.

'Don't kill it,' Jen said, but Alice was already pounding her fist against the wall, hammering the spider into the paisley wallpaper with quick, vicious blows. If it had been human, the room would have swum in blood.

Alice stopped and stared at the smashed remains. Her body was shaking, her breathing quick. She turned to Jen, who stood pressed against the door, open-mouthed.

'I didn't mean for you to . . .' Jen said in a whisper.

'Like you said, you don't want it bothering you any more.' Alice brushed her hand against the wall. 'And now it won't.'

Jen stared at her friend, seeing her for the first time.

On the ministry a week later, Jen leant down to smell the roses in someone's front garden. She faced the door as she did so, careful to keep her feet on the path. When the woman opened the door, Jen greeted her warmly.

'We've been admiring your beautiful garden,' she said, taking out her Bible. 'Have you ever wondered where our love of nature comes from? Because we all have it, don't we? A shared appreciation for the outside world. If I can just read this one little quote . . .' and she turned to a scripture.

Alice waited further back, the obligatory smile plastered on her face.

When the door closed, they walked back down the path. Jen wrote down the woman's details as Alice leant in and inhaled the scent.

'What are you doing?' Jen hissed, holding the gate.

'Oh, I forgot how we're only to notice things on the way *up* to the door,' said Alice. 'There's no seeing for the joy of seeing. Only for manipulation.'

At school Alice began tormenting the male teachers. She left tampons on their desks if they refused her request to go to the toilet. Mr Bates, the geography teacher, was known as a lech who would rub himself against the desk when talking to the class. Alice once coloured the corner with a stick of chalk so it smeared all over his groin. She got a week's detention for that.

'Something's happened to you,' said Jen one day, and she jumped back as Alice lunged forward.

'And what would you know with your perfect family?' she spat. 'Your elder dad and his elder's wife and his Lina and his Jen. Untouchables.'

Jen stared at her, her face draining of colour. 'Why are you being like th–'

'Like what? Maybe this is how I've always been, only now I can't ignore it.' She gave an over-the-top cackle, then her eyes filled with tears. She pressed her face into her hands, shook her head and ran.

They were hanging out with the boys in the congregation by the time they turned fourteen, and Saturday evenings were spent with them. Mike lived in the centre of town, and they would use Vince's brother's ID in the off-licence before heading to the park to smoke and drink bottles of Hooch. Once, Mike's mum was out walking the dog and almost caught them. They hid their hands under the picnic table, and somehow she didn't notice the smoke wafting through the gaps. Jen said no to cigarettes but tried the Hooch. It was her first taste of alcohol. On the walk back to Mike's house, they had to smuggle her up the stairs almost passed out. Angela didn't notice at pick-up that her daughter couldn't walk in a straight line. She assumed she was just tired. There was no reason for suspicion if Jen was with Disciples. You trust the brand on the can.

In Mike's room they sat on his bed and listened to music. Alice got off with the boys. She always did. They loved Alice for her boobs, which had exploded in size at the start of that year. She wore tight tops that made them look bigger and black chokers that spelled BABE in silver letters. When once Jen lined her lips in brown to copy Alice, her father marched her straight to the bathroom and called her a whore.

Their friendship ended when they were sixteen.

Rumours did the rounds at school that, as well as boys, Alice liked kissing girls.

'So what if I do?' she said, when Jen asked.

Jen stared at her. Alice knew that homosexuality was unacceptable in their world. She had read the scriptures condemning such urges, declaring those who practise such things as deserving death.

'But you're not . . . gay?'

Alice took a dramatic pause to blow a bubble with her gum. 'You mean *bisexual*. Dunno. Don't think so. But it's fun.' She saw Jen's face. 'Don't worry, I don't fancy you. I have standards.' She ran away before Jen could slap her.

The following weekend they were at Jen's doing their make-up before heading to Mike's. 'Here,' said Alice, flinging a box on the bed. 'Will you do my lashes? I'm rubbish at doing them on myself.'

Jen stood in front of her friend and pieced the gluey lashes on to her eyelids, frowning as she concentrated.

'You look cute when you do that,' said Alice.

Jen smiled and leant back to inspect her handiwork. She put her hands on Alice's cheeks as she looked from eye to eye, checking they were even. 'There,' she said. 'Beautiful.'

There had been the briefest of moments when their eyes met and they shared an understanding. Alice reached up and kissed Jen on the mouth, and Jen stood there and let her. Their tongues touched. Then the flame went out, and Jen shoved Alice against the wardrobe. 'Get out,' she hissed, and threw Alice's bag at her. 'Get out of my house.'

That was the final time they spoke. Jen avoided her at meetings, and once, when Alice pressed a note into her palm after the final prayer, she went to the Ladies' and ripped it to shreds before pulling the chain. As she watched the unread paper swirl and go, Jen felt the same dread in her stomach as when Alice had pushed her mouth on hers. A sensation so strange, so familiar, it made her heart quicken. My mum was right, she thought. You have to watch yourself with girls like that.

A year later, Alice was disfellowshipped, and, by then, Jen was engaged to Pete.

Eden

Zelda

'Alice.'

Zelda leans against the door, eyeing her old friend. It is almost eighteen years since she left that life and took on another, but Jen still looks as she did. The same petite features, straight blonde hair, neat clothes hiding her body. 'I'm Zelda,' she says. 'It's years since Alice.'

'Oh.'

'You probably shouldn't be talking to me,' says Zelda, rubbing her finger against a rough part of the wood. 'I went over to the bad side, remember.'

'Is there room for me?' says Jen, then smiles at Zelda's surprise.

Seeing her friend makes the memories of those days sharp again, and Zelda presses a hand on her stomach to stop herself from trembling. 'You're here now,' she says. 'May as well come in.'

Jen steps over the threshold with a dazed expression. It's rare that others are invited in, and Zelda loves to watch new faces take in her dad's old workshop. Tin tabernacles are rare, and even rarer converted. When her dad died, she spent her tiny inheritance fixing it up.

'This is where you live?' says Jen.

Zelda tries to see it as a stranger would. The open-plan kitchen and living area that are separated by a small black stove in the middle. Wooden panelled walls that stretch up into the vaulted ceiling, giving the house the heavenly aura its Victorian inhabitants wanted. The metal, spiral staircase in the centre leading up to Zelda's room, the only upstairs space. The furniture is tatty and old-fashioned, but sofas have new life with colourful throws, and the walls are adorned with embroidered fabric. Light floods the space from the arched

94

windows along both walls. It is incredible. Zelda never gets bored by it.

'The kitchen's a little more old-school than you're used to,' she says, tapping the stained worktop and remembering Jen's immaculate childhood home. The cupboard doors are roughly hewn wood, as if someone has chopped down a tree there and then. 'There's not much in the way of hot water . . . well, enough for a few sinkfuls, but then you have to wait for it to reheat. And the cooker's a bit old, but . . . there we go. It's fine for me.'

Jen nods, pushing her hands into her pockets. 'No, it's nice. Very . . . rustic.'

Zelda laughs. 'Don't worry, it's not everyone's cup of tea. Some people don't like sharing their home with insects.'

Jen looks up at the churchy windows, then down at the pews lining the walls, the stained glass throwing coloured shapes on the floor. Zelda knows there is no way she'll say yes.

'You want to take a look at the room on offer?'

Jen follows her to the door at the back.

'What's with the dead flowers?' she says, stopping by a glass vase of wilted lilies.

'An experiment.' Zelda pushes open the door.

She has always loved this space. It was once a junk room where her dad stored old trunks and broken mannequins, and where Zelda would play. If her dad had to measure expensive fabric, he'd shoo her out with a promise of a biscuit from the tin in exchange for five minutes' peace. She'd arrange the mannequins so they faced each other or looked out of the window, and she'd chat to them like they were old pals. An only child makes friends where she can. As she got older, nine or ten, she'd lay them down on top of each other and try to position their legs for the s-e-x of her schoolfriends' whispers. She always stood them back up before her dad came to find her.

The room is darker than the rest of the house, but cosy. A single bed sits in the corner beside an old chest of drawers, a window looks out on trees, and a handmade rag rug lies over the floor. The smooth nakedness of two mannequins catches the light.

'I can get rid of those,' says Zelda.

Jen drifts, letting her fingers brush along the furniture. When she reaches the mannequins, she stops to examine them. 'No,' she says. 'There's something other-worldly about them. They belong here.'

Outside, the air is getting hotter. The honeysuckle trailing along the tin wall is thick with bees, and Jen takes a deep inhale of scent. 'Did you do all this?' She waves at the blooms.

Zelda nods. 'You probably don't remember my dad – he was a costume designer – and when he saw this place in an auction, he snapped it up. It used to sit in the middle of some shitty town before he brought it here to be his workshop.' She looks up at the spire. 'It needed a garden to match its beauty.'

Jen looks towards the path. 'Who lives in the house?'

Zelda smiles. 'You don't recognize it, do you? Of course not. The untouchable Jen never saw it.'

'Oh. But –'

'My mum closes the curtains whenever I go by. I'm dead to her unless I go back to that life.' She bites her bottom lip. 'Christian love, eh.'

'Well . . .' Jen stares at the flowers. 'I've never seen anything like this. It feels hopeful. Like nothing bad could happen here.'

Zelda gives a sad laugh. 'I made my own Eden.'

Jen smiles, and there's a moment of connection between old friends, when years can go by but it doesn't matter.

'So what's your story?' says Zelda, and listens as Jen fills her in. 'Fuck,' she says when Jen's finished. 'Fuck, fuck, fuck.'

Jen almost laughs. The sound of swearing usually shocks her, but Zelda is right. There are no other words that fit.

'So you're out?' says Zelda, then frowns at Jen's expression. 'Surely you don't want to go back. After all that?'

Jen looks down at her fingers twisting together. Leave? She has been put outside, but, after proving herself, the door will reopen. Did Jesus abandon the truth when the religious leaders put him to death? No, Zelda would not understand. She is worldly, and therefore her instinct is corrupt.

'Look,' says Zelda. 'The rent's cheap for obvious reasons, but I'll knock another fifty off. Desperate times and that.'

Jen looks away. The elders would never approve of her living with Zelda, but what choice does she have? Perhaps they won't find out, perhaps she can work more at the shop and save for a flat, so that by the time she is up for reinstatement all this will have been forgotten.

'Perhaps,' she mumbles.

'God, Jennifer, you've not changed. Stop being so damn polite.'

A blush spreads across Jen's face at being rumbled, and she looks relieved at permission to be open. 'It's just . . .' she starts, then her eyes travel upwards. 'Was this ever a church?'

Zelda knows what she means. 'No idea. Probably.' She watches Jen stare at the roof. 'It's two pieces of wood nailed together. It doesn't mean something unless you make it mean something.'

Lipstick

Isobel

Isobel lays out her clothes on the Sunday night. She has no idea what the receptionist at a dental surgery wears and chastises herself for not looking more closely when she went for her interview.

In the end, she decides that meeting-wear is the most appropriate. She selects a dark green linen skirt, a white blouse and a brown tailored jacket. The blouse has a silver thread running through its weave, and so she picks out a scarf and bracelet in the same shade, just as her mother taught her. Isobel assembles the outfit and hooks the hanger over the wardrobe. Before she closes her eyes that night, she looks across at the woman she is now supposed to be.

She had informed the elders the previous week. Brother Connell took her into the back room, and she sat upright with her hands folded as she delivered her speech. Afterwards, he smiled and patted her hand.

'It's okay, Isobel. We understand.'

'It's not that I don't want to minister full time any more,' she said quickly. 'And I'll still do it every Saturday morning. But Steven left me with limited funds, and the rest is tied up in the house.'

'No need to explain,' he said. 'Full-time ministering is a personal decision. Of course, the preaching work *is* more important than secular employment, especially this close to the end, but we must still survive in this system before we make it through to the next.'

'I want to be clear that I'm not stopping out of desire. I have no choice.' Once the house is sold, she will be financially secure enough to quit her job and go back three spaces to her old life.

'Isobel, please. If you must take paid employment, that is perfectly understandable. It wouldn't be right to continue ministering if you seek benefits from the government, but you know that.'

Isobel's face burned. He thinks she's on the breadline. She, Isobel Forge, who six months ago had entertained Les Connell and his wife for a five-course meal with a Château Margaux 2010 from their wine cellar.

'Perhaps you should change your car for one more economical,' he went on. 'More modest. You may find that lowering your out-goings will help you get back on your feet quicker.'

'Actually it's Steven's,' she said, her face still hot. She had never been counselled in her life. 'The car. It's in his name. Everything is in his name. So it's not quite that simple.'

'Don't be offended, Isobel,' he said. 'A bit of friendly counsel, that's all. I say it because I care.'

'Thank you. As I said, it's not that simple.'

At the following meeting, Isobel sat in the audience as the announcement was made. *Sister Forge is no longer serving as a regular minister.* She knew it was coming, but the shame still overwhelmed her. It was not hers to own, but it made no difference. The announcement was worded the same as it would have been had she committed a sin. It made no allowance for context, and now perhaps everyone was thinking of her what she had always thought of others. The silent translation: you are not good enough.

She arrives at the surgery at 7.37 a.m., eight minutes early. The Victorian building is large and detached, multiple extensions feeding from its bulk, and its white-painted bricks in need of a fresh coat. As she is first to arrive, Isobel reverses with ease into a space, then sits and stares at the surgery.

For the past thirty years, she has never spent longer than a few hours in the company of an unbeliever. *Keep yourself without spot from the world*, Jesus said. Even if the organization didn't warn her against people of the outside world – which it frequently does – she would not have needed friendships elsewhere. Her days were spent minis-tering and socializing with other sisters, and there had never been a reason to step outside the bubble. Many of her friends had their babies when she did, and so her coffee mornings and play dates were spent with them. She didn't need to linger at the school gates, and half hoped the other mums noticed how she didn't join in with meet-ups or their jokes about too much wine. Perhaps it will make them curious, she thought, and lead to an opportunity to preach. And, if they thought her snobbish, well, that was to be expected. Hadn't Jesus warned his followers they would be hated on account of his name? It made her feel powerful to know she was taking a stand for truth. I am good, she told herself. I am more righteous than them.

Today is the start of something new.

But Isobel doesn't want new. She liked the hamster wheel of meetings, ministry and wholesome recreation, the weeks blending together, her routine of designated meals on designated nights, the certainty of her existence as true and correct. What is the point of new when the end of the world is coming? This is not my choice, Isobel keeps repeating. I liked my life how it was.

The clock on the dash reads 7.47 as a car turns off the road and hurtles down the driveway. It's one of those little Italian cars that inspire Isobel to say, without fail, *But you can't get anything in the boot!* It skids to a stop, and out hops a young woman with blonde hair that bounces.

Isobel gets out and starts walking across the tarmac, her handbag pressed against her waist.

The girl looks up and smiles. 'Hello! Nice to see you again. I'm Sadie. I'm on reception too. It's Isobel, isn't it?'

She nods and smooths her hair. 'I was told 7.45 and it's now' – she looks down at her watch – '7.49.'

'Oh, I know. Slept through the alarm, didn't I? Do me a favour and don't say anything to Carol. We've still got ten minutes before opening, so plenty of time to switch everything on. Now where are the damn keys . . . Ah, got them.'

Inside, Sadie flicks a switch and there's a momentary fizz from the fluorescent bulbs before the reception is bathed in light. She had seen it once before, at her interview, but that day her attention had been fixed on her nerves and not the decor. Now, Isobel takes a closer look at the room where she will spend her days. It is a large open-plan space with green threadbare chairs in a u-shape around a coffee table that overflows with tatty books and magazines. The reception is divided from the waiting room by a low mahogany counter, and the walls are coated in thick Artex plaster, stippled like meringues. The vibe is army-green and dark wood with brass fittings. Isobel notices that her skirt matches the carpet.

'Retro, huh?' says Sadie, dropping her bag and firing up the computer. 'Did Carol tell you we're closing for a few days soon so it can be redecorated? Don't worry, we're getting paid. First thing I checked, ha. But, yeah, this will all be ripped out. Out with the old.'

She sings a modern pop song as she wanders out to the back.

Her first day goes well. When Carol arrives, she introduces Isobel to the dentists and tells her to shadow Sadie, just until she gets a feel for the software and calls. But Isobel finds herself picking up the phone when Sadie is with a patient, and she smiles when Carol gives a thumbs-up as she passes. You don't knock on strangers' doors all your life without learning a thing or two about initiative, she thinks, and feels a warm pride for everything her faith has taught her.

Sadie handles the job of reception with the ease of someone used to being noticed. She types away with the phone receiver cradled into her shoulder and flashes a Hollywood smile at patients whose names she always knows. *Well, hello, Mr Godden, and how are we this morning?* Her confidence is a bold lipstick. Vivacious. Teeming with life. Isobel finds her exhausting.

Sadie and Carol insist on taking her for a welcome drink at the pub next door after they finish. Isobel tries to refuse, but Sadie loops her arm through hers and gently pulls her across the car park. 'Nonsense,' she says. 'Five minutes. Everyone can spare five minutes.'

They make an odd trio, sitting around a sticky table in the corner, Sadie and Carol with their vodka and Cokes, and Isobel with her juice. Her handbag stays on her lap, and her eyes flick to the door each time it opens, terrified that someone she knows will catch her having a drink with worldly colleagues. She tries to think of an excuse in case this happens.

'Who's up for another?' says Sadie. 'I know you are, Carol. Isobel? I'm sure another OJ won't push you over.' And she floats off to the bar before Isobel can answer.

As Carol talks about the office, Isobel recognizes the man chatting to Sadie as a patient from that morning. Her eyes dart up and down his motorcycle leathers and his long pony-tailed hair, and she looks down as Sadie points towards their table.

A minute later, he is taking the seat beside her as Sadie sets down their drinks with a splash. 'They're on Mr Godden,' she trills, dropping into her chair.

He gives a shy smile. 'I see you ladies so often these days that it's the least I can do.' He leans slightly towards Isobel as he taps his cheek. 'Extensive work in progress.'

Isobel shifts further away.

'To your first day,' says Sadie, raising her glass.

'Ah, congratulations!'

'Thank you,' mumbles Isobel, tucking a strand of hair behind her ear. She blushes despite herself, and is relieved when he notices and turns his attention away.

The Maker

Jen

1999

The first time she felt the clay was in her final year at school. Ms Orr, the art teacher, had set up a wheel in the classroom for the girls to try. They were taking exams the following summer, and when they discovered this was a fun exercise on which they weren't going to be tested – 'Life isn't just about what you *have* to do, girls' – most of Jen's classmates chose to work on their coursework instead.

Why not, thought Jen. She wasn't bothered about exams. Her fellow students were preparing for sixth form and university, but she would be choosing a different path. Her career would be educating people on a much more important subject.

That's how she saw ceramics at the start of that art class. A bit of fun. Her hands hadn't yet touched the clay, her fingers hadn't dipped into water, she hadn't felt the rhythm of the wheel or discovered how a nudge could transform the entire shape. All she saw were tools and a cold lump of grey. Everything else was invisible.

A dam burst inside when she took the wheel. She looked at her stained hands, the clay, her teacher's face, and thought, *Oh*. Ms Orr stood near her shoulder, murmuring and guiding her gently. A flash of anger burned through her when she had to make way for someone else, and she scraped back her chair. When Ms Orr told the class they could have another go the following week, Jen maintained her poker face, but after school she went to the public library and borrowed every pottery book they had.

The following week, more students wanted a go, and Jen tapped her foot as she waited. When the lunch bell rang before she'd had a turn, Jen slammed down a book and blushed when everyone looked over. 'Sorry,' she muttered.

Ms Orr stopped her on the way out. 'It's a shame you didn't get time today, Jen.'

She gripped her bag strap, embarrassed by her anger. 'I'll just have to wait another week.'

The teacher hesitated. 'You can do it now if you like?'

'Really?'

Ms Orr smiled. 'My sandwich will taste the same here as in the staff room.'

Jen rushed over to the wheel, forgetting to thank her. She dropped her bag and set about readying the clay. Everything from the previous week came flooding back. It was as if she'd always known what to do.

'You're a natural,' said Ms Orr from her desk.

Jen was bent over her work. 'Oh, I doubt that.'

'You are.' She spoke between bites. 'The pot you made last week, and the way you touch the clay. You're a beginner, but you have an affinity with it.'

Jen couldn't take her eyes away from the wheel.

'What does it do to you?'

'Sorry?'

Ms Orr paused while she finished her mouthful. 'Working the clay with your hands. How does it feel?'

Jen didn't answer straight away. She finished the pot, using the wire to cut it free, then scraped the wet remnants from the surface. She sat with her legs either side of the wheel and thought of how to reply. How to explain that it made her feel powerful, directing the clay and being responsible for its future. She was a maker. *Her*. It rooted her to that specific moment, to the physicality of the world. The smooth pulse of the wheel was like the heartbeat of someone you loved.

She stared at her hands, smeared with clay. 'It just makes sense.'

As well as her regular class, Jen went along twice a week to the art room. On a Monday Ms Orr sat at her desk eating lunch and marking papers as Jen worked the wheel, then on Tuesdays she left Jen alone before returning later to lock up. She fired Jen's work in the kiln, she lent her books on ceramicists, she repeatedly told Jen she was a natural.

Jen lived for these sessions. She wished the days and weekends away until she was back at the wheel, forming and making and feeling. She learnt how the firing process transformed colour so the end result was nothing like the start. She discovered through practice how to centre the clay using her whole body and not just her hands, to prevent her back from hurting. Now and again, she looked up at the classroom walls, at their chaos of colour and texture, and warmth would bloom through her chest. And then there was Ms Orr, standing so close that Jen almost felt drunk. But schoolgirl crushes on teachers were normal, or so she once read in a magazine.

'I'm staying later at school on a Tuesday,' she told her mother one night as they washed up. 'I'll take a later bus.'

A pause. 'Why?'

'Oh, you know,' said Jen. 'I've got exams, so . . .'

Her father stuck his head round the door to ask for a cup of tea. Football blared from the lounge.

Angela switched on the kettle and turned back to Jen. 'But it's meeting night.'

'I won't be late. Promise.'

And she wasn't. For three months, she stayed behind on a Tuesday before racing to the last bus. She'd walk in as her family was sitting down to dinner, then change her clothes and go to the meeting. She was exhausted but happy.

But one day the bus never came. She waited, the minutes taking hours, then she rang her dad to come and get her. They were silent on the journey home.

The following week, as she cleaned the wheel at the end of Monday lunchtime, Jen told Ms Orr that she would no longer stay late on Tuesdays.

'Really?' said Ms Orr. She peered at Jen over the top of her glasses. 'But I thought you loved it?'

Jen cleared her throat. 'It's complicated.'

Ms Orr handed Jen a piece of paper from her desk. 'Well, you might find this interesting, seeing as decisions on sixth form must be made. This school is useless with anything creative.'

Jen glanced at the printout of a ceramics course at the local art college. She smiled, surprised that Ms Orr thought her good enough to specialize, but it was soon replaced with a frown. 'Oh, I couldn't go to an art college.'

Ms Orr watched her for a while, then started bundling up some papers. 'You know, Jen, it's easy at sixteen to think you know your future. But a talent like yours . . . You come alive at the wheel. Don't waste that.'

Jen looked at the paper, then back at Ms Orr. Well-meaning, kind Ms Orr, who would never understand the world she lived in. 'I'll think it over,' she said, folding it into quarters and stuffing it into her bag.

That weekend, she worked on the ministry with Bill Norris, an elder in the hall. After they had exhausted their general chit-chat on the walk between doors, he said, 'I hear from your mum that you're considering art college?'

Jen stiffened. Of course her mother would look through her bag. Of course she could never be afforded even the slightest privacy. To want privacy must mean she has something to hide, her mother said once. 'Not really,' said Jen, looking away. 'It was just an idea. Silly, really.'

'I can imagine you are very creative.'

Jen looked at him. 'Really?'

'Your demos on the doors are always imaginative. You look for an angle to appeal to the householder, like the one back there whose car window was covered in stickers for their local church. You spotted that and adapted your presentation to appeal to their belief in a god. That's creative, Jen.'

She blushed. She'd never considered this. 'I've been making ceramics at school.'

'And are you any good?'

'My teacher thinks so. She suggested college.'

'And what are your thoughts?'

'Oh . . . I've always planned to leave at sixteen and preach full time.'

'Well, that's obviously a wonderful goal.'

Jen paused. 'Yes.'

'Is it still your aim?'

She nodded.

'Did you know I was in a rock band when I was young?'

Jen looked at him in surprise. Brother Norris often played guitar at congregation parties, and he was known for his booming singing voice. She and Alice would stand behind him at meetings and try not to laugh.

He told her of how he toured the country, playing guitar and singing lead vocals on the occasional song. When people asked what he wanted to be when he grew up, the answer was always a rockstar. And then, at the age of nineteen, he signed with a record label and became one. He said the name of the band and Jen looked at him, shocked.

'But they're huge.'

He nodded. 'They were pretty successful even back then.'

She tried to imagine sweet, dull Brother Norris thrashing a guitar as girls screamed his name. 'What happened?'

'I came into the truth,' he said, lifting his chin. 'I was high on drugs when someone knocked on my door, but I liked the look of the magazines. I went to a meeting, started a study and quit the band.'

'Just like that?'

'Playing songs seemed silly in comparison.' He rapped his knuckle on his Bible. 'What I do now, what *we* do . . . It's saving lives.'

Jen stuffed her hands into her pockets. That week, she had allowed herself to dream about a different life. One that involved art college and the wheel. Meetings and ministry would still come first, but perhaps she could work for herself, making ceramics, selling her own creations. She wouldn't let it take over her life, just pay her modest bills while she ministered. She told her mother. Not a word about college, just that the teacher said she had talent. But what is it good for? said Angela. You can't make a living out of it. Why would anyone pay more for a cup from you than from a supermarket?

Alice had loved the pieces Jen showed her. She examined them with care, before declaring her *spectacularly* talented.

'Do you miss it?' she asked Brother Norris.

'I still play in my evenings and weekends, when I have the time.'

'But the band. Do you miss being on stage and having people love what you do? The rush of creating music.' She thought of Ms Orr, her praise shooting through Jen's veins.

He smiled as he opened the next gate. 'We will have eternity for that, Jen. Any day now, but we must survive this system first. There are more important things.'

The following week Jen told Ms Orr that she would no longer take the wheel at Monday lunchtimes. She'd wait her turn in the lesson along with everyone else. She used it as an opportunity to preach, to tell her that she was going to be a full-time minister of the good news of God's kingdom, and, as much as she loved ceramics, there were more important things. Ms Orr listened, a sad smile on her face. 'Well, okay, then,' she said, when Jen finished.

Jen nodded and left the classroom.

Perhaps she could do it as a hobby, Bill Norris had suggested. Like his music. Perhaps she could put the kingdom first but enjoy it in her time off.

Jen had murmured in agreement, but she knew she never would. A hobby was something for fun, kept for designated moments, that you could happily leave when it was time to do other things. It would be dangerous to love your hobby more than your work. When your job requires a hundred per cent dedication, you can't allow room for distractions or resentments to build. You can't marry a faithful person, then live for the nights when you have an affair.

She would bury those urges. Any day now.

She will wait for eternity.

Cellophane Flowers

Isobel

Isobel is at reception when Victor returns to the surgery. They have only just opened, and the room is quiet. His biker boots thud on the floor.

'Hello again,' he says, his voice friendly.

Isobel looks up at him leaning on the counter with a small bunch of flowers wrapped in plastic.

'Hello,' she says with a blank smile. 'Name, please?'

'Godden. Victor Godden. We met the other day. And yours?'

She looks at the screen. 'Ah, yes. Take a seat and they'll call you in.'

He clears his throat, and she glances up again to see him waving the flowers at her. She reaches out to take them. They droop inside the cellophane, which bears the tacky remnants of a reduced sticker.

'She's running late today,' says Isobel, nodding at Sadie's empty chair. 'But I'll see that she gets them.' She's already been informed by Sadie of all the patients who fall in love with her. This one must be at least thirty years older than her colleague, but there we are, thinks Isobel.

'No, love. They're for you.'

She blinks. 'I'm sorry?'

'They've seen better days, I suppose, like me,' he says with a wheezy laugh. 'But they were all I could afford.'

'Oh, I couldn't possibly.' She hands them back, but he shakes his head.

'Well, it was hard enough bringing them on my bike. Look, if you don't want them, chuck 'em in the bin out there.'

Isobel's hand hovers, unsure. She tries to study him in two-second bursts. He's about her age. Grey-brown hair to his shoulders.

Fairly ugly – definitely not her clean-cut type – but a good smile. One that lights up his whole face. Nicotine-stained fingers. Not particularly tall. Kind eyes, she'll give him that.

He could not look more different from Steven.

'Thank you,' she says to the desk.

The dental assistant calls his name, and he smiles and disappears into the treatment room. Isobel immediately brings up his record. He is fifty-eight and lives in the block of flats in town that can be seen from everywhere. His next of kin is his daughter. He has a history of problems with his teeth.

Sadie arrives and sees the flowers on the desk. 'Ooh, lucky lady. Who's your beau?'

'Not my beau,' she says, blushing. 'A patient just brought them in. Silly, really.'

Sadie looks at her for a moment. 'I'll get a glass of water,' she says and disappears out back. When she returns, she stands the bouquet next to Isobel.

'I don't know why you're bothering. They're practically dead.'

Sadie looks closer. 'No, they're all right. Another shot at life. Just snip the bottoms and pop them in boiling water for a sec when you get home. That'll perk them up. Take it from someone who knows.' She hums to herself as she sits back down.

When Victor comes out, Sadie greets him warmly while Isobel keeps her eyes on her work. She frowns in concentration as Sadie arranges his next appointment. She doesn't plan to look up until he has left, but then he slides across the counter and clears his throat. Isobel feels Sadie watching.

'Can I help you?'

A smile lights up his face, and Isobel squeezes her pen to steady herself in this unknown land.

'I wondered if I might take you out sometime.'

Isobel almost laughs at the absurdity. Technically, she's still married, and the very idea of going on a date with a worldly man is unthinkable. She purses her lips, knowing a laugh would be cruel. 'I'm married,' she whispers.

'Oh. I saw no ring and made an assumption. My apologies.' He smiles again, but it's not as bright.

'Separated,' says Sadie, and, when Isobel looks at her, she winks and says, 'I asked Carol. I wondered about the lack of ring too.'

Now Isobel's face is burning. Her life is fodder for the water cooler. She wonders if it would really be that rude to crawl underneath her desk.

'I don't want to make you feel awkward,' he says, stepping back. 'And I am, so I'll be off. It would be nice to know your name, though. I mean, you have all of my particulars.'

'It's Isobel,' says Sadie, her hand under her chin.

Isobel closes her eyes and declares mutiny against her colleague. This is all a game to her. *Flirting.* This is what she does for fun. This is what worldly people do for fun.

When the day is finally over, Isobel walks to her car, the bouquet of flowers feeling ridiculous wedged under her arm. She rests them on the passenger seat and steals glances at them in traffic. The brightness of the petals catches the lateness of the sun. They lie across the seat like a casual lover.

At home, she trims and sears the ends like Sadie told her. She arranges the stems in a vase of cold water, then heads upstairs to take a bath. When she comes downstairs in a robe an hour later, there on the kitchen island are the roses, revived and happy. Isobel drops the towel from her hair and reaches out to touch the petals. There is little scent with cheap roses, but she leans in and imagines the aroma. Myrrh, perhaps, or vanilla.

She thinks of Steven. If he could see her now.

She moves into the flat the following weekend, and Patrick takes the day off to help. 'You didn't tell me it was the third floor,' he says, struggling with a box on the stairs. He walks into the lounge and gasps. 'Wow, look at that light.'

Isobel follows his gaze to the ceiling, where celestial sunlight beams down. 'Yes, I shall have to get something rigged up or I'll go blind.'

He stares at her.

'So?'

Patrick folds his arms and takes in the room, slowly nodding. 'I think it's great, Mum. Really, really great.'

'It's very small.'

'As you said, a five-bedroom house was too big. This is perfect. And far easier to keep clean.'

Isobel nods, knowing it wouldn't do to protest that cleaning brings her joy. Because, as she's discovered throughout her life, cleaning is not supposed to bring joy. It is something to be complained about, that people seem to rejoice in complaining about, and really she should be finding happiness in shopping or manicures and Chardonnay.

'You should get Cass over to help you decorate,' says Patrick. 'She'd know exactly what to do.'

'Hmm. I wonder if your sister's taste is a little out there for me.' She feels his stare.

'When did you last speak to her, Mum?'

'Oh, you know Cassandra. I've tried calling, but she never answers. I can take the hint.' Isobel sniffs, recalling how Cassandra moved to a different hall as soon as she married, ensuring their paths would rarely cross.

'Maybe try going over there?'

'And have my ringing of the doorbell go unanswered too?'

Patrick sighs. 'You know how you both are. Here's the perfect opportunity for you to do something together.'

Isobel purses her lips. She can't remember the last time she heard from her daughter. 'Perhaps.'

He brings up the rest of the boxes, and she unpacks the kettle to make a drink. Her fingers are already itching to start scrubbing the skirting boards, but she also doesn't want Patrick to go. She hands him a cup, and they stand in the poky kitchen, sipping tea.

'I have news,' he says. 'Jude's pregnant.'

Isobel's hand flies to her neck. 'Oh, Patrick.'

'Crazy, huh? We've just had the scan.'

'Darling,' she says. 'I don't know what to say.'

'Are you ready to be a grandma?'

A memory appears of them driving to Oxford for a day-trip, shortly after Patrick and Jude married. Isobel turned round in the passenger seat to see Jude's arm draped across the back, her fingers stroking Patrick's neck. 'Jude, what *are* you doing?' Isobel exclaimed, laughing, and her daughter-in-law gave a confused shrug as Patrick looked away. Steven glanced at his son in the mirror. 'Leave them alone,' he said quietly. She has never forgotten it.

Isobel steps forward to kiss his cheek. She pats his arm, and there are tears in her eyes. 'My boy,' she says. 'My little boy.'

When Steven first left, she read a tip in a magazine that suggested writing down the emotions in a diary or letter addressed to the one who hurt you. Isobel already keeps a diary, a few lines of what happened each day, but she's never examined her feelings. The thought makes her want to vomit.

But a letter, she thinks. I could write him a letter and then tear the paper into pieces and bury them in the bin.

Steven,

I have received no correspondence from you, but thought it incumbent upon me to write to you regardless.

The weather here is cold and vile, and it was such a promising spring. But then the snow came, and the sunshine went for what seemed forever. It appears occasionally now, through cracks in the clouds, and I watch a square of bright light appear on the neighbour's roof outside my window. Sometimes I stretch out my arm into the open air to feel it on my fingers. You would laugh at my ridiculousness – I use a stool to climb on to the sink and lean out. I suppose there's a risk of slipping and falling three storeys, and smashing my head on the pavement. You would probably laugh then too. But here I am, stretching my palm in the sunshine, my brain aching for warmth. It's been a long winter.

I expect France is hot. I expect you are sunning yourself on a lounger, letting her rub cream on your back. I wonder if she sees those grey spiral hairs on your shoulders, the ones I always wanted to rip out. You think you look so perfect, but you can't see yourself from behind. I could. And I hated every single one.

I am working now. I know you do not approve of women working, but what choice do I have? The funds you left have almost gone, the rent on this flat is the same as our mortgage, and surely I must eat? It has been so long since I've had any kind of job, apart from that of a wife and mother. Those few years that I continued working at the bank after our wedding seem like a distant memory now.

Do you remember that, our wedding? I wore your sister's dress — tailored, of course, as I was always much smaller than Helen at the waist — and had a veil like you said I should. Our cake was three tiers of boozy fruit with marzipan, Greek columns and piping round the rim. Everyone brought a dish, and we laughed in the car on the way home at the hideous bean salad Aunt Rose had made. Do you remember, Steven? Because I think that if you looked back and saw how perfect that day was, you would not be doing this now. We had hardly a penny — our rental house was filled with tatty furniture that people gave us, we ate dinner from our laps, and I gave you everything I earned. I helped you build that business from nothing, I was there from the start, I supported you. Does she, Steven? Does she ever say no to you, like I never did?

And here I am, at a kitchen table hardly big enough for two. You can't see the room so I'll describe it. Small and square with yellow walls (*yellow!*), a window that faces north, rickety wooden shelves — the kind we had in our first kitchen — from which I hang cups that gather dust quicker than I can use them. And the kitchen itself? Fifties painted units without doors. Doors. I can't even afford *doors*. Instead, I have grubby curtains that must be removed every week to wash, and my pans with their burnt little bottoms must hang on hooks above the hob like strung-out laundry for the neighbourhood to see.

Oh, Steven. What have you done to me.

Champagne

Zelda and Jen

Jen lies in bed, watching morning light spill over the mannequins. Their arms reach out to each other as if dancing, and their faces are lonely.

Today she will help Zelda photograph a wedding. She was unsure initially about attending a worldly celebration and being out in public with Zelda, but then she heard a number she couldn't refuse. It is more than double what she makes in the shop.

Jen can still remember how Alice kissed her. She remembers the very texture of the day, of the minute and second. The force that charged through her body and shot from her fingers, slamming Alice against the wardrobe. When a power is unleashed, it has to take hold of someone. A sacrifice must be made. She thinks of the torn pieces of Alice's note in the toilet bowl and her fear of what may have been written inside.

Jen's eyes wander back to the female mannequin.

It is sad how some friendships die. How we mutiny our revelations to maintain our own denial, and break with friends who show us who we are, not who we want to be. We choke the truth to make it quiet. To make it go away.

And, now, a resurrection. They have broken bread together, silently healed their rift. Jen is intrigued by how natural it feels to be with Zelda. In the week since she moved in, there has been no conscious work on either's part to restore the friendship. It has come back to life on its own.

She sits up as a thought takes her over. Her reconnection with Zelda had come from her need for a cheap room, but didn't Jesus say a shepherd should leave the flock to rescue the one sheep that strayed? Perhaps God has led her back here. To rescue and save her friend.

When she emerges from her room, it's impossible to ignore how Zelda looks at her knee-length skirt and lace blouse. Jen's fingers fumble with the collar. 'Is this okay?'

'Mm-hm,' says Zelda, turning away and sipping her coffee. 'However you feel comfortable.'

'It's just . . .' Jen gestures at Zelda's outfit. 'Bit different from yours, that's all.'

Zelda holds out her cup and looks down at her trouser suit, emerald-green brocade with red roses embroidered along the lapel. 'They book Zelda Bloom, they get Zelda Bloom.'

They are almost walking out of the door when Jen sees the flyer on the table. Her stomach contracts as she reads the print along the top. *Evening pottery class.* 'What's this?'

'Oh,' says Zelda, fussing with her bag. 'I remembered you doing that when we were kids. Thought we could give it a go. Together.' She shrugs and walks out.

Jen stares at the bold letters on the flyer. She folds it in half, running her fingers along the crease again and again.

'So how many megapixels is your camera, then?'

Zelda turns to the man – it's always a man – and fixes the dazzling smile she wears for such inane questions. She recognizes him as the one shooting over her shoulder after the ceremony. 'Pfft,' she says, waving her camera. 'No idea.'

He scoffs, his baldness reflecting the sun. He wears a crumpled linen suit and his ruddy cheeks suggest the glass of champagne he's holding is not his first. 'How can you not know the size of your camera's resolution?'

Zelda glances at the drooping flower pinned to his lapel. Bridal party. She'll have to tread carefully here. 'It's not all about the size, sweetheart. It's what you do with it that counts.' She gives a cheeky wink and moves off through the crowd before he can answer.

When she started photographing weddings a decade ago, Zelda quickly learnt the art of fakery. She couldn't dropkick the shit out of every best man or usher who leant in for a drunken hug – their hands lingering on her backside – or roll her eyes whenever a male guest asked if she were a family friend, as if this could never be her full-time job. She learnt how to set her face.

Zelda sighs and rolls back her shoulders, craning her neck to look for Jen. She's not feeling it and an energy boost is needed. She reaches out to take a canapé from a passing tray, and then, just as she takes a bite:

'Well, well, well . . . Zelda Bloom.'

She turns and looks into the eyes of Matt Fish. First love. Heart-breaker. The one that got away. He inhabits all her tropes.

Her cough is a little louder than she intends, and people start turning as Matt thumps her back. This is not the reunion she's waited for all these years. This is not how it's supposed to go.

'Well,' she says, finally swallowing every crumb. '*Well.*'

'Hi,' says Matt in that devilishly calm way, and leans in to kiss her cheek. He smells of aftershave, the same fucking aftershave, the one that half the male population wears and causes her to follow strange men down the street.

Zelda's cheek is slick with sweat. Fuck, she says in her head. Fuckity fuck.

'You good?' he says, looking her up and down.

'Mmm, fantastic,' she replies, picking up her camera and wishing she'd worn a dress. 'How come I didn't see you at the ceremony?'

'Oh, I was there.' He sips his champagne. 'I watched you from the shadows, doing your thing.'

There are a hundred and fifty guests, so it's no surprise she hasn't seen him. But something inside says she should have known. She grabs a glass of champagne from the waiter. For the first time in three hundred weddings, she will break her rule of not drinking on the job.

'You alone?' she asks, the bubbles tickling her throat. Why does he still look so good?

'Mel's here somewhere . . .' He gives a brief look around. 'Did you ever meet Mel?'

Another gulp. Melissa, the girlfriend that came straight after her.

The one he turned into a wife. 'No,' she says. 'I didn't meet Mel. How is Mel?' *Why is she saying her name?*

'Mel's good, Mel's good. Maybe I'll introduce you.' He is looking her over, his eyes lingering on her chest.

Zelda puts down her glass on the table behind them. 'I wish I could chat, but' – she shakes her camera – 'work. Later, maybe.'

Matt nods – although she hadn't asked a question – takes hold of her arm and leans in. 'You look fucking amazing,' he whispers, then stares into her eyes and strolls away.

Zelda is seething. She was the one who was meant to leave first, right after she'd doused him with champagne. How dare he take the last word, a word she's wanted to throw back at him for sixteen years.

And yet.

And yet.

Her body brims with torturous delight.

Disco Ball
Zelda

He was her manager at the bowling alley where she worked at seventeen. From the moment he led her into the tiny windowless room for an interview, she knew she was a goner. It didn't seem to matter that she was wearing her school uniform, but Zelda had learnt by then that it only made men love her more. The local club gave two-for-one drinks if girls tried to look underage. On Friday nights the men swarmed like flies.

Matt was an older man by three years. He asked questions and looked serious as he pondered her answers, leaning back in the chair and tapping his lips with a pen as she spoke. It was twenty-five degrees outside, and the air-con didn't seem to be working, but he looked immaculate in his shirt and tie. Top button done up. No sign of a sweat. 'We'll let you know,' he said, as he showed her out, then rang her the next morning to say she had the job.

She fitted in with the young staff right away. She'd changed her name to Zelda the month before and this gave her a confidence that radiated from her fingers and toes. What shall we call you, they asked. Zelda, or something short, like Z? I don't know, she thought. I've only had this name five minutes. Nicknames take years to be earned. Z, she said, as if that were normal to her. You can call me Z.

Here were new people, this was a different place; finally, she could be who she was meant to be. Alice could be left in a previous life, discarded like old skin.

Their relationship was entirely professional at first. He talked to her like he did any of the others, and there wasn't the slightest hint of partiality. But then Zelda began to notice how he always arranged the rota so they worked the same shift, and, when she was closing, it was just the two of them cashing up. He would ask about her favourite films or music, and they'd have semi-serious discussions about politics or current world events. As Alice, she'd been banned from having feelings on the former, and talk of the latter always made her uneasy, as if she should be preaching to him about the end of the world. It had been almost a year since she'd put down her Bible, but those religious rivers still ran deep.

He took any legitimate chance to touch her. Nothing inappropriate, just a brush as they passed in the corridor, a light touch of her finger as she gave him a pen.

Perhaps it's all in my head, she thought. She made a habit of that, people used to say. But then other staff began to notice, and, although she laughed it off, she was secretly glad because that meant it was true.

'You have beautiful hair,' he said once as she cleaned the kitchen out back. He was looking down at his clipboard, checking stock levels against the contents of the fridge. 'Anyone ever tell you that? The colour . . .' He licked his finger and turned the page. 'It's like fire.'

'Thanks,' she mumbled.

'Is it real?' His pen scratched into the paper.

'The red?'

Finally he looked at her. He held the clipboard against his chest as he waited for her to reply.

'Of course it's not real. No one has this hair without putting in the effort.' Zelda bent forward to clean a cupboard door and her shirt fell open. After a few seconds she straightened up. 'Everything else is, though.'

He continued watching her for a moment, leaning against the stainless-steel counter before tapping his biro against the top. 'Good to know,' he said, as he walked away.

She went to a schoolfriend's house on her eighteenth birthday. It was a small gathering of her closest friends, and they made her down shots and wear a paper hat and threw the first party she'd ever had. A few hours in, one of the girls called her boyfriend to invite him round. 'He's bringing some mates,' she said with a wink. 'With the parents away, kids will play.'

When Matt walked through the door, she felt a warm sensation inside as she imagined herself looking back at this moment. Her present, past and future converging in one slow, violent second: the frantic heat of her teenage crush entering a room.

He smiled and came over. 'Happy birthday,' he said, leaning in to kiss her cheek.

'Do you want a drink?' The shots in her stomach made him look even better.

In the kitchen she mixed him a Red Bull and Coke in a plastic cup. Someone had turned up the music, and he leant in to speak in her ear.

'Have you really never celebrated your birthday before?'

She shook her head.

'That's mad. How come?'

Zelda made a face to suggest there was more to her than meets the eye. 'It's a long story.'

He came closer. They were next to each other now, resting against the worktop, observing everyone else from a shared view. 'Well, that's good, because I've got all night.'

She laughed, delighted that he was asking her to talk about herself. He wants to know me, she thought, and she wondered if she'd ever felt so happy.

They escaped the noise by going out to his car. In the front, Zelda talked about her upbringing. She gave him the PG version that wouldn't scare him away. Her old religion was becoming a party trick, something to hold people's attention when she craved it. Their faces would contort in fascination as they contemplated a childhood without birthdays or Christmas, where Bonfire Night and Mother's Day were forbidden, where every Saturday and Sunday were spent at meetings or knocking on doors. She described how she was never allowed to attend after-school clubs or discos, that they were considered tricks of Satan to lead her astray. She never went to a schoolfriend's house. She never took part in a raffle. She'd never made a celebratory toast with a drink.

'So you're not a Last Dayers now?' Matt said, when she finished.

Zelda ran her finger over the upholstery and shook her head. She sealed the reason shut. This was not the moment for honesty, for sobbing into his sleeve. She had never told anyone why. Well, almost anyone. Besides, all that happened to Alice, not her.

'I had to get out,' she whispered. 'I couldn't breathe.'

'That's very brave,' he said, turning to her. 'It can't be easy, leaving everyone you know.'

She was relieved the alcohol soothed her throat so it no longer felt sore at the thought. 'I figure that if people love me, they should love *me*. It shouldn't be that I have to pretend to be someone I'm not.'

Matt opened his mouth to speak, then stopped. He smiled and the look on his face was tender. 'You're clearly not like other people.'

Oh, but I am, she thought inside. I need to be loved, just as they do. 'Let me ask you something,' she said.

The streetlight glowed dimly on his face.

'What would you do if I kissed you?'

He laughed, unsure. 'What would I do, or what should I do?'

'Both.'

Matt stroked the steering wheel. 'I *should* be aware of our professional relationship. I *should* say no.' He paused. 'I can't promise that I would, though.'

Zelda could still feel the fuzz of the vodka as she climbed on to his lap. He made no move to push her away. Instead he reached down to the lever and slid back his chair so she was no longer crushed against the wheel.

It was definitely a case of *her* kissing *him*. She put her mouth on his, she searched for his tongue, she led the way. There was reluctance in his kiss, but he didn't protest. She knew how seriously he took his job, and this only made her bolder. This was how much he wanted her, that he didn't push her away. If she had been just anyone, if he hadn't cared at all, his job would still have been at the forefront of his mind.

'Touch me,' she said.

He bit his lip. 'I'm not sure I should.'

'Not like that. I mean, just touch me. Put your hands on me. Put your hands on my back.'

She wore jeans and a red cowl-neck top made of crushed velvet, and, when he put his hands on the bare skin of her back, she let out a small cry of pleasure. This was the thing that did it. This was what made him give in. He pushed against her skin and felt his way up her spine, winding his fingers around the gold chain that hung across the backs of her shoulders.

'Do you know how gorgeous you are?' he said, as his hands crept under her top. 'We all sit in that office and talk about you.'

Her body shivered. She tore at his tongue with her teeth. 'I don't care about the others,' she said, and this made his hands grip her harder.

It didn't happen in his car, though. He asked if she wanted to get in the back, but she shook her head a little too forcefully. 'It's not that,' she said, when she saw his face. 'I want *that*. I just don't want it there.'

Again, she kept the truth to herself.

They waited another week. On the Friday night they went out with the work crowd. She felt his eyes on her all night. He asked if she wanted a drink, and when he returned, he leant in and said, 'You look so good in a dress.' She laughed and stepped away from him, swinging her hips as she moved on to the dance floor. Zelda felt strong. Her chainmail dress glittered under the lights like a disco ball. When all the managers stood there, watching her dance, she felt like the most powerful person in the world.

The next day they worked the same shift, and then she followed him back to his house.

It was a council house on the north side of town. She parked down the road in case anyone drove by, and, as she got out, she looked at the graffiti and dented bodywork of the other cars and wondered if it'd be rude to ask if she could leave it somewhere else.

His Ford Escort was parked on the driveway. Why do you have a purple car, she asked once. He bristled and said it was navy, and if ten per cent of the world was colour blind, who was to say which was right? The other ninety per cent, thought Zelda. Instead, she changed the subject and said she liked the spoiler he'd had fitted on the back.

He took her virginity in his single bed, with his mum and little sister asleep on the other side of the wall. Taped to the fleur-de-lis-patterned wallpaper were basketball posters and photos of him with his friends on his last day of sixth form. A weight bench took up most of the room. The next morning Zelda woke in his bed and stared at the light dancing through the net curtains. That was it, she thought. All her life she'd been told her virginity was sacred, that if she lost it before she was married, she'd be a ruined and immoral woman. Forever changed.

'How do you feel?' he said, when he awoke and turned over to hug her. 'Any different?'

She lay on his chest and stared out of the window. 'I feel exactly the same.'

He smiled and kissed the top of her head. 'You didn't bleed.'

She turned to him. 'Am I meant to, then?'

'Some do.'

'Oh.'

'Not always.'

'How many virginities have you taken, exactly?'

He laughed. 'Whoops. Brought that upon myself, didn't I?'

When he didn't elaborate, Zelda asked about his tattoos. He had a tribal pattern on his upper arm, thick black wavy lines – 'A phoenix rising from the flames' – and two Chinese markings on his chest that had faded to green.

'It says *free*,' he said, touching his pec. 'I wanted something that symbolized the breaking away from people's expectations.'

Years later, when she showed her Chinese friend Anne a close-up shot of Matt with his top off, Zelda discovered that the symbols did indeed mean free, but not in the way he intended. 'Free,' said Anne, when Zelda looked confused. 'As in *no charge*.' They had laughed until their ribs hurt.

'Why a phoenix?' Zelda asked, stroking the bleached tips of his hair. She remembers sunshine bursting into the room.

He took a while to answer, looking at his arm as if the pattern itself would explain. 'I want to get out of here, Zelda,' he said. 'This place. My mum . . . she's trapped in this life, and I want more.'

He told her how his dad left when he was eight and moved to California, and his pregnant mum brought him up on her own. She spent his early years doing cleaning jobs to make ends meet, leaving him and his sister with babysitters while she did evening work. She was never there, he said. She sounds amazing, thought Zelda. She listened as he talked about one day finding his dad. Maybe he had done all right and now lived in a house big enough to share. Maybe, if he saw Matt again, he'd see how hard his son worked to get out of poverty and make something of himself. Maybe he'd be proud.

Your poor mum, Zelda thought. Left with the kids, puts food on the table, then becomes the object of her son's pity while the absent dad plays hero.

Zelda thinks this now, years later. But, at the time, in his arms, she had nodded and said she understood. She knew how it was to miss a father, especially one you adored.

'Where will you go when you get out of here?' she asked.

'America,' he said, his eyes dreamy. 'They let you work hard and make something of yourself in the States. I'll be so successful that they'd never turn me down. That's the place. Out West.'

He reminded Zelda of the mouse in *An American Tail*, singing of how the streets would be paved with gold.

'I don't want to be average, Z,' he said, and she felt euphoric at his shortening her name. 'I don't think there could be anything worse than being average. I want to be great.'

This was why an ironing board was almost permanently set up in his room. He picked out his clothes each morning and ironed them, even the jeans and underwear. He had to be the best every time. Not a crease out of place.

She met his mum and sister Esme at breakfast and could tell straight away that they liked her. His mum rushed around making pancakes and asking Zelda about herself. Esme said she had hair like a Disney princess.

Zelda can't remember the first time she said she loved him, but she knew it from the start. A few days after she stayed, she handed in her notice to one of the duty managers – he smiled at her as if he knew why she was quitting – and got a job at the Pizza Hut in town. She didn't care how she made her money. All she wanted was Matt.

He changed his single bed for a double, and she slept over most nights. This was the other thing. She loved fucking him. There was beauty in the way their bodies fit together, and hours flew by in minutes when he made love to her on his polycotton sheets. His bed was a time machine where she could lose and find herself all at once. When she rode him, she'd feel the way he looked at her and how his hands clung to her hips, and the very idea of him craving her flesh gave the only high she needed. If he teased her in front of people, well, she could forgive it when he spent an hour kissing her skin. If she met him after work and he jokily called her *shit-head* or *fuck-face*, who cared about name-calling when he could lick parts of her body that took her outside of herself? She knew it was rare, this physical connection, even if he had really been the only one she'd known. It couldn't be this good with everyone. A few flaws could be ignored. Nobody was perfect.

When she discovered he hated smoking and thought it a sign of weakness, she resolved never to light up around him. She walked to the park on her break and took sneaky puffs in secret, drowning herself in perfume and Polos to cover the scent. He would never know the extent of her addiction.

His room was filled with Americana. There was a vintage Coke sign on the wall that lit up and a film clapperboard leaning against the JVC stereo. A Magic 8-Ball sat next to his bed, and, when Matt went down to make a morning tea, Zelda held it close and whispered questions. She shook it until it gave the answer she wanted.

You're not yourself when you're with him, a schoolfriend said once. You're so quiet. He presses all the air out of you like a flat balloon. Zelda stopped texting her back. Hadn't she been told all her life that a woman should be quiet, meek and submissive, so wasn't it good that she wasn't as fierce? She wondered what more she had to do to be what people wanted.

One day, when the mercury hit twenty-eight in October, she was lying on his bed and listening as he argued with his mum in the kitchen. The sound of his feet on the stairs made her sit up, and then he told Esme to fuck off. He slammed his bedroom door as she started to cry out in the hall.

'You okay?' said Zelda, going over to him. 'What happened?'

He pulled away and pushed his arms against the door. 'I just want to get out of here,' he said. 'I want to get OUT!' And he kicked the door frame.

'Hey, don't,' said Zelda, gently pulling him in. She wrapped his arms around her body, soft like cotton wool. 'You will. Shh. You will get out.' She soothed his back with her hands.

His neck pulsed with sweat. He let her stroke him, and she heard his heavy breathing in her ear. After a minute he put his hands on the damp skin of her waist and pulled up her t-shirt. Esme was knocking on the door, sobbing, begging Matt to let her in.

'Your sister . . .'

He ignored their pleas. He started kissing her neck – hot, wet gashes of saliva – and pawing at her bra. Zelda wanted to open the door and console Esme, but not as much as she wanted Matt to fuck her again. So she let him undo his shorts and pick her up and ram her hard against the wall as his little sister cried on the other side.

Afterwards, she went to the bathroom to clean herself up. She leant against the avocado sink and turned to see in the mirror an imprint of the fleurs-de-lis on her shoulder. Zelda stroked it with a finger and wished it would sear into her flesh forever.

At the end of December, she stayed at his house and had her first proper Christmas. They all went over and above to make it a celebration to remember. His mum asked if she'd help to dress the lounge, and Zelda took decorations out of the boxes from the loft and pinned them to the ceiling. She felt so much love within her as she touched ornaments that Matt had known all his life. His mum asked if she'd put the star on top of the tree, and Zelda had watched enough Christmas movies to know this was an honour.

He spent an entire month's salary on her presents. She opened box after box and looked up at him with joy in her heart.

Then, for Valentine's Day, he gave her six red roses and a card with a shitty rhyme. He wrote inside, *Dear Zelda, I think this says it all. Best, Matt*. She stared at the *Best* until her head spun.

A few days into March, he messaged to say he wouldn't be about that weekend. *Are you away*, she typed back. *Just got a lot on*, came the reply. *Work's nuts and I need to sleep.*

That Friday, she was leaving the cinema with a friend when she saw him in the queue for the nightclub next door. He stood with his friends – in his white t-shirt with the slogan *Chalk my cue and I'll pot your pink*, ironed jeans and loafers – and they were laughing alongside a group of girls.

After three hours of sleep she went the next day to confront him. He was outside his house when she drove up, and he climbed into her passenger seat instead of inviting her in.

'Why did you go out if you were meant to be sleeping?'

Matt sighed. 'The lads invited me last minute. I haven't been out in weeks, you know that.'

'Why were you with a load of girls?' She couldn't look at him. 'Girls?'

'I saw you in the queue.'

He shook his head. 'Oh, Zelda. They were just waiting to get in like us. Do you know how paranoid you sound?'

She looked at him, confused. Did seven months mean nothing? 'I don't get why you'd want to spend a weekend apart, and one of those nights at a sweaty club watching your mates pair off with people?'

He took a deep breath and looked out of the window at the overcast sky. The clouds were drab and heavy. 'I think . . .' He exhaled.

'Our expectations are very different. You want a *happy ever after*, but my story is just beginning. I don't want average, Zelda, and that's what this feels like to me. Average.'

And then her world ended. Who knows the words he said. She screamed at him to get out and then somehow drove the three miles home. She can't remember it raining, but she remembers the wetness of her skin as she ran down the path to her little tin house.

White on White

Zelda

She cannot decide between black or white.

Zelda holds the black against her, pressing the cool fabric to her waist. It's her sexiest dress, with spaghetti straps and silk that clings. Tiny red hearts – real, not cartoon – are embroidered around the waist, the only nod of colour. The dress is a potion that always works.

But perhaps sexy is too much for the cinema. Her fingers brush the white. The soft tulle ruched at the waist, the fun, flared skirt, the sleeves that drape off the shoulder. Sexy. Effortless.

Her phone hums five times, but she ignores it. Not tonight.

The previous weekend Matt came to find her during the wedding breakfast. She had sat in the grand foyer, scanning through her shots while Jen went to fetch their dinner. Matt collapsed into the empty armchair beside Zelda.

'I may be slightly pissed,' he said, his hands behind his head.

Zelda didn't look up. 'Some things never change.'

He watched as she flicked through the memory cards to check she had what she needed. She took her job seriously and was rewarded with a steady stream of clients. They always said there was something about her photos that moved them, that was different from everything else they'd seen. Her passion shone through.

'Hey,' Matt said, nudging her with his foot. 'You need to drop that camera and let me get a proper look at you.'

Zelda put a finger to her lips and continued until he began to stir. She put down the camera and turned to him. 'I'm all yours.'

'Don't tempt me.'

'Where's Mel?'

Matt sighed. 'In there being Mel. Using every occasion to net-work. If I have to listen to another anecdote about her C-lister clients . . .' He motioned a gun to his head.

'I hear she's very successful,' said Zelda, recalling the countless articles she'd read on the local news. *Girl Boss Takes Over PR World . . . Blonde Boss Beats the Boys at Awards Show.*

'Yeah, yeah. I bite my lip and be supportive. That's what being married's about, right? Keeping one's gob permanently shut.'

'I wouldn't know.'

'No. You're too much of a free spirit to be pinned down.'

The tips of her ears burned. She licked her lips.

Jen returned and set the plates down on the table. Chicken driz-zled in sauce with some delicately stacked vegetables.

'Mmm, delish,' said Zelda, turning her attention to the food.

'Is that all you get?' he said, screwing up his face.

Zelda dipped a finger in the sauce. 'What's wrong with it?'

'You've been on your feet all day. It'll take more than that to buck you up.'

'I'm used to it, sunshine,' she said. 'And you're in Jen's seat.'

Jen waited politely for Matt to get up. He threw her a brief glance, then leant across and dragged his finger through Zelda's sauce. 'Mmm,' he said, licking the tip of his finger. 'Delish.'

Zelda smiled. Damn it.

Half an hour later, after photographing tables of tipsy guests, Zelda was looking for Jen when a hand pulled her into a side room. She turned to see Matt closing the door. He was drunk. Happy drunk. He stood between her and the exit, forcing her to reach around his body to grab the handle.

'Wait,' he said, laughing, his hands on her waist. 'I've got a surprise.'

'But I'm working,' she said, pushing him away. He only gripped her more.

'Go back to all that in a minute,' he said, leading her over to a table. He let her go and picked up a dessert. 'I felt sorry for you with that poor little plate of food. They should be ashamed, treating you like a servant.'

'Well, I'm here to work.' She half wished his hands still held her. 'And I need to get back. I do enjoy my job.'

'Wait,' he said in a serious tone. He cut the cake with the fork and fed it into her mouth, his eyes not leaving her lips as they closed around it. Slow mouthful after mouthful. The wedding went on outside the door. When there was one piece left, he went to feed it to her, then put it in his own mouth instead. They stood in silence, a foot apart, the room filled with heat. 'There,' he said. 'Better.'

Zelda couldn't look away. She was thirsty and there he was, ready to drink. 'Can I go back now?'

'Only if you promise to meet up next week.'

'Matt, I –'

'Somewhere public. As friends.'

She paused. The tartness of the cake lingered on her tongue. 'If I say yes, will you let me go?'

He tucked a strand of hair behind her ear. A classic move. 'You would never actually say no, though, would you? I know you, Zelda Bloom.'

Jen is at the sink drinking water and wearing one of her usual outfits. She holds the glass mid-air when she sees Zelda coming down the spiral staircase. Zelda leaps from the final step, then reaches down to work her feet into her highest, strappiest shoe.

'Where are you going dressed like that?'

'Cinema with an old friend,' says Zelda, then laughs to herself and looks at Jen. 'Meeting night, is it?'

Jen squints at Zelda's dress, reaching out to touch the daisies embroidered in white thread around the waist. White on white. She frowns. 'Shouldn't these be yellow or a colour that contrasts with the background? You can hardly see them.'

Zelda strokes the flowers. 'I know they're there. That's what matters.' She straightens up. 'And hardly seeing them is the point. You have to look closely. You have to really look.'

When Jen moved in, she asked Zelda why breasts were drawn everywhere – on door handles, mirrors, etched into the table. Voluptuous *u*'s or *o*'s with jewel-coloured nipples. Jen half closed her eyes to see if they were eyeballs, but, no, they were very clearly breasts. Zelda shrugged. Men are always drawing cocks on everything, so what's so bad about a tit? At least a tit is for nourishment. Jen replied that perhaps the solution was for everyone to stop drawing genitalia altogether. Zelda rolled her eyes and said, 'God, Jen, you're so conservative. There are tits under your top in case you've forgotten.'

'So when will you be home?'

Zelda smiles. 'Later.'

'I'm not going to find you in bed with a bloke, am I?'

'Would it be a problem if you did?'

'It's your house.'

'Oh, thanks so much.'

Jen takes a deep breath. 'But . . . don't you think you might be happier if you didn't? Maybe come to a meeting sometime and try that again. It's quite a different hall now. People have moved on.'

Zelda looks like she's going to cry, then steels herself. 'Don't ever ask me that again.'

'I just think if you gave it another chance –'

'Jennifer!'

'But . . .' Jen's eyes dart around the room. She has to find the part of Zelda that once believed.

'I like shagging around, okay?' says Zelda. 'I love sex and don't see why I should apologize for that. And, if you think my idea of fun is listening to *men* dictate how I should live . . . well, we differ on what constitutes fun.'

Jen knows the way to show true friendship is to speak the words Zelda doesn't want to hear. How the end of the world is coming. How her friend will die if she doesn't return to the truth. A vision of Zelda dead beneath rubble appears, and she rubs her eyes. No. She cannot knock on the doors of strangers and not do everything to save her friend.

'Don't you want your life to have meaning?'

Zelda looks at her. 'I tried that life, Jen. It wasn't for me.'

'Love is for everyone, Ali . . . You haven't been forgotten.'

Zelda gives a cold laugh. 'You have no idea what I went through. The fact you think it's God's will that your family and friends refuse even to look at you is proof it's an abusive cult. Like my mum, out there . . .' She trails off. 'Don't talk to me of love.'

Jen closes her eyes. Her heart weighs heavy as she sees how far Zelda is from her. 'It's not a cult.'

'People in cults never think they're in one.'

This is where the stranger's door would slam in Jen's face, but she wedges her foot in the gap.

'I lost a baby and almost died, yet I didn't give up. How is your experience worse than mine?'

Zelda places her hands in front of her face. That she is meeting Matt in less than an hour is the only thing keeping her calm. Matt is what keeps her grounded. Matt. Matt. Matt.

Finally, she takes her hands away and goes to the mirror, where she dabs the inner corners of her eyes and fixes her hair. This is not the time for confession. She turns to Jen. 'I would never dream of telling you how to live your life. Don't tell me how to live mine.'

Fat drops of rain start spilling on the windscreen as she drives into town.

'Shit,' says Zelda, as she feels around the rear footwell and remembers lending her umbrella to Jen. No coat either. It was sunny when she left. 'Shit, shit, shit.'

She looks for a space in the cinema car park, but everyone else had the same idea. He'll be waiting, she thinks, as she checks the clock.

By the time she finds a space a quarter of a mile away, the rain is tropical in beat and the wipers can't clear it. Zelda sits in the car, drumming her fingers on the wheel. If she runs, she'll get soaked, but if she stays, Matt will go without her. He won't wait. She knows he won't wait.

Zelda begins texting him, but her battery dies before she can press 'send'.

'Fuuuuuuck!'

Her clutch bag makes a poor umbrella. She can't look up as she runs because of her painted face, and so she doesn't see the cars that drive into puddles that drench her twice. As she crosses the road, she slips and breaks the heel of her shoe and now all she hears is the sound of internal screaming as it reverberates through her body.

She is one turn of a corner away. She has to check herself before she sees him, and so dives into the covered doorway of a nearby shop. Warm lights shine a glow in the window, the mannequins dolled up in finery, their headless bodies advertising the polished perfection that is usually Zelda's brand. The clock on the wall says she is ten minutes late.

She begins to cry when she sees her reflection. There are black streaks under her eyes, and her styled hair is flat and sodden. She holds her bag and the heel of her broken shoe against her face. The woman she is right now is a horror show. Too far gone for fingers and spit.

A car slows down and beeps, and she slowly turns to see Matt's face as he rolls down the window. So he wasn't even there.

'All right?' he says, when it's obvious she is not.

She throws up her hands in defeat and looks away down the road, the headlights of passing cars lighting up her stained face.

The door opens and Matt jumps out. He pulls off his coat and wraps it around her, rubbing her arms to pump her blood. *Here*, he says, and holds her like she's a girl, soothing her back. She breathes against him. *Come on*, he says, and shields her as they run to the passenger side of the car, where she dives in. When he gets into the driver's seat, his shirt is soaked through.

They drive in silence through town and gradually leave civilization behind. A mile into the countryside, Matt pulls off down a lane and parks at the padlocked gate to a field. Rain thrashes the roof as the windows start to fog.

'You okay?' says Matt, stroking the back of her head.

Zelda laughs, or sobs. 'The state of me.' She looks down at her ruined dress.

'Listen,' he says, putting his hand on her chin and turning her face towards him. 'You have never looked more beautiful than you are right now.' His finger presses hard against her lip.

Of course this was going to happen. Of course Zelda would kiss his mouth and climb on to his lap like the day she turned eighteen. Of course she was going to let him rip the dress from her wet body and moan as he pushed himself inside her. Of course she would get just as much pleasure imagining how she looked to him as she would from doing the looking. Of course he would flick the switch back on. Of course he would bring her to life.

This is a dream, she thinks inside. This is all a dream and I'll wake up in a minute. I have to live it while I can.

Angels

Jen

1995

They are all sitting down to dinner one night when Jen's mother drapes a striped tea-towel over her head. It's the one she used to bring in the roast potatoes, and there are black stains around the edges.

'What are you doing?' Jen asks, confused.

Her mother gestures to her father, who sits at the head of the table, his head in his hands. It's the third day of flu, and the infection has moved to his throat. Tonight is the first time he has left his bed to join them, but he still looks weak, his skin pale and wet.

'Your dad's not well enough to say the prayer so he's asked me.' She sits oddly straight to prevent the tea-towel falling into her lap.

Jen's mouth gapes open. 'But why do you have to look like a shepherd?'

Lina sighs. 'Read your Bible, Jen. A sister has to cover her head if she prays in front of her husband.' She turns to inspect her lipstick in the mirror.

They stare when she laughs. 'Are you serious?' Jen says, but their faces suggest her amusement is a mistake.

Her father clears his throat, and they bow their heads.

After the meeting the following evening, Jen tells Alice, who gives a bored nod.

'You think that's bad,' she says, as they sit in the cold foyer by the coats. 'My mum does it *every time* she says a prayer. Because of my dad, innit? I hardly notice any more.'

'But why? The scripture they say explains it doesn't make sense to me.'

Alice yawns with her arms outstretched. 'Something about the woman having a sign of authority on her head because of the angels. Who knows? I swear they make it up as they go along.'

It is the first time Jen has questioned a teaching, and she puts it to the back of her mind.

Nobody Would Ever Know It Wasn't Real

Isobel

'It has the most incredible light,' Toni says, walking round the flat with an approving nod.

'So everyone tells me.'

'Don't you think so?'

Isobel looks up from stirring milk into the tea and watches Toni swan about in her ridiculous floaty kaftan. 'Mmm,' she says. 'It's quite glaring when the sun's out.'

'Let me guess, you're planning custom blinds to darken it.' Toni smiles as she takes a cup. 'You'd only be complaining with a basement flat.'

Isobel shrugs and looks around. 'It's hardly big enough to swing a cat in, though. I'll have to buy all new furniture. None of the old stuff will fit.'

'A whole new place to decorate. Oh, what a bind!' Toni's laugh is a cackle. 'This place is wasted on you. A little pied-à-terre. I'm quite envious, you know.'

'I don't actually want to be living here, Toni.'

'Oh, come on. Surely you wouldn't take that pig back if he came crawling home now?'

Isobel hesitates. 'No.'

'There you go!' Toni throws up her hand, and her silver bangles clatter. 'The only way is forward, and so you should embrace what this place represents.'

'And what does it represent? What exactly does single at fifty-five mean? Other than a spinster or failed marriage?'

Toni sighs and tilts her head to look at Isobel, more with boredom than sympathy. 'You're still adjusting. I get that.' She hums under her breath. 'Any movement on the house?'

'The sale's going through.'

'Then you'll have money to go somewhere else. Money buys you freedom. He never let you have any beyond your *allowance*, but now you'll get an equal share and can move on. Get divorced pronto, and we'll fix you up with someone dashing.'

Isobel doesn't flinch as the tea burns her lip. 'And how many of those are there likely to be? A single man in the truth at my age is either divorced for good reason or alone because nobody wants him. Besides, my best years are behind me.'

'Life is what you make it, Isobel.'

'It feels very different when it's happening to you.'

'Well, we can't all have what you have. Some of us would like out of our marriages. If Armageddon comes tomorrow, I'm stuck with Bill forever.'

'Toni!'

'It's true. I made my vow and I'll keep it, but it doesn't mean I *enjoy* my situation. You can't force yourself to think a certain way. You do or you don't.' She looks at the cup in her hand and places it on the kitchen worktop. 'Now, why on earth are you giving me tea? Let's crack open that bottle.'

Isobel calls Toni her best friend, but, really, Toni is her only friend. Despite trying to live an honest life, Isobel doesn't mind bending the truth on that.

'I wondered' – Isobel gestures at the blank walls and empty corners – 'maybe you could help dress this place?'

'Don't tell me you haven't got a bottle opener,' says Toni, rummaging through a drawer. 'Oh, thank goodness. Hmm? Oh, love to.'

Toni has her finger on the pulse, Isobel knows. She lives for current trends. Ten years ago, she was polka-dot plates and shabby chic, wearing clothes that looked to Isobel like they were from a jumble sale. She went through a brief Scandi phase – stripping the pastel paint from her dining chairs back to bare wood – and now she favours pencil-drawn sketches of naked women, terrariums, clay earrings in wonky shapes. Isobel rolls her eyes at Toni's fickleness, but she could use this know-how, this ability to size up a space and make it sing.

140

Toni pours the Prosecco. 'So . . . we'll put up mirrors to bounce the light over to the darkest areas. Illuminate those corners. Then maybe some sisal rugs over these floorboards. Perhaps sheer curtains for the windows – nothing too heavy – although you'll probably opt for drapes.'

Last year Toni started placing houseplants in every room. There was one with variegated leaves that reminded Isobel of a plant her late mother had. She couldn't face a live plant – all that maintenance – but tracked down an artificial version that she placed on a shelf above the bath to give the room a pop of life. It was too high up for anyone to touch. It looked the part. Nobody would ever know it wasn't real.

Toni's face lights up. 'Hang about. Forget curtains. Did you hear the news about Pete Musgrove?'

'What now?'

'That customer he was having it off with . . . Well, he got a slap on the wrist – this is confidential because I'm not supposed to know – but he's only gone and moved in with this woman. He's sure to be disfellowshipped now.'

Isobel's mouth drops open as she remembered Pete as he'd always appeared: an upstanding member of the congregation, volunteering to help and giving public prayers. The last time they spoke was when she dropped off a chilli after they lost the baby, and of course Jen must have been up to no good because she was disciplined soon after.

'*Minister. Deacon.*' Toni shakes her head and swills her wine around the glass. 'You never really know who people are.'

Isobel doesn't pay much attention when Carol starts talking about the vacancy on Monday morning. Her computer is slow to start, and she begins to panic that a long queue of patients will form when the door is unlocked and she won't be able to access the calendar to tick off their arrival, and then the dentist won't know who is waiting, and then . . .

'Isobel? Are you okay?'

Carol's voice cuts into the chaos and she looks up, trying to appear calm. 'Sorry. I'm just having problems with my computer and I know we open in two minutes, so —'

'Here,' says Sadie, wheeling across and leaning in to press a button. 'Your screen's on standby.' She scoots back.

'Oh,' says Isobel with her hands mid-air. 'Easy as that, then.' She turns back to Carol, her face pink.

'As I was saying, Louise is leaving and Anish would like to find her replacement in-house preferably. Someone he can train up from the start. Dental-nurse experience not necessary.'

Isobel listens as she details the hourly rate — better than reception — and what would be required. Her mouth sets in the rigid line it takes when change is first suggested. No, she thinks. Not for me.

'Let me know by tomorrow if you're interested. If not, we'll open it up to outside.' Carol checks her watch. 'Isobel, could you get the door?'

Victor is outside. He smiles and nods, and she turns away, blushing.

'Come in,' she says to the carpet.

'Hello, there.'

'Mr Godden,' says Sadie, waving from the desk. 'We tried calling Friday to say Dr Hall is ill, and today's appointment must be moved. I left a message.'

'Oh, dear,' he says, putting a hand to his head. 'I'm having endless problems with my phone, and it doesn't alert me to voicemails.' He approaches the desk where Isobel now hides behind paperwork. 'When's the doc back in?'

'We have a space on Friday at ten if that suits?' says Sadie. 'Remember we close next week for the refurb.'

'That'll work well, thank you.'

'Anything else we can help you with?' She gives Isobel a sidelong glance.

The door tinkles for another patient, and Victor moves aside. He is now directly in front of Isobel.

'Did the flowers make it out alive?'

'I'm sorry?' Isobel says, raising her head but keeping her eyes on the paper. She's read the same line ten times.

'The rather pathetic bouquet. Did they have any life left?'

Isobel smiles, despite herself. 'Actually they flowered quite beautifully.' She smooths her lapel. 'It was very thoughtful.'

'Ah,' he says, shrugging it off. 'Don't mention it. Unless, that is, you've reconsidered my invitation? Drink? Or dinner?'

Isobel frowns, wondering at his persistence. She looks down at herself – what is it he's seeing? She shakes her head and ignores the rare heat in her chest that comes from being noticed. A tingling warmth through her veins. 'I really can't. Please don't ask again.'

He puts up his hands to reassure her, then does a jokey lock of his mouth. 'So long,' he says, smiling, and then he is gone.

The landline phone is ringing as Isobel walks in. It's the solicitor with an update on the house. In addition to the mortgage, there is a vast amount of secured debt in Steven's name that will need to be repaid before any equity can be divided.

No, says Isobel. No, I didn't know about any loans. They were nothing to do with me. Steven handled everything financial.

She can hear the frustration in the solicitor's voice, how the woman is tempted to ask how she could have been so stupid as to not have her name on the deeds. We were one flesh, Isobel wants to say, but now she knows this means nothing.

She hangs up and stands there, still clutching her bag. The amount left over will be enough to cover a holiday. She has no private pension, and her state one will be a pittance because of the years spent ministering and as a housewife and mother, exactly how she was meant to spend her life. What was the point of a pension when the end of the world was coming any day?

Armageddon had been coming all her life. She remembers as a child being told she would never grow up in this world. In 1975, when it was believed the current world would end, her parents – like many others – sold their business and postponed medical treatment to wait for Judgement Day. When bills were still arriving well into 1976, the leaders began to erase the previous year from their followers' consciousness. Some brothers made assumptions, they said, but we never set a date. They did, said Isobel's father. He grumbled for a couple of years, but it faded from memory. *Any day*, became the new mantra. *Any day now.*

Over forty years later, Isobel is still waiting to never grow up in this world.

Trying to Disappear

Alice

1996

The day is bright in the train carriage. They choose a four-formation on the shaded side, Alice's mum taking a seat that faces forward. Alice and her dad flop down in the opposite seats, to which Marjorie cries out, 'Your dress! Your suit!' and father and daughter exchange looks and laugh.

With each stop, the train gets busier, and Alice and her dad begin talking in whispers. This is how she has been raised, not to draw attention, not to make a fuss, but the whispers only frustrate.

'Speak up,' says Marjorie. 'It's rude to whisper. Wilfred, you know better.'

'I doubt you'd hear under that thing on your head,' he replies with a wink. 'It could sink the *Titanic*.'

Marjorie's hands fly to her hat. Its blue satin perfectly matches her frock coat and bag. Her shoes are silver, and they sparkle on the carriage floor. She strokes her lap with gloved hands.

'You look like the Queen,' says Alice with a snort.

'I fail to see why that's an insult.'

'Ah, your mum's always been a vision,' says her dad with a nudge.

Marjorie smiles, despite herself.

As they draw closer to London, trees and fields merge into houses, narrow gardens, streets. Alice presses up against the glass. She loves looking through the lit windows of other houses, catching sight of someone else going about their life. The houses morph into flats and Victorian warehouses, casement windows and the grime of old brick. Years later, Zelda will love taking the Charing Cross train, seeing the same rooftops and remembering her dad by her side.

When they emerge from the station, Alice and her mother are overwhelmed by the traffic and crowds swarming the Strand. Alice steps closer to her. In twelve years, she has never been to London. The city is a foreign thing.

'Well?' says Marjorie.

'Where to, Dad?'

Wilfred looks towards Trafalgar Square. 'There. I'm sure of it.' He loops their arms through his and guides them to the crossing.

They pick their way through the square, stopping occasionally to watch a mime or listen to the strum of a pop song. Alice takes it in, soaking up the colours and music, so she can relive them tonight when alone in her bed. London is too much, and yet it is the very fizz and whirl that excite her. That hint of danger; the knowledge that, among these crowds, anything can happen, anything at all.

'We need a quieter street, Wilfred,' calls her mother from behind.

Leaving the square, her father stops and looks around. He loosens the tie at his neck.

'Are you lost?' says Marjorie, reaching him. 'You're here all the time?'

'But I go straight to the theatres. Tea at the Ritz isn't regular life.'

Alice points down the road. 'It's that way.'

'How do you know?' Marjorie clutches the lapels of her coat, looking about with suspicion.

'It's Piccadilly, right? So follow the sign.' Alice marches off.

Her parents look at each other and hurry to catch up.

They are sitting down in the Ritz when the waiter offers to take Marjorie's hat. She looks at him in horror. 'Oh,' she says, touching her hair. 'Can I not keep it on? Only my hair will be ruined, taking it off.'

'Whatever you like, madam,' he says and leaves.

Marjorie looks about at the gilded cornicing, tall Greek columns, the ornate flower displays. She catches sight of herself in the mirror and shifts about in her chair.

The afternoon tea is as sumptuous as they had hoped. They pour the tea from a silver pot, sip from fine bone china, take tiny bites of cream puffs and cucumber sandwiches and fluffy scones.

Alice and her dad smile over the rims of their cups. Her mother, however, eats in silence. She folds her arms and legs inwards, and occasionally lifts a nervous hand to the rim of her hat, which she had been so proud of earlier but that now seems excessive. She looks around. The realization that she is the only one in the room wearing a hat turns her cheeks pink. Alice, watching her, knows she is trying to disappear. Her mother, who taught her not to make a fuss.

When it is time to go, Marjorie pulls Alice in and says, 'We forgot the prayer.' And then she whispers some words in thanks for the food they have eaten, the tea they have drunk, the love God has shown by granting them another day of life. Alice's instinct is to pull away towards her unbelieving father, to laugh and roll her eyes, but the memory of her embarrassed mother prevents her. She bites her lip and waits until Marjorie says *Amen*.

At the theatre, cars and photographers mill about outside, and a long red carpet stretches from road to door. Alice squeezes her dad's arm, and they fake screams of delight.

When they take their seats in the auditorium, the person behind Marjorie asks her to remove her hat. And so she does, without fuss, her hands shaking as she tries to locate the pin. 'Here, Mum,' says Alice, and reaches up to do it. Marjorie places the hat on her lap as Alice smooths her stray hairs.

When the award for 'Best Costume Design' arrives and her father's name is read out as the winner, Alice jumps up and cheers. She watches him rush up to the stage and accept the award, stare at it, then blink as he approaches the microphone. She hears the nerves in his voice. The mumbled words are hard to hear, but she catches her name and feels a pain in her heart. She looks down at her mum, sees her trying not to cry.

On the train home, they sit in the same formation – Marjorie opposite Alice and her dad. Alice speaks in fast sentences, overflowing with pride. She rubs her thumb over her dad's name engraved on the plaque. 'Can I have it in my room, Dad?' she asks. 'On my shelf?'

'Don't be ridiculous,' says her mother. 'It's your father's award, not yours.'

Her dad squeezes her hand. 'It might say Wilfred Kay, but what's mine is yours, pet. Of course it can go on your shelf.'

Alice sees her mother stare at their entwined arms, then purse her lips and look towards the window. The warmth in her chest fades as her eyes move to the empty seat beside her mother. The seat that's always empty. The one she never takes.

When they get off the train, it is raining. Her father leaves them at the entrance and hurries off to fetch the car. Heavy rain pounds the flat station roof, the noise almost deafening.

'Mum?' says Alice, an olive branch forming in her mind.

Marjorie is staring out at the black night. She grips her hat by her side.

'I was thinking of getting baptized. In the summer, maybe.' Strange how fast a thought can be spoken, how it comes to life in a flash.

Her mother turns slowly to her. She opens her mouth to speak, and Alice recognizes her expression. She sees it sometimes when her dad makes a cup of tea without being asked, and her mother's face turns pink and glad, as if their state of intimacy goes deeper than words. They have not been required to articulate their needs, but, through closeness, they have been understood. 'Well, I . . .' That is all she can manage.

A car starts up in the distance. Headlights swing their way. Alice notices the stoop of her mother's back, her smart blue coat puckering at the shoulders, how she bends away from the light.

'Here's your father now,' says her mother, and they step out into darkness.

Hot Water

Isobel

There is no answer when Isobel taps on the treatment-room door. She has to knock harder to be heard.

'Come in.'

Dr Ramini doesn't look up from his laptop. As she waits, she looks around at the polished surfaces and gleaming silver instruments. If everything out there is cluttered in an eighties time warp, the treatment room sings modernity with its sparse and glossy vibe. A thrill pulses through her as she imagines swapping the outside world for this one, a talent-show contestant reborn by walking through smoke.

Anish closes the laptop. He folds his arms against his scrubs and looks her up and down, his chin hidden by his medical mask. 'Carol says you're interested in the position?'

She nods, pulling at her sleeve.

'And . . .' Anish waves at her to continue.

'Oh. Yes, I am very interested in oral hygiene. The health of one's teeth is extremely important, and I would be intrigued to learn more about the process.' She hopes the words do not sound as forced out loud as they do in her head.

He studies her. 'Ideally I want someone new to the profession. If I take on a nurse from elsewhere, I'd waste time unpicking bad habits. But the most important skill for a dental nurse is initiative. Is that you, Isobel?'

If only she could be honest, pull him to one side and say: Look, Anish, you don't realize how much I need this. My world has crashed and needs rebuilding. I want a distraction, and this could be a way to discover who Isobel might have been if she hadn't left the bank all those years ago. If she'd kept a little something for herself.

149

Instead, she jerks her head and says, 'Yes. That's me. I have initiative.'

Back at her desk, she watches Sadie toss her blonde hair and stride in for her turn. The door shuts, and there is silence, punctuated by the occasional burst of Sadie's laughter. Isobel listens. Anish is laughing too.

The decision is made by the end of the day.

Isobel nods as Carol gives the reasons.

'You've done a fine job settling in, Isobel, but the impression is you do better when given direction. It may be you're still finding your way, and that those confidence levels will rise. But, right now, you're more *reactive* than *proactive*, and a nurse must anticipate what the dentist needs before he does. Anish decided Sadie would be better suited.'

Isobel is only half listening, distracted by Carol's hair. It reminds her of a thatched roof, dense and from a forgotten era. Instinctively, she reaches up to touch her own. Carol is probably the same age as her. Of course she is being passed over for the younger, brighter thing.

Out in reception, she attempts her best smile. 'Congratulations,' she says.

Sadie touches her arm. 'Thanks, Isobel. I am sorry. Joe and I hope to buy a house next year, so I need the dosh, and, seeing as you drive a Range Rover, you're clearly doing all right.' She smiles and turns back to her screen.

Isobel clicks the mouse to wake her computer. She doesn't tell Sadie that when checking her bank account an hour ago, she had hardly enough to fill her car with fuel.

It is raining as Isobel drives home, and the only empty space is at the end of the road. She runs to her building, the key slipping from her hand, and by the time she enters the foyer she is soaked. She shakes her hair, and the droplets fly in all directions. Like a dog, she thinks. Her feet are heavy on the stairs, the soles squeaking with every step, and Isobel pushes on faster to try to outrun herself.

One storey.

Two storeys.

Almost three storeys.

'You stupid girl,' she says to her reflection in the window. Her voice echoes on the empty stairs. 'You stupid, stupid girl.'

That evening, she bakes a chocolate cake and eats every last crumb.

Friday morning is bright with a heat that shrugs off jackets.

Victor arrives and smiles at Isobel as he takes a seat. She watches him lay his leather jacket on a chair and pick up a magazine. The pencil in her finger doesn't move against the paper, but then she looks down and sees it has bored a hole.

When he comes out of his appointment, he nods at them both, then heads for the door. Isobel panics. She assumed he'd walk up to the desk and she could ask Sadie to make a drink. But now he is leaving, and she hasn't a Plan B, and so she jumps up and calls, 'Mr Godden!'

He stops and turns. Sadie covers the phone receiver and looks up at her. The room is silent as they wait for her to act.

Oh, goodness, thinks Isobel. Oh, for goodness' sake. She grabs a piece of paper from her desk and holds it up. 'You forgot this,' she says and moves around the desk towards the door.

Victor lets go of the door handle as she approaches. His eyes are on the paper, which she now realizes is the order form for the stationery cupboard. It crumples in her hand. Sadie resumes her phone conversation, and Isobel positions herself so their lips cannot be read.

'Mr Godden, I-I –'

'Please, call me Victor.' His voice is quiet, like hers.

'Victor,' she says, and looks at the floor. 'I wanted to thank you again for the flowers.'

He smiles, and Isobel loves how he looks at her. 'They reminded me of you. That was all.'

She frowns, remembering how the heads drooped. Really? And

then she thinks of how it took only a little hot water to bring them back to life. 'Oh,' she says with a faint laugh. 'I don't know about that.'

'I thought, there's a woman who needs something to make her smile again.' He shrugs. 'Silly, I know.'

'No, not at all. I –'

'It's okay. I won't ask you again, so don't be nervous about me coming here. I'll leave you be.'

'No,' she says, taking a deep breath. 'That's not it. Actually, I would like you to ask me again. If that would be agreeable.'

He looks at her, surprised, then down at his leather jacket. 'Well, now . . .' The room is silent. 'Would you like to go out with me sometime, Isobel?'

'Yes, Victor, I would.'

People Will Like You Then

Jen

Mid nineties

The day she got her first period, Jen pulled down her knickers and saw a reddy-brown stain. Oh, she thought. I've put on Lina's underwear by mistake. But then a drop of the same colour started running down her leg. 'Mum,' she shouted. 'Mum!'

Angela had known just what to do. She found her daughter fresh underwear, stuck in a pad and made a hot-water bottle. 'You're becoming a woman now,' she said to eleven-year-old Jen, patting her head as she explained the meaning of the reddy-brown.

'Wait, you mean this will happen every month, *forever*?'

'Not forever, darling. Just the next forty years. Give or take.'

Jen looked at her mother as if she had cheated her, as if she had committed some unforgivable act by bringing her into the world and making her female.

Angela Owen raised her two daughters to be thankful. 'Always say please and thank you,' she said. 'People will like you then.'

When the girls were small, she felt an adrenalin kick whenever they received a compliment. Their beautiful blonde hair, their sweet little outfits, their politeness – all translated by Angela as *You are a good mother*. She had learnt through life the currency that came from commendation. If she ever felt blue, her tonic was to go out and have someone ask where she bought her dress. It was a drug, the praise of another woman. Their admiration gave a sense of worth she had craved all her life.

She tried to impart this wisdom to her daughters. There was much of her in Lina, and her elder daughter absorbed every word.

She brushed her hair a hundred times, she followed the religious three-step of cleanse, tone and moisturize, she bought only clothes that suited her. Lina was a natural extension of Angela, and this brought her joy. *We will all be made perfect in the next world, girls, but that doesn't stop us reaching for it now.*

Jennifer was a different matter. At first, her younger daughter allowed herself to be dressed. She showed little interest in clothes, happy to wear whichever outfit had been laid out, but aged eight or nine she found her own opinion. *I am not*, she'd say about ruffles or flowers or anything pink. She insisted on choosing her clothes, and Angela noticed her friends' faces when Jen ran by in jeans, torn from climbing trees.

When she became a teenager, Angela resorted to bribery. She gave extra pocket money if Jen swapped trousers for skirts, she stopped nagging her to tidy her room if Jen wore make-up. Gradually, with a little work, her daughter stopped being so obstinate. Jen curbed the pert opinions and sat quietly in the corner, watching the world go by. Angela realized the push-back had all been a phase, a way of testing boundaries, and Angela's persistence had won out.

See, she was a good mother. She never gave up on the girl.

Jen remembers differently.

When eight years old, she went to a gathering in someone's garden where the boys began to kick about a football. She was the only girl there. As the sun beat down, the boys pulled off their tops and ran around half naked. She joined them. In the blur of the game, there was little difference between her prepubescent body and theirs.

Her father came striding across the grass and yanked her away from the others. 'Put your top on,' he hissed, throwing her t-shirt in her face.

'But everyone else is doing it,' she said.

'Girls are not boys, Jennifer. Don't ever do that again.'

She didn't understand the difference. Nobody explained why it was so wrong. Whenever she tried to make sense of it, they always got angry. *Why can't you be more like Lina? Look at Lina. Lina gets it, so why can't you?* It didn't matter to them that the ribbons and frills made her feel like a stranger. That she felt dishonest each time her mother chose her outfit in exchange for money to buy her own things. With one hand she was given independence, while the other snatched it back.

They don't like me being truthful, she realized. They are happier when I give them what they want.

And so she buried that part of herself, and let her smile do the work.

Kill the Sun

Jen

Jen cuts her hair as soon as she hears about Pete.

She enters the salon on her Saturday lunch break, and the girl on the desk says, 'You're in luck, as we've just had a cancellation for five thirty if that suits?' Jen nods before she can change her mind. She spends the next few hours at work catching sight of her reflection and saying goodbye to her hair.

At five thirty she settles into the chair and brings up a picture she's saved for years.

The stylist looks surprised. She is tall and willowy, with perfect hair, and Jen imagines how easy her life must be.

'Are you sure?' she says, letting Jen's hair fall through her fingers. 'It's a great look, but that's a good fifteen inches off. Have you had it that short before? Should we try something chin-level first?'

Jen shakes her head. 'No, I've thought it through. I'm ready.'

The woman smiles at her in the mirror. She must have seen many women like me, Jen thinks. People who make out they know what they want and just hope they're not asked twice.

Zelda is in the garden when she arrives home, digging and planting flowers. She doesn't turn as Jen drops her bag on the step, but gives a *hey* and continues singing along to the stereo. Her fingers are dirty, stained with soil. There is always much to do.

Jen hits the 'pause' button on the twenty-year-old boombox and Zelda looks up.

'Oh, Jen . . .' She examines her from every angle. 'Very Mia Farrow.'

'You like?' Jen hasn't stopped stroking her neck since leaving the salon.

'*Love*. Not many people can pull off a crop like that. What made you do it?'

'Oh . . .' She smiles at Zelda's response. 'I've always wanted short hair. But something always held me back.' She tells Zelda about Pete moving in with the woman.

'Oh, screw him,' says Zelda, waving him away. 'He's gone, and taken your hair too.' Her face brightens, and she peels off her gloves to take Jen's hand. 'Come.'

Upstairs, Zelda throws open the doors to the huge wardrobe that runs along one wall. Jen noticed it when she first moved in – its Art Deco burr-walnut-panelled doors are so intricate that they cannot help inviting attention – but she has never seen them open before. Behind the doors are compartments filled with colourful clothes and accessories, rails of jewel-hued dresses, vibrant froths of feathers, silks and hats. It is a steamer trunk on steroids.

'How did this get up here?' she says, glancing at the staircase.

'It's always been here,' says Zelda. 'I used to call it the dress-up box, as if the clothes were characters I could try on.'

'These silks . . .' Jen runs her fingers through.

'Incredible, aren't they? The theatre allowed Dad to keep some of the costumes. The torn ones weren't worth anything, so he took them away and made them like new.' She looks at Jen. 'Come on, then. What's your style?'

'My style?'

'Yeah. What do you like? Who do you want to be?'

Jen shrugs. 'I don't know.'

'That's the problem. You never do.'

'But why does everything have to look a certain way? Why can't it just *be*? I'm tired of having to work out who I am for others before I even know myself.'

Zelda watches her for a moment, then pulls out a long pair of silk palazzo pants and holds them up. 'Try these. Or not. Whatever you want.' She grabs a blouse from the rail to pair with it, but Jen shakes her head.

'No, that one.' She points to something else.

'Good girl,' says Zelda, pushing Jen towards the screen in the corner. 'Now go. Be reborn.'

When Jen comes out, Zelda claps her hands and stands behind the long mirror that leans against the wall. 'Look,' she says, tapping the glass. 'There's your audience. *You.*'

They spend the evening drinking wine and trying on costumes, laughing as they strut about the room as other people. The booze makes everything funnier. When they're done, they collapse on the bed and talk shit while draining the bottle.

'This is nice,' says Jen, making shadow puppets on the wall. 'I've missed this.'

'Yeah,' says Zelda. 'It's good to fuck about.'

Jen wakes in the morning at the end of Zelda's bed, her mind fuzzy like the feathers on her waistcoat. She groans at the sun as Zelda snores beside her.

She swears under her breath at the sight of the clock and tries to stand, forgetting her feet are strapped into seventies platforms. Her fingers fumble with the buckles.

Zelda throws out her arms and stretches herself awake. 'God, kill the sun.'

'It's half nine on a Sunday, and I have the hangover from death,' says Jen, putting the shoes back in the wardrobe.

'So stay home this morning. Christ, Jen, you can afford to miss one meeting.'

Jen doesn't reply. There is little point reminding Zelda that her biggest chance for reinstatement is to be regular at meetings. Even if it's the loneliest two hours of her week, it is her only way back to Jacob.

Zelda watches her. 'You're serious about this, aren't you?'

The room is silent as Jen takes off the clothes. In spite of the time, her movements are slow and careful as she slips off the silk palazzo trousers and picks up her blouse, climbing out of one skin to put on another.

'All your friends refuse to speak to you, Jen.'

Jen turns, but not to Zelda. She is drawn to the sunshine pouring through the circular window, the way the dust drifts in the light. Its dance has no purpose or consciousness. Oh, to be dust, she thinks, and looks through the light at Zelda.

'It's because they care that they do it.'

Zelda tries to steady her voice. 'There's the script again, ingrained in your fucking DNA. You lost a baby and almost died. Those people should be lining up to hug you, not guilt-trip you for being alive.'

Jen shuts her eyes. She is in limbo between craving mentions of Jacob and almost vomiting when they come. He is rarely acknowledged outside her own head. He exists in the silences that greet her encounters with family, his name amplified each time they turn away. They say you begin to forget, but Jacob defies tradition. He grows more real with every passing day.

'They want me to gain everlasting life,' she says, clinging to what she can. 'To hold Jacob again. That's why they do it, Zelda. They want what I want.' She looks at her childhood friend. 'Do you?'

Jen tries not to fall asleep as she sits in the back row of the Worship Hall. The fluorescent lighting wages war on her pounding head, and she cannot escape the brother's monotone pumping out from speakers around the room. Across the hall is a row of elderly sisters, where two have already nodded off. They're allowed, she thinks. I must do better.

She could do with fresh air. There are windows, but the panes have been replaced with mirrors, and behind the frame is solid wall. So not really windows at all. Just the illusion of them, with glass that reflects the room. Jen knows from experience that those sitting close to these mirrors can watch other congregants without their knowledge. She sits as far away as she can.

She gathers her things together before the closing song so she can rush to the door. If she can get into her car without passing anyone, her heart rate does just fine.

But, as she slips away, a hand reaches out to touch her. She jumps as she sees Brother Connell.

'Jen, a word?'

She takes a seat in front of three elders in the back room. They sit with smiles and Bibles, and she bites her lip as she waits.

'How are you, Jen?' says Brother Norris.

'Fine.' She nods. 'Thanks.'

'It's encouraging to see you at every meeting,' says another brother.

'I've nowhere else to be.' She stares at a speck of ketchup or blood on his collar. 'My place is here.'

He smiles and then Brother Connell says, 'It's come to our attention, Jen, that you're living with Alice Kay. Is that right?'

She knew this day was coming. 'Yes.'

'Are you aware Alice is disfellowshipped?'

She nods.

'Is it wise to associate with her, seeing as she has no wish to return? Let's not forget that disfellowshipping is a loving provision in the hope of making the sinner return to truth. It is God guiding the elders.'

Like he did with Pete, she doesn't say. And how do you know she has no wish to come back? Have you ever asked her? Doesn't she have a voice? So many thoughts. So many thoughts she has learnt not to say.

'I understand,' Jen says, 'but what can I do?' Must she remind these men that she has no home or husband, that her family won't speak to her, that she works only three days a week so cannot afford to rent alone. She has barely any qualifications due to leaving school at sixteen to minister. No. They already know this. She cannot bring herself to repeat it. 'I'm homeless.'

Brother Connell opens his Bible. 'Let's turn to a scripture we know well. 1 Corinthians 15, Verse 33. Jen, perhaps you can read it.'

She hardly needs to open her Bible – this scripture has been drummed into her since birth – but still she turns the pages.

'*Do not be misled. Bad associations spoil useful habits.*'

'And another,' says Brother Connell, licking his finger to reach it more quickly. '2 John 1, verses 9 to 11. Jen, again.'

Then he slams his Bible shut.

'Jen, do you see how serious this is? It is clear how our God feels. If Armageddon comes while you live with a disfellowshipped sinner, not to mention in that state yourself, our Father is unlikely to reward you with life.'

She leans forward. They are not interested in logistics, so she must change tack. 'But I know I can do some good here, find the part of her that still believes.'

Brother Norris looks at Brother Connell. 'Jen, it is not our place to go above scripture. We cannot set aside the commandments, no matter how good our intentions. Alice is not your concern.'

'Correct,' says Brother Connell. 'She is not your responsibility. But your way back to your heavenly Father and your relationship with him *is*. Yours alone. His spirit decides whether an individual can be reinstated to the congregation, and, frankly, Jen, we could never consider that while you live with a disfellowshipped person.'

Jen hears the hum of voices from the foyer. Loneliness pierces her heart.

Brother Connell clears his throat.

'Also, your hair.'

Jen touches her neck. 'My hair?'

His finger is pressed against his lip as he studies her. 'Do you think the shortness of your hair is befitting a Christian woman?'

Jen takes a deep breath, but it does little to steady her heart.

'There's a scripture that . . . It quite escapes me now.' Brother Connell perches his glasses on the end of his nose. 'Jim, Bill, do you remember the scripture about how it is detestable for a woman to look like a man?'

They confer for a moment, flicking through their Bibles and whispering. Jen looks at the floor as the walls close in.

'Ah, yes, Deuteronomy 5, Verse 22. It says . . . Jim?'

'*A woman must not put on the clothing of a man, nor should a man wear the clothing of a woman. For anyone doing so is detestable to God.*'

'So the scriptures are very clear,' says Brother Connell, removing his glasses. 'It's a minor point, but one that bears thinking about.'

★

Zelda is out when Jen returns. She goes to the sink and drinks three glasses of water, one after the other, as if quenching an insatiable thirst. Then she drifts towards the staircase and climbs the spiral up to Zelda's room.

Jen looks at the clothes, the ghosts of other lives, before finding herself in front of the mirror. She starts to undress. Her meeting clothes are kicked into a pile.

Behind is a collection of bare mannequins, like the ones Zelda left in her room. Jen looks at them, then back at her reflection. Her underwear slips off. Her belly is rounded from the glasses of water, and she turns so her body is in profile. The water is a baby. Her hand rests on the top of the curve.

She looks at herself, looking at herself.

'Jacob,' she says.

Eating the Apple
Alice and Jen

1999

'Hello, it's nice to find you home this morning. Isn't it a beautiful day? Chilly, but look at that blossom . . . It's refreshing to see beauty after the news events this week. I'm only fifteen but I do wonder what kind of future I'll have. Did you know the Bible promises a time when there will be no more war? Isn't that a wonderful prospect?'

Jen's voice is smooth and unforced, years of practice behind her. She asks questions to encourage a dialogue with the householder, then summarizes the magazines she is trying to place.

Stood behind Jen, Alice glances at the cover of the top magazine. A mushroom cloud of death, the city below concealed by bold type: WAR, WHEN WILL IT END? She tightens the scarf around her neck.

Two minutes later, magazines accepted, they approach the next house. Alice puts out her hand and waits for Jen to hand her some literature. She ignores Jen's raised eyebrow. 'They don't fit in my bag, okay?'

Alice taps lightly on the glass.

'They're not going to hear that, are they?' says Jen.

Alice swears mildly when a key turns in the lock. The door opens and a man looks out with a blank expression, hair and pyjamas still creased from bed.

'Hiya,' says Alice. 'We're calling with our magazines. Interested?'

He shakes his head.

'Thanks for your time,' says Alice, already stepping away. She shoves the magazines in Jen's bag and ignores her expression as they walk down the path. 'It's Saturday. Let them have their breakfast.'

'What's the point in spending a whole morning doing this if you don't do it properly?'

Alice grabs an apple from her bag. 'I don't know, Jennifer. What is the bloody point?'

They wait on the corner for the rest of their group. Two by two, brothers and sisters come from all directions, until there are ten of them on the kerb. The brother in charge frowns at the sight of Alice's legs under her long jacket. 'Run out of clothes?' he says to her, rubbing his hands together to warm them.

Alice continues to eat. 'Show me a scripture that says women can't wear trousers on the ministry.'

He laughs. His eighteen-year-old skin is pimpled and cut from shaving. 'Oh, Alice. If you knew your Bible, you'd know it's the principle that matters, not the law.'

'Oh, *Pete*. The principle is that it's freezing and trousers keep me warm. And surely trousers are more modest than the shape of my legs.'

There is silence. The only sound is Alice eating her apple. Everyone looks at the ground as they wait for Pete to react. He pulls his black overcoat tight over his suit.

'Let's move further down the road. We'll work over and over until midday.' He strides off, and everyone starts to follow. They dart glances at Alice, the older sisters giving her dirty looks.

Jen stares at her.

'Oh, you too?' says Alice, tossing the core into a bush. 'So he's allowed to be sarky with me, but I can't dish it back? Give me a break.'

Jen goes to speak, then sighs and takes out fresh magazines.

The door opens at the next house, and Jen repeats her presentation, but when she says *Don't you think this world is getting worse?* the woman shakes her head.

'But . . .' Jen stutters. 'You don't?'

'There's never been a better time to be alive.' The woman's voice is calm. 'In the Western world, anyway.'

Jen gives a small laugh. She glances at Alice, then down at her magazines. 'But the wars and diseases . . .'

'There have always been wars,' the woman replies. 'There have always been diseases. But now we have a good shot at curing the worst ones. We live to be eighty or ninety. It's normal for children to survive childhood and outlive their parents. Education is open to everyone, not to mention there's less poverty. And, as women, we have more opportunities than ever. It's rare that we die in child-birth. We can have a career. We have choice.'

After the woman closes the door, they both walk down the path in silence.

Jen shuts the gate and forgets about the woman.

Alice is alive in thought.

Watch Out

Zelda

It's strange, she thinks, how someone can be connected to you for one intimate minute and then never be seen again.

Then one day, as Zelda is leaving the cinema, Will brushes her arm as he walks through the door. He opens his mouth, but then he sees Matt and goes by without a word. When Zelda turns back a moment later, his eyes are fixed on Matt's palm shoved down the back of her jeans. He looks away.

'Pizza Hut?' says Matt, nodding at the nineties brick building in the corner of the leisure park.

'Really? Can't we go somewhere –'

'Nah, I fancy a Meat Feast. And it's fun in there.'

Inside, an eight-year-old's birthday party is in full swing, complete with balloons and raucous shouting. It is five o'clock, still early, and now she has no appetite. She excuses herself and leaves Matt alone with the menu.

Zelda stares in the Ladies' mirror. Her face looks different. She examines it from various angles, but can't put her finger on what has changed. A sharp pain in her tooth makes her wince, and she holds her cheek, waiting for it to pass. It's years since she went to the dentist. Perhaps it is time.

As she's returning to her seat, she glances through the front door and sees Will, leaning against a bollard. He wears the same corduroy jacket he wore on their date, and looks to be waiting for someone.

Zelda throws a quick glance at Matt, who is smiling to himself as he fills his bowl at the salad bar. She pushes open the front door.

'Hello, stranger,' she says.

He looks up and his expression changes. Not shock or surprise, not a reaction she can describe, exactly. It is as if he sees right through her. Yes, she thinks, that's it. He is looking at me. Actually looking. Actually noticing who I am. And then her cheeks flood with warmth, and she is back on that street corner with one foot in a taxi, the memory of his touch still on her skin.

'I wondered if I would see you again,' he says.

'Well, Pizza Hut's my favourite place.'

He raises an eyebrow as he glances at the neon sign. Another party of children stream in through the door.

She tucks her hair behind her ear. 'Waiting for someone?'

He rubs his hand against his lip in a way that seems familiar. It surprises her. One date, and he is stamped on her consciousness.

'Here comes your Prince Charming now,' he says, and, before she can ask, the door swishes open and Matt sticks his head out.

'You all right?'

She turns. 'Oh, hey. Just coming.'

Matt looks Will up and down, his tongue pushing hard against his cheek. 'Sure you're okay?'

Zelda almost laughs. To Will she says, 'Are you a danger?' and then to Matt, 'I said I'm coming?'

Matt stares, his face hard. 'Come on,' he says, putting out his hand. 'I'm hungry. I want to order our mains.'

Zelda sighs and starts walking backwards towards the door. 'Bye,' she mouths to Will, who watches her, frowning.

At the table Matt cranes his neck to look out of the window, but there is no sign of Will. 'Who was that?' he says, eating a slice of cucumber.

'Oh, just a guy I know.'

'Did you fuck him?'

Zelda snorts at the absurdity of his question. 'What?'

'Did you fuck him?' He is louder now.

She looks around, confused. 'I don't think that's appropriate language or topic of conversation for Pizza Hut.'

'Tell me.'

Zelda is amused by his jealousy. 'Yeah,' she whispers. 'I fucked him. Good and proper.'

Matt's jaw tightens. 'I should have laid him out.'

Now she laughs louder. There is something faintly ridiculous about a grown man threatening to destroy a rival while children celebrate their birthdays at the next table.

'Oh, he's all right,' she says, taking the menu. 'He's quite lovely, actually.'

Matt reaches across and grips her wrist. 'Did you tell him you're with me?'

Zelda stops smiling. She looks down at his hand, sees how easily his fingers fit around her wrist, how, if he wanted to, he could snap her bone. She is filled with both dread and desire. 'Am I with you, then? Are you with me?'

'You know you're with me.'

Zelda's eyes flit from his fist to his face. She can almost smell the air between them, the delicious, toxic scent of excitement, the petrol hype of an explosion that everyone knows is coming. Fear mingled with craving. His body is a known thing, her only knowledge of love. He is a hot summer, causing her to strip off and beg for a cold drink.

There it is again, that smell of petrol. Listen up, it says. Something here is about to happen. Watch out.

Something Softer

Isobel

There is now no sign of the previous century.

The Baked Alaska surgery walls are smooth and bright, the heavy, dark wood ripped out and replaced with honey-blond accents. In place of the green threadbare chairs is an L-shape length of blue banquette seating, plush and modern, on which Sadie bounces and declares it *sooooo comfortable*. Dotted around are plants – real ones – to purify the air, and the mahogany counter is now pale ash. Isobel runs her hand along the grain. The floor is engineered wood instead of carpet, and she sees how much easier it will be to keep clean, now that dark corners have been revealed and there is no fabric to stain.

And the light has changed. Tubular fluorescent bulbs have been swapped for spotlights. The room is still bright, but the bulbs are now warm, not cool and stark. Softer.

The focal point is no longer a rickety coffee table strewn with magazines, but a large tank of exotic, colourful fish. Everyone leans in to decide their favourite, apart from Isobel, who looks around in silence.

Five days, she thinks. A complete transformation in five days.

She calls a hair salon on her break and makes an appointment for tomorrow.

'Early finish, eh,' says Sadie, when Isobel turns off her computer the next day. 'Is tonight your date?'

'No,' says Isobel in a posh voice. 'And I did work through my lunch break and clear it with Carol.'

'All right, keep your hair on. I was only fishing, that's all.'

Well, fish off, thinks Isobel as she walks out.

★

In the chair, she shows the stylist a picture from a surgery magazine. 'You should do this, Isobel,' Sadie had said when the magazine came in the week before. 'I mean, your hair's nice, but it could do with an update.' Isobel pretended not to hear, then cut out the picture when Sadie took her break.

'Oh, a *lob*,' says the girl, leaning in. She looks barely old enough to have graduated from shampooing. 'That's what everyone wants right now.' She inspects Isobel's hair. 'It's more choppy than this feathered cut you have. It'll look great. Take years off.'

Isobel frowns. She never understands why young people consider it a compliment to say you don't look your age. What is so wrong with being fifty-five? Is she meant to walk around with a bag over her head? 'Hmm,' she says.

'And we're doing highlights, right? What colour?'

Isobel has avoided the mirror so far, but now she takes herself in. She remembers the fish tank. 'Honey-blonde,' she says. 'Something softer.'

It's a hit with Sadie. She lets out a piercing scream across the car park the next morning, and Isobel is surprised by how flattered she feels by the reaction. She rolls her eyes in any case.

'A-ma-zing,' says Sadie, pushing open the door. 'You look ten years younger.'

Isobel goes with it. Her hair bounces as she walks down the corridor, and it's true that she feels a spring she never realized had gone. She flicks the switch, and the reception room lights up. Still fresh, still new.

Her phone buzzes with a message from Victor. *Okay for the weekend?* She smiles and goes to reply.

'Is that our Mr Godden?' Sadie says, as she walks out to the kitchen. She runs the tap and calls, 'So when's he taking you for a night on the tiles?'

Isobel bristles. *Our* Mr Godden, indeed. 'Saturday. I haven't yet made up my mind if I'm going.'

Sadie sticks her head out. 'Oh, but you can't do that. He's such a sweetheart. Do you know, he's the only patient who doesn't stare at my tits? I actually wondered if he was gay.'

Isobel doesn't quite know how to reply. 'No, I didn't know that, Sadie. But thank you for enlightening me.'

'What are you going to do?'

'We haven't discussed that. He mentioned dinner, but –'

'But?'

How to explain to this girl that, if she is spotted with him in public, she'll be forced to explain to the elders. Dating a worldly person is shocking in itself, and she isn't even yet divorced. She has thought all week of cancelling, but cutting her hair has made her feel reckless. She's not ready yet to shut down the feeling.

'It's hard to explain,' she says, knowing she should be honest. It's hardly right for her to knock on strangers' doors when she's not open with people she sees daily.

'Well, I think you should give the bloke a chance. He did buy you flowers, after all.'

'So I owe him an evening in thanks?' she says, alarmed. Is this how it works?

'Don't be silly,' says Sadie, coming back with two mugs of tea. 'I just mean he likes you. May as well have some fun.' She puts down Isobel's cup. 'What are you planning to wear?'

Isobel follows her colleague's eye and smooths her blouse. 'I'm not sure yet. Why?'

'Oh, it's just . . .' Sadie tips her head from side to side, looking her up and down. 'Don't take this the wrong way, Isobel, but you don't do yourself any favours. I mean, you're wearing a tweed skirt. In *summer*.'

Isobel sits up straight and starts sorting through paperwork. 'I didn't realize my clothing offends you.'

'Don't take it like that.' She folds her arms as she scrutinizes her. 'You don't realize what a knockout bod you've got, Isobel. I hope I have a figure like yours when I'm old.'

'Well . . .'

Sadie's eyes widen. 'Hey, how about when we close for lunch, you and I go to the outlet and find something for your date?'

'It's not a date.'

'I reckon we can find an outfit that will blow Victor's little socks off. Have you got nice underwear?'

Isobel looks at her, her mouth open. 'I'll probably just cancel, to be honest,' she says, fumbling with her bag.

'I've put the fear of God into you now, haven't I? Oh, ignore me. Forget the knickers. Let's just find you a dress.' She taps her fingers on the desk. 'I'm offering my services for free here. I only say this because I think you could do with a bloody good sha–' – she coughs – 'time.'

Isobel sits with her phone in her hand, the flashing cursor waiting for her reply. She should cancel. Oh, but her hair . . . She would like to know what he thinks of her hair.

Yes, okay, she types to Victor. 'Yes, okay,' she says to Sadie.

Fear

Alice and Jen

1997

'*We must prepare ourselves, brothers and sisters, for the war that will take place here on earth. It is clear from the state of the world how far we are into the last days, and the Apocalypse that awaits us will be unlike anything the world has seen before.*'

The air in the windowless Worship Hall is stuffy and smells of wet woollen coats. The sound of rain pounds on the roof above the congregation, whose stares are fixed on the brother on the platform.

Jen awaits a poke through the chair from Alice, who is sitting behind her. There is usually a jab whenever Brother Connell gives a talk, or at least a note of the rudest order. But, fifteen minutes in, and still no sign.

'*Do you feel upset at the sight of a dead animal in the road? Well, brothers, when our God has won His war, there will be piles of dead people in the streets. Scorched, mangled bodies. Imagine the smell. Most likely, it will be our job to dispose of them. So it's essential that we get our minds off ourselves during these last days, because there are people out there who need our help. We are on the right side in this war. We are fortunate. Our job now is to preach to the world, so that they may not be on that rotting pile of corpses.*'

Brother Connell pauses for dramatic effect, and a toddler screams from the back row. There is shushing from the parents, and then the child is hurried out to the foyer before the crying disturbs the talk.

Jen turns, pretending to look at the clock, to sneak a look at Alice. She sits poker straight, her eyes on the brother as she holds back a frown. A sharp dig in the ribs from her mother, and Jen turns back to face the front. But she no longer listens.

She cannot stop thinking of Alice's expression, the fear etched into her face.

Afterwards, they hang around the foyer with other youngsters. The boys talk of Premier League football, while Alice stands apart, staring at a wall vase of dried flowers.

'Earth to Alice,' Jen whispers. 'Where are you?'

Alice blinks, shaking her head as she rejoins the room. 'That talk . . .'

'What about it?'

Alice doesn't reply. She looks from Jen to the boys who are laughing at some joke, then pulls Jen away into the corner.

'He said we're all on the same side. The *right* side.'

Jen frowns.

'At Armageddon!' Alice hisses. 'He said the worldly people are going to die, and that we're all on the right side together.'

'Yes. And?'

'So are we all on the right side, just because we're here? We'll all survive because we wear the same badge?'

Jen does her best to follow. 'Well, only God can judge. That's what the Bible says, isn't it? He decides who's good and bad, who lives or dies.'

'But that's not what he said,' says Alice, slowly. 'He said we're all on the same side.'

'He's talking generally. I suppose he can't get into details in a thirty-minute talk.'

Alice stares at her. 'But it's all *about* the details. How can you talk generally about this? It's life or death. Surely you have to be specific.'

Jen shrugs, unsure of what to say. She has never seen Alice so worked up about spiritual matters. She is usually bored at meetings, stifling yawns or slouching down in her seat. Ever since she got baptized last year, she seemed to lose all interest.

'But I guess we are all on the same side, aren't we?' Jen says, trying to offer hope. 'We're not murderers or rapists or thieves like in the world. None of us are perfect, but I wouldn't say we deserve to die.'

The door to the main auditorium opens and three elders come out, all talking in hushed, serious tones. Jen smiles as they pass, and one, Steven, gives her a friendly wink. They go into the back room and close the door. Jen glances at the keyhole. There must be something ominous going on for them to gather like that after the meeting.

She turns back to Alice, who leans against the wall with an unreadable face.

Alice looks at her. 'So none of us are baddies? We're all going to make it through?'

Dead Flowers

Jen

Jen takes each day as it comes. She ignores the deep ache in her stomach that doesn't fade after eating, and hardly notices the angry red spots that spring up along her chin and neck. Plates clatter, mugs chip, and she spends a long time staring out of windows.

'What's up with you?' Zelda asks, when Jen forgets to turn off the tap.

'Nothing,' she says.

On Wednesday, she goes to work as usual and a steady stream of shoppers keeps her mind off the dilemma that wakes her at night. She pushes her problems away as she picks up clothes and repeats *Sorry to keep you* to strangers.

After work she will meet Zelda for their class. She imagines her hands in the clay, throwing a lump on the wheel, watching it spin as her fingers tease it to life. The act of creation usually settles her head, but today her ache is too strong.

At around four o'clock, she drops the dress she is folding and doubles over behind the till, breathing hard and trying not to faint. 'Are you okay?' asks a customer, as her boss comes rushing over. 'I'm fine,' she replies, putting her hand to her mouth and trying not to vomit. 'Honestly, I'm fine.'

She is sent home to rest, and drives with the windows down and music blaring to sober herself up, one hand fixed to her forehead, which feels ready to break. She dreams of sleep.

Maybe she will tell Zelda everything. If she is home, perhaps Jen will explain that she must move out, that she has no choice, that it is not her decision to make. Zelda will see that it's out of her control, like Pete and Jacob, and everything else that makes her crave darkness.

Or perhaps she can wait a while longer. Whatever the elders say, she knows there is a yearning in Zelda for something out of reach, and Jen can bring her back. This is the way I can show her my love, she thinks. This is the only way. The thought floods Jen's body and cures her sore head. *I will try, Father,* she prays. *Please see how I try.*

The garden is empty when she returns and the house, quiet. Wasn't Zelda's car out front? Jen drops her bag and walks over to the sink, where she runs the tap. She lets it spill down the sides of the glass.

There's a shout from upstairs and a loud thump, like something falling off the bed. Jen puts down the glass and listens. There it is again, the sound of Zelda crying out in pain.

Jen takes the stairs two at a time, bursting into the room to see Zelda naked on the bed, a man behind her with one hand on her throat and the other yanking her hair. There is no time to think. Jen launches herself at the man and punches his back, pulling him off her friend. He falls on to the ground, his nakedness splayed out as he puts up his hands against the bruises Jen rains down. 'Get the hell off me,' he yells.

And then Zelda's arms hook around her waist and push her on to the bed.

'What are you doing?' screams Zelda.

Jen blinks. 'Wait, what?'

'I'm bleeding,' says the man, cross-legged on the floor and holding his forehead. 'You've made me bleed, you crazy bitch.'

Zelda goes over and touches the wound. 'It's just a graze, you're fine.'

'But I heard you scream,' says Jen, 'and I thought . . . wait.' She sits up. 'You're that bloke from the wedding. The one who wouldn't leave us alone.'

He puts his hand out. 'Matt. Fucking pleasure.'

'But . . . you're *married*.'

Zelda puts on her robe. 'Go out,' she says, avoiding Jen's eye. She bends over Matt to inspect his wound, then half turns towards the door. 'Go.'

Jen gives her a filthy look and retreats downstairs, her body

177

boiling with heat. She perches on the edge of the sofa, then puts her head between her knees. There is no customer to ask if she's okay. There is nobody.

'I'm sick of this,' she says, when Zelda comes downstairs in overalls, stained with clay. 'I've lived here for months and I still don't know why there are dead plants everywhere. Here.' She flicks the curling leaves on a cheese plant. 'It's *dying*. Just give it some damn water.'

'This is about houseplants?'

Jen cannot look at her. 'He's married, Alice. Married!'

'Trust me, I'm aware.'

'But why was he doing that to you?' Jen points upstairs, where Matt is dragging his feet around the room. 'Making you cry. No wonder I thought you were being attacked.'

'Oh, enough.' She looks at her watch. 'We'd best get going.'

Jen turns away. Roses drift in the breeze outside the window. Scarlet, carmine, crimson, shades of romance and blood. 'You can't sell this to me as *love*,' she says, 'not with it looking how it did. Nobody who truly loves a person would do that to them.'

Zelda snorts, shaking her head. 'Maybe it shows how comfortable I am with him that I can enjoy that side of myself. Love doesn't equate to missionary, Jennifer.'

Jen hugs the ache in her stomach. 'What he's doing to his wife is what Pete did to me.'

'I'm sorry you saw it, okay?' Zelda's voice is softer. 'But that's my private space. You had no right barging in or framing it now as if I've deliberately hurt you. I don't care how things *look*, but about how they actually are. Try it sometime.'

Zelda's bedroom door slams open. They look up at Matt in the doorway, his bulk taking up the space. He comes down the stairs casually, then slings his jacket over his shoulder and kisses Zelda on the mouth, again taking his time. Jen looks away. When he is finished, he strolls towards the door and whistles over his shoulder. 'Bye, girls.' And then he is gone.

'You call yourself a feminist, but what about his wife?'

Zelda is touching her lip where he kissed her. 'Oh, come on.'

'Not your problem, then? He's an idiot bloke, but you should know better.'

Zelda throws up her hands. 'Why is it men screw around and everyone accepts it? Nobody says they should be standing in solidarity with other men. Why is it different for us? For me? Why should my freedom take into account half the population of the entire world? I mean, no, I'm not a fan of the situation, but don't tell me what to do. I'm tired of people telling me what to do. I want to be free. You think birds have marriage ceremonies? You think they put little rings on their skinny feet and sign bits of paper that they send to big fancy nests in some capital city of birds where all the biggest, fattest ones make laws that tell others how to be? You think a bird puts up with shit from another bird because it has to? In case of what the pigeons in the next tree think? Well, I want to be a bird. A free fucking bird.'

Jen looks at the vases of dead flowers, their heads weeping and sad. 'You're a fraud. You talk about honesty and being open, but everything is fake. Your hair, your name, your costumes, the way you morph your body in photos . . . it's all just to hide the truth.'

Zelda tips her head with a mocking expression. 'Because you're so honest? Like that day in your bedroom, all those years ago, when you denied your own truth.'

Jen feels the blood in her veins. She is still, her thoughts fighting, and then she lifts her chin. She knows now she cannot stay. 'Alice,' she says.

Zelda shrugs. 'Call me Alice if you like. She's still there somewhere. But maybe her life was too fucking sad. Maybe she had the chance to create a new one, to reinvent herself. Do you blame her?'

'But it's not real. Your hand can pass straight through it.'

'So I should face up to the realities? That my dad's dead and my mum won't look at me, that my life fell apart when I was a kid and an old man raped me with his finger? Is that real enough for you? Tell me, would you want that existence?'

Her voice breaks on the final word, and she turns and runs out.

The Cut

Alice

1998

'That is an extremely serious allegation, Alice.'

Alice sits in front of them, unsure where to look. Not at the man speaking, with his balding head and fish-hook nose. She has never liked Brother Connell. He doesn't notice the younger ones, unless they need chastising for running in the hall or wearing their hair in a worldly fashion. Then he is on them like a pox, bending scriptures to suit his preference. The other two brothers watch her. No, she doesn't want to look at them either. She is fifteen years old and done with older men.

'Do you realize how serious it is, what you're saying?'

Alice shrugs, unsure. All she has done is tell the truth. Was she meant to examine its seriousness before she did that? How does that work, exactly?

'Perhaps we should start at the beginning,' says Brother Mason, smoothing his tie. 'When did this all start?'

'About two years ago,' says Alice to the carpet.

'*About* two years ago?'

Alice frowns as she thinks back – did they want an actual date? 'It was summer. I was almost thirteen. So two years ago.'

Her answers are staccato. Headlines on a telegram. They have lived as graffiti on her insides, no extra words softening their truth.

'How do you remember so clearly?' asks Brother Boyd.

'Because I got baptized the week before. I wore a dress with no tights and he noticed a cut on my knee.' Alice blushes as she remembers the hack job she'd done of shaving her legs. 'He touched my leg and asked about it. That's how I remember.'

Brother Boyd shifts in his seat and looks down at his Bible.

'And how had it got there?' asks Brother Connell. 'The cut?'

Alice's face burns. The last thing she wants to do is explain her puberty to three middle-aged men, but her mother will know if she lies. She is there, outside the door. She knows about the cuts. 'I don't remember,' Alice whispers.

One of them writes this down.

'Start at the beginning, Alice,' says Brother Mason, his voice gentle. 'How that first day happened.'

Alice takes a deep breath and listens to the silence. No laughter or voices come from the foyer, because there is nobody else here. The Worship Hall has been unlocked just for her.

'He stopped by to pick me up. Josh Townes was in the front. He knocked, and I went out and got in the backseat.'

'What kind of car did he have?'

Alice swallows. 'I don't know the name – he doesn't have it any more – but it was white and had a spoiler on the back.' And hot leather seats that burned her legs.

Brother Boyd waves at her to continue as he writes down her words.

'We were doing country territory, so there was a short drive between houses. He asked me to do the first one with him. Then we went back to the car and drove on to the next house. Josh went along that time. We swapped over for a while, and then he asked Josh to try a door on his own.'

'Why would he do that?' asks Brother Mason.

Alice frowns. Surely this is obvious in light of what she's told them. 'The house was at the end of a long path. We could see the door from the car, and I guess he thought that, if Josh needed him, he could wave and we'd see.'

One of the brothers talks quietly with Brother Connell. Alice tries not to listen but hears every word. 'I'm not sure he'd remember,' she says. 'If you asked him.'

'And why's that?' says Brother Connell.

'Because it was two years ago and just a regular ministry morning for Josh Townes.'

He nods for her to continue.

'Josh got out, and then he turned in his seat. He asked about the cut, then reached out and touched it.' She squirms and presses her legs together. 'He carried on talking, but his hand went up my leg and under my dress.' Alice imagines her mother sitting upright outside the door.

'I know this must be hard, Alice, but we must know the facts. Please tell us exactly where he touched you.'

Alice stares at the shelves of books behind the three men. Rows of heavy books in glorious hues with spines in the fashionable font of the decade in which they were written, from the organization's late-nineteenth-century beginning down to the present day. She has known these books all her life. She has known this back room all her life. Everything here has always been her anchor.

'He put his fingers inside me. He talked the whole time. As if what was happening wasn't happening.'

'What did he talk about?'

'The Spice Girls. The weather. That he had a public talk the following week. I remember it perfectly.'

'What were you wearing?'

Alice blinks. 'Pardon?'

'What were you wearing?'

'A dress my mum had made. It was red with gingham pockets.' And now lies buried at the back of her wardrobe.

'What shape was it?'

Alice doesn't understand why they need to know, but says, 'Like a loose summer dress. It had little straps so I wore a cardigan unless it was very hot.'

'Were you wearing a cardigan that day? How short was the dress?'

'Yes, I think so.' Her heart is deafening. 'Erm, about here.' She touches her knee. 'What's that . . . Why is that important?'

Brother Connell clears his throat. 'Alice, it has been noticed that you have a tendency to wear clothing that borders on, shall we say, the inappropriate. A few comments have been made on the low-cut nature of your tops. Are you aware of that?'

Alice's hand flies to her chest, and she sees their eyes follow. I thought that day in the car was the worst of my life, she thinks, but I was wrong. I was so wrong.

'I-It's hard to find clothes that fit properly . . .' Sorry my body has suddenly transformed, she thinks. But if it offends you, why do I feel you all watching? Even when I don't dress for your gaze, your eyes still find me. Perhaps listen to Jesus, who said to tear your own eyes out when looking at a woman, not make it the job of a fifteen-year-old to police her changing body. This is what she wishes she could say. 'I don't really see what that has to do with this.'

Brother Connell watches her. 'Alice, how many times did this event occur? Was the time in the car an isolated incident, or not?'

'Five times over the following year.'

'And did you at any time ask him to stop?'

She shrugs. 'I would try to move away, sit up against the door. But he just climbed in the back. Nothing I did worked.'

'When was the last time?'

'About a year ago.'

'Why do you think it stopped?'

Alice doesn't understand why they are asking *her* this question, but she knows the answer. 'He started not to notice me when I stopped looking like a little girl.'

'How did you know that he didn't notice you?'

'Because he didn't look at me any more. He would watch me all the time, start a conversation. But when my body started changing, he stopped taking me on the ministry.'

'You knew he looked at you. So you looked at him back?'

Alice hugs her arms to her chest, trying to disappear. 'Sorry?'

'Well, for someone to know they're being looked at, they must also be doing the looking.'

Alice doesn't know how to reply. She makes strange little noises, like the beginnings of words, but none of them complete.

'Did you tell anyone else?' asks Brother Boyd.

Alice bites her lip to stop herself from crying. 'It would have devastated my parents. My dad . . . I couldn't do that to them. But I wrote it down in my diary. In code.' Her skin turns clammy as she imagines them asking to read it. The secrets of her heart laid out on purple paper.

'Code?'

'I called him a different name. I described it as him feeding me ice-cream.' She gives an embarrassed laugh. 'Stupid, really.'

'Why didn't you tell anyone?'

Alice wants to laugh again. Is he serious? Tell who? She is telling now and they don't believe her. 'He's an *elder*,' she says.

Brother Connell gestures to Brother Boyd. 'Let's bring him in,' he says, and Brother Boyd moves towards the door. 'Now, Alice . . . the Bible is very clear on the evidence required to establish guilt. Either the accused admits the sin, or there must be the testimony of two witnesses to the act. You count as one, but, without a confession, we need another. This is a Bible command, so as to ensure that false accusations don't proceed. The brother will now join us and hear your account.' He looks up at the door behind her and snaps his fingers.

Alice's blood runs cold. He is out there in the foyer with her mother. Waiting as if for an appointment. As if this is a regular day. The door is opened and the brother enters.

He sits beside her. 'All right, Les? All right, Tim?'

Everything He does she will see from the corners of her eyes.

'Alice,' says Brother Connell. 'Perhaps you could repeat what you told us?'

'All of it?' she whispers.

'Yes, if that's not too much trouble. We need to establish the truth of the matter.'

And so, with her face scarlet, Alice sits alone in the back room in front of four men and recounts what one of them did to her. She tries to repeat it exactly, so as not to be accused of making it up. She tries not to imagine her mother crying outside. It is not hard to remember the details, because the details of that day are burned on her brain. As this one now will be.

When she has finished, she bites her tongue and awaits further direction.

He denies everything.

There is no second witness.

Alice is not sure what all this means.

Her mother comes in to take her home. They sit side by side in the car, silent. They do not mention the moment Brother Connell asked her mother why she allowed Alice in His car without adult supervision, as if Marjorie bears all responsibility. Alice folded her body in knots as her mother, petite and quiet by nature, apologized over and over. Neither of them spoke of their happy nervousness that first morning, when her mother had picked her outfit and said what a privilege it was that He was singling her out as a ministry partner, how it showed the congregation's love that they gave special care to young ones with fathers not in the truth.

Nor do they speak of Brother Connell fixing his eyes on Alice and advising her to keep it to herself. 'Without two witnesses, we must leave this in God's hands,' he said. 'Trust in God's love, and God will sustain you. Keep approaching our Father in prayer. We mustn't threaten the unity of the congregation with gossip. And, Alice, you may find these articles helpful.' He handed her some photocopied papers, stapled together. The title on the first page was *Dressing in a Modest and Attractive Way*. Alice had held them against her chest, confused as to why he had prepared homework before hearing what she had to say.

To her mother, he murmured, 'Best not speak of this to anyone, Marjorie. You know how worldly institutions are. They're just looking for reasons to attack God's people, and we mustn't give Satan the pleasure of seeing what havoc he can wreak. If you have any concerns, come and see me. But we must leave this in the hands of our heavenly Father and not bring reproach upon God's name.'

They speak of nothing. The noise of the wipers squeaking across the windscreen is their only soundtrack, until they pull up outside the house and Marjorie half turns as she grabs the door handle.

'Don't breathe a word of this to your father,' she says. 'This would break him.' And then she gets out of the car.

Inside her bedroom, Alice throws the papers on her bed.

'So that's it?' she says to nobody.

That day remains in Alice's head and never takes the past tense. It is always on repeat.

Forget-me-nots

Alice

1998

The only hint at change was when Marjorie came into Alice's room the next morning and sorted through her wardrobe. Anything immodest was thrown out. She took Alice shopping, but finding clothes to fit her petite frame and full chest was an impossible task.

'You're just not the normal shape,' she'd say, tutting and shaking her head.

'Yes, apparently I'm some kind of monster.'

'I'll have to make you things instead,' said Marjorie, and she ran up voluminous blouses and dresses on her sewing machine that swamped Alice's frame.

'I'm not wearing any of it,' Alice said, when her mother hung them in her wardrobe. 'I'm fifteen, for God's sake. I don't want to look like a balloon.'

'I won't have a daughter that dresses like a slut,' Marjorie said. 'And don't blaspheme.'

Alice began spending her pocket money on clothes. She went to the cheap shops in town, places where a tenner would stretch across several outfits. Fabric that puckered and itched, just as it did on other girls. She'd dress up to go out and then pull on one of her mum's creations. When she was clear of the house, she'd whip it off and stuff it in her bag.

She didn't set out to deceive. This was the body she'd been given. Tell a young girl something enough times, and she'll start to believe it. Call her body offensive and vile, and see how she will crave attention. See how she lets their hands creep, just to feel of value. Do not be shocked by this, she recited like a proverb to the outraged voices in her mind. Love is what we are born wanting.

The real me is not allowed, she thought. If I hide myself away, I am not true to myself. If I am true to myself, they do not want me. Either way is dishonest, and so they must prefer trickery over truth, just as they favoured His words over mine . . . and His were deceitful.

Her voice dried up. She'd been warned not to speak of it and so she didn't, not even to Jen, who'd always listened when the lights went out. Schoolfriends were off limits – *They're worldly people, Alice* – and, even with the ones she was close to, a voice inside said they would never understand her world. She was six of one, half-a-dozen of the other. Limbo.

At meetings she continued to sit in the audience as He continued with talks and prayers. She watched Him conduct Bible studies and take other young people in His car on the ministry. No two witnesses meant no proof, and so He kept His innocence, as well as her own. He lost nothing. People kept loving Him.

Alice lost herself with boys. By the time she was sixteen, she had kissed every boy in the hall and allowed a few to put their hands up her top. On holiday in the South of France, she spent an evening making eyes at a handsome French waiter while at a table with her parents. When she spilt red wine on her white crochet dress with daisies appliquéd on the hem, her mother sent her off to the toilet to rinse it. She sashayed through the tables towards the back and let him follow her into the cubicle, where she locked the door and let him finger her until she came. When she returned to the table, her cheeks were as red as the stain she had forgotten to wash.

She kissed girls for a while too, but her heart wasn't in it. They were practice for the real thing. That real thing would come speeding into her life in a purple car with bleached tips and a smile that made her feel she was beginning again.

But, before then, at age sixteen, her mother finally relented to her pleas and they moved to another hall twenty minutes in the opposite direction. But memories don't stay in buildings or the backseats of cars. They follow like a shadow.

Her dad begged her to sort herself out. He spent hours teaching her sewing and embroidery, using their time together to talk and find a way through. 'I feel like I don't know you any more,' he said to her, wiping his eye. 'What happened to you, pet?'

And so she told him. She sat in his tin workshop by the warm stove and poured out all she had worked hard to bury. It came fast and furious, and she realized then that it would never leave her. It would hover under the surface of everything she did and everything she would ever do. The thought of this made her want to sink and slip through the cracks in the floorboards.

Her mother was right. It broke him. When Marjorie refused to go to the police and begged him not to either, he withdrew from living. Months later, he was diagnosed with terminal brain cancer. 'No surprise there,' he said, when he found out. 'Of course the heart's connected to the head.'

Three months after her father died, Alice was taking her seat at the Sunday meeting when she heard the announcement *And now we have a visiting brother for today's talk,* and He walked up to the platform. She ran out and vomited into the toilet, then sat in the audience for two hours and listened to His voice.

That week, she went on a rampage. She kissed three boys at a congregation party on the Saturday and smoked a cigarette in broad daylight in town, where she was seen by an elder's wife. She got her belly button pierced. She smoked weed. She tried to feel every damn thing.

Her jury was the standard three men in the back room. It was a different hall, but all back rooms look the same. The same rows of books, the same suspended ceiling, the same vibe of catching her out. These elders knew nothing of what had gone on before. Those allegations were filed away in some cabinet, strictly on a need-to-know basis. Her words had not been allowed to take flight. But what had followed her from the last hall was her reputation as a girl who wore tight clothing and loved nothing more than being chased.

You're naughty for making me do this to you. It's all your fault. His words that first time. She couldn't bring herself to tell this to the men when they asked her to keep repeating her story, because perhaps they'd ask *why*, as if somehow she had the answer.

Part of her wanted to make them understand. Listen, brothers, she would have said. When I was a modestly dressed child, He did what He liked, because I was no threat in that state. It was only when my body transformed that He was done. These lumps and bumps are my weapons. Becoming a woman set me free. This is why I must celebrate them, show them off, be thankful for their birth. Don't you understand? I want to scare. I want to chase. I must reclaim my power.

But all this existed as mere colour in her seventeen-year-old brain. She hadn't yet made sense of it. And so, two years on from when she first told three men her secret, Alice folded her arms across her offensive chest and bit her lip whenever they asked a question. I can't bring all that up again, she thought. Besides, they didn't believe me the first time. So she stayed silent and was deemed unrepentant. *Haughty. Worldly. An independent spirit.*

Disfellowshipped and cast out.

She became Zelda shortly after that. Her inheritance she spent converting the workshop and she moved her things in as soon as she could. There was no final hug or conversation with her mum. Marjorie locked the door behind her.

Zelda loved living in her tin house. Love surrounded her in the form of her dad's costumes and mannequins and the hours she had shared with him there. This had been his space and sanctuary, and now it was hers.

She tried to love again. She did. First love filled her veins with fire. Even when it ended, like everything does, Zelda was sustained by a strange and beautiful pain. It was her own desire that had awoken.

At nineteen, a boy fell in love with her, and, although she knew he wasn't right, she tried him on for a while. He was a new dress in a shape that everyone said would suit her. He wrote her letters and poems and spoke of how their souls were entwined. Once, when they were lying in a field, he stood up and took her picture and said that she would now forever be linked to forget-me-nots. Oh, not forget-me-nots, Zelda said. That's so obvious. But you *are* obvious, he replied. You're cold water on a hot day. You're the ink that gives paper meaning. Forget-me-nots are exactly what you are. And then he had dropped to his knees in the long grass and kissed her.

Why couldn't she have fallen for him? Were her symbols of love now forever tainted by cheap tattoos and basketball posters? She had kissed him back and stroked his hair and thought *If only I'd met you first*.

Fully Formed Beings

Zelda and Jen

Zelda doesn't look up when Jen enters the workroom. She is at the trestle table, its surface stained and marked, pummelling the silver clay. Zelda prefers hand-building. She cannot speak the rhythms of the wheel. It is too precise for her nature.

Jen sits beside her and makes no move to begin. She shakes off her jacket, which is splattered with rain, a storm starting up outside. Wind whistles through the roof, and the room is bathed in sunshine.

'You were right,' says Jen. 'That was your private space. I shouldn't have assumed that . . .'

Zelda pounds the clay.

'Jen,' says Mara, entering the room. She wears her usual dungarees over a colourful shirt, her curls held back with a ribbon. 'You on the wheel? It's just you both today.'

Jen finally looks away from Zelda. 'Actually, I think I'll hand-build.'

Mara glances from one to the other. 'Well, I'll be out here. Holler if you need me.'

She goes out, and they are alone again.

The minutes go by. Jen looks at the cluttered shelves of pots, books and canisters of paint. They have done a month of Wednesdays, and it is the highlight of Jen's week. She wishes away the weekend so she can begin again. Here, amid this mess, in a room that smells of earth and summer rain, she can sit with Zelda and make. If she were good with words, she would describe the sensation it gives her – this act of creation – deep down in her stomach, deep down in her fingers and toes.

'I never once orgasmed with Pete,' she says.

Zelda looks at her, astonished, and a sharp burst of laughter fills the room. 'What?'

'I faked it from the very first time. I'd pretend to love it, just so he'd stop touching me. Just so he'd leave me alone.' She shakes her head. 'So messed up.'

Zelda stares at the clay. 'We're all so messed up.'

Jen goes over to the sink and fills a bowl with water. She sits down at the bench, making no attempt to start.

'Do you know what I first felt when I found out he'd cheated?' She gives a sad smile. 'Relief. I had a way out. And then I felt bad for being happy.'

'That's what I don't miss about that world. Guilt over every little feeling.'

And then Zelda tells Jen everything. The backseat of an elder's car, Matt, her dad. Jen listens, her hand over her mouth. The only sound is the rain hitting the roof.

Zelda leans forward. 'I see everyone else as fully formed beings. And, yet, what am I? Still stuck in the back, not knowing how to get out. People look at me and think, Why can't she be good. Why can't she *be*. And I think, I don't know. Why can't she be?'

A quiet flash of rage unfurls in Jen as she thinks of how life could have been if she'd known all this. She would have found Alice and thrown her arms around her. She would not have let her go.

'That's why I like what Matt was doing. Because, this time, it's my choice. I can relive it, and I can stop whenever I like.' Zelda pulls apart the clay. 'I had no power for so much of my life, and it probably sounds fucked up, but this gives it back to me.'

There is a loud bang, and they turn to see a branch beating the window. A cloud moves in front of the sun, and shadow darkens the room. It falls away as quickly as it came, and, in a split-second of light, everything is heightened.

'I'm sorry for kissing you that day,' says Zelda.

Jen leaps up and goes over to the peg board on the wall, where she scans the tools with her finger. She takes her time. It startles her how quickly she'd moved, as if Zelda triggered a reflex. 'There we go,' she says, and picks one up.

Back at the bench, she sits down and stares at the useless tool. It's a wooden rib, used only for the wheel.

'Jen,' says Zelda, reaching out. 'I wanted you to see . . .'

She closes her eyes at Zelda's touch. 'I assumed it would stop when I married Pete. When I found the life I was meant to have. I didn't know until it was too late.'

'You know it now.'

'And what can I do with that? This habit of falling in love with the wrong kind of person.'

Zelda shakes her head. 'Jen, don't you want to be honest?'

She stares at the cold clay. 'I want Jacob, Zelda. I knew when I felt his first kick that his was the only love I wanted. Unconditional.'

'Because you knew that, if you were honest with everyone, you'd discover their love had conditions.'

'Maybe that's why I want him so much. I'm allowed that kind of love.'

'But do you want to live a lie?'

Jen stares at her friend. Are there really people who take any path they like? She should tell Zelda how she pinches herself when her head turns towards a woman, squeezes her skin each time she has an impure thought. Perhaps she should show her the bruises. She has been taught all her life that these urges are wicked. Her kind of love is wrong. Even as she feels it, she is begging her brain to stop, commanding her heart to cease with its excitement. She would be lying if she said she hadn't sometimes wondered. But to lose her family forever and watch Zelda waste herself on cheap men? It seems a worthless trade.

'Some days, I wish I had died.'

'Jen.'

'If I'd just slipped away, I would open my eyes and be with Jacob. I told the truth for nothing. I would have him back quicker if I'd done what they said.' She begins to shake, and then Zelda is hugging her, calming her, soothing her pain.

'Listen,' says Zelda. 'There are people who rip through you, and, when they're done, you know you'll never be the same. What was there before will never be again, and that's fine. Because you'd rather feel a river of pain than be a lake of nothing. You'd rather something fucks you up, because at least then you know you bleed. At least then you know you're not stone.'

There is a lightness to the air when two people have shared their secrets. They turn to their clay.

Mara comes in a few minutes later, carrying a vase fresh from the kiln. Its belly shape forms upwards into several tubes, like a human heart. Thickly painted red-and-pink stripes flame upwards from the base to merge into one colour around the tubes, setting it alight. Jen imagines it would scorch her fingers.

'What's it meant to be?' she says.

'Be?'

'It's a heart, right?'

Mara leans her head to one side and looks at the vase, as if seeing it for the first time. 'Never explain your work. Put all your love and soul into the thing, and let others do the interpreting. They'll only see what they want to, anyway.'

Mara's pieces are hard to define. They are coloured with abstract shapes, batik lines, stripes and zigzags; traditional motifs, but with an unusual form. At their first class, she told them how influenced she is by her homeland, a place she left as a child. She will never go back – this country is her home now – but it will always be with her. The hot and arid air, the heated scent of spices, the light that exists only in that corner of the world. It is entwined with her. You take your roots everywhere, she says. You just make them into something new.

Zelda studies the form she's made, then crushes it with her fist. 'I'd like to know how many great tragedies would be avoided if every parent threw their arms around their kid and said they fucking loved them.'

Falling, Falling, Falling

Isobel

Isobel feels ridiculous as she gets off the bus. People are staring. She is sure of it. What does that woman look like, she imagines them thinking. Trussed up like a twenty-five-year-old . . . look how she can hardly walk in those silly, strappy things.

She had made similar judgements when Sadie threw open the changing-room curtain and gushed.

'It's perfect,' Sadie had said, to which Isobel replied, 'It's red.'

'Exactly. The colour of romance, the colour of love. Just what you need.'

'But it's so red,' Isobel kept saying. 'And it's a meal, Sadie. Let's not get carried away here.'

But she'd bought it. They had only forty minutes once they'd factored in the time spent walking there and back, and she knew Sadie would say if it looked bad. Besides, Isobel was well accustomed to the attention that came Sadie's way. Perhaps she could try a spoonful of that. Just a taste. It wasn't as if her work colleague's good opinion really mattered, and, compared with Sadie, she was a nun.

Sadie grabbed some high-heeled shoes on the way to the till. 'These are lush, and thirty per cent off. What size are you, Isobel?' and then gave them to the sales assistant. 'Just return them if they don't fit,' she said, when Isobel looked unsure. 'Come on. Carol will have a fit if we don't get back.'

Two inches are skyscrapers to Isobel, and what with the stiletto heels . . . She is learning to walk again. But at least the dress isn't short. It fits snugly over her chest with a hint of skin, but her shoulders are covered and the light, floaty skirt moves like water.

Victor said to meet outside a French bistro in the back streets of town. She hasn't heard of the place before, which bodes well for avoiding attention. The sun is starting its descent as she totters across the road. Outside, the restaurant window boxes are crammed with geraniums, and warm light spills out through the bay windows. She peers inside. Red-and-white-checked tablecloths. Real flowers. Candles to be lit. Steven would love this, she thinks, and then suddenly remembers that she is here in foreign clothes, waiting for a stranger.

When a taxi pulls up, Isobel recognizes the passenger's silhouette and presses herself into the doorway of the adjoining building. Toni and Bill Norris laugh as they jump out and hurry into the restaurant.

They didn't see me, she repeats, as her heart runs lengths around her body. Of course they wouldn't recognize me dressed like this. But, oh, what would they think if they did . . . She is hobbling away when the purr of a motorbike sounds behind. She turns to see Victor coming to a stop. His bike is shiny black and chrome, and its roar fills the street.

'Leaving already?' He removes his helmet, and his newly fixed teeth flash in a friendly smile. He is not wearing leathers today, but jeans and a floral shirt with seventies cuffs and a pointed collar. Isobel tries not to stare.

'I . . .' She looks at her bag, embarrassed. 'Someone I know is in there, so –'

'Oh, me too. The maître d' is a mate and reserved me the best table, so shall we?' He puts out his arm.

'I can't.'

He watches her. 'Well, now, I'm sure we can find somewhere else, although good places may be booked on a Saturday.'

Saturday night. Busy. Eyes. She grips her bag against her body. 'I should go.'

'Oh,' he says, looking down. 'In that case, let me give you a ride? I came prepared.' A spare helmet is strapped to the back of his bike.

Isobel has never been on a bike. Cars were more Steven's vibe. Bright, flashy cars that scream youth. She shakes her head. 'I'll get the bus.'

'If you're in town, I can have you back in no more than five min-utes. The beauty of the bike, see.'

She hesitates. Bikes have always seemed reckless, dangerous, but the chance to not limp to a bus stop and fight for a seat is tempting. She looks down at her red dress. Nobody would see her on a bike. Not with her head covered and her body like that of someone else.

'Go on,' he says, clenching the handlebars and smiling. 'Live a little.'

Perhaps it's the dress or the hair or the rarity of a man showing her attention on a warm summer's night, but two strange words run through her head: why not?

The breeze shoots up her legs and over her body as they glide through the streets. Isobel can tell he is taking it slow, but her arms fix tightly around his waist, and she clenches her thighs against the seat. When they pass a mirrored building, Isobel turns to their reflec-tion. A blur of black, chrome and red. Her skirt billows behind her. She could let go of his torso with one hand to pull her dress over her bare legs, but she doesn't. She leaves her legs on show. A heady mix of thrill and desire shoots through her body as she wishes every-one she knew could see her now. Isobel Forge on a bike.

When they pull up in front of her building, he climbs off and helps her dismount. Pain shoots through her toes as she steps on to the pavement. 'My first and last time on a motorbike,' she says with an embarrassed laugh, as she smooths her hair and worries about its appearance. She rushes on when she sees his face. 'But thank you for the lift.'

'Nice place.'

'Oh, it's just the top floor. The two other tenants usually smoke on the front stoop, and I wish they wouldn't, but it's a rental, so you're going to get that sort, aren't you?' She wants to sew her mouth shut.

'Beautiful architecture, though,' he says, pointing to the roof. 'Those circular dormers. You don't see those much. Stunning.'

She looks up. 'Right.'

'Sorry,' he says. 'I bore people to tears with the details. But you miss so much if you don't look up.' And they glance back up together.

'I'd better be going,' says Isobel, touching her hair. 'Sorry about this.'

'Perhaps another night.'

Isobel draws a sharp breath at the thought of dressing up again. 'Why don't you just come upstairs now?'

'Really?'

This had sounded better in her head. 'A cup of tea? There's not a lot of food, maybe cheese on toast . . . That's not much of an offer, I know, so it's fine if –'

'No, I'd love that,' he says, with a big smile.

On the walk up, Isobel is gripped by panic. What is she doing? She doesn't know this man. He could be anyone, do anything. The knowledge that his personal details are just a few taps away on a keyboard does little to calm her nerves – what if he kills her? – but, deep down, she knows she has nothing to fear.

In the flat the skylights have soaked up summer, and the rooms are damp with heat. Isobel goes straight to the mirror to check her hair.

'What an unusual space,' says Victor.

'The light, right?'

'Isn't it something?'

'Mmm.'

He looks around. 'Still got unpacking to do?'

Isobel turns. 'No. Why?'

'Oh, it's just . . .' He gestures at the walls. 'You don't have any pictures, that's all. No photos.'

Isobel glances at the blank spaces. 'Yes, well. I'm not sure what photographs I would put up.'

'You can't move in my flat for the damn things. They're everywhere. Mollie, my daughter, sends me pictures of my grandson which I stick on the fridge. I have so many that I keep running out of magnets.'

'That's nice.'

'My son Sam's the same. Sends old selfies of us fishing or at a bike meet. He lives up north and I don't see him much, so the pictures help. And it's funny being reminded of how you've changed over time, isn't it?'

Isobel stares at her reflection.

'That's what you should put up,' says Victor, snapping his fingers. 'Pictures of yourself over the years. Doing things.'

'I don't really have any pictures of myself.'

'In storage, are they?'

'No.'

'Ah, I get it. Camera-shy.'

Isobel looks at her new hair that he hasn't even mentioned. 'I was always the one holding the camera,' she says. 'Nobody ever offered to take my picture. And I never thought to ask.'

The room is quiet.

'I suppose I could put up photos of my son and daughter. Patrick and Cassandra. I don't see them much either. But they don't live up north.'

He looks at her for a long moment, then clears his throat and walks with purpose into the kitchen. 'I'll sort that cuppa.'

The landline starts to ring, and Isobel looks at the screen to see who could possibly be calling. Patrick. Her heart quickens. If she ignores the call, he'll try her mobile, and, if she doesn't answer that . . . Well, she always answers. What might he do if she doesn't?

'Hello?'

'Mum,' says Patrick, and his voice is tight. 'How are you?'

Isobel coughs as Victor bangs a cupboard door. 'Fine. Just making a tea.'

'Mum, I have news. Are you sitting down?'

'News?' She turns away from the kitchen to shield the phone.

'Are you sure you're okay? Your voice sounds strange.'

'I'm fine,' she hisses. 'What is it?'

He takes a deep breath. 'Dad just rang.'

'What?'

'I hung up. Refused to speak to him. So he texted.'

She doesn't reply.

'She's pregnant. *Amber*. Due the same time as Jude.'

Isobel drops the phone.

'Mum? Mum?' Patrick's voice is small and distant from the floor.

Isobel sinks to her knees. 'I'm here.'

Patrick says he knows he's not meant to talk to him, but he had to tell his dad he's a piece of work. That he'll be a dad again the same time he becomes a grandad. That this is meant to be a happy time. That his girlfriend is a decade younger than his son. Every sentence from Patrick's mouth is about how catastrophic this is for Patrick.

'I've got to go,' says Isobel, and places the handset back on the cradle as he talks. The sisal rug burns her knees.

'You okay, love?' says a soft voice over her shoulder. Victor. She'd forgotten he was there. He leans down, his face creased with concern, and offers a hand. She stares at it, unsure if it's real or an apparition, then places her hand in his and climbs to her feet. Her sore, tired feet, which are still in those ridiculous shoes. She kicks them off and looks at the walls of her flat, which now no longer seem so temporary.

'I took the liberty of having a look at what food's on offer,' says Victor. 'I could rustle up a posh beans on toast?'

He hands her a tea, and she stares at the dullness of the brown, trying to read her future.

A wave of nausea floods through Isobel and the cup slips in her hand. She reaches out to grab the side table as the tea drips on to the floorboards.

'Careful,' says Victor, leaping across to take the cup from her hand. He pulls out a chair from the kitchen table and guides her into it. 'There, sit yourself down. Maybe tea was a bad idea in this heat.' He looks around. 'Fresh air is what you need.'

'There's no garden. That's why I can afford the rent.'

'Well, what's this?' He leans across the kitchen worktop, and the window opens inwards like a door. He points to the flat roof outside, the ceiling for the tenant below. It's a small space, about six foot square, with a slight slope that overlooks other people's gardens. 'Bingo,' says Victor.

Isobel looks at him as if he's insane.

'There's your fresh air.'

'I'm not crawling across a kitchen worktop to sit on someone's roof.'

'Doesn't this whole building belong to someone else? So what difference is a roof? Okay, it's a somewhat awkward entrance, but beggars can't be choosers. Here, I'll help you.'

He pushes a chair against the counter and clears the side. A hand is extended Isobel's way, and she stares at it and thinks of her husband.

'That's quite a handshake,' says Victor, wincing.

She climbs through and looks out at the pink sky. The black roof is warm under her feet, its pores having soaked up the sun. There is still some to be had, and she stands so the rays fall on her face. A breeze stirs through her, just as it did on the bike.

'Here,' says Victor, passing over some cushions from the loveseat. 'Tuck these behind yourself. Get comfy and grub will be served up pronto.'

Isobel settles down, leaning carefully against the tall skylight windows that look into the lounge. She attempts to settle her mind, unsure of how to process the strange reality of a man finding his way around her kitchen.

'Shall we crack this open?' Victor waves a bottle of red through the window that Toni brought on her last visit, along with the sisal rug and mirrors. Isobel nods and listens as the wine glugs into glasses.

When the food is ready, Victor passes two plates through the window along with their drinks. Isobel stares at the pattern etched into the crystal. A wedding present. The best for special occasions. Isobel has kept them all this time, and now she considers dropping both from the roof and listening to them smash on the ground. No. Too romantic. Instead, she will sit back and watch another man drink from Steven's glass.

They tuck in. The end of yesterday's sourdough is loaded with butter beans and red onion, all mixed in a rich tomato sauce and doused with grated cheese. It is delicious, and clearly the work of someone who knows how to cook.

'Spicy,' says Isobel, and sips her wine.

'I did go a tad overboard with the smoked paprika.'

'Is the kitchen a mess?'

'I tidied as I went, so everything's soaking in the sink. Here, this wine's delicious.' He picks up the bottle to inspect the label. 'Expensive?'

'Probably,' says Isobel, picking up her glass. 'I wouldn't know. I don't usually drink.'

'Take it slow, then,' he says, gesturing with his fork as she drinks half the glass in one hit.

'What does it matter now?' she says under her breath, as she notices the sky turning plum. 'Shame we can't see the actual sunset.'

Victor puts down his plate and leans his arms on his knees. He smiles at the sky. 'Ah, but you get a sense of it. That's what matters.'

She drains the glass, waving it in Victor's direction until he picks up the bottle and pours some more.

'Go easy there, lass,' he says.

'I'll decide, thank you.' She pulls her dress over her legs and touches her bare ankles.

'I just don't want you falling off and taking me with you.' He peers over the edge. 'Looks like quite a drop.'

'Well, I wouldn't want to put you out.'

Victor gives a grim smile. 'I think we're getting our wires crossed. I didn't mean anything by it.'

'Like you don't mean to insult me by not saying anything nice about my hair? Or my dress? Both of which were bought specially.' She stifles a belch and blushes at her self-pity. Perhaps she could roll off the roof. Splat.

He stares at the glass in his hand. 'I'm sorry,' he says after a while. 'I was taught it wasn't polite to comment on what someone looks like.' He looks up at her. 'But would you like me to be honest?'

She bites her lip. Can she take honesty right now? She nods, regardless.

'Your hair looks very nice. Then again, it looked just fine before. And your clothes . . . well, same. But I don't think *you* like your new clothes. Am I right?'

Isobel looks down at her dress and her feet, which still bear the imprint of the tight straps. 'I hate them.'

'So why do you care if *I* like them?'

She shrugs. 'Isn't that what I'm meant to care about? Everyone tells me I'm out of date. Old model. Past it.'

'But why care so much about what other people think? Why does the appearance of things matter so much?'

Isobel opens her mouth to reply, but she has no answer to this question, because not once in fifty-five years has she ever asked it. Of course appearances matter. Perhaps it would be better if they didn't, but that doesn't change the fact that they do.

'Look at me,' says Victor, tugging at his hair and shirt. 'I'm a walking advert for not giving a damn. And you know what? I'm happy as a bird.'

Isobel takes him in. His horrendous shirt, purple with psychedelic flowers, with a pointed collar and cuffs that are forty years out of date. His hair is thankfully tied back but sits past his shoulders. His beard is clipped but covers the bottom half of his face. He is absolutely not Isobel's type. And, yet, hadn't she said yes? She'd spent a chunk of salary on an outfit for him to admire. She rode his motorbike. She held on to his waist. There must be something about Victor Godden that transcends type.

A meow sounds from above, and a black cat appears on the roof. It jumps down next to them, choosing Victor to rub against as Isobel edges away. She notes the absence of its collar. 'Careful, might be a stray.'

'Then it needs extra love, don't you, mate?' He rubs the cat between the ears, and it throbs with gratitude. 'Now there's an animal that doesn't care what others think.'

Isobel checks from a safe distance for fleas.

The cat collapses by them, rolling around and enjoying the heat.

'Cat on a hot tin roof,' Victor jokes, to which Isobel replies, 'But it's bitumen.'

He laughs and gives a deep sigh. 'You're hard work, aren't you.'

Isobel drinks more wine and notices the air feeling softer. She has an urge to give him something. 'Here,' she says, tugging down her dress slightly to reveal a two-inch scar on her chest.

Victor sucks in air through his teeth. 'How did you get that?'

'A car accident when I was eighteen. Happened in the middle of the night when I swerved to avoid a cat. My car rolled over. I remember sitting there, alone, thinking I was going to die.'

'Bloody hell.'

'Luckily another car was passing.'

'Were you badly hurt?'

'My parents were told I wouldn't make it through the night. A shard of glass hit me' – she touches the scar – 'and missed my heart by a whisker. I lived, but this was left behind.'

'A reminder of how things could have been worse.'

She looks at the sky. 'I often wake up in the middle of the night. I can never fall back asleep, so I get up and clean. Hoover, scrub the kitchen. Then when the sun starts rising or lights come on, I know it's safe to go to sleep. I know I've made it through the night.'

He watches her closely.

'Steven hated me getting up, said I always disturbed him. As if my mind and body were within my control.'

'That's your ex-husband, is it?'

She gulps the air. Ex-husband. It's the first time she's heard it. A nod is all she can give.

They finish the bottle. Their talk is so easy and steady that they don't notice when the sun sets the sky on fire. Isobel tells him of her faith and her children and her life up to now. Victor lets her talk. At one point he goes in to the bathroom, and on the way back does the washing-up. She listens to the tune of plates clattering on the draining board and wishes they had more wine.

When she starts to get cold, she climbs in through the window, and he takes her hand. But her feet slip on the clean counter and she tumbles down on to the floor, flailing against his arms as he tries to catch her. The wine has done its work. She is almost hysterical with embarrassment, and they dissolve in a pile on the floor, each going to speak before laughing.

As Victor starts to say that he really should go, Isobel feels a deep ache and leans across to plant a clumsy kiss on his mouth. She doesn't know what it means. Perhaps gratitude for the nicest evening she's had in years, or for the washing-up, or maybe something else. For once, she doesn't stop to analyse the sensation. He kisses her back. It's the first time in far too long that she's been kissed back.

When they break apart, she looks away and smiles. He lifts her up, but her feet don't work as they should, and then she is falling, falling, falling and everything goes black.

She wakes the next morning on her bed, fully dressed, with her brain the texture of soup. Sun streams through the skylights and she thinks to herself: Enough. She doesn't care what people say. Tomorrow she's buying blinds. It's the first time in her life that she is consciously choosing to do what other people think she shouldn't.

There are sounds coming from the kitchen – the light clattering of utensils – as if someone is trying not to be heard. Isobel pulls her dress over her legs and peers out from the bed. Did she leave the window open last night? Has someone climbed in?

But burglars don't whistle. And they don't fry bacon. She sniffs the air and crawls to the end of the mattress. Through the glass windows, she sees Victor moving around her kitchen. His movements are slow and deliberate, his face upbeat. Isobel smooths her hair and grabs a cardigan. She feels her way down the mezzanine stairs. A movement distracts her through the living-room windows, and she sees the black cat sprawled out on the flat roof.

Victor holds a pan aloft as she comes through the door. 'Greetings!'

She pulls the cardigan tight. 'What's going on?'

'I took a punt on you waking soon, so I've started the bacon, and, now you're up, I'll crack on with the eggs.'

A glance at the clock says it's a quarter past nine. On a Sunday. A hand flies to her neck. She'll never make the meeting now. Not looking like this and with him still around. 'Did you stay over?'

'Down here on the floor,' he says, pointing at the lounge. 'I thought about going once you were safely in bed, but it didn't feel right leaving you in that state. You were out cold. I thought you might vomit.'

She tries to remember the previous night. The roof, the wine – oh, the wine – the cat, the kiss . . . The kiss. It repeats like a siren.

'We didn't . . . Please say we didn't . . .' Isobel hugs her body.

He turns away to the hob. 'Of course not.'

'I'm sorry, I just . . .' She catches sight of herself in the window and recoils. Without another word, she goes to the bathroom and locks the door.

She showers quickly, anxious not to compound her rudeness by spoiling the breakfast. She towel-dries her hair, then fastens her robe so her entire body is covered. Her fingers wipe the foggy mirror to reveal her tired face. Her reflection doesn't tame her thoughts, which are racing and cloudy. I'm sorry, Victor, she wants to say. I shouldn't presume that your first inclination is bad. But you're a worldly man and worldly men only think one way. They cannot help themselves.

On the other side of the door, she hears him laying the table.

So unlike Steven, she thinks. Good-looking, successful Steven, the belle of the social ball. Steven, who threw parties and gave talks and was labelled *a good one*. Steven, who never set foot in the kitchen except to ask when dinner was ready. Steven, who ran off to the South of France with his eighteen-year-old employee who now carries his child. Steven, who had been an elder. Not a worldly man. A *good* one.

Cheap, Laminate Floor

Jen

It is late summer when Jen moves out. She sees a falling leaf outside by chance as she folds her clothes and packs her few possessions. A lonely stab of gold. It's too early, she thinks, then remembers it is almost September. Now there will be no stopping the fall.

Two weeks have passed since their confessions in the workroom. The air between them has been calm. Zelda has taken care with her words, and Jen has made feasts that take hours. They have allowed the other to be.

But it comes as no surprise when Jen tells Zelda she is renting a flat. Zelda continues to eat the lamb that Jen spent hours slow-cooking, and the only hint of emotion is the way she stabs the meat with her fork. 'That's great,' she says, without a smile, and they continue with their food.

I love you, Zelda, Jen says inside. I have loved you since Alice, and not just in the way that friends do. This is why I must leave. I know now I can never bring you back, but I must try to save myself.

She says this by reaching across and dabbing her napkin at a spot of sauce on Zelda's chin. Their eyes meet for a second, before Jen pushes back her chair.

'I'll see you at class, at least,' Zelda says.

Jen wipes her hands on her apron. 'I told Mara I'm not going back.'

Zelda looks at her with a blank expression.

'There's no point. Hopefully I'll get more hours at the shop so I won't have time for much else.' She hasn't told Zelda of the new credit card or the cost of her rent. The numbers give her a headache.

'No, *I'll* quit. Not you. I was only doing it for you anyway.'

'It's not about you.'

Zelda pushes away her plate. 'Then what?'

Jen cannot look at her.

Zelda jumps up. She stands there for a moment, her palms resting on the table, her fingers feeling the knots in the wood. She searches Jen's face for doubt.

'Are you really allowed nothing of your own?'

Jen fills her car. She moves back and forth between the driveway and house, her eyes fixed on the path. Zelda is in the garden, dead-heading roses. There is no offer to help, no acknowledgement that this is a day different from any other.

Inside, Jen takes a final look at where she has spent her summer, where a childhood friendship came back to life. The air is heavy with talk, the absence of many years made up for by an intense three months together, and in this room live days she will not forget.

She notices a white vase she made in her first class, sitting on a cabinet by the door. Jen's fingers stroke its curves as she remembers Zelda's deep intake of breath when it came out of the kiln. She lays her keys down beside it. A piece of her will stay.

The sun is low in the blue sky, and the morning is hazy with long shadows. Jen brushes a bee from her jumper. It is drunk, probably from the apples that have fallen nearby and now lie bruised on the ground. She inhales the citrus air. The place where she is going has none of this beauty. She will fill her boots with its scent, steal its tonic for the darker days.

'So goodbye,' she says, putting her hand over her eyes so she can see Zelda.

Zelda clips a faded pink rose and drops it in the trug looped through her arm. She wears a loose white dress, and there is something ethereal about her standing barefoot in this Garden of Eden that is all her own. 'Bye.'

'Can we at least part without thunder this time?'

'You want me to be happy to see you go?'

'Not happy.'

'You're making a huge mistake.'

'Let me make it, all the same?'

Jen takes a snapshot in her mind of this exact moment: Zelda walking towards her in sunshine, surrounded by roses and colour and life, the tin walls of her home rising up behind. She feels a sudden lurching sickness, the fear of a step that can't be retraced, but then she presses her hand against her stomach and pushes away the pain.

'It's a control thing,' says Zelda. 'The houseplants. I deliberately neglect them, just to see how much they need me. It reminds me I'm in control. It's a comfort.'

'You're quite mad, you know.' Jen's voice is soft.

Zelda stares at the ground. 'They never actually die. I just let them get to breaking point.'

Jen takes a final look at Paradise. The elders would say that somewhere in these bushes lives a snake. She has a sudden urge to tear a limb from her body and plant it in the ground; leave it here to grow with Zelda, to be watered by her, staked, tended, loved. I want life and death, she thinks. I want polar opposites. I want, I want, I want.

'I'm not strong like you,' she says.

Zelda reaches out to hold Jen's cheek and leans in to kiss the other. It is the soft kiss of friendship, of the past and future. 'Goodbye,' she whispers.

Jen puts her arms around her friend and pulls her in.

This is not the end, she tells herself, rewriting her present. But the start of something else.

The flat is a studio in the heart of town. It's in a tall nineties block, with a front door that jams, a broken lift and a stairwell that reeks of urinated beer. Jen has arranged a futon to be delivered on moving day, but the driver looks up at the building and shakes his head. 'Kerbside only,' he says and leaves it in the lobby. Jen knocks on the door of a ground-floor flat and introduces herself, then asks if they'd mind helping her lift the box up four flights of stairs. 'Sorry, sweetheart, dodgy shoulder,' comes the reply, and the door shuts in her face. She rests her head against the wall and sighs, then spends the next hour easing it upstairs by herself.

In the flat, Jen unpacks the futon and pushes it against the wall. She drops down and yelps at the hard mattress. From this vantage point, she can survey her entire kingdom of a draughty front door, a line of kitchen cupboards, a floor-to-ceiling window – view of the bins – and the door to a dated bathroom, where the tiles are chipped and the tap is dripping. All for an entire month's pay.

She bought a cheap drill for hanging pictures, but the walls are the hollow kind that need special fixings, and so the framed prints lean along the cheap, laminate floor.

The pulsating throb of dance music thumps through the wall.

Tomorrow I'll buy some houseplants, Jen decides. And then I'll watch them die.

Unbelievers

Isobel

It is after the Sunday meeting that the elders call Isobel into the back room. She doesn't even have time to chat with Patrick. Her face burns as the brothers and sisters try not to notice her being led away. The whispers. It is rare that *Can we have a word* means anything other than trouble.

The door shuts as she sits down and waits for the men to start.

'Isobel, how are things?' says Brother Connell, his voice grave.

'Fine.'

'I know many sisters miss working with you in the ministry during the week.'

'Well, hopefully one day I can minister full time again.' She frowns, wondering if they are under the misapprehension that stopping was her choice. 'You realize *why* I can't right now? I told you before –'

Brother Connell raises a hand. 'It's okay, Isobel. We're well aware of the mess you're in.'

She purses her lips. Over twenty years of voluntarily spending almost a thousand annual hours in the ministry, and she doesn't even get so much as a *thank you* or *well done*. Of course, everyone does their best, and so she is no more deserving than those who manage only an hour or two each week, but still . . .

Still.

'We wondered if there was anything you wanted to tell us?'

Isobel's throat tightens. 'Is there?'

Their stares are silent.

She takes a deep breath as her mind races through a hundred different thoughts. 'I'm not sure . . .'

'Bill says he saw you in town at the weekend.'

Her heart falls into her stomach.

'Saturday night?' says Bill Norris. 'Outside Henri's near the back of the town.'

'Oh. Saturday? Quite possibly.'

'You were dressed very differently, I hear,' says Brother Connell looking down at her meeting clothes, which today are blue and grey.

'The man you were with,' says Bill, avoiding her eye. 'Clearly not a brother. The hair, the beard . . . Just a friend?'

Isobel gives a forceful nod. Yes, that's it. Because really that's all Victor is, isn't he? 'Mr Godden is a patient at the surgery. He's been very kind and offered to accompany me for the evening. In a public place, you understand.'

'Yes, except you didn't dine at the restaurant, did you?' says Brother Connell. 'I understand you left when Bill and Toni arrived. That's right, Bill?'

'Yes, Les,' he says, his face red. 'Toni noticed you as we pulled up, and then we saw you walk off.'

'Almost as if you knew the situation was quite, shall we say, inappropriate,' says Brother Connell, turning back. 'What would you say, Isobel?'

She bristles. Leslie Connell rarely saw eye to eye with Steven, and, as they were one flesh, she knew the same critical feelings had extended to her. 'I know how things can appear, but, as I explained, he is a patient and we spent a few hours together. That is all.' She picks her words with care.

Brother Connell's mouth curves downwards. 'You were seen riding away on his motorbike.'

Her mouth is dry. 'Possibly.'

'Presumably to somewhere private where you wouldn't be seen and therefore unchaperoned?'

Six months ago she would have nodded along, but now Isobel seethes with embarrassed rage. How dare they interrogate her like a teenage girl, as if she is unable to make her own decisions? Hasn't she taken care of herself for months? She smooths her lap, her hands trembling. 'Anything else?'

Brother Connell adjusts his glasses. 'Remember, Isobel, that before any divorce, which – as the wronged mate – you are within your rights to seek, you are still married in the eyes of the world *and* God. Any romantic considerations must wait until you are in a position to remarry, and of course the Bible condemns marrying an unbeliever.'

'We say this out of warm Christian love, Isobel,' says Brother Norris. Bill – passive, simple, ineffectual Bill, whom Isobel and Steven holidayed with and assisted financially when he lost his business a decade ago. The very same Bill now delivering her up.

'Thank you for your concern,' says Isobel, her voice cold. She stands with her arms folded and walks out.

Isobel changes out of her meeting clothes and ties on her apron. She places a large mixing bowl on the kitchen table along with utensils and baking ingredients. The recipe isn't required. She knows this one by heart.

Two hours later, Isobel puts the finished cake in the centre of the table. It sits on a milk-glass cake-stand, the one she chose as Steven's gift to her on their thirtieth wedding anniversary. Pick your own present, he always said. She cuts a slice from the perfect circle and lays it on a side plate. With a fork, she eats every last crumb.

Her eyes look down at the cake. Nobody will know if she eats the rest, because there are no elders' eyes here. She is quite alone.

A meow sounds through the open window, the cat with its mournful eyes. She reaches out, and he nuzzles against her fingers. 'Hello, you,' she whispers, then picks up the mixing bowl and puts it outside the window. The cat turns its attention to the streaked batter with long, hungry licks. 'It's a treat. Don't make yourself sick.'

She remembers how once, in another life, she made cakes for the workdays at the hall. The sisters took care of the teas and coffees, and there would be the low rumbling of tins when time came for the brothers to make their choice. Her mood for the rest of the day depended on the weight of the tin she took home and how many brothers had favoured hers. She once ate seven rejected slices to convince herself she was of some use.

Isobel stares at the cake. She is no longer hungry. The yearning in the pit of her stomach has gone.

'Dear Steven,' she says aloud, her foot on the pedal to open the bin. 'You loved my red velvet cake. Said it was the best you'd ever tasted. That the frosting was like heaven.'

The cake-stand smashes at the bottom of the bin, and Isobel takes her foot away to watch the lid slowly fall.

'Dear Steven,' she says again. 'Fuck. You.'

Orchestra
Isobel

Isobel parks up and looks through the car window at the little terraced house. Neat, red Victorian bricks, with black-painted sash windows and white roses climbing the wall. Victor's bike is parked in the front garden behind three balloons waving from the gate. It is a child's painting of home.

She checks herself in the mirror and considers driving off.

Since her conversation with the elders, she and Victor have met up several times for low-key lunches in the park behind the surgery. Their casual meet-ups end with a kiss, and Isobel has almost counted down the minutes between the end of the last and the start of the next. How strange to be kissed. How many years it has been since someone deliberately reached out and touched her.

The front door opens and there is Victor with a smile, his arms wide. 'There you are,' he says as a dog pushes past. 'I was just about to call.'

Isobel pulls her skirt in tight around her legs to avoid the Labrador or retriever — she can never tell them apart — who sniffs her before presenting its wet, unwelcome tongue.

'Dave, oy, away,' says Victor, giving the dog a gentle push and reaching in to kiss her cheek.

'Dave?' says Isobel. 'For a dog?'

'Dad!' comes a voice. 'We're ready!'

'Am I late, then?' she asks, following him in. 'I thought you said two-*ish*.'

'It's okay, don't worry. Mollie just wants to do the candles now as Joey's getting impatient. You know how kids are.'

Isobel spins round. 'Is this a birthday party?'

'Didn't I tell you? Oh, don't worry about a present. My fault. I'll scribble your name on my card.' He shuts the door and is about to walk through to the kitchen when she grabs his arm.

'Victor, I-I can't go to a birthday party.'

He looks at her, confused. 'Why?'

Does she really have to explain? He had called it a party. Surely if you invite someone to a birthday party, you explicitly say *birthday party*. Because it's not just a party. It's a *birthday* party. She closes her eyes and puts a hand to her forehead. Why are men so bad at the details? Because if the devil is in the details, this is a cartoon version of hell.

'I don't celebrate b—'

'You must be Isobel!'

She turns to the warm sound of her name and sees a young woman coming towards her. She looks in her early thirties, the same age as Cassandra, blonde hair with her father's smile.

'Mollie,' she says, reaching in to kiss Isobel's cheek. 'It's so nice to finally meet you. Please come through . . . It's a bit chaotic . . . Overexcited kids on excess sugar . . . Can I get you a drink? . . . Dad, grab Isobel a plate.'

She has been led by the hand into a small kitchen that opens on to a long garden. Fifteen or so adults mill about outside, surrounded by balloons, banners and a throng of sweaty kids. Brightly coloured presents lie beneath a crêpe-papered table, which is decorated with metallic ribbons that catch the sun. A large banner hangs above the patio doors – HAPPY BIRTHDAY, JOEY! Isobel's heart is an orchestra.

'I'm just prepping the cake,' says Mollie. 'But it won't be anywhere near as good as the carrot one you made Dad.'

'Oh, it's an old family recipe.'

'Isobel makes me a cake every week.' Victor pours their drinks and pats his stomach. 'I'm going to need a bigger boat!'

Mollie laughs and nudges Isobel, who looks around for a place to hide.

Armed with drinks and food, Victor leads her out into the garden and introduces her to everyone in turn. Their names do not compute. She blushes at their hellos and covers her mouth with sips of sugary drink.

'Best get the video ready,' says Victor. He takes out his phone and clicks on the camera.

Isobel doesn't know what he means. And then she does. And it's too late for her to do anything but turn scarlet and shrink back against the fence.

'It's Sam,' calls Mollie, waving her phone as a face talks on the screen. She passes it to a friend, who holds up Sam from hundreds of miles away.

'Happy birthday to you . . .' The chorus begins, and Mollie appears through the doors holding a homemade cake with sugar-paste characters and five candles awaiting a wish. Victor leans forward, smiling as he films an excited boy jump up and down as his mum walks towards him.

Isobel watches Joey blow out his candles. Everyone claps. Victor cheers and high-fives his grandson. They all look so pleased, and yet they do not realize that what they have just done is manifestly evil. God hates birthdays, Isobel told Patrick and Cassandra throughout their childhoods. The only time birthdays are mentioned in the Bible is when something dreadful happens. Do you want to displease your heavenly Father? So turn off that television show. Rip out that page in the colouring book. 'But what about dogs?' Cassandra asked when she was twelve. 'Whenever they're mentioned in the Bible, it's always horrible. Does that mean people shouldn't have dogs?'

She looks about at happy faces. Joey throws his arms around his grandad and Victor squeezes him tightly as someone takes their picture.

Evil, she thinks. Evil? Then smiles as Joey claps his hands.

Later, when the guests have gone, Mollie comes out and sits next to Isobel. Victor's whistling can be heard through the patio doors as he washes up. Joey has spent half an hour playing with the Scalextric set that Victor – and Isobel – bought him. He squeals with delight each time a car takes a corner.

'Thanks for that,' says Mollie, settling back into the chair. 'He's wanted it for months.'

'Oh, that's okay,' mumbles Isobel, brushing invisible crumbs from her skirt. She has been watching Joey and thinking of her own grandchild, soon to be born. It's a fortnight since she heard from Patrick, and months since his sister has been in touch.

Plates clatter in the kitchen, and they wince as they wait for a smash. Then a shout from Victor. 'It's okay! Slippery hands. All fine.'

Mollie laughs. 'Thank God for Dad. I plan and he tidies. Teamwork.'

'Right.' Isobel turns to look at Victor through the window. She had offered to help, but he waved her out with a glass of wine, along with a refusal of any cash for the present. Your money's no good here, he said. She sits back in the chair and feels Mollie's eyes.

'I haven't seen him this happy in years.'

Isobel's back goes rigid. She forces a smile.

'Thank you,' says Mollie, quietly.

Isobel drains her glass.

'Would you like another?'

'Oh, no,' she says, getting up. 'Actually I should probably head off now. Miss the traffic.'

'On a Saturday? You're welcome to stay for longer.'

Victor comes through the doors, wiping his hands on a towel. 'Done!'

'Dad, persuade Isobel to stay for the evening.'

'That's very kind, but I really must get back.' She roots through her bag for her keys.

Victor watches her for a moment, then says to Mollie, 'I'll head off too, love. It's getting late and I'm sure Joey will want his bed soon after all the excitement. Won't you, son?' He ruffles the boy's hair.

'Dad, you can't ride home. You've had far too much wine.'

'Nah, I'm all right. Three glasses, tops. And not for a good two hours.'

'Nope,' says Mollie. 'Not happening.'

Victor gives a good-natured huff. 'Isobel, mind dropping me? I'll get the bus over in the morning to collect the bike.'

When they drive away, Victor turns to wave until Mollie and Joey fade from view, still flinging their arms from side to side. He laughs as he turns to the front.

'They couldn't bear to see you leave,' says Isobel, half to herself, and pulls her sunglasses down over her eyes.

Teeth Marks
Zelda

Zelda takes up with Matt as if they've never been apart.

They usually meet at her house, and, now that Jen has moved out, there is no risk of being disturbed. He often comes straight from work, in his suit and tie, and Zelda takes pleasure in pushing him to the floor as he enters, causing creases that must be ironed out before he leaves. Afterwards, he walks around naked while she sets up the board and moves a hot iron over his clothes, erasing all sign of her passion. They have an hour of hot sex and thirty minutes of domesticity, and then he goes back to his life.

They have car sex too. He drives out to country lanes or parks up in the emergency-access gate to the motorway, and they fuck as the lorries charge past.

Zelda has never told him the reason she always says no to the backseat. Those memories rarely appear in her head when she is with Matt. Her mind is cloudy with glorious distraction, leaving no room for sadness.

Her clothes have also changed. Ever since he leant in on a dance floor to declare how good she looks in a dress, she has yoked Matt with a feminized form of herself. She has put away her loose trousers and blazers, exchanged her suits and ties for floaty, easy-access slips. This costume change has altered her demeanour. No longer does she stride or walk with purpose, her brogues pounding the floor. Now she drifts and glides and makes no sound.

Zelda cannot cook, but, when she dares to imagine their future, there are table spreads of roast dinners with gravy, rich with know-how, and potatoes roasted in goose fat (because *of course* that's the only way they should be done). She stands by in an apron as Matt and the kids tuck in, which is strange, as she has never wanted children. The scenes are safe, though. They do not scare her. They take the form of childhood fantasies, from reruns of *The Waltons* or *Little House on the Prairie*, shows her housewife mother had deemed acceptable.

I'd even take your name, she thinks. I'd forgo Bloom for Fish if it would make you happy. I'd do anything to make you happy.

This is what love does, she thinks. It transforms you. It's a plaster over the pain.

Matt tells her that Mel has affairs of her own. They have an open marriage, he says, but this doesn't make Zelda feel better. Would you do that if we were together, she wonders. And does that mean you'll never give her up? Instead of asking questions, she leaves little teeth marks on his body. Her branding, like the fleurs-de-lis he once scored into her.

Sometimes, when alone, Zelda tries to define her feelings. It leaves her breathless. If she tried to explain, she would say the experience of making love to him is like swimming upwards through water, that gulp of air as you break through the surface. The experience is overwhelming. It is drowning and survival. Hard to explain, simple in feeling.

There are no games. She is always available. Life is too short to play it cool.

One afternoon, she tries to tear herself from his arms in bed. I have a shoot, she says, as he nuzzles her neck. I have to go. His hands crawl over her. Stay, he whispers. Tell them you're ill. I want you for myself. She laughs, considering it. But her work has been neglected these past months – clients having to chase, checking her phone too often at weddings, not marketing enough for the following year. She is not eighteen any more, and there are bills to pay. She has tried to tell him this, how next year has too few jobs to pay expenses, but he never hears her. He is calling her over or putting her hand on his body, taking her mind off worries in other ways.

Even on weekends, when he is with Mel, her minutes are haunted by his absence. She tries to reconnect with her creative spark, setting up her large-format camera in the garden to capture it bursting with life, but the pictures are barren and flat. The sight of sewing exhausts her. She doesn't understand. She should be alive, with Matt as her muse.

One afternoon in August he picks her up, and they drive to the park in a town thirty minutes away where he doesn't know anyone. Zelda is prepared. She has a bag of stale bread for them to throw to the ducks, and wears her sexiest underwear. Feed the ducks or fuck like rabbits. She has all bases covered.

The one she doesn't consider is the one that happens. Sitting cross-legged on tarmac watching Matt shoot hoops. Over and over again.

I'm thirty-fucking-four, she thinks.

He scores.

'Nice one!'

Zelda leans in to kiss him as they walk to the car and he pushes her away. *Someone might see.* A sharp pain burns in her chest, and they drive to hers in silence. She knows her mouth will speak sobs if it opens, so she looks at the road instead.

He follows her down the path. The sulky air is hot between them, and Zelda can't work out why he didn't drive off. When she unlocks the door, he comes in behind, and for the first time in her life she wishes he would leave.

'Well?' he says.

'*Well?*'

'Aren't you going to say anything?'

She stares at him, fire raging inside. All the hours she has put in, the effort of being what he needs her to be, and still she is expected to do the work. An urge to sleep overwhelms her.

'Shut the door on your way out.' She kicks off her shoes and climbs the spiral staircase to her room.

Her phone beeps with a message from Will. *Hey, stranger. You're probably living your 'very best life', but you appeared in my head tonight, so thought I'd see how you are?*

She smiles. *Good timing*, she types, hearing Matt on the stairs. *I'm about to commit a murder.*

The door handle turns as she's pulling her dress over her head. Despite her exhaustion, there's a lick of satisfaction at his following her up.

'I'm sorry, Z,' Matt says from behind, and she shivers as his arms slip around her waist. 'It's not what you think. I want to touch you in public. You have no idea how much.'

'Then why don't you?'

He sighs. 'Everyone acts a certain way in front of people. It isn't real. I hate performance, how people pretend to be something they're not. With you, I get to be a version of myself that the world won't accept. I want to guard you and keep you safe, because you're special, Zelda. You have no idea how fucking special you are.'

She leans back against his chest as his hands travel her body. 'Keep talking.'

'I like it being our secret.' His hand slips between her legs.

'Stop.' She pushes away and walks over to the bed, pulling off her underwear. She lies back naked and wills him forward.

'Let's not ruin this with other people,' Matt says, unbuckling his jeans. 'Keep it between us. We know what we have.' He sinks down on to the bed.

'Tell me how you feel about me.'

Hot kisses on her neck.

'You're the one I should have been with.'

Zelda lets out a moan as his soft cotton t-shirt drapes across her waist and the jeans he hasn't bothered to remove chafe her legs. She sees her phone on the floor light up with a message, and her skin takes on a delirious fever. 'You want me, don't you.' She says it like she already knows.

He sticks his tongue out as he slides a finger inside her. She licks her lips and arches her back. Window-light spills over the sheets.

'I have to put you down,' he says, rocking her gently.

'Like a dog?'

'Yes, like a dog,' and he flips her over on the bed.

Afterwards, while he is dressing, Matt asks if she'd like to go away for a long weekend.

She sits up. 'Really?'

'Why not?'

'I just thought . . .'

He fastens his belt. 'Mel's away for work next month. Why don't you and I take the chance to get away?'

She kneels on the bed and looks up at him. 'Where would we go?'

'There's somewhere I've always wanted to visit. I used to think about taking you.' He strokes her hair. 'It'll be a surprise.'

Zelda's stomach lurches. Could it be . . . No. Surely he doesn't mean there. 'For a weekend?'

'Yeah, it's a bit of a trek, but . . . we're only young once.'

'Will I need my passport?'

Matt laughs. 'Oh, Z. You're like a kid at Christmas. Stop trying to guess.'

'Well, I need to know what to pack.'

He leans down and gives her a long kiss. 'Yes, to the passport. Dress for heat. Swimsuit. Make it that sexy *Baywatch* one I've seen pictures of you wearing.'

Zelda returns his tongue with added intensity. It must be ninety degrees in California this time of year. She has a vision of them at a beachfront diner with sand between their toes, drinking freshly squeezed orange juice and kissing like they're never coming home.

You're not yourself when you're with him. Her old schoolfriend's words appear in her head.

No, she thinks. I'm better.

Her Heart, Her Heart

Isobel

Victor's flat defies categorization. Open plan, but the use of room dividers and plants creates zones that feel private. Tidy, but lived-in. Isobel swipes a finger along the top of a cabinet when he turns to close the door. There is no dust when she wants it.

She hadn't intended to come in. Her inclination was to go home and run a bath, see if Patrick calls, perhaps some mindless television. But, like always, Victor sensed her mood, and when he asked if she'd like to come in, she found herself nodding. Besides, there was a curiosity to see how this man lived. What he looks at each morning, and whether his habitat is clean and neat when visitors are unexpected.

There is a flutter of disappointment when she sees he is quite capable of looking after himself.

'Coffee?' he says, throwing his keys in a pot.

Something stirs her into action. 'I'll make it,' she says, dropping her bag and heading through to the kitchen, still in her jacket. Isobel looks inside the kettle and the sight of scale pleases her. She could do some good here.

They stand at a tall lounge window with their coffees and look out over the town. The evening sun renders everything the softest pink, and Isobel feels strangely moved by the ring-road traffic and the houses with their matchbox windows, the lives going on behind each one. There is order and industry in the form of deliberately made buildings and cars, and chaos in the hearts of those who use them. It will cause a headache if she thinks of it too long.

'You are loved, aren't you,' she says.

Victor gives a half-smile, not wanting to make a big deal over the fact that, yes, he knows this.

'They don't just tolerate you, your kids. They don't even *like* you. They love you.'

'Most kids love their parents,' he says. 'Different ways of showing it, that's all.'

Isobel remembers holding the soft pad of her son's hand as they walked along. How she placed her body between him and the road. And Cassandra. Hadn't Isobel made the effort each year for her daughter's school play, sitting with other parents on those low, hard benches? She loved those plays. She would tune out the discordant singing and watch Patrick, his face lit up, in the front row. Cassandra was always in the chorus, way off in the back, hard to find.

It has been weeks since she heard from one and months since the other.

Victor gives his cup a little shake. 'Kids are like instant coffee.'

She gives a blank look. 'Sorry?'

'You bring up a child the way you make coffee. You don't put the milk in last, because the pale will be swallowed up by the dark and it'll always look bitter. Put the light in first, and then, however much dark you add, the light simply absorbs it. Turns out a much more pleasing colour. Same with kids, see. Give them all the love in the world when they're babes, before they know themselves, before they know how the world can be. If you give them the light, they can handle the dark when it comes. They absorb it, like milk with coffee. They don't let it get the best of them. They don't let it take them over.'

Isobel looks down at her dark, bitter cup.

And then Victor is pulling her close. It is still foreign, the sensation of being held, hands reaching out with intention. She has felt anger when someone knocked her arm in the supermarket or brushed past through a doorway. A wasted touch. Who are these people, she would think, so used to physical contact that they throw it around without care.

I should go, she thinks as he holds her.

He draws back so they are facing. His fingers stroke her cheeks.

When his mouth meets hers, she is torn between unfolding herself like a flower and sharpening her thorns. But his lips are soft.

'Victor,' she says, breaking away. 'I can't. You know what I mean.'

He holds his mouth and nods slowly. 'Shall we have some wine?'

She stiffens. 'You think wine will make me give in?'

Victor steps further back. 'Hey, now, you really need to stop.'

'Stop sticking up for my principles?'

'Always thinking I'm out to get you.' His tone is gentle but firm. He is tiring of her. She knows it.

Isobel places her hands over her face and lets out a long, guttural moan. It surprises her as much as Victor, and she backs away into the corner. Now the sobs come. She puts a hand to her chest. Her heart, her heart. It pounds.

'Come,' says Victor, guiding her over to the sofa. He rushes to the kitchen and bangs a few cupboard doors before pressing a tumbler of whisky into her hands.

Isobel takes hungry sips, her hands shaking. She leans forward to put her head between her legs, and Victor soothes her back.

'Oh my,' she says to the floor.

'Enough,' says Victor, taking the empty glass. 'Your body's trying to talk.'

She sits up slowly and leans back against the sofa. He returns to the kitchen, and she listens to the noise of him moving around his flat.

'Stay here tonight,' he says, pausing to look at her. 'You can't drive now anyway. I'll sleep out here. Or I'll call a cab if you like.'

Isobel lies down, her mind easing into calm. She has never cried like that or drunk a whole glass of whisky. She has never sprawled out on a sofa. Everything is upside down.

What if everyone she knew could see her now?

But they can't, and they won't, and, here, she knows she is safe.

Victor is at the kitchen counter when she comes out the next morning, his gaze on the outside world. She has to shut the bedroom door hard to wake him from his trance, and he turns with a smile.

228

Isobel blushes at the knowledge that she slept in his bed. I was awake most of the night staring at the walls, she wants to say. I wondered which side was yours. I think it's the left, so I slept on the right, stretching out my hand to the space where you would be.

'It's hard,' she said. 'Your bed.'

He doesn't reply. His cup of coffee sits neatly in his palm, the other tucked in the front pocket of his turned-up jeans. Isobel imagines him making his coffee, putting the milk in first, and she thinks of all the words she could say.

'I have to go.'

He puts down his cup.

'I don't think I've told you this before about my religion. That I have to be married.'

Victor picks up the kettle and runs the water. 'I did wonder.' He flicks on the switch, and Isobel waits for the whirr. She finds the sound a comfort. Especially now, in this room, when she has said she must go and he is boiling the kettle as if she will stay.

'I should be honest, though,' Victor says. 'I'm not sure I want to get married again.'

The hot breath of the kettle bursts upwards into the room.

'Oh.'

'It didn't mean much to the first person I married, and then, well . . . It was slapping a contract on the thing that made the spark go out.'

'I see,' she says, looking down at her hands. Of course it would be this way.

'And I'm an atheist.' He gives an awkward laugh.

'Oh, Victor,' says Isobel, putting a hand to her forehead with a slight laugh. 'What are you doing to me?'

'You don't want to get me started on religion.'

There is something comical about the air in the room. Isobel – who has spent a life of Tuesdays at meetings learning how to stop a door from shutting – has no idea what to say. All she knows is this is a door she doesn't want to close.

'Well, I guess that's that,' says Isobel, straightening up and taking her keys. She hurries to the door, where she works her feet into her shoes, moving fast before her body shocks her again.

She opens the door.

Coming out of the opposite flat is a sister from her hall. Isobel mouths her name, and, with striking clarity, looks down and sees herself as the sister does. Dishevelled, tired, clearly having spent the night, Victor in the background. In this out-of-body experience, she now hangs on a gallery wall as a painted scene from the sister's point of view. Isobel looks across the corridor, but, instead of the sister, she sees the gallery visitors who point at her as they whisper. They hold grey Bibles. They are all men. The painting's name is *Jezebel*.

The sister holds a black refuse sack and stares open-mouthed at Isobel, who covers her mouth with her hands. No, she wants to scream, it is not how it looks. Fear floods through as realization takes hold: that, in the world she shares with this sister, how it looks is all that really counts.

Camera

Jen and Zelda

The month after Jen moved in

Jen stares at the antique camera. Old-fashioned, the kind with bellows and a hood, it stands beside a vase of faded sunflowers that droop despite the light flooding from the clerestory windows. She glances at Zelda, who has just come in from the garden and is arranging roses in a jug.

'My experiment, remember?' Zelda swears as she pricks her finger. 'They're not quite ready yet, but soon.'

'I didn't realize you photographed them.'

'Don't you think they're beautiful? Even when they're dead – or almost – they still teem with something.'

Jen frowns. 'Decay?'

'There's a death rattle, yes.' Zelda sucks the wound. 'But it serves a purpose. We forget about life, until it's gone. We need that contrast to see the beauty. And then, because it's too terrifying to accept that everything ends, we can't help but use our imagination. We can't help but wish it back to life.'

Jen squints, trying to see, but the smell of dank water is overpowering. 'They're just dead flowers.'

'To you, maybe.'

Jen turns away, done with death. She no longer wants to see it.

Smoke without Fire

Isobel

Tuesday, 28th August

Was called into the back room after the meeting. They asked me to explain, so I did. How I felt unwell and that he slept in the lounge. I was almost sick when they asked if anything of a physical nature had occurred. Of course, those aren't the words they used, but I cannot write it here. It sounded so clinical, the way they phrased it, like he and I were a problem to be solved. It felt like someone had set fire to my face. A jury must be formed, they said. Next week. Almost thirty degrees.

Wednesday, 29th August

Work. Felt sick. No word from V. Les Connell rang – jury is set for 3 September. Couldn't eat dinner. Weather hot.

Thursday, 30th August

Work. So hot, fan broken. Sadie brought in a cake she'd made. She told me to have the last piece. Think she sensed I was melancholy. She is thoughtful, even if her sponge is much too dry.

Friday, 31st August

Still nothing from V. Perhaps best this way. Better to end it before it really begins. Work. Too busy to think. Best this way too. They say a storm is coming.

Saturday, 1st September

Didn't go on the ministry as the heavens opened. Tried ringing Patrick, left message with Jude, but he probably won't get it. Couldn't concentrate on telly so tried reading scriptures. Couldn't focus. Headache. Waited for Patrick. Tried the landline from my mobile to check the connection was okay. Maybe there's a fault his end. Went to bed late. Lightning.

Sunday, 2nd September

No idea of weather as slept the whole day.

Monday, 3rd September

I don't know what to write. I cannot think now.

Dear Patrick,

You left here in such a hurry. I could see it in your eyes, the way you looked at me, like I had transformed into a different person. But I am still your mother. Do you hear me? I am still the woman that was.

You said there is no smoke without fire. But, dear boy, this is the strange thing. Nothing has happened. Of course, I know how it looks, staying the night in a worldly man's house, but perhaps, just perhaps, *looks* isn't the same as *is*. I have told you the truth. I told them the truth. And yet . . .

They read scriptures, they said prayers, they emphasized that disfellowshipping is loving discipline from God to bring me to my senses. But this is what I don't understand. If it is from God, then surely He knows nothing actually happened? If decisions are made through holy spirit, surely holy spirit knows the truth?

I have known this all my life, and yet, this is a different thing entirely.

Oh, Patrick, please do not keep me from the baby. The words you said . . . I have done nothing wrong. I would never lie to you. Please do not take this away from me, the promise of my grandson, any day now. I do not know why they did it, Patrick. I told the truth. I told the truth.

Who do I have now?

PS Tell Jude I tried everything, but first babies are often late. Curries, exercise, pineapple. I even swallowed half-a-bottle of castor oil. Nothing made your sister budge. She came when she felt like it.

I didn't try any of the methods with you, though. I couldn't bear the thought of asking you to leave.

Isobel makes herself go the following Sunday, slipping in as the song begins, as is the custom with those who are shunned. It removes the simultaneous awkwardness of being seen and unseen. Once it was her eyes that pretended the black sheep weren't there. Now here she is. Sliding in late. Taking a seat in the back row, usually reserved for latecomers, screaming babies and those judged to be wicked.

If asked what she took home from that Sunday meeting, Isobel would not have been able to recount a single word. But there are screenshots in her head. The sight of other people's embarrassment. Toni looking away. The first Sunday meeting in decades where she has not raised her hand to comment. If she were to be asked, those are the things she would describe. Except, of course, nobody will ever ask her.

She is being deceitful. There is one moment when she heard every word:

'And now we have a happy announcement. Brother Patrick and Sister Jude Forge gave birth yesterday morning to a bouncing baby boy named Noah. Isn't that wonderful? I'm sure they will appreciate any cards or dinners at this very exciting time.'

Victor's door feels cool and smooth beneath her fist. She has probably moments before the sister who lives opposite returns from the meeting. Isobel cannot risk bumping into her on the stairs. Please be in, she whispers and starts slapping the door.

She almost falls inside when it opens. Victor stands there with his mouth open, wearing a loose shirt – the floral print turns Isobel's stomach – and shorts. 'Why . . .' he begins. 'Come in, come in.'

She stumbles in, clutching her bag. Victor makes apologetic noises as he moves through, swiping old cups and plates from the tables and piling up books. 'Sorry,' he mumbles. 'I wasn't expecting company.'

Isobel is crying as she looks at the mess. 'No, don't apologize. You have no idea how happy this makes me.'

He looks confused, as if confronted by a trick question. The crockery is deposited in the sink, and then he stands awkwardly by the sofa, his hands in his pockets. It's been three weeks. He hasn't yet earned back the right to console her, and so he nudges a stack of books with his foot until it topples on to the carpet. 'How's that? Happier still?'

Isobel laughs, wiping her tears with the sides of her hands. She hasn't cried around people for years. I'm the same woman I was, she'd said to Patrick, and yet here she is, new.

'Oh, Victor . . .'

This brings him across the room, and he puts out his arms for her to walk into. They stand there for a moment, feeling each other breathe, then sit, and she lets it all out. But speaking the words makes it real. She covers her eyes with her hands.

'So they refuse to talk to you? Patrick too?'

Isobel explains about her grandson, how she heard of his birth at the same time as everyone else, and he gets up and goes to stand by the window.

'What about Cassandra?'

'She wouldn't answer the phone anyway.'

He gives a slight shake of his head. 'I thought Christianity was about love?'

'The disfellowshipping practice is actually a loving provision. It helps bring wrongdoers to their senses, so they can rebuild their relationship with God and gain everlasting life.'

He turns to her. 'But you're not a wrongdoer.'

'Well, no, but –'

'See, you're spouting the script drummed into you. But, Isobel, surely now you can see it's not love. *They're* wrong. You told the truth, and they chose not to believe you.'

She looks down at her hands. It is odd to defend it, but defending it is what she has done all her life. We think in the language we know.

'You just don't understand,' she says.

'No. I don't.' He looks down at the streets. 'I know what love is, though.'

Speaking of love. Questioning love. All this talk is making her hungry.

Isobel looks up at the silhouette of his body. The window-light is so bright that she can hardly make him out, but she gets up from the sofa and walks over. He turns, surprised by her touch, and allows her to embrace him. Soft kisses. He surrenders.

Don't analyse it, she thinks. Right now, you're dead to everyone you know. This doesn't count.

Double jeopardy.

It is nothing like she is used to. Victor takes the time. He looks at her throughout, kissing her scar, and she is happy and embarrassed in equal measure.

She was right. He sleeps on the left side of the bed.

Hidden Picture
Jen

Each autumn, she waited for the leaves to change. Will it be this year, she'd think. Will this be a year they look like they are burning, like they did in that year once, whose number she can no longer remember? Most years, the leaves turned their regular shades of mud. But, now and then, the trees revealed their truth. They would blaze on each side of the road as people went about their day. They would hang like mystical orbs, catching the light just after the rain, beating red and orange hearts above people's heads. Look up! she screamed inside. Look at the magic just inches above you. Why is this not headline news? Why do the newsagent displays not scream *Look up! This is the year! Look up!*

Jen said this once to her friend Leah on the school bus home. Leah – who had taken the window seat as usual – looked at the trees with a frown and back at her, then turned to talk to the boy behind.

It was just one instance in her life when she realized she was not like other people.

Jen thought like this in spring too, when new life pulsed from every branching finger, but by then she'd usually learnt her lesson.

Keep it to herself.

'Do you regret your decision to take blood?'

She is prepared. Many conversations have been had in front of the mirror, where she has answered this question to every part of her face, excluding her eyes. The words have been repeated within that crummy little flat so often that they are now just sounds inside her head.

'Yes, I regret it.' But she doesn't leave it there. 'I regret leaning upon my own understanding. I have meditated on this and wondered if the humble course of action is not to think I have the answers. God is bigger than I am, and His organization has been tasked with spiritual direction.' Jen hopes she has covered all bases. Please don't ask more questions, she prays. Please don't force me to lie.

The brothers look at each other, communicating through eye gestures and a holy spirit of which they alone are beneficiaries. Jen bows her head. Her hands are neatly folded, her ankles modestly crossed. She is dressed smartly for this meeting of four.

'So you no longer believe it acceptable to take blood?' Brother Connell's eyes do not leave her.

Jen's hands tighten in her lap. She remembers her father when he caught her years ago with the book in his study, his trick questions, the disappointment on his face. She counts a beat, then another. 'It was foolish to lean upon my own understanding.'

He smiles. 'So you said. To be clear, you no longer believe it acceptable to take blood?'

Another beat. 'No.'

'You believe your course of action was the wrong one?'

Jen relaxes her vision, like she did as a child when looking at a hidden picture. She'd blur her eyes and then would come a 3-D dog, an elephant, an eye. It was there all the time, she just had to choose how to look. 'These months have given me time for thought and reflection.' *Jacob.* 'You have no idea how much I regret taking blood.'

When they call her back into the room and inform her that her application for reinstatement has been successful, Jen's body dissolves into sobs. She has impressed them with her consistent meeting attendance, they say, as well as her willingness to heed counsel, and they appreciate that her current living arrangements are resulting in increasing levels of debt. She has demonstrated repentance by going to such lengths and proved that her conscience is being moulded by truth. They recommend she seeks alternative accommodation and reduce what she owes. An announcement will be made at the next meeting, but until then she will continue as a disfellowshipped person. No contacting family or friends until the congregation is informed. Does she understand?

Jen nods without really hearing. She knows there is truth in the words unsaid. That her reinstatement in such a short time is not down to her alone but to her willingness to help other members of the congregation in the clutches of sin. *Her conscience is being moulded by truth.*

She ignores the memory of her fellow sister's face in the flat opposite, how she silently screamed Jen's name. The terror and the fear.

A life for a life? No.

Jen tells herself that her actions have saved Isobel Forge from destruction.

Don't Cry

Jen

The following evening, Jen's ears fill with music as the entire congregation claps. They turn and smile, and Jen sees her parents shake in the front row. Afterwards, everyone gathers around, kissing her cheeks and telling her how missed she has been. I was here all the time, she thinks, but pushes the thought away. Her sister, Lina, whispers *Well done* in her ear and hands over Jen's niece as her mother and father wait for the crowd to disperse. They pat her on the back, her mother wringing her hands.

'Don't cry,' Angela says. 'You'll ruin your make-up.'

Strangely, when Jen will look back at this day, it will not be the hugs she remembers.

When she first arrived, she walked through the car park with the evening sun on her shoulders. The brothers and sisters were singing, and their voices carried through outside. Summer was fading into autumn. Soon the air would have a different scent. Her footsteps took her up into the foyer and through into the windowless hall. As she put down her bag in the back row, her attention was drawn to a stream of sunshine through the open doors. It poured down in shafts. She looked forward, but the rays kept pulling her back. As the song ended, two brothers came forward to close the doors. The light was shut out, and Jen turned back to the front.

Some people choose death.

PART THREE

Americana

Zelda

Zelda's watch says Matt is fifteen minutes late, as she cools her heels on the road, ignoring the net curtains that stir in the window of her childhood home. Nothing today can touch her. The sun beats down, and she is being whisked away by her lover. She wears a floral jumpsuit and, just as the song commands, flowers in her hair.

She checks her watch again. Her small suitcase waits on the gravel beside her. Pack light, he'd said. It makes it all the more exciting, being free of material things.

When his car speeds down the road towards her, Zelda leans casually against the fence as if she hasn't waited weeks for this moment.

A glimmer of pain throbs in her cheek, and she taps it with her finger. The ache has lasted all summer. She should have seen a dentist before the trip, but every moment passed in a daydream until they were all used up. She has packed painkillers and hopes endorphins take care of the rest.

The boot opens as he slows, and Matt stays in the car as she heaves in the case. He kisses her as she gets in. 'Hey, beautiful. Ready?'

She smooths her hair. 'I've even worn flowers as a little nod to San Fran.'

He looks her up and down. 'Well, you're knockout, as always. I've prepared some tunes to get us in the mood.' The car turns loud with 'California Dreamin''.

Butterflies fill her up. Here we go, she thinks, as his car purrs into life, and they leave her road behind.

Zelda first suspects something is off when she looks down at Matt's feet and sees he is wearing sliders. Hardly suitable for a plane.

'Won't your feet be cold?'

He glances down, then at her. 'Cold? It's boiling.'

Zelda gives a slight frown and stares out at the mirage blur between sky and motorway. 'Shame to leave this behind, really. It's crazy warm for autumn.'

'I'm sure it'll be hot at our destination. Maybe the weather will be too.' He winks.

Halfway through the next song, they pass the airport turning. She looks at him, confused. 'Did you miss the exit?'

Matt glances up as they drive underneath a sign. 'No, straight on.' He continues singing as she looks at the wedding ring on his hand.

An hour later the sky is a dismal grey, and Zelda no longer bothers with talk. She is staring out of the window when she remembers Will and the way he kissed her. His hands on her face.

Another hour. Rain lashes down. Matt has eaten all of Zelda's snacks.

Finally, three hours after they left home, he pulls off the main road into a car park next to a diner. He reverses into a space and cuts the engine.

'Do you need a piss?' says Zelda, staring at her phone. She just wants to be wherever they're going.

'Ta-da,' he trills, throwing out his arms.

She looks at him. She looks ahead. No. Surely this eighties box of a building – with its salmon-pink pebbledash walls and uPVC doors and windows with garishly coloured picnic tables on the concrete out front that partly obscure the diner windows that flash with neon signs, and are those bedroom windows above, so really this is a motel, and he is not whisking her away to *actual* California with palm trees and orange juice and cool vintage thrift stores but instead an incarnation of an American diner on a busy A-road in the West Midlands and what the fuck this must be a joke – is not the place he is taking her for their romantic long weekend?

Zelda murders him with her eyes.

He looks at the diner, then back at her. 'Okay, it doesn't look fantastic on a grey and rainy day. Some imagination is needed. But it's *so cool* inside.'

'You said I'd need a passport.'

'Well, I thought we'd go to Wales one of the days. It's only half an hour on.'

'You don't need a passport to go to Wales.' She enunciates each word.

'Yeah, found that out afterwards. But I didn't say anything because I wanted it to be a surprise.'

She looks ahead, biting her lip so hard she draws blood. 'Wish granted.'

They carry their bags across, dodging the puddles in the potholes that litter the broken tarmac. On the other side of the boundary fence is a second-hand car garage with a sign screaming WE BUY CARS FOR CASH! They go through the side door, which sits under a flat roof supported by imitation Greek columns.

'Welcome to Heartbreak Hotel!' sings the woman behind the reception desk, her face painted up like Marilyn Monroe's.

Sweet Jesus, thinks Zelda.

'Reservation for Fish,' says Matt, drumming his fingers on the counter.

The receptionist hands him a form and talks them through their stay. Her accent is Australian. Her blonde, fifties curls are frozen with hairspray. Zelda stands behind Matt, her arms folded as she takes in the barely there retro styling of the lobby. A fake cactus stands in the corner beside a pink plastic flamingo, a long cobweb stretching between them.

'Now you're more than welcome to use the pool, and the diner is just behind you, through there. Tonight we have a fifties-themed event you may be interested in –'

Matt turns from the desk to wiggle his eyebrows at Zelda.

'Twenty English dollars will buy you each an evening with our resident Elvis, who will be performing the hits, as well as an all-you-can-eat buffet of all your diner favourites. However, it is a ticketed-event, so if you'd rather not, there's a Harvester down the road. Sign here, please.'

Matt asks her to send up an ironing board.

Upstairs, Zelda follows Matt down the poky corridor. She looks out through the windows on the right and stops at the sight of the pool. A kidney-shaped block of blue in a mile of grey pavement, surrounded by weeds that stand in for grass. Around one end of the pool is a crescent of artificial tropical plants, coated with algae. She stares at the scene, then at Matt, who is walking further and further away.

'Bingo,' he calls, putting the key in a door near the end.

She doesn't hurry. He is outstretched on the bed when she enters, typing on his phone.

The room is small and square, with teal carpet, lime-green walls and orange curtains. A Sputnik ceiling light throws out a dismal glow. Behind the bed is a feature wall of palm-tree patterned wallpaper. When Zelda reaches out to touch the leaves, she realizes just how much she'd been looking forward to the real thing.

She has taken in the whole room in sixty seconds. He oversees a national chain of bowling alleys, and this is the best he can do. A room with no hope of emotion. No armchair in which to curl up with a book, no double-ended bath that invites conversation, or a chance to linger and think. No. All she is good for is a cheap place to fuck.

Zelda drops down on to the bed.

'It's warm, right?' says Matt, reaching up to open the window so the sound of rushing traffic fills the room. He kneels on the bed and kisses Zelda's neck. 'Or maybe it's you making me hot.'

She doesn't look at him.

'Hey, all right?'

'Fine.'

He moves her hair away and nibbles her earlobe with his teeth. 'C'mon, you're like an ice-cube.'

'I'm not really in the mood.'

Matt frowns and pulls back at the sound of words she has never spoken. He follows her eyes to the dusty radiator, its grooves covered in drips of dried paint. He sighs. 'All right, it isn't Beverly Hills.'

'How generous.'

'I thought you'd look past all that, though.'

She stares at him. 'Look past it? What am I missing? It's called Heartbreak Hotel, for God's sake.'

'Mel would never come here —'

'Don't mention her name. I don't want to hear her name. Got it?'

'All right.' He glances towards the window. '*She* would never come here. Nothing's ever good enough, but you're not like that, Z.'

'What am I, then?' Her voice is bored.

'You're not obsessed with *stuff*. You exist on a deeper level. Here we are having a dirty weekend away, just you, me . . . a bed.' He makes a face but she doesn't smile. 'Isn't this what your Hemingway was into? Cheap hotels and cheap food and drink. Just being together.'

'*Hemingway?*'

'I read his book. That Paris one. *Moveable Banquet* or something.'

'When the hell did you read that?'

'You told me it was your favourite book, so . . .' He shrugs, embarrassed.

Zelda looks at him, amazed. This would be something at the best of times, but, coming after the potholes and fake palm trees and the WE BUY CARS FOR CASH!, it is like finding water in the desert. A mirage turning out to be real.

He leans in to kiss her, and she doesn't pull away.

'Wait,' she says after a minute. 'You must be starving. Shall we go down and get food?'

Matt starts unbuttoning his shirt. 'I fancy eating out up here.' He nudges her back on to the bed.

They have sex under the glare of the Sputnik light. As Matt pushes Zelda against the MDF headboard, she tries to ignore the drone of the A-road, but it fills her ears until she's drowning. She panics and fakes an orgasm for the first time in her life.

They dress and go down to eat. The diner is exactly how a diner is expected to be. Checkerboard floor, plush booths, melamine counter tops, touches of chrome and neon and Americana adorning the walls. Matt is in heaven. 'Oh my God, a jukebox!' He fills it with coins.

When they sit down in a bubblegum-pink booth, Matt looks around and sighs. 'My dad would love this place.'

Ah, thinks Zelda.

She orders fries, but halfway through loses her appetite. 'I'm going to take a shower,' she says, as Matt sucks the last of his Oreo milkshake through a straw. 'I feel a bit . . . you know.'

Matt gives a thumbs-up. 'Cool. I'll check out the pool after I've finished. Dip a toe.'

Upstairs, Zelda edges round the bed and closes the window. She looks at the road outside. A bus is pulling up at the stop in front of the diner, and a woman about her age gets on. The doors swing shut, and Zelda watches the bus move on down the road. She doesn't look away until it's out of sight.

The bathroom extractor fan has packed up, and, when she gets out of the shower, the room is swamped in steam. She wipes the mirrors with a towel. Her cheeks are stained with black mascara.

The door slams and Matt appears, pulling off his clothes. 'Got us two tickets for that shindig tonight.'

Zelda rubs her hair with a towel. 'We're going, then, are we?'

'Well, I am,' he says, kicking off his shoes.

She looks at him and then back at her fuzzy reflection. 'Are you going to take that off?'

'What?'

'You don't think it's strange that you're here for the weekend with me and wearing your wedding ring? You don't think that's the slightest bit weird?'

Matt looks down at his hand and gives a bored shrug before sliding it off his finger and tossing it into his wash-bag. He pushes past to get in the shower. Zelda stares at the bag lying casually on the bed.

They go for a walk down the road in the late afternoon, but she sees nothing but second-hand cars and telegraph poles and a boarded-up Indian restaurant. Matt tries to talk as they walk single-file along the overgrown path, but his words are stolen by passing lorries.

They spend an hour on the bed, Matt scrolling through his phone as Zelda reads the book of short stories intended for an aeroplane. The words swim on the page. I can't take three days of this, she thinks.

She goes down to the pool. Her bare feet linger on the hot, cracked concrete. Sitting on the edge, she dangles her legs in the water and rips out a weed with her fist. Closing her eyes only amplifies the A-road. She picks up her book to forget.

The first story is of a divorced man who returns to his hometown after two decades away. To relieve his sadness, he decides to reconnect with the places and faces he once knew. The years he spent there are burned on his brain. They shimmer. They are destinations his mind returns to when days are dark. He takes a room at a cheap hotel and calls his old friends. They arrange a get-together in the pub where they used to hang out, and he gets there early, eager to pick up where he left off. But his friends are no longer boys. They are pickled with middle age and broken hearts, the fantasies of their futures turned sour. At the end of the night they all say goodbye and mean it. When he passes the girl he adored in the street, she doesn't know him. The roads where he walked and drank and loved are dirty. The evergreen trees that lined the pavements are now stumps, chopped down to save costs. His memories allow him to recall skin and hair and the texture of conversations. But they are fossils. Relics, frozen in a flash flood. He knows there is nothing left for him here.

When the story ends, she stares at the book and throws it into the pool. She watches it float. The shiny cover catches the sun.

At six o'clock, they begin to get ready. Matt irons his clothes as Zelda does her make-up. The ironing board takes up much of the floor, so they have to climb over the bed to move around. Zelda puts on her dress – a nude floaty slip embroidered with red dragons and balls of orange fire, with gold-thread swirls running over the silk. The dress has a deep 'V' at the front, and she tapes her tits to best effect.

She is working her feet into a pair of high heels when she turns and sees Matt, half dressed in a shirt and socks.

'Is that a tiki shirt?'

He looks down. 'What's wrong with it?'

'Just wondering what happened to *Chalk my cue and I'll pot your pink*.'

'Eh?' He pulls up his trousers.

'Forget it. Shall we go down?'

The diner is already busy when they walk in. An Elvis impersonator fiddles with an ancient-looking amp as his cartoon quiff rests on a chair beside him. The jukebox booms out David Bowie. Zelda laughs.

'What?' says Matt, smiling.

'The song. Which era are we in?'

'This is absolutely brilliant.'

A waitress zips by on roller-skates. 'Food's coming up,' she calls over her shoulder. 'Order drinks at the counter.'

Zelda finds a booth near the window as Matt gets in line. They are definitely the youngest there. The women are in poodle skirts and twinsets, the men in turn-ups and checked shirts over vests. She looks down at her outfit and comes to the strange realization that she is both overdressed and not making enough of an effort. Matt, at least, nods to the theme with his tiki print. It's just her who's out of place.

She has a sudden urge for a cigarette.

Matt comes back with beers and a red plastic basket of fries. 'Even the bowls are just like America!'

Zelda takes a long gulp of beer and mutters, 'You've never even been.'

Everyone flinches as microphone interference pierces the air. 'Testing, testing,' comes a voice, and they look over to see Elvis raising a glass to the crowd. 'Good eeeevening, everybody! And how are we feeling today?' His American accent is as fake as the palm trees, but the diners all whoop with delight. 'Are we cruisin' for a groovin'?'

Zelda exhales loudly through her teeth and looks out of the

window as a bus pulls up, this time on the other side of the road. She frowns as a woman about her age – *another one?* – rises from the bench and climbs on. The doors shut, the figure sits down, the bus moves away.

When the buffet opens, Zelda is first in line. She piles her plate high, and, when it's all gone, she returns for more. Matt watches, uneasy. 'Enjoying that, are we?' She drops the bone of a sticky rib and licks each of her fingers in turn.

'Let's dance,' he says when 'Suspicious Minds' starts up, and he stands and waves at her to follow.

She stares at his outstretched fingers that jig to hurry her up. 'I'm all right. But you go.'

'I can't dance on my own. Look, they're all couples. Come on. I want to dance.'

'Well, I don't,' says Zelda as Marilyn from reception struts by their table.

'Hey, there,' Marilyn says, and rests her elbow on Matt's shoulder. 'I'm up for a boogie-woogie if you are, sweetheart. If your wife doesn't mind.' She gives Zelda a flirtatious wink.

'Not at all,' says Zelda, smiling. 'Go and enjoy yourself . . . hubby.' She takes another sip of beer.

Matt takes the receptionist's hand, and she leads him on to the dance floor. Zelda sees them in flashes. The crowd is too thick for a clear look, but Matt's hands are definitely on the polka-dot hips in the Lycra dress. As Elvis sings about not letting a good thing die, Zelda imagines the woman taking Matt out to the office behind reception and letting him bang her against the wall. Or inviting herself upstairs for a threesome in their tiny double bed. Would she care? She turns the thought over in her mind and drains her can.

In the Ladies', she sucks the remnants of rib from her teeth and reapplies her lipstick. A woman in *Grease* clothes and a pink wig exits a cubicle and washes her hands. As she takes a paper towel, she gives Zelda a suspicious look.

'Your dress isn't very fifties.'

Zelda runs her tongue over her teeth and snaps her lipstick shut. 'No, well, I'm not very fifties.'

They oversleep the following morning. The room is hot and cramped with stale breath, and Zelda leans over from the bed to open the window. The sound of the cars no longer registers. Not even a full day has passed since their arrival, yet the room speaks of eternity, with each hour an endless loop of the last. I'm going to die in this coffin of teal and orange, she thinks, staring at the dusty plug socket.

He wakes, they tangle and fuck, and, as she comes, Zelda's mind and body feel holy. Her skin is torrid with his touch. Yes, she thinks. Yes, yes, yes. Nothing else matters when there are moments that will exist like this. His mouth on her flesh is his confession. I forgive you, she moans inside.

He repeats the yes, yes, yes, when she returns the favour, but the words come hard and hollow. He lies at the end of the bed, holding his face as his body pants for breath. 'Bloody. Hell.'

Zelda leans back against the headboard. 'Male orgasms are such mindless, easy things. Like throwing scraps to a dog.'

He laughs and rolls on his side to face her, begins stroking her feet. 'You're good. Very, very good.' He crawls up the bed to kiss her.

'Wait,' she whispers, as his hands cup her face. She taps his finger on the side of her head. 'Do you ever want to get in there?'

He frowns. 'A blowjob?'

She looks at him for what seems forever.

'It was a joke,' he says, laughing as she gets up from the bed.

They finally emerge from their room at midday. The diner is quiet now, still heavy with retro. Zelda slides down her sunglasses.

'What can I get you, folks?' asks the waitress, taking a pencil out from behind her ear.

Zelda's head starts to ache.

'I'll have the Triple-stack Burger,' says Matt, his face hidden by the laminated menu. 'Strawberry milkshake and a large side of cheesy fries and onion rings, please.'

'Cheeseburger and fries for me,' says Zelda. 'And a small Coke.'

'Regular is our smallest size.'

'Well, I'll have your smallest size. If you call it a regular, that's up to you.'

The waitress's smile loses a little of its sheen. She walks off, and Zelda peers over her glasses at Matt. 'What?'

'You know she'll probably spit in our food now.'

Zelda shrugs. 'But, hey, at least it's *American* spit.'

They discuss plans for the afternoon. He suggests a designer outlet an hour away. She nods while striking a sachet of sugar against her nail, satisfying her desire for careless gestures that pass the time.

A song clicks on the jukebox, and Matt's face creases with delight.

'Ah, tune.'

'Isn't this from *Toy Story*?'

'Yeah. Classic.' He starts tapping out the beat on the table as Zelda cranes her head towards the kitchen for a sign of their food.

'Mel never got *Toy Story*,' he says, 'but, when we went to Disney World on our honeymoon, she finally saw what all the fuss –'

'Wait, what?'

'Mel never got *Toy Story*, but –'

'Disney World? You went on your honeymoon to Disney World?'

'So?'

She stares at him. 'Nothing.'

'The Florida one,' he says, making sure she understands. 'Not Paris.'

'Ah, okay,' she says. 'Right.'

The waitress brings over their order, and Zelda watches Matt smother his fries in ketchup before taking a long sip of milkshake. He pushes away his glass. A long, satisfied sigh.

'I'll get to the California one when I finally set off.'

She looks at him, fry mid-air. 'You still want to move to the States?'

'Yeah, course.'

'Even with everything going on there?'

'Meaning . . .'

She looks about for a candid camera. 'You know who they elected as President, right?'

Matt shakes his head. 'Oh, not you as well. All right, the guy's a bit much, but he only says what everyone's thinking.'

She drops her fry. 'Whoa, back up. What?'

'I can see why Americans are upset. What did Obama achieve in eight years? Nothing. He bombed the Middle East – conveniently forgotten, by the way – and refused to listen when the people said they didn't want free healthcare . . . they're not communists! He wanted to be Mr Nice Guy rather than get anything done.'

Zelda stares at her burger, cooling on its plate. 'And if your guy had been a woman? Do you think they'd elect a woman who's twice divorced, has children with multiple men, is accused of sexual assault and just spouts whatever shit comes into her head. Hmm?'

'Why are you being like this?'

She stabs a chip into her ketchup. 'I'm just asking a question.'

'Exactly.'

Zelda picks up her Coke and takes a long gulp as the cars rush past. Now she sees them again. One long blur.

'Can I have the room key?' she says, holding out her hand. 'Just need to grab something.'

Matt fishes in his pocket and hands it over. 'Don't be long,' he says with a mouthful of burger. 'I'd like dessert. Fancy sharing a banana split?'

As she walks along the upstairs corridor, staring out at the pool, a memory comes back of the day she passed her driving test. Excited to be alone at the wheel, Zelda drove for miles without looking at the dash. When it ran out of petrol, her car spluttered to a halt on the dangerous curve of a steep hill. She rang her dad, and he arrived an hour later with a can of fuel and a smile. Back when he was there to save her from herself.

She never has known when to stop.

★

256

In the room Zelda applies her lipstick straight from the bullet. Bright pink, her favourite since forever. When she has blotted her lips, she stands back to check her reflection. She frowns. The colour makes her skin look sallow. It has always been old faithful, the one she has worn since she was eighteen. But it no longer serves her well.

Her eyes wander down to the shelf, where Matt's toothbrush leans against hers, his razor next to her mascara. It is their bathroom. It is what she has always wanted.

Zelda moves fast on autopilot. Everything is chucked into the bag. She cleans her teeth and packs her toothbrush, leaving any shared items behind. He can have them all.

The covers are still a mess, and so she walks around the bed, pulling them into place with hospital corners. Her passion, she will take.

'Is there a train station nearby?' she asks the girl on reception.

'You can take the No. 3 bus from outside. It comes every fifteen minutes and goes straight there. Are you checking out?' The girl sees the key fob in Zelda's hand. 'Only we have you down for two more nights?'

Zelda turns to look through the door into the diner, then back at the receptionist. 'He's staying.' She places the key on the counter. 'It's just me.'

The girl smiles. 'I'll let him finish his food first.'

Zelda slips out the side door, where she bums a smoke from a guest before making straight for the bus stop. It sits twenty feet in front of Matt's window. The glass reflects the cars, so Zelda can see him only faintly, like a double-exposure photo. Two scenes at once, only half a picture.

She could wait further back, hide behind the wall and run out when the bus is in sight. But she's done with hiding.

It takes less than five minutes for him to start shouting her name.

She doesn't turn. The ridges in the bench dig into her legs, which are dimpled with cold. She is dressed for the scorching Californian heat, not a bus stop in the overcast English Midlands.

'Zelda, are you going to answer me?' He is facing her now, his hands in tight fists.

'I don't want to be here any more,' she says, looking at his sliders, at his comical toes.

'You're not enjoying it?' He stares at the cigarette. 'Since when do you smoke?'

Zelda exhales upwards. 'Since always.'

'Who *are* you?'

She smiles and places her weapon between her lips.

'Look, we'll go somewhere else,' he says, stepping forward. 'There's bound to be some five-star country pile around. I'll make good.' He strokes her hair, and she looks up at him.

'You think it's luxury I want?'

'Z . . .' His hands move slowly down her face. 'I won't let you leave. You make me feel invincible, like I'm the man I'm meant to be.'

Something inside breaks at his touch.

'Yeah, well, I don't want to exist just to make you come alive.' She drops the end of the cigarette.

'You know I love you.'

'How would I? You've never told me.' She stares at the ground. 'And we've never been on the same level when it comes to love.'

'Yeah, well, you're so full-on with it all. You feel things too deeply.'

Zelda holds her cheek as it throbs. 'You say that like it's a bad thing.'

He sighs. 'Listen, I can be a shit. But, come on, Zelda. It's you and me. We can't escape each other, like all those years ago when you kept coming back.'

Zelda looks at him as memories swirl through her head. Night after night of following him home from some sweaty club, hoping his hands on her body would heal the heart he'd broken. She bartered fucks for a chance to get close. Then no word until the next time. She had to learn, like a child – falling and falling, until . . .

'My friend was right all those years ago,' she says. 'I'm not *me* with you. I'm this broken, damaged thing that wants to take care of you so badly that she forgets about herself. You know, I used to dream about being your wife and making you dinner? I can't fucking cook. I don't *want* to fucking cook. I'd think about being this good little fifties housewife, some dirty version of my mother, as if that would keep me safe.'

Zelda looks down the road at an approaching bus. She sticks out a hand which Matt tries to bat away.

'Come on, Z. At least let me drive you home.'

Three hours in his car with a broken heart. She picks up her bag and pushes past.

'You know you'll just come back eventually.'

As the bus slows, Zelda thinks of Jen and how she couldn't leave that life. Even when it threw her out, she still crawled back, crushing the truth of herself so she could be whatever they wanted. She couldn't break the bond.

The doors swing open. She half turns to see Matt with his arms folded, his head cocked, his face questioning her ability to survive alone.

'I'm done with you, Fish. The truth is I've outgrown you. I don't want average, and that's what this feels like for me. *Average.*'

She gets on the bus.

Face the Wall

Isobel

She thinks later how she wasn't even meant to be there. Carol usually makes the deposits, but that day she sent Isobel to town instead.

Isobel clutches the envelope to her chest as she enters the bank that afternoon. She is always nervous handling other people's money, and knows it is a positive sign that Carol trusts her with the task. She must have *some* initiative, she thinks, recalling the feedback when she didn't get the dental-assistant job. Yes, she can take charge for herself. They'll see.

As she waits in line, she looks around at the place where she worked thirty years ago. Like the surgery, it too has had a facelift, and the purple carpet and mottled wallpaper have been replaced with wood and floor-to-ceiling glass. Everything changes, she thinks. Even if you keep the shell, it can still be made to look completely different.

She is distracted by the movements of the woman in front, who searches through her bag in a way that is familiar. Her hair is like Toni's, and Isobel smirks at the frizz. But then the woman is turning, throwing a brief glance over her shoulder as she adjusts her strap, and Isobel sees that, yes, it is Toni.

'Oh,' she says, then clamps a hand to her mouth.

Toni spins round to face the front, and Isobel drops the envelope. She leans down, patting the floor, her eyes remaining on the back of her best friend's head. I'm not even meant to be here! she wants to shout.

She stands and looks around. Everything goes on. The cashiers serve, the woman at the door steps forward to greet customers, the world continues to turn. And yet, suddenly, this normal place has become completely different.

Isobel knows Toni is blushing by the shade of her neck. And me, she wants to say, but instead she moves to the back of the queue.

Minutes take years. Isobel positions herself so she cannot be seen and watches Toni. When her friend reaches the desk, she casts side-long glances at each person going by. She is looking for me, Isobel thinks. Despite herself.

For a moment she fantasizes about pulling her to one side. Look, Toni, she'd say. I simply didn't do it. They cut me off because they didn't believe me, but that doesn't change the truth. And what is the point of truth if it isn't acknowledged? If it isn't heard?

But, no. More outrageous than ignoring the truth is to go against the elders. There is no power in words unless spoken by them. To speak to Toni when they have commanded her not to is worse than being convicted of a sin she didn't commit.

Besides, she knows Toni. She knows her friend will toe the line. Isobel would joke about her fickleness, but now, as she sneaks glances at Toni's trendy outfit of a prairie dress with white trainers, Isobel understands. Toni adapts. She does what she must to fit in.

She turns to the wall as Toni walks out.

This is the first time, but it won't be the last. Isobel knows the drill. She has often bumped into disfellowshipped ones, felt pity and moral righteousness at the sight of their shame, experienced the lurching fear when catching their eye. Although she never knew the reason for their expulsion and had not been privy to their time in the back room, it didn't matter. They were guilty, plain and simple. Nobody was disfellowshipped unless they deserved it. It simply wasn't possible.

So she once believed.

Not Long Now

Jen

'It's Jen, right?'

Jen drops her slice of Brie as she turns to the girl on her left at the cheese table. She smiles and leans down to retrieve it from the floor, next to the girl's feet.

'I'm Susanna,' she says, before explaining how she knows Lina. She's from a local congregation, early twenties in age, and Jen knows she has never seen her before, because she would never forget a face like that.

'Hi,' she mumbles.

'Lina's so happy you're back. She cried buckets when it happened. We did our best to rally round, support her, but she just wanted you.'

'Right.'

Jen had turned up on Lina's doorstep that evening expecting only her family, but instead found half the congregation there for a cheese and wine. 'Didn't I say?' said Lina, when she took Jen's coat. It was her first visit to Lina's since her reinstatement the previous month. 'Oh, well. It's been arranged for ages. Go, if you'd rather. No one's making you stay.'

Jen has spent the evening in the kitchen, in a constant state of movement so she doesn't feel alone. After several months of being actively avoided, she can't run the risk of standing still in the crowd and discovering they all still have nothing to say to her. These people she has known all her life. The ones she came back to. The thought makes her want to vomit.

But here is Susanna, seeking her out.

'Tell you what,' says her new friend. 'Grab those seats in the corner, and I'll get us some P'sec'.'

Jen wants to kiss her for multiple reasons.

When Susanna still isn't back after five minutes, Jen starts to shift in her seat. Back in a mo, she wants to say to the curious glances. She's just getting us wine. You'll see.

Susanna returns with two flutes and brushes Jen's leg as she sits. 'I had to fight two little old sisters for these.'

Jen laughs, and the Prosecco bubbles tingle on her tongue.

'I'm sorry about the baby,' says Susanna, touching Jen's arm. 'It must have been awful.'

Jen stares at her cheese and biscuits.

'I didn't know whether to mention it,' she says, quickly. 'But my cousin lost a baby, and she said the worst thing is people acting like it never happened. Sorry if that's not right.'

'No, she's right,' says Jen. 'You're the first person to mention him, that's all.'

Their corner of the room falls silent.

'What was his name?'

'Jacob.'

'That's beautiful.'

'He was beautiful.' Jen feels Susanna's hand on her shoulder.

'Not long now,' she says with a kind smile. 'You'll hold him soon.'

Jen sips more wine.

Two girls enter the room with a scream and rush over. They are about Susanna's age, although their excitement at being at a cheese and wine suggests younger. Susanna introduces Claire and Donna to Jen, who recognizes them vaguely from parties over the years.

'I like your hair,' says Claire. 'Very brave.'

Jen touches the nape of her neck. 'Oh, I'm growing it out.'

'The elders would have a field day if I did that. Probably call me a *lesbian*.' She whispers the word.

There is talk of leaving early to meet boyfriends in a bar, and, when Susanna asks Jen if she'd like to join them, she shrugs and says, 'If you like.'

They apologize to Lina, who bats them away – 'Ah, go where the fun is' — but then takes Jen's arm and pulls her back. 'You know they're all, like, twenty,' she whispers hotly in her ear.

What choice do I have, Jen almost says. None of your friends have anything to say to me. She pulls her arm free and follows the others.

Jen feels every one of her thirty-five years when they walk into the pub and join the men. Lina was right, they are all so young. Boys. Women can flit anonymously between late teens and early thirties. Make-up buys time. But men's faces fit their age. Teenage acne and hairlines place them more or less where they are.

The lads nod at Jen with little interest. They turn to the girls and start their own conversations.

After her first drink, Jen already feels tipsy, and then remembers the Prosecco and abandoned cheese plate. Her stomach may be rumbling, but the room is too loud to be sure.

'We should do shots,' she shouts, and the lads turn round, a little more interested now.

'Really?' says Susanna, surprised.

Jen feels excited by how they look at her. Clearly, she has been underestimated. A raw, nervous energy pulses through as she enjoys the thrill of being unknown in this new crowd. 'Tequila?'

'Go, Jen,' says Donna, raising her glass.

'Not for me,' says a tall, lanky lad they call Simeon. 'I'm reading tomorrow so I need to be in reasonable shape.'

'We'll all sit in the front row and make drunk eyes at you,' says Claire, squeezing his arm.

Jen returns with six shots of tequila and side plates of lime. She makes two trips, then a third for the salt. Everyone else is heavy with conversation. She lines the glasses up along the table then raises her voice to be heard – 'Guys, the tequila, remember?' – and they count 1-2-3 before performing the ritual of the salt-tequila-lime. Susanna shakes her head at the offer of the shot glass, so Jen has another. Donna nudges her in solidarity.

'Ugh,' someone says. 'I always forget that I hate tequila.'

Jen floats on a fuzzy high, the sharp edges rubbed off. This is nice, she thinks. Keep myself here.

She buys another round of drinks on her credit card.

'I'm going to leave my car in town and collect it tomorrow,' Susanna whispers in her ear. 'You okay if we all share a cab?'

Jen nods, forgetting her car is at Lina's. Susanna looks even more radiant to her tequila-soaked brain. Don't go there, Jennifer, she tells herself and drains her glass of drips.

The conversation about moving on must have been had without her, because now she is following them out into the cold autumn air. She stumbles on the threshold of the sixteenth-century pub. Somebody laughs.

As they walk over the bridge, she stops to tie her shoelace. 'Wait,' she calls, but her voice is swallowed up by traffic. Cars rush by, their headlights blurring. When she finally looks up, they have gone. Quickening her pace, she comes down over the bridge as they disappear up the stairs into the bar.

Jen's hands fly out to steady herself as she stumbles on the first step. Her body hangs forward and a groan emerges from her dry throat. Several drinks swirl around in her empty stomach.

'Up, Jennifer,' she mutters, gripping the balustrade. She climbs the steps to the bar.

'I don't think so,' says the bouncer, as she nears the top. 'Sorry, love. You're far too gone.'

'But my friends are in there.'

He folds his arms.

'What' – she burps into her hand – 'am I supposed to do?'

His walkie-talkie crackles as he points to the taxi rank. 'There.'

'But . . . my friends. They won't know where I am.'

'So ring them. Text them. It's amazing what tech can do these days.'

'I don't know their numbers.'

'Thought they were your friends?'

Jen looks at her phone as if she can magic Susanna's number on to her screen. A small group passes by, backslapping the bouncer as he stands aside to let them in. Her loneliness is deafening.

But then, as she's walking down the stairs, she sees Claire with

Simeon on the balcony. He stands close, and his hand rests on the small of her back.

Jen has to shout several times before they hear her. Claire peers over the railing and frowns, as if trying to recall who she is.

'Oh, it's you,' she calls. 'We wondered where you'd gone.'

'They won't let me in. Say I'm too drunk.'

Claire nods as Simeon whispers in her ear. They both laugh and continue talking.

'Erm, hello?' Jen calls up.

'Hi?'

'Well . . . think we could all go somewhere else?'

Drunk as she is, Jen recognizes the look on Claire's face. Disdain. She swallows a sob.

'Not really,' says Claire in a fake-sympathetic voice. 'We've all just got our drinks, so . . .'

'There's a taxi rank over there,' says Simeon.

'Can you ask Susanna to come to the door?'

Claire sips her drink. 'Sure,' she calls, and pushes Simeon back into the bar, leaving Jen to sit on a brick wall and wait.

Minutes tick. The cool night air has not sobered her up, and neither has her abandonment. Drunks walk past, all with an arm to cling to.

I can't stay here, Jen thinks. She doesn't trust her woozy head, and a vision comes of her falling backwards off the wall and being dragged into a corner. The taxi rank is one long queue with not a cab in sight.

I'll sober up soon, she thinks, gripping the wall and widening her feet for balance, but, as the minutes blend together, her head continues to swim. Her drunk brain wants to sleep, and even in her stupor she is terrified by the idea of passing out alone.

After several attempts she finds the number. It answers immediately.

'Please help me,' says Jen, but her tears smother the rest.

Orange Blossoms
Zelda

Zelda sees Jen slumped on the wall as soon as she turns in. It is half past ten and too early for collapsed drunks, but there she is, oblivious to the people who point and laugh as they pass. She comes to a stop by the kerb and sticks on the hazard lights, ignoring the beeps as she leaps out to rescue her friend.

Jen falls hunched to the side, her head resting on the brick wall. Zelda checks she still has her phone and then loops Jen around her body.

'Geroff,' Jen groans, her feet rooted to the ground.

'It's me,' says Zelda, and Jen half opens her eyes.

'It *is* you. There you are.'

'What the hell's going on, Jen?'

'I've missed you, Alice.'

Zelda inches Jen towards the road, where a long line of cars waits behind the Volvo. She sticks her finger up at a man screaming through his window. When Jen is safely inside, she runs round to the driver's seat and blows kisses to the queue.

'Wow, this car stinks of dog,' says Jen, huddling against the door.

Zelda sniffs. 'No, it doesn't.'

'It's always smelt of dog. I've just never told you before.'

'I'm not sure I like drunk Jen.' She rolls down the window, then inhales her sleeve. 'Wait, do *I* smell of dog?'

Jen, bleary-eyed, throws herself against Zelda. She draws an exaggerated breath. 'You smell like citrus . . . and dog.'

'Piss off.'

'I mean a cute poodle. Not an Alsatian, or one of those dribbly . . . what they called . . . the big, slobbery things. Beethovens.'

'A St Bernard.'

'That's it!' Jen claps her hands. 'Yeah, you're not one of those.'

'Can we talk about why you were passed out on a wall in the middle of town? Where exactly are your *friends*?'

Jen rests her head against the door. 'You don't smell of dog. You smell beautiful, in fact. Like orange blossoms on a hot day. Have I ever told you that?'

Zelda gives her a sidelong glance. 'Did you bang your head?'

Jen's mind is still thick with drink, but she can feel warmth flood back as she sits beside Zelda. Several weeks apart has done nothing to temper the heat.

'Let me know if you're going to be sick,' says Zelda. 'I don't want to add vomit to the list of crap my car smells like.'

As she glances out at the never-ending blackness, the town left behind, she catches Jen watching her. 'You okay?'

'You know I love you, don't you.'

Zelda takes a moment to reply. 'I know.'

'No. I mean love you. Like nobody else.'

'Don't go all Timberlake on me.'

'It's like, the lid was screwed on tight. And someone tried to undo it, but they couldn't. Well, now the drink has loosened the lid. It's off and you can see inside the jar. Because *I'm* the jar . . . the jar is me. I'm a jam-jar full of feeling.'

'Are you sure you're not high?'

They are nearing her house. When Jen complains of feeling sick, Zelda makes her roll down the window. She starts the CD player, and the car throbs with a nineties pop song.

'Tune,' she says, turning up the volume. 'Remember? When we wore combats and I wanted a tit tattoo like Shaznay.'

Jen doesn't reply. She tips her head back and watches the road.

When they get out, Zelda loops Jen's arm around her. The kitchen light shines in her childhood home, and Zelda glances through the open curtains at the dining table and sees how it looks the same. But then a silhouette appears at the window. Zelda hides Jen's face, and the curtains are quickly drawn.

They make it down the path. As Zelda releases her grip, Jen pushes herself away and vomits on the flowers by the door.

She groans. 'All over your beautiful roses too.'

'Ah, it's fertilizer for the soil. You *have* spoken shit all night.'

Jen cringes. 'Don't. Can't laugh. Hurts.' She staggers back, looks down at herself. 'Oh, no.'

'Here, I've got you,' says Zelda, taking her arm and leading her into the house, which is warm from the wood-burning stove. They go into the bathroom, where Zelda carefully peels off Jen's clothes as her friend stands half asleep. She tests the water for temperature before guiding Jen into the bath and showering her down.

Jen leans against the chipped tiles and gently moans as the night is washed off her skin.

The Harder Road

Jen

The dreams come often.

She has learnt to doubt the state of her mind. On better days, when the ache is not so raw, when she slips into sleep, then it will be a nightmare. The nights when she tosses and turns, unable to settle, when her insides feel scraped to the bone, she will be gifted a vision of his face.

The harder road gives the greatest reward.

She never wants to wake from the good ones. Here, Jacob is two or three, safe on her hip. They stand in wild gardens, drinking in scent and colour. He plays on a lawn of wildflowers and picks her the prettiest blooms. Their home is a small, simple cabin of wood and metal, salvaged offcuts from buildings that came before. Ahead is nothing but eternity. Mum, he says. Mum.

And the bad.

Buildings crash. The ground splits open. People burn alive. Thunder and lightning clap as she scrambles over rubble, over dead children, over the bodies and carcasses of those judged to be wicked. She waits to see if she is wicked. There is often a flash of light, and she wakes in a sweat before she has the chance to know.

The worst is the one she sees most. He is perhaps a year old, lying there amongst the flowers, sleeping. Alone. His name is called from a distant cloud, and he wakes. For a moment he looks about, plucking daisies and watching them fall through his fingers. Then he climbs to his feet and trundles off through the wood.

She is screaming his name.

He does not hear her. She is not there to be heard.

Fiery Coals

Zelda

Zelda also dreams.

She is dressed in white and lies in a painted circle in a dark field. Her dress is loose and modest, but torn at her chest and hips, so she is exposed. The elders stand around, Bibles in their hands, chanting scriptures as they heap fiery coals upon her head. This is to make you better, they say. This is to cleanse your soul. Her mother is not allowed in. The women must stand far back outside the circle. She is an outcast and to be comforted only by men.

The elders console her with their hands. They drop their coals while pawing at her body. Their eyes drink her in, while they shake their heads and say she should cover herself. Sister, they say. *Sister*. You bring this upon yourself. And then they take it in turns. She is not believed, because they draw a curtain and so there is no second witness.

When they are done, they pick up their shovels and load more coals upon her head. I can't breathe, she shouts, but they ignore her cries or cannot hear them. Her voice is drowned out.

She wakes. Even in the dead of night, she showers the sweat from her body, turning up the heat until the pipes rattle and the water scalds. All these years later, she still remembers their faces as they made her repeat it, again and again.

She tells herself that they didn't believe her. This is kinder than what she fears is true.

That in her, they saw their downfall, and so they burned the witch.

Wonderwall

Jen

Jen wakes the next morning in her bedroom. Or what was her bedroom. It takes a moment to remember the what, when, why, and then the ache of past lives blooms in her chest.

She strokes the brushed-cotton pyjamas that she knows are Zelda's. Why does her body feel so clean? Pieces of the night start to connect: the sensation of water on her body, Zelda drying her with a towel.

Sounds float under the door. The clatter of plates and cutlery. Jen eases herself up and goes out into the main room, where the ceiling reaches up into a holy point. Here is where the light floods in.

Zelda stands in the kitchen, eating something from a bowl. Former days come to mind as the spoon scrapes against the china.

Jen recognizes Zelda's suit from the wardrobe, pale pink with blue and orange flowers stitched along the lapel. Her red hair is piled high, a few strands loose. She is smart and casual together. Her camera bag sits by the door.

Zelda turns, and they smile; a brief pause, then Zelda grips her cheek.

'Still no dentist?' Jen shakes her head. 'You'll never be told.'

'I know, we're just the same.' Zelda puts down her bowl and leans down to study her itinerary. 'Heard from your mates?'

Jen walks around, taking in the room. Nothing has changed, but the air feels different. She stops by the stove, where her skirt and top hang over the airer. The cotton is warm to the touch. She inhales the fabric. 'So I wasn't sick,' she says, revising her memory of the previous night.

Zelda turns over the paper. 'Oh, you were. Chunky vom, the lot.'

She inhales again. 'But they're fresh?'

'Because I washed them.'

Jen looks at her. Zelda doesn't have a washing machine. Almost all her clothes are delicate, and so are washed by hand in the kitchen sink with soap flakes and a scrubbing board. Jen hugs the clothes to her body.

'Where are you now?' asks Zelda.

Last night, after Zelda helped her into bed, Jen told her she'd been reinstated. She laid against the pillow and watched Zelda in the doorway, waiting for a droll or cutting reply. But Zelda's face was without expression. She stood still, then turned away with a soft 'Goodnight'. The room went dark as she closed the door.

'I've a few months left on the flat,' says Jen, wrapping the clothes over her arm. 'Then . . . I don't know. Move in with Mum and Dad? Sad, eh?'

Zelda doesn't answer at first. She folds the paper into quarters and slips it into her pocket, then pushes open the window and lights a cigarette. 'Live here.'

Jen cannot look at her. 'I shouldn't even be talking to you.'

Zelda takes a long puff and shakes her head. 'So those idiots who left you drunk and alone – those people are holy, are they? They're better association than the Good Samaritan who came along and cleaned you up?'

'Listen –'

'Those bastards who abandoned you' – she pauses, forcing herself to stay calm – 'they're not your friends, Jen.'

'Zelda, you know the drill.'

'*Drill?*'

Jen still cannot face her. She has been here before; she knows how this will go. She doesn't want anger, and yet there is comfort in knowing that, here, confrontation is allowed. She thinks of her childhood home, the Worship Hall, Lina's, all the places where she behaves. With Zelda, she can argue and it will still turn out fine, because they have been here before and yet came back together.

'I haven't gone through all this for nothing,' she says. 'I won't blow it now.'

'By having me in your life, you mean.'

Jen steps forward. 'Come back to the truth, Zelda. I can't jeopardize my relationship with God. Doing what He and the elders say is the only way I can –'

'The *truth*? Did you speak truth? When they met with you, the elders would have asked if you regretted taking blood. Your answer?'

Jen watches Zelda ferry the cigarette to her lips, her wrist shaking. 'I do. I regret taking blood to prolong my life.'

Zelda stares at her and shakes her head, red tendrils of hair slipping down. They both know what Jen means.

'So you believe it?'

Jen still clutches her clothes, but their warmth is gone. 'Which life shall I choose? The one where my family treat me as if I'm dead? Where I'm not qualified to do anything but work part time in a shop?'

'But you could create, Jen. People would pay good money for your talent.'

Jen looks down at her empty hands. 'It's cold clay. It doesn't have a heartbeat.'

Zelda's eyes penetrate her skin, roving through cuts that never heal. Her voice is quiet but hard. 'Wanting something to be true doesn't make it true.'

His name is unmentioned and its absence reverberates through the room. Jen floods with rage. 'Have you ever held your dead child? Hated your own body for not keeping them safe?'

Zelda stubs out the cigarette. She steps forward and puts her arms around Jen, holding her as she sobs, tightening her grip as Jen tries to pull back, letting her know she isn't invisible. Her pain is welcome.

Pressed against Zelda's neck, Jen smells her citrus perfume. It is the scent of spring and high summer, of long days and nights. It is another thing too: the shutting of a door she desperately wants to open. Zelda's touch both calms and riles her, and her final sob is not just for Jacob. 'You don't understand,' she says.

'I know.'

They let go and step back into silence.

'Breakfast?' says Zelda.

'You have to go.' Jen rubs her cheek with her sleeve.

'You know I always arrive too early. I have time. Sit.'

Jen sits at the table as Zelda makes them a meal. She looks about, taking it in, making an inventory. The embroideries on the walls, the dead flowers in vases, the riot of colour and white. She grieves its loss already.

They chat over plates of scrambled egg and toast. Snippets of talk of teenage days, when they drank Hooch in the park and leant out of boys' bedroom windows, singing 'Wonderwall' to the night. They acknowledge the end of their time together with talk of pleasure, not of pain. This is where they will exist now, for this short moment.

'I wish . . .' Jen looks down at her empty plate.

Zelda, generous with touch, leans over and takes Jen's hand. She goes to speak. She stops. They both know these crossroads, the sunshine and shade that awaits them as they go their separate ways.

And then Zelda's chair scrapes back against the floorboards, the noise echoing up to the rafters, and she cannot look at Jen. 'Leave the plates,' she says, her tone casual. 'If I don't see you later, lock up and put the key in the usual place? You know.'

She goes over, picks up her bag and walks out.

After a while, Jen gets up and washes the dishes before getting dressed. She calls a taxi and writes DENTIST on the front of an old envelope before propping it on the table. She gathers her things. A final look.

Over on a side table is a laid-out collection of loose black-and-white photographs. The glossy paper picks up every detail of the flowers. The background in shadow, the dead petals in light.

'Some people like to take photos,' says the midwife. 'They find that a comfort. Is that something you'd like?'

Jen starts to feel light-headed, and lets her head rest on the pillow. 'I'm not sure. What do most do?'

Pete is shaking his head. 'I don't want any pictures.'

The midwife – the one who rubbed her back and has a kind,

older face – gives Pete a sympathetic smile, but it is Jen she turns to. 'There's no rule, love. Everyone's different. There's no right or wrong, just however you feel comfortable.'

Jen's first thought is to say yes. A photo might be helpful, a way to make sense of the day when she looks back in future. But the idea of fishing in her bag for her phone, reading notifications on the home screen, pointing the camera at Jacob and hearing the sound of the fake shutter feels distasteful, abhorrent.

There are black spots in her vision.

Jen looks down for the last time and knows she won't need a picture. 'I need to give him to you while he's still a little warm from my body. I can't think of him cold.' She puts her lips against his forehead and feels the bone beneath his skin.

Touch is all the memory she needs.

Jen looks at the photo, the flowers, then holds up another and stares. She sees it now, what Zelda meant.

'*We forget about life, until it's gone. We need that contrast to see the beauty. And then, because it's too terrifying to accept that everything ends, we can't help but use our imagination. We can't help but wish it back to life.*'

She drops the picture.

Outside, she locks the door and slides the key under the cracked terracotta pot. She passes the rose bushes, where petals lie scattered. The winter will soon be here.

Jen walks away down the path. She doesn't turn back, but continues through the woods towards the patch of light ahead.

Jacob.

She will hold him again.

Jacob.

I am coming, my darling. I am coming for you.

Now There to be Seen

Isobel

Isobel recognizes her as soon as she walks in. It must be twenty years since she saw her last, and her hair is now a ridiculous shade of red, but, for the most part, Alice Kay looks just the same. Alice takes in the fish tank as she shuts the surgery door. Her hand clutches her cheek.

She stops when she sees Isobel behind the desk, and blushes.

It's okay, Isobel wants to say. I'm like you now. But instead: 'May I help you?'

Alice doesn't move. 'I've had this pain for months. It's agony.'

'Do you have an appointment?'

She shakes her head.

'Well, that will be tricky, as we're full today.'

'Oh.'

She wears a loose shift dress covered in red and pink roses with metallic stalks. The roses are wilting, and their petals lay embroidered around the hem. Isobel stares at the pattern, struck by its ability to be both modern and traditional. *Extraordinary* comes to mind.

Sadie comes out of the treatment room, a medical mask around her neck. She holds two empty cups and hums under her breath.

'Sadie,' says Isobel. 'This young lady isn't booked in, but she's in great pain. Any chance of an emergency appointment?'

Sadie looks at Alice. 'Ah, you poor thing. I'm sure the doc will try if you don't mind waiting? Can't promise when.'

'I can wait,' says Alice, her voice oddly stilted. She winces with each word. 'I can't take the pain any more.'

Isobel holds up a clipboard. 'Fill out this new patient form, and I'll get you on the system.'

Alice hesitates, then steps forward and takes it. She sits and stares at the form, making no attempt to write. Isobel watches her between calls.

When Alice hands it back a while later, Isobel smiles before typing up the details. She frowns. The name says Zelda Bloom. Isobel looks up again. It is definitely Alice Kay.

What to do? Isobel knows her name is not what is written. Should she ask for ID? It is not standard procedure, but surely, if someone is lying, she should ask for proof. Her heart beats faster. Carol is out. There is nobody to ask.

Sadie opens the door. 'Isobel, we can see that patient now. Quickly, though. Her details aren't on the system?'

Isobel stands. She looks from Sadie to Alice and back again. 'I'm just inputting them. It's . . .' She looks down at the clipboard. 'Zelda?'

Zelda stands, still holding her face, and walks into the treatment room. Sadie shuts the door behind her.

When she comes out, her demeanour is calm. They have taken temporary care of the abscess, Sadie tells Isobel. Zelda is to come back in a week.

Her details now added, Isobel makes another appointment. She writes it on a card that she places on the counter: *Zelda Bloom. 8th November. 2 p.m.*

Zelda goes to leave when Isobel says, 'Did you sew your dress yourself?'

She stops and stares at the counter. 'Yes.'

'It's a work of art.'

She looks down and touches the roses as if to check that they are real. 'Thank you,' she says to the floor, and then runs out.

The surgery is closed for the afternoon, and when Isobel gets home she makes a salad. The cat meows as usual, so she pours food in his bowl and sets it down on the roof. It feels wrong, feeding a stranger's cat, but he just keeps coming back. One day, fed up with his cries, Isobel had gone to the pet shop and bought a bowl and fish-shaped food. Now he is quite happy as she fusses, attending to his needs. He purrs when she joins him on the roof and rubs against her. At first she would whisper, worried the neighbours would hear. But now she talks as if he is family. 'You are a handsome thing,' she says, tickling his chin.

They sit outside, enjoying their lunch, the sounds of the world going on below. Isobel can see the tips of trees. For weeks they have been red or yellow, but strong winds mean all colour has drifted to the ground. She is left with bare branches and a view of the distant park. Hidden all summer, now there to be seen.

There is a knock at the door and Isobel frowns at the cat. 'Who's that?' But he only flicks his tail.

She climbs through and jumps down, straightening her skirt. Another knock. Isobel opens the door and cries out at the sight of her son.

Patrick stares at the floor as he gently swings a car seat. Isobel hears a soft whimper. 'Can I come in?'

She steps back to let him through. 'Oh,' she says, her hands twisting. 'Oh.'

Patrick heaves the car seat up on to the kitchen table. They stand apart as the baby takes soft breaths in and out. Isobel cannot bring herself to look at his new, fresh face.

'You look tired,' says Isobel, reaching out to almost touch Patrick's arm.

He still holds the nappy bag, a plain canvas tote filled to the brim.

'It must be hard finding things in that,' she says. 'Surely Jude could get something with pockets? In my day we had quilted bags with several compartments that made it much easier to locate what you needed. You'd have to empty *that* bag just to find one item.'

Patrick doesn't answer. He looks around the flat.

'Was it raining out?' she asks.

A pause. 'No.'

'Oh. Only there was a wind earlier and it felt like the weather was about to turn. I was pleased to get back in time because I'd left my brolly here.'

He finally looks at her.

'Well, it didn't rain,' he says. 'And it's not raining now.'

'That's good.'

The baby continues to sleep. Isobel still cannot look at him, in case of what she might do.

'Did you watch the local news last night? There was a segment about a man in town who collects miniature —'

'It was Jude's idea,' he says to the floor. 'Coming here. She said it was cruel for you not to meet your grandchild. So here he is. For you to see him.'

So her daughter-in-law had really been her ally. Isobel looks at the baby, her hand reaching out, but his sleep is peaceful, and she doesn't want to make him cry. Not after they have come so far to see her. All this way.

'It's Noah, isn't it?'

'Yes.'

'He looks like you when you were new-born. All that black hair.'

'I had black hair?'

'Don't you remember pictures? It fell out when you were six months, then you were bald for a year. I always had to dress you in blue so people would stop asking what you were. It was blond when it grew back.'

Patrick clears his throat. 'Yes, well, he probably gets his hair from Jude.'

Isobel clasps her hands together to keep them busy. His bluntness, at least, comes from her.

'Does he have a middle name?'

'Laurence.'

She looks at him in surprise. 'My dad?'

'Well, he's named after Jude's brother.'

'Oh.'

The sound of the bin lorry filters in through the open window.

'I guess it can be after your dad too,' he says.

'Except it's not. It's for Jude. Like his hair.'

The baby begins to stir. He uncurls his fingers, stretching them

280

out. His eyes blink until they are fully open to the world, and, when he looks at Isobel for the first time, she can hardly breathe.

'Do you want to hold him?'

'Can I?'

Patrick unclips the strap and picks up his son, his movements slow and careful. His palm is outstretched against the baby's chest. Isobel looks at this palm, the wide palm of a man, and remembers how she used to hold it within her own. She would gently press the soft pads of his hands, the indents where the knuckles would be, and close her hands around them.

When Noah is placed in her arms, she cannot say a word.

Patrick leaves her for a moment, and when she hears the click of the bathroom latch, she looks into Noah's eyes and says, 'Hello, little one. I'm Grandma.'

She holds his hand and inspects his fingers, which are long and slender and in constant motion. They crawl through the air like spiders. She tries to hold one still. The fingernail is long and curls under, and Isobel leans down and clips it with soft bites. 'Are you smiling at me?' she says, when his lips bend upwards. She imagines them taking off in her car.

When Patrick comes out, she straightens up and goes to hand Noah back. Patrick shakes his head. 'Hold him a while.'

She rocks him gently. 'He'll be a piano player with those fingers.'

They stand there for a moment, not talking. Isobel considers offering a drink, but she doesn't want to risk Patrick waking up and realizing his mistake. I will hold on for a moment, she thinks. Take it while I can.

'Haven't seen you at the last few meetings.'

Isobel purses her lips. How to tell him that the sight of the three of them is like drowning. 'I've felt a little out of sorts, of late.'

'Don't suppose you've seen Cass?'

Isobel gives a slight shake of her head. 'Your sister has always seen things differently.'

Patrick stares at her. 'Are you joking?'

'Why?'

'You know *I* shouldn't be here, right?'

She bristles. 'I don't see why I can't exist as your mother, and a grandmother.' She is surprised by the words as they leave her.

'Mum . . .' He looks at her, uneasy. 'You know how it works. For goodness' sake, you taught it to *us*.'

'Yes, well . . . I thought that if they disfellowshipped someone, they must deserve it. That's what I thought.'

'It's not just the rules,' he says, swallowing. 'It's everything. You cut people off if they did something you disapproved of, you never forgave, your opinion of someone was formed by what kind of meat they served for Sunday roast. We copied you.'

Isobel closes her eyes.

'Look . . .' He sighs. 'We got all the stuff you thought mattered. The right-sized shoes and holidays and being everywhere on time. Maybe it's greedy to have wanted more.'

'I gave you all I could. You, especially.'

'Yeah, I know that.' He pauses. 'So does Cassandra.'

They look at each other then, and Patrick is the first to turn away.

'I'd best get going. He'll be due a feed soon.'

'Jude feeds him?' She bites her lip. 'Lucky girl.'

Patrick takes him from Isobel. She forces herself to let go. Noah is strapped back in the chair, and he gives a dozy look as he drifts off. They watch him together.

'I'll bring him to see you now and then. We'll have to keep it quiet.'

'Really?'

'You've got Jude to thank. She says you should still have a relationship with him. Despite everything.'

Silence.

'Thank Jude for me, Patrick.'

He goes, and her grandchild goes with him.

Years before, when she'd finish hoovering the downstairs of the house at some ungodly hour, Isobel would run outside to watch the sunrise. The dew on her feet felt cool and private. Nobody could see her out there in the garden in her nightgown. Nobody but her knew where it felt so good, on the damp soles of her feet. Once, she watched the sunrise and thought of Patrick as a baby, how he would wedge himself into small spaces and clasp his hands in his satisfied lap. Patrick, who couldn't yet string a sentence together, but who knew when something was just right.

The first sight of the sun, the dew on bare feet. She did not have the language to put the feelings of these things into words.

They were just right.

That night, she wakes suddenly. The clock says 2.33. Isobel lies there a while, her leg searching for a cool part of the bed. The air is chilly, but her body drips with sweat. After ten minutes of trying to still her mind, she pads down the mezzanine steps. The hoover waits in the corner. She walks to the wall of windows to stand in the spotlight of a full moon, its pale light on her face as she looks up from her stage.

A memory comes of giving birth. How she felt so powerful. *I've done something no President of the United States has*, she declared to the room, high on gas and air. Okay, dear, Steven replied, rolling his eyes at the young nurse. You make fun, she wanted to say. Keep pretending you know more than me.

Nobody ever asked about her experience of birth. It was all about the baby. The moment when she felt giddy with power and pride in her strength, no one was interested. Her husband belittled her. Everyone else wanted the name and the weight and the gender. Not details of how she coped, how it felt for a human head to tear through her skin, not the animal sounds of her screaming. They were footnotes. Not important enough for the paragraph.

She was glad that she had Patrick to soften the blow. Love blotted out pain. For a while.

This is the nature of being a woman, it seemed to her. The constant giving way to someone else.

Now she stands in the spotlight of her one-woman show. The only one who needs to clap is herself.

Our Cat

Isobel

On the Saturday, Victor comes to meet her, and they walk from her flat to the park. They have made a picnic, and they sit on the river bank in warm jumpers and eat cheese sandwiches, scotch eggs and leftover chicken pie. It is almost November and the trees are nearly naked, but those along the river are still the colour of fire.

Victor buys them coffees from the drinks-stand and adds whisky from his hip-flask. He hands her a cup, then holds his out. Isobel laughs as she shyly clinks his paper cup with her own.

'What's so funny?' he says.

'That's another thing I'm not meant to do. Make toasts or knock drinks together.'

'Why ever not?'

Isobel watches the steam rise. 'I think it comes from toasting the gods. Something pagan.'

'But it doesn't mean that any more.'

'No, but the origins of things . . . they matter.'

Victor shrugs. 'The names of months and days of the week are pagan or from ancient gods. Sunday is Sun Day. You don't have special words for those.'

She frowns as she thinks this over. 'No, I guess not.'

'So you speak pagan names every day without realizing.' Victor lies on his side, looking up at her. 'Seems a big fuss about things that don't matter.'

Isobel touches her cup to his, and a blush creeps over her skin. 'To the things that matter,' she says.

They are just turning into her road when they hear screeching tyres and the dull thud of metal. They watch as a car stops, reverses and drives off. A man walking on the opposite pavement shouts and raises his fist as the car disappears.

Isobel and Victor step into the road and see a black mound. Victor murmurs, but Isobel knows. She is already running. When she gets up close, she sees the cat lying still against the tarmac, its stomach split open to the light.

'Our cat,' Isobel cries. 'It's our cat.'

Victor holds her. He rubs her back as she sobs.

The other man stands in the road, his hands on his knees as he leans down to examine the dead animal. 'Your cat, is it?'

Victor shakes his head.

'I saw who did it,' says the man. 'Young kid. Teenager. Going way too fast. That generation don't care about anything but getting everywhere in a hurry.'

Victor soothes Isobel's cries. She can tell he doesn't understand her reaction. It's just a cat, she knows he's thinking. Why such violent feeling for something that wasn't even hers?

But she cannot calm down. How to explain that it's not really the cat she is crying for.

The Not Quite

Alice

1996

'Don't believe a word,' Alice's mother whispers loudly in her ear.

The guide breaks off for a moment and glances at Marjorie.

Alice has an urge to dive into the dinosaur skeleton that stretches across the room, creating a distraction so loud and outrageous that the group will forget her mother is there.

'Imagine thinking we came from monkeys,' says her mother. She huffs to underline her point.

'Mum –'

'Is everything okay?' says the guide, a woman about Marjorie's age. Her sleek, polished hair reflects the museum lights, and her hands are clasped in front. HILARY, says her badge. No nonsense.

'Fine,' says Marjorie. 'Just chatting with my daughter.'

'Please feel free to share,' says the woman.

Alice closes her eyes. She knows her mother is mentally rolling up her sleeves, ready to preach. Don't, thinks Alice. Please just accept that this woman has a PhD or a Masters, has probably spent a lifetime studying the very subject you know nothing about.

Marjorie clears her throat. 'Alice and I believe that all things were created. We do not accept the theory of evolution, because that's all it is. A *theory*.'

The woman smiles. 'Well, the scientific definition of that word is different from the everyday meaning. We call gravity a theory, or there's the theory of electromagnetism. But we don't question the validity of those.'

Alice's mother makes a noise at the back of her throat, but she doesn't continue. Her daughter stands beside her, staring at the mosaic floor, praying: *Please don't mention the ark.*

'But the ark,' says her mother. 'And the dinosaurs . . .' But the group has already started splintering off, Alice's classmates giving her looks as they drift towards the next exhibit.

'I knew this was a mistake,' says her mother. 'Filling your head with all this stuff and nonsense. Good thing I came. Now, where's the loo.'

Alice stares at the picture on the wall that illustrates the evolution of humans. Six figures in a gradual process from hunched over to fully erect, shedding their hair as they go. It is quite ridiculous, she thinks. How could they have changed so much? And why are apes still apes if they became humans? She remembers Bible talks over the years from the platform, the brother asking these questions of the audience, encouraging them to share in his incredulous laughter. It does seem absurd.

'What do *you* think?'

Alice glances at the guide who has left the group at the next exhibit. She instinctively looks round for her mother, then back at the wall. 'It's hard to believe,' she admits.

The woman doesn't reply but also studies the picture.

'All that change,' says Alice, rushing on, torn between not seeming stupid and her loyalty to her mother. 'How can something look so different from where it started? Change its essence, almost.'

Hilary gives a slow nod. 'But you've changed.'

'Sorry?' Alice stares at her, as if the woman has seen beneath her skin.

'You were a baby once. And, before that, a speck. Now you're twelve or thirteen or so, but one day you'll be a woman. It's a different process, of course, but if all that change can happen in eighteen years, what can millions of years do?'

'But, how can it . . .' Alice takes in the middle drawing, the figure that is not quite primate and not quite man. The *not quite*, like her. She lets the guide's words sink in and listens further.

Then comes the swish of her mother's boots, the flat soles being

287

dragged along the polished floor. Her mother arrives, breathless, and Alice knows she will have rushed when she saw the guide.

'They put it too far away,' she says. 'The loo. Stupid.' She frowns at the woman, who fills her in on their conversation. Marjorie replies that humans have only existed for six thousand years. Oh, says the guide, how then does that explain the *Homo sapiens* fossils we have that are hundreds of thousands years old? Marjorie clears her throat. I haven't got the answer to hand right now, she says, and Alice knows that means the Bible literature that tells her what to say.

'Come on, Alice,' says her mother, giving the woman a nod and pulling her daughter away.

Alice doesn't pay attention to the next exhibit, or the soundtrack in her ear. Her mind is on the guide's words as her mother walked towards them: 'You change every single day, but you don't see it. Little by little. Until one day, you're completely transformed.'

Time Travel

Zelda

She sees him first.

He comes through the front door of the building, a coffee cup in his hand, a scruffy bag over his shoulder. Zelda doesn't call out. She sits on the stone bench across the road and watches him push his blond hair back, just as he did on their date in the spring. This is an experiment. Sitting here on this warm autumn day. She wants to know what the fresh sight of him will do.

He sees her as he's crossing the road and spills his coffee down his jeans. His crumpled shirt and the triangle of skin at his collar — something about them gives her a thrill.

He is still rubbing at the marks when he reaches her. 'So you found my trail of crumbs.'

Zelda smiles. She has yet to meet a woman her age who can't piece together a life from social media, track a person down. 'You said you did something in science.' She nods at the brick building behind. 'Science.'

'Renewable energy,' he says, turning to look at the building, then back at her. 'Chemistry.'

'Right. Chemistry.' Zelda stares up at him. She knows he is seeing her worst angle, that the left side of her face looks better than the right, but she pushes through the feeling. 'What do you do in there all day anyway?'

A shiver down her spine as he takes her hand. His shirtsleeves are rolled up, revealing soft blond hairs that catch the light. 'Come with me,' he says. 'I'll show you.'

She had called him the previous week and he answered on the second ring. He was with his friends, he said, and when she offered to call back, he replied, Are you kidding? I've been waiting how-many-months for you to ring. You're not going anywhere. She laughed and they had talked, minutes slipping into hours, his friends vanishing without a word.

I don't want marriage and kids, she said almost immediately. I want to make that clear. Well, good, he said, because I've only met you twice so I don't want them either. She paused, then said, I mean it. And calmly, he said, That's fine.

She was surprised by how easy he was to talk to, how she felt completely herself as she spoke. With Matt, she had morphed into his desire, craved a traditional life she had never wanted for herself. But, with Will, she could make jokes and be funny, not reduce her voice to a whisper, not constantly check the mirror for how she was being seen.

But maybe that means we're friends, she thought. Not lovers. Not people who can fall in love. If I'm not trying to impress him at the start, when fireworks should be raging, where can it hope to go? She is a thirty-five-year-old child, her experience of love so narrow and fixed.

Two hours in, she told him of her past, something she had never told Matt. He listened. He didn't interrupt her. And, when she had finished, he asked if she wanted his honest opinion.

Go to the police, he said. Find a therapist. Ask for help.

The turbines stand tall and proud, their long limbs mirroring the flatness of the marsh. There are no hills on the horizon. A straight line divides land from sky, interrupted only by the occasional house. The blades turn and go nowhere. Zelda stares, transfixed by their rhythm.

'You make these?'

Will leans against the car door, his hands in his pockets. 'My job is figuring out how to store their energy.' When she frowns, he says, 'It's not all about the physical. The invisible parts need nurturing too.'

She looks at him.

They stand together. The air is silent except for the slicing of the blades through the wind, their sound a distant storm.

'So where did you go?'

Zelda turns up her collar against the breeze, shoving her hands in her pockets. 'Do you believe in time travel?'

'I'm a scientist,' he whispers, nudging her. 'Anything is possible.'

Her feelings change shape at his touch. 'Well, I gave it a go.'

'Forwards or backwards?'

'If they invented time travel, I doubt people would go forward.'

'Where would they go?'

'Their happiness. Or the time they felt closest to it.'

He pauses, looking down. 'Did you not find yours?'

'Would I be here with you if I did?'

He smiles at her. 'I'm glad you made it back alive. Some don't, I imagine.'

Yes, she thinks. This is the way to see it. She is alive. He did not break her this time. All those years spent trying to emulate the only real relationship she'd known. She would test every new man for the physical, making that the holy grail. Now she had returned to the mouth of the beast and conquered. She had seen it was not as she remembered.

The wind picks up, and Zelda hugs her arms to her chest. 'You ever been in love?'

'I'm twenty-four, not twelve.'

Zelda takes a side step towards him until their arms touch. 'I so wanted it to be true,' she says.

'If this is the guy from Pizza Hut, then . . .' Will stops.

'Were we that ridiculous?'

He stares at her, a slight frown. 'You're bold, Zelda. You should be with someone who loves that.'

She takes his hand and examines his fingers, then his face. This man was just a boy when all her things happened. The tears and the hopes and the never agains. But there is an oldness to his ways. She has ten years on him, but not in the parts that matter.

'I should be honest with you. That time, those people, that

world . . .' She shakes her head. 'It's not done with me yet. I'm pushing it away, but it keeps coming back.'

'See, that's where you're going wrong. You have to make room for it. Give it space to wear itself out. It will fade without you even realizing.'

Zelda remembers Matt's reaction to Will. I should have laid him out, he said with narrowed eyes. She had laughed, partly at his over-reaction, but also delighted by his jealousy. Now Will is looking, and she realizes she is laughing again. 'I never knew calm, rational thinking could be so sexy.'

Will turns her towards him, wrapping himself between her and the wind. As their noses touch, her muscles start to soften. His mouth is familiar. There is a warmth here, in the space between their breath and limbs. Now she allows the idea of Matt to dance through her for a moment. And then here is Will, cutting in.

She lets him.

Chalk

Jen

Jen folds the clothes into piles, righting the mess of the first day of the sale. Her movements are slow. It is the eighth time she has tidied the shirts that morning. They will be untidy again before the day is out.

A spark of light in the corner catches her eye, and she looks up at the CCTV camera that points straight at her, watching.

'Most people see themselves as the lead player in the story of their life.'

It is the month before Jen leaves. They are lying in the long grass behind the tin house, listening to the bees and lounging in heat. Often when they talked, Zelda would jump from the sofa or table and pull Jen towards the door to the garden. Words sound better in colour, she said.

'I don't see myself that way,' Jen continues. She stares at a cloud in the sky. 'Before I buy a dress, I imagine myself walking around a kitchen in the dress. Or leaning over the table as the kids do their homework. But I'm never actually there in the head of that Jen. I stand further back, where a camera would be, watching the action, watching another version of myself. A calm, pacified Jen who knows she's being watched. *Good* Jen.'

Zelda doesn't reply. She is looking up at the sky, her hands behind her head. The air is drunk with summer, with lavender and the sweetness of Portuguese laurel.

'It's not just buying dresses,' says Jen. 'I do this with every decision. I wonder what that Jen would do. I watch her moving about a room, this person who's not really me.'

Zelda pulls at the grass. 'Women are never allowed to just be.'

'It's more than that, though.' Jen stares at the sky. 'I'm never the star, even in my own story.'

There is a long silence, during which Zelda reaches out to touch Jen, who flinches. She throws a side-glance at Zelda's hand as it strokes her skin, comforting her. But Zelda's touch is tonic and poison. She pulls back.

'Jen,' says Zelda, softly. 'Don't you want to be who you are? Not some idealized version. *You.*'

Jen looks at her. 'You think it's that easy?'

'I don't see how loving anyone can be so dreadful.'

'Like Eve eating the apple? How she traded eternity for a taste.' She shakes her head. 'Zelda, I'd feel nothing but guilt. It's not worth it.'

'But you're looking for something to love.' Zelda's tone is urgent. 'I know you, Jen. How you need that. Fuck, don't we all?'

Jen looks at her friend, this woman who knows her better than anyone. She wishes she could keep her close.

She says, 'The version of myself I see right now is one whose arms are empty when they should be full.'

Her mind floods with the image of the delivery room, their taking Jacob away, how her eyes detached from her body and went up to the ceiling. The clarity of the memory is crystal. She willed herself over to him. For the first time in her life, she was the one looking out, listening to her own voice. She came alive and almost died in the same moment.

Jen closes her eyes. 'There is only one person I am allowed to love. I must go to him.'

This time, Zelda ignores her. She takes Jen's hand and parcels it with her own. This time, her grip is strong. This time, Jen doesn't pull away.

The bell announces the postman's arrival. The young girls on the checkout nudge each other. They are all in love with him, and constantly moan that Jen steals his attention. It is true that he always comes to her with the parcels, brushes her fingers as she takes them, spends longer than he should making talk.

294

'All right?' he says, giving her an up-and-down glance. He goes to hand her a package, but Jen shakes her head and nods at the checkout.

His grin loses its edge, and he swaggers over to where they are pushing each other aside.

Jen continues to fold. She looks at him again. It is true that he is exceptionally good-looking, the kind of face that made Zelda elbow her in the street. She can appreciate his beauty, acknowledge it, even. Could she . . . Jen tries to imagine his hands on her skin. His mouth on hers. She tries swapping his face for those of other men who are considered attractive. It is not even excitement she is hoping for, but the settling of her suddenly queasy stomach.

She shuts her eyes and thinks of how she won't feel like this in Paradise. One day she will awake and all will be made new. The harder road is the right one. This is her test, and Jacob her reward.

Jen looks at the clock as she picks up a shirt. Three hours to go. Every shift, she is begging the seconds to pass, wishing minutes into hours. Another day done, she thinks when she climbs under the covers each night. Another day waiting for colour.

A tally scored in chalk on the prison walls inside her.

Bloom

Isobel

Isobel leaves the little white house with green shutters each morning to walk the paved path along the cliff above the sea. There are quicker ways to the café, but she enjoys the scenic route. The heat that radiates from the stones, the tile-chipped walls of pink, blue, green and gold, the cacti and palms deliberately planted to soften the black reality of volcanic rock.

This is her twelfth morning here. She likes to nod to the women sitting outside their front doors on white plastic chairs. Their faces are ruddy and weathered, their sundresses faded. The open doors to their home are obscured by chain curtains or strips of plastic that ripple in the breeze. The women return her nod. Her sandals seem to amuse them. Isobel gives a polite smile and imagines herself living here, stopping and conversing with the women in their native tongue, the words flowing from her mouth as she makes passionate declarations on the price of fish or the never-ending stream of tourists. Her teacher at school used to say she had an ear for languages. Where might she be now if she had listened?

The houses along this part of the seafront are low and square with crumbling white walls. Electrical and telephone wires are strung between buildings, cutting through the view. Further along, where the walls are pink and gold and terracotta, is where the tourists pose. But her money can stretch only further along the path to where the vibe is more *bombed-out Beirut*. This is how Isobel describes it. Or how she would if there were anyone to tell.

She doesn't want beautiful, she tells herself. Imagine Lake Como or Provence. All those vistas and lushness and a hotel room for one. No.

The café's name is Bloom. It is in the style of an eighties boudoir, with marble floors, pink wallpaper and lime-green upholstery. Accents of brass and mirrored panels give the illusion of depth. It is brash, bold and, to Isobel, terrifyingly exciting. It is not her usual sort of place. But then who wants to be expected, she thinks as she enters the café, and goes up to the bar as usual to order her usual drink.

When she takes a seat, her eyes fall on the *Bloom* at the top of the menu, and she conjures up a vision of the disfellowshipped girl in her dazzling embroidered dress.

'Here's your latte,' says the waitress, 'as usual.'

She has imaginary conversations with this waitress, who looks about sixteen. Isobel places her accent as Yorkshire, but in these fantasies the girl speaks with a native Spanish tongue. Her name is not Paige but Esmeralda. She comments on Isobel's preference for the café, and marvels at her ability to eat pastries while maintaining a trim physique. Isobel takes it all in her stride.

'Oh, Esmeralda,' she says in reply, 'I came here once years ago. My son Patrick was a few years younger than you. We stayed in the hotel on the hill, the one that looks like a cruise ship. I would sit on our balcony – we had a two-bedroom suite – and watch the sunset. And in the distance, beyond the pools and the sunbathers, there was a pink neon sign that flickered. It said *Bloom*. That's right, this very café! I would sit on that balcony and wonder what went on behind these walls. Yes, a son. I have a son. Would you like to see a picture?'

She forgets about Cassandra. How, to Isobel, she was still just a girl before that week in Tenerife. Until one morning, as they sat on the loungers, Isobel watched a middle-aged man put down his book and track her fifteen-year-old daughter as she got up and slipped into the pool. When Cassandra came up to the surface and floated on her back, the man watched her still. And when she climbed out, saltwater dripping from her hair. He watched her still.

Isobel looked with new eyes. The flicker of recognition in her daughter as she noticed the man. Isobel was sure she parted her legs even further.

Gouge out your eyes, she silently commanded the man, and threw a towel at her daughter.

She is walking uphill towards the hotel when a message arrives from Victor.

So how is it? When are you home? It's not the same here without you. x

She slips the phone back into her bag.

It all started when she found the wind chime.

Patrick brought over the final bits and pieces the day before the house sold. When he left, Isobel began opening boxes, then closing them again. Years had passed since she'd last seen their contents, and she had survived just fine. She had no use for clutter.

She began to stack them in a neat pile by the door when a familiar sound from one of the boxes stopped her. Slowly, Isobel opened the lid and lifted out a small wind chime – pearlescent discs of Capiz shells that tinkled. She held it up towards the light.

'That's not very *you*,' Steven had said, when she picked it out in the gift shop in Tenerife. 'The noise will drive you mad.'

Isobel waited for him to pay. You think you know me, she didn't say. 'It's nice to buy a memento. And we may never come back.'

In the end, it was Steven that made her take it down. The sound drove him insane, he said. Like pigeons squawking.

She took a hook from the drawer and screwed it into the kitchen ceiling. All the windows were opened, the breeze invited in. She stood against the kitchen counter with her arms folded and waited for the sound. Come on, pigeons, she said. Make a racket.

The cat died two days later.

The house sold three days after that.

She'd just got in from work when the solicitor rang to say her share of the proceeds from the sale had gone into her account. Isobel opened the post as she listened. She slid her nail under the seal of the first envelope as the solicitor talked.

She dropped the letter. There it was in black and white, with no grey areas.

Divorced.

She flew to Tenerife the following week.

The gate to the resort is locked, but, from where she stands, Isobel has a good view of the balconies. Their glass balustrades reflect the light, and dotted behind them are bikinied bodies or wet costumes draped over a chair. Isobel leans against the hot, volcanic-rock boundary wall and feels sunshine burn her calves.

Sixteen years ago she woke early every morning but not for the sunrise. She came for the women and their mops. As the lifeguard removed the parasol covers and folded them neatly away, the ladies went to work. In silence they glided around the pool, mopping away the footprints of the previous day. Isobel took pleasure in watching. *Good job*, she wanted to call, and, sometimes, *You missed a bit*.

Down by the pool, Steven watched every woman from behind his sunglasses. A Japanese couple appeared a few days in and took the loungers beside them. She knew Steven noticed, because she once overheard him telling a group of friends how much he loved Asian women. It was at one of their parties, when the husbands gathered around the bar and barbecue as the wives took root in the kitchen. A few beers in, Steven waved his pitchfork and declared his thing for Japanese girls, or Chinese, for that matter. He wasn't picky. He took them however they came. And then the men had laughed.

Steven's eyes moved each time the woman walked by their loungers. There was a slight shift of his head. Isobel was sitting upright, a book against her knees. She noted every flicker. Her eyes had scanned down Steven's body, stopping to rest on the pool of sweat in his belly button.

Isobel goes into the village shop on the way back down. She passes the inflatables and tourist tat, and chooses a few items for dinner from the food aisle along the back. Food here is so expensive, she thinks, as she picks up a bag of dried pasta. Flies buzz around the open fruit. She selects a tray of tomatoes wrapped in plastic.

The woman at the checkout is speaking urgently with someone buying cigarettes. Isobel stops and listens as the words bleed together. The gaps between them are lost to her. I came here looking for life, she thinks, but the world is going on and I cannot understand it. She empties the basket on to the checkout and pays as fast as she can.

That evening she watches the sunset on the sea from her rickety balcony. The sounds of music and laughter float through the air from the tourist areas. Isobel eats her pasta. She drinks a bottle of wine.

So far, she has ignored all messages. There's been the occasional logging on to social media, just to prove she's still alive to anyone who cares to check. But, otherwise, she has left well alone. You can do this, Isobel, she tells herself. Call your own shots.

Steven never sat with her for sunsets. Bloody mosquitoes, he'd go, slapping his arm before going inside. How alone she was even back then, with a gold ring on her finger.

The sun dips down and sets the sky on fire. Not even the ocean can put it out.

Isobel sits there, the breeze cooling her skin, her mind on the time she rode a motorbike and fixed her arms around Victor's waist.

Some people are with you even when they're not.

Kintsugi

Isobel

Isobel is walking back from the café the next morning when she looks up and sees Victor waiting outside her front door.

She drops her bag.

'But how did you know to come?' she says, as he reaches her. 'And where I was?'

His hands are in his pockets, and his smile kick-starts a rush inside of her.

'Oh . . .' he says. 'We're in sync, you and I.'

Isobel blinks. 'We are?'

'That, and the booking confirmation you left up on my computer. It was almost like you wanted to be found.'

He puts his arms around her waist, and Isobel kisses him. She takes his hand, leading him to her little rented house, where he follows her inside and sucks the loneliness clean from her skin.

Later, they walk along to the tourist area for an alfresco lunch. Isobel has walked past these tables often, always packed with couples and families, and she has never felt brave enough to pull out only one chair.

They drink sangria with their elbows on the table and their faces leaning in. The waiter makes a joke about turning on the hose, and they laugh before going back to each other.

'I've not seen you with your hair up before,' says Victor.

Isobel blushes as she remembers scraping it into a bun. She forgot to check a mirror. 'Oh, sorry, it must look awful.'

'You look wonderful. And stop saying sorry.'

'But my neck?' She touches the edges of her face. Her skin is glowing.

'What about it?'

She finishes her sangria, and, after lunch, they walk around the town. Isobel recognizes the shop where she bought the wind chime, and she stops by the window, Victor's hand in hers. There are the usual shell decorations and other seaside gifts, but her attention is caught by a trio of ceramic vases in the centre. Black, pot-bellied, with rivers of silver and gold through the matt clay. A card sits propped up in front. *Kintsugi*, it says in both English and Spanish. *A Japanese way of fixing. Broken things are mended with metallic glue so the breaks are visible. Lost pieces are replaced with patches of gold or silver, giving a beauty to their absence.*

'Where are you going?' says Victor, as she lets go of his hand and steps into the shop.

'A memento,' she calls over her shoulder. 'I may never come back here.' She chooses the pot in the middle, the one with the most breaks.

She is still glowing when they arrive back at the house.

'I bet you've spent hours in that water,' says Victor, nodding at the sea as she unlocks the door.

She looks at the beach, and her smile falters. 'I haven't been in once.'

He frowns.

Who would I go with, she wants to ask. Who would watch my things while I swam? But she doesn't. She likes him thinking she is braver than she is.

'Take me?' he says. 'It looks quiet.' He points to some hidden steps that lead down to a patch of flat, brown rock.

When they have changed, they walk down to the sea. There is just water and rock and coastline, covered in brown brush. Everyone else has chosen the beach with raffia parasols and cocktails that never run dry. Here, the rock is like pumice stone. Its pores have soaked up the heat. Isobel looks around at the barrenness of this place and decides it suits her just fine.

'I thought maybe we'd get married,' says Victor, looking out to sea. He stands with his hands on his hips and his tone is careless, as if he's made a comment about how the rain's coming in. 'You changed your mind on things, so maybe I should too. See what you're doing to me?'

'Victor –'

'Think about it.' He dives in.

They swim in the sea together. He holds her hands as they tread water, and she doesn't give the slightest thought to her neck.

After a while, they get out and sit on the warm rocks. Isobel watches the water drip from Victor's beard and ponytail. His shoulders are sloping, and his waist is thicker than she's used to, and she doesn't want to change a thing. It doesn't even occur to her to make him different from the man he is.

'I like that you're the only one who knows where I am,' she says, hugging her knees.

'You didn't tell Patrick?'

She shakes her head. 'I thought he might try to talk me out of it. But you didn't.'

He doesn't reply, and Isobel sits on her hands to stop herself from asking: Why didn't you stop me? Why didn't you ask me to stay?

His answer is low, quiet. 'You've had quite enough people telling you how to live.'

Isobel puts her hands flat on the stones. Her black one-piece glistens against her skin.

'I do like it, you know,' she says. 'Being told what to do.'

'Because it's what you're used to.'

The hairs on his arm brush against her own, and she shivers. 'But then I'm not used to *you*,' she says. 'And, yet, here I am.'

They listen to the waves on the rocks as the tide begins turning. The breeze picks up, whistling through and cooling her skin. She feels Victor look at her.

'I'm not sure you've been loved enough,' he says. 'By anyone.'

Isobel turns away, out to sea, remembering the bare walls at home. 'Cassandra would pinch me when she was small,' she starts. 'Pinch me hard. She'd grip and set her teeth, and I'd smack her hand with a *no*. I keep thinking of that, wondering if it was her way of

303

showing love. The emotion was too big for her. She confused the intensity with pain. And I kept telling her no, Victor. I kept pushing her away.'

She is silently crying now.

'You'll get there,' he says, stroking her back.

'And then there's you.' She half turns to him. 'I thought you were a bit of fun. Your opinion didn't matter. Until, suddenly, all I cared about was being seen by you. A worldly man. By the time I put my guard up, you'd already got in.'

His hand moves up to her neck. 'I love you too, old girl.'

She had loved the structures of her life, the cachet of what Steven brought her: the marble kitchen island and a wall of bi-fold doors, the guests' faces when they clocked the wine vintage served at dinner, the knowledge that every question could be answered, that life's every twist and turn would eventually lead to the future she knew was coming. It wasn't the love she had craved, exactly, but the certainty. The rightness of living within walls that she had always expected to house her. It was not Steven she had grieved, but the doors he had opened. The social standing. The appearance of good conduct. And it had all gone to pieces. She had climbed the ladder, then slipped down a snake. Now she was left with the oddity of being truly seen by a man who brought her no currency in the world she had thought was true.

'Nothing's as it should be.' Isobel presses Victor's hand to her cheek. 'And yet it's never felt so right.'

I Don't Make the Decisions

Jen

She goes into the fair in search of warmth. A cup of tea, a hot chocolate, anything to bring colour back to her cheeks.

It has been a long ministry morning, a cold day where the chill
gets into the bone, and hardly a door had opened. She is used to the
dash of a curious face at the window, then the interminable minutes she must allow to pass before moving on. I know you're home,
she thinks, as she goes toward the gate. I know and you know that
I know, but we'll just keep pretending that neither one of us exists.

Houses beam with Christmas. Today she worked the more
expensive streets, so outside decorations were confined to a wreath
or a tasteful string of lights around a pot. But she saw the glow of
fairy lights through stained-glass doors, the top halves of trees in
bay windows, kids wearing red-and-white hats as families ready
their houses for joy.

The one person she found in gave her a strange look when he saw
the magazine on offer. *Christmas – Delightful or Dangerous?* She got
through her presentation, but felt no surprise when he politely
refused. I'm sorry if it seems disrespectful, she thought, as she
slipped it back into her bag. I don't make the decisions.

She hadn't taken her car that morning, the forecast being clear
and the street walkable. Jen told herself she could do with the exercise, not to mention conserving the petrol, but now she pulls out
her purse to buy a drink to warm her through.

It's a maker's fair, under the old corrugated roof of the market
near the town centre. A hundred or so stalls all huddle in rows, selling homemade soaps and macramé and other gift-worthy wares.
She pays for her hot chocolate and wanders down the aisles, nothing
on her but a ten-pound note.

She is nearing the final row when her thoughts turn to the evening, when she is due at her parents' for dinner and, no doubt, silence for dessert. Her dad has hardly looked at her since her reinstatement. Perhaps he can see the foreign blood swirling round my body, she thinks, and then remembers how he always wanted a son.

She shakes her shoulders a little. Chase the thought away.

One of the final stalls catches her attention. A table crammed with ceramics, spread out on a linen tablecloth. Bowls, cups, plates, all simply made, in plain and quiet colours. A woman of about her age sits behind, reading.

Jen smiles at the woman, who looks up briefly before turning back to the page.

The pieces are thin in form, expertly made. Not loud in shape or colour, they are the kind that lets the food or drink be the star. Modest, humble. Jen picks up a cup and sees herself at a country table, setting two places for dinner, a roaring fire in the inglenook, Jacob at the window and pointing at clouds.

She examines the cup. It is tactile, with a pattern of ridges around its rim, and a solitary faint drip of dried glaze running down one side. Something about its pure and honest form makes her think of Zelda.

'Your pieces are beautiful,' she says, almost without thought.

The woman looks up and smiles. 'The one you're holding is my favourite.'

Jen looks at the sticker on the base to find it is more than double what she has in her purse. 'Oh,' she says, with regret. 'I can see why. You'd have the perfect cup of tea in that.' She sets it back down on the table and notices the flicker of disappointment on the woman's face.

She has probably not sold anything all day, thinks Jen. Sitting here, freezing under this flimsy metal roof, the walls open to the elements, hoping someone will be drawn to a bowl or cup.

Jen immediately looks for something that would fit her budget. She picks up a tiny black teaspoon with a handle reminiscent of hammered metal, and turns it over. It is beautiful and would leave her with change. The cup is out of her reach but perhaps a spoon to stir in the sugar.

She hands it over with the ten-pound note, and feels a lick of power and goodness at the sight of the woman's gratitude.

See, this is why it would never have worked, Jen thinks, as she walks away. Creating things. Being so dependent on someone liking what she'd made. What did her mother say all those years ago? *You can't make a living out of it. Why would anyone want to pay more for a cup from you than from a supermarket?* She was right. There is something so desperate about craving attention from strangers, their money and good opinion the measuring stick for the maker's validation. Yes, Jen thinks. It is desperate, disgusting, and here is where her mind makes more of it than necessary. Her mother was right, the elder was right. Spending time on worldly pursuits is pointless when the end of the world is near. Better to preach, better to teach, better to bring people through.

Yes!

Jen turns back, her hand reaching into her bag as she approaches the woman. 'I just want to leave you this,' she says, placing a leaflet on the table. *Life without End – When?* She steps away before the woman can refuse.

She has come too far to turn back. She has lost too much. Instead, Jen allows her eyes to see things as she wants to, so that she can be convinced that she was right.

Calico

Zelda and Isobel

Zelda's fingers are deep in the earth as she pulls out the last of the weeds. She has spent almost a week out here, avoiding the silence of her house, as she tries to make the outside breathe again. She neglected it too much this summer. Her mind had been elsewhere.

Even on chillier days, when she works a needle and thread, she curls up outside on the porch swing and listens to birds, sewing summer on to silk as the winter creeps in.

It's been weeks since that final morning with Jen, but time has changed pace. As a child, she would experience moments when life slowed down or sped up, when people's mouths moved differently from the speed of their voices. It was explained as growing pains, or her imagination. What is it now, then? Every minute takes an hour. Every hour takes a day.

And yet her hands have been busy. She has made dresses and photographs, taking time to experiment and see where it takes her. She has set up a makeshift darkroom over the bath and lost herself in the alchemy, the smell of the fixer, the hours of solitude. Zelda is startled by how the ideas rush out. She had felt so alive all summer, but creation escaped her. How euphoric it had been to bathe in distraction, numbing her fingers and toes. But a buzz always fades. A plaster must eventually peel off and expose the wound to light.

Zelda stands up straight, lifting her chin to the sun. Long shadows fall around her. The smell of the earth is on her hands.

She hears a footstep and turns to see a ghost. The woman from the surgery. The elder's wife.

'Is the pain all better?' she says, before looking away. 'This is very unprofessional, but I took your address from the surgery. The details you left.'

Zelda puts a hand to her cheek, the other pressed against her heart. 'Why? Why are you here?'

She looks down at a scrap of paper. 'I don't know if you remember me. It's been years. I'm Isobel F—'

'I remember.'

Isobel smiles, relieved, then glances up at the house. 'You live in a shed?'

'What do you want?'

'That dress you wore. It was . . . something else. I need a dress, you see, for a special occasion, and thought about having it made. Rather than off-the-rack.'

Zelda shakes her head. 'I only make for myself.'

'I can pay, if it's a matter of money?'

She tries to steady her heart. 'It's not.'

'I just . . . when I saw your dress, it made me feel a certain way. The pattern of the roses as they wilt. It was as if you were wearing your pain outside of yourself. That probably sounds ridiculous.' She gives a nervous laugh.

Zelda frowns, confused by the clash of the reality of this woman with the memory of her.

'I'm getting married. And I need a dress.'

'Married?' Zelda stares.

Isobel smiles, glad to be surprising 'Yes. I'm divorced. And disfellowshipped. Things are quite different.'

Zelda drops the clumpy weed she is holding. She pushes open the front door, then stands back to observe Isobel take in the room. She sees her frown at the sight of dead flowers, how she goes to speak but stops herself.

Consumed with a sudden raw energy, Zelda gathers pencils and paper, then gestures to Isobel to sit down at the table. She does so, perching on the edge of a stool as if ready to bolt.

'Maybe we can talk about what you have in mind,' says Zelda. 'That doesn't mean I'll do it. But we can talk.'

They sit and start a conversation. Zelda takes the lead. Her pencil dances across the paper as she listens to Isobel, who speaks words like *freedom*, *beauty*, *love*. Zelda makes suggestions. Isobel clasps her hands.

'Does this mean you'll do it?'

'I haven't decided yet,' says Zelda, pressing the pencil into the page.

'Name your price.'

'It's not about money.'

Isobel looks around at the old, tatty furniture. 'Then what is it?'

Zelda stares at the drawing. She does need a project, and maybe there is something in this. A way for her to set all that down, use her talent to put it to bed. 'Have you got time now?' she says. 'I have some calico. I can start pinning together a shape.'

Isobel claps her hands.

Zelda sets down a low stool in the centre of the room. She goes to the sink and pours two glasses of water, then downs three cuploads herself. When she looks back, Isobel is on the stool, waiting.

'I need to take your measurements.'

'Yes.'

'So . . . you should be undressed? To your underwear.'

'Oh.'

Zelda looks away as Isobel steps down and begins removing her clothes. There's the sound of fabric being folded, and Isobel clearing her throat, then Zelda runs her tape measure between her fingers and gets to work. She measures Isobel, jotting down the numbers in a notebook. The room is quiet apart from the birds and trees outside, and the light whistle of wind through the roof. Life goes on around them. When she's done, she holds up the calico. 'Shall I start?'

Isobel nods, relieved to hide her skin. She stands still as Zelda drapes and pins, occasionally stepping back for a better look. Sometimes Zelda explains her intention, but mainly they are silent.

'Do you remember me?' she asks Isobel. She stands behind her, pulling the fabric taut. 'All those years ago.'

Isobel nods.

'What did you think of me?' Her voice is quiet.

'Oh . . . I didn't really know you.'

'But you must have had an opinion. Everyone had an opinion.'

'Perhaps a little wild,' says Isobel. 'But, as I said, we didn't really mix.'

'No, I was wild. Too wild for all that. Even I knew that.'

'What did you think of me?'

'Prude. Frigid. Cow.'

Isobel looks at her, surprised, and they both burst into laughter.

'I'm sorry,' says Zelda. 'You did ask.'

'There is a way you're meant to be in that world, isn't there?' says Isobel, after a moment. 'What to do when you don't fit in?'

Zelda doesn't reply, but her fingers soften. 'What happened to your husband?'

'Let's just say I wasn't young enough.'

Zelda stares at her. 'What?'

'He left me for an eighteen-year-old. And now she's having his baby.'

Zelda drops to her knees and picks up the hem. She stares at it, pulling the calico through her fingers. 'I've often wondered what happened to my story,' she says, after a while. 'Whether it ever got passed around over coffee, or if it's still sitting there in that filing cabinet at the back of that hall.'

Isobel frowns. 'Story?'

Zelda looks up. 'So you never knew?'

'What? What did I not know?'

Then Zelda tells Isobel. The memories are brought to light from where they live in darkness. Here is someone she never thought she would tell. And, at the end, she says, 'It was Steven Forge. The elder. Your Steven.'

The words hang in the room.

Isobel puts a hand to her mouth as life slows down, then she is sick down the front of the calico.

Truth

Zelda and Isobel

Zelda begins scrubbing the fabric, but soon drops the brush. There's no point. She has plenty of calico. She'll just start again. She leaves the mound in the bath and goes out to the main room, where Isobel sits in a heap on the floor, right where she left her.

'I'm sorry,' says Isobel. Her voice is distant, no longer here. 'Is it ruined?'

Zelda unrolls more calico. 'The shape wasn't right, anyway. We'll try something different. Better.'

'It's just . . . Perhaps I should apologize.'

Zelda looks up.

'I was one flesh with him, after all.'

'You were married to a stranger.'

'Thirty-three years. Was there no truth to any of it?' Isobel shakes her head. 'Of course you went wild.'

Zelda remembers the dread at each meeting, how she would murder the elders with her eyes. You all protect Him, she would think. You speak of God being a refuge, when I feel anything but safe. 'I died each time I saw Him in a suit and tie.'

Isobel sees the years of Steven watching girls, his hours on the ministry, the backslapping and spending their money – *her* money. The generosity was less about love and more about currying favour. She rewrites the context of all her memories.

'Did you not go to the police?'

Zelda looks at her. 'You know how this works.'

' "Don't bring reproach on His name," ' Isobel recites in a low voice.

'My mum would never go against the elders.'

'Is that her house out there?'

Zelda nods, picking at a loose thread.

'But how dare they? He could have done this to other girls. He could have . . .' Her hand flies to her mouth. She grips the table. 'No, this can't be true.'

'It *is* true.'

Isobel looks at Zelda, but she is in a different time and place. 'I don't understand. Everything is done by God's holy spirit. He wouldn't allow this to be hidden. If He is guiding their decisions, if God is there, this cannot happen. This covering up of truth.'

'*If.*'

Their eyes meet.

'Go to the police,' says Isobel, and her tone is brisk. She knows what needs to be done.

'And if they do nothing? I don't think I could stand it again.'

'We'll make them.'

Zelda closes her eyes and nods. She feels Isobel's hand squeeze her own.

After a while, they start again. Zelda pins fresh calico to Isobel, this time draping something looser and more free. When she comes round to the front, Isobel is staring upwards at the circular window, where sunshine floods in.

'I went to the Tate once on a school trip,' Isobel says, not turning away from the light. 'I got lost from the group and spent a while searching, but in the end I gave up and looked at the pictures. There was one in particular. A small painting of an empty room with a window, bureau, some chairs. There were some books scattered around, but not a single person. Nothing of interest. Just a plain, bare room. And I remember thinking, What a strange thing to paint. How odd. Then I read the name underneath. *The Room in which Shakespeare was Born.*'

Isobel turns to Zelda. 'I looked at the painting again. It was completely different.'

Exile

Zelda

As soon as Isobel leaves, Zelda takes the muddy path towards the road. She moves without conscious thought. Something is guiding her there.

The painted wood on the front door is peeling and porous, its once brilliant red now faded. Zelda knocks three times and waits.

When the door opens, Zelda almost cries out. Her mother must be in her early seventies, but she looks much older. She has shrunk, her head now hardly past her daughter's shoulders and the bones almost visible beneath the papery flesh. Her hair is thatched with neglect. When she sees Zelda, her first instinct is to step back.

'No,' she says. 'No, no, no. You cannot be here.'

'Mum.' Zelda grips the door frame for support.

Her mother walks away, but leaves the door wide open.

Zelda steps over the threshold and closes it. She stands in the hallway and inhales the air, dense with dust and old breath. Her mother rarely opens the windows, afraid of what may come in. The same scenic pictures hang on the walls, the same ornaments on the shelves that moved from her grandparents' house when they died to stand undusted in this one.

Their only contact has been notes through the door, and only for essentials. A bill that needed splitting, a letter addressed to the other. They have shared a country but built a wall.

Her mother sits in the armchair in the corner of the living room, her arms folded across her chest.

'What is it, then?' says Marjorie. 'Has something happened? Are you ill?'

'No, I'm not ill.'

Her mother breathes out.

Zelda looks around. The living room still lives in damp darkness. All the lamps are off, despite the setting sun, and a smudge of daylight filters in through net curtains. Everything is as she remembers, except the photographs are gone. Their faces taken down.

'Where are Dad's pictures? The one of him getting his award?'

The day is bold in Zelda's memory. The afternoon tea at the Ritz, standing to applaud her father, her embarrassed mother in a hat. For years afterwards, when Zelda asked to take it out of the box, her mother would tell her to be careful with her *when-your-father-won-his-award* hat. It was precious.

'Never you mind,' says Marjorie.

'Are we at least in a drawer? Or did we get thrown out on bin day?' No reply.

'How can you bear it in here?'

Her mother looks at her. 'What choice do I have?'

Zelda stares at her father's armchair. It is still slightly turned towards the television, next to her mother's own seat, as if he is coming in at any moment to watch the news and weather, or their favourite murder mystery.

'You should state your reason for coming,' says Marjorie, her eyes fixed on the carpet.

Zelda can hardly breathe. 'I'm going to the police, Mum.'

Her mother sighs. 'Are you really still on that?'

'How was I supposed to forget?'

'Oh, Alice,' she says, looking at her daughter. 'Throw your burden on God and He will sustain you. People go through things all the time. Why are you so special?'

Her mother's words from teenage years reverberate through her brain in bold, underlined italics: *Cling to the truth. Move on. You're dwelling on the past because you're forgetting the future.*

'Where's Dad?' Zelda starts rooting through drawers. 'What have you done with us both?'

Her mother turns away and draws her cardigan tight. 'I am waiting for the new world.'

'In this coffin of a house.'

Marjorie's voice is sharp. 'I warned you not to tell your father, that it would *break* him, and look what happened.' She stumbles on the words, on her loneliness.

Zelda is slamming drawers. She has a furious urge to see her father, not his flesh in some abstract future, but now in a photograph. She remembers journeys home at night, when she would pretend to fall asleep in the quiet backseat just so he would pick her up and carry her to bed. Dad, it was always Dad. Never her mother. She wasn't strong enough, she said.

'You still think it's my fault,' says Zelda. 'All of it.'

Her mother flinches. 'I tried telling you. Your clothes, the way you carried on . . . What did you expect? Dress like a slut and people will think you are one.'

Zelda leans against the dresser and breathes out, remembering how she'd hoped baptism would bring them closer. She had always taken her dad's side, never her mum's, and no sibling to pick up the slack. Baptism had seemed an easy bone to throw, allying with her mum in something that – to Alice – didn't really matter. She had been thirteen years old, with no idea of the consequences. Was this how it was always to be? Splitting apart to be all things to all people? For everyone who wanted a piece? Never completely herself.

'I was a kid, Mum,' she says.

'I brought you up to know better.'

'You brought me up to be meek and submissive,' Zelda almost shouts. 'You taught me not to make a fuss, that men were meant to lead, that I was to give in to *them*.'

'Not like that. You should still have said no.'

Zelda turns to her. 'When did you teach me how?'

She purses her lips. 'Don't try to rewrite your history simply because you don't like how life turned out.'

'You put me in a world that took away my voice. Look what happened when I told the truth. What good would *no* have done?'

Marjorie huffs. 'They couldn't do anything because there weren't two witnesses. You know that.'

'When are there ever two witnesses to *that*?'

'You can't change scripture.'

'No, I guess obeying a two-thousand-year-old book when it goes against humanity is much more sensible.'

Marjorie sucks air through her teeth. 'Alice, you will always think whatever you want. It's always been your way.'

Zelda closes her eyes, feels the glass door of the dresser against her forehead. She knows her mother sees her as *other*. Every word Zelda speaks is scrutinized for danger and viewed with suspicion, poison from a worldly person controlled by the Devil. She can no longer grasp her mother's love, but just because a thing is hidden doesn't mean it isn't there.

'Mum,' she says, kneeling down at her mother's feet. 'I was expected to sit there, week after week, watching him get up and have his voice be heard. And when I couldn't take it any more – the lies, the hypocrisy, his smiles – they threw me out. They called me *weak*. They took everyone from me. Even you.'

Marjorie gets up and leaves the room.

Zelda leans forward, almost foetal now, her body struggling for breath. She takes a moment, then goes into the kitchen where her mother is putting away utensils.

'Mum, look at me.'

A cupboard door bangs.

'Look at me, Mum.'

Zelda starts to cry. She leans against the door frame, her face resting against the pen marks and etchings that show how she grew over the years. Her fingers touch the tallest line. *Dad.* She is taller than him now.

'I'm showing myself to you,' she says, her cheeks hot. 'I'm not hiding or putting on a disguise. This is me. And you don't want her.'

Marjorie drops a pan. She leans against the sink, looking out of the window. 'That's not true, Alice.'

'What, then?'

'I've had trials of my own.'

Zelda sits down at the kitchen table, taking the place she did as a child. She lets the silence build.

'All right.' She wipes her hands on a towel, keeping her back to Zelda. 'My father . . . he would come home, drunk with his fists. When my mother went to the elders and asked what to do, they told her to stay, because only adultery can end marriage. You're surprised at that? Well, she was to endure it, along with us kids, because, perhaps by her own peaceable action, he would be moved to change. And he did. He came into the truth, and so my mother saved his life.'

Zelda puts her head in her hands.

'I'd watch him with her, with us, and think why is this happening? Why isn't God stopping this? But it all worked out. She kept her faith and he found his. That would never have happened if my mother had gone against the elders.' Marjorie nods with certainty. 'God knew what would happen.'

'That's the saddest thing I've ever heard.'

Her mother lifts her chin. 'It's marvellous.'

Zelda stares at the ceiling, the corners drowning in cobwebs, too high for her mother to reach. 'But why should women and children have to wait around for men?'

'Oh, Alice. You would say that.'

'Told they are weaker, then made to suffer unspeakable things. Forced to be victims. Have to delight in the pain.'

'You think that shows her as weak?' She makes a clicking noise with her throat. 'My mother was strong. She endured.'

Zelda looks at her. 'Oh, Mum.'

Her mother takes a seat at the table. They are opposite each other now.

Unable to look at her, Marjorie stares through the back door at the rusty metal chains of Alice's childhood swing. 'See. You think you are strong. But you ran. Like *him*' – she nods towards the window, towards the tin house – 'blaming me for what happened. You always were like your father.'

'I thought I was going to die.'

'*I* endured it,' Marjorie says, pressing the tip of her finger on the table. 'The bruises on my mother's face and sometimes on my own. Why are you so different?'

Zelda sees now the futility of her attempt. Confronting the darkness of her daughter's past would force her mother to examine her own pain in a new light. Marjorie would have to surrender the idea of her mother being strong as she bears the brunt of punches. To give up the illusion that Zelda is weak, she must abandon her mother as a saviour. Zelda looks at her sitting across the table, shrinking into death. What good would it do now for her mother to discover her truth was a myth? She was right when she said she wasn't strong enough to lift her. There is only so much sadness a person can take.

Marjorie leans forward. 'Don't you want to live forever?'

A timber lorry passes. Its thunder shakes the house.

'I'm living right now, Mum, and you want nothing to do with me.'

'Now you're being deliberately ignorant. You went through a bad thing. So do many people. Scripture doesn't change just because you decide to view it differently. Come back and all will be made right.'

Zelda sees the pictures on the front of the fridge. Finger paintings, felt-tipped drawings, *Alice* scrawled along the top. She always drew houses the same, and a trio for a family. Here, photos of her have been replaced by childish dreams. Here, her mother wants the child, not the woman she became.

'You can't force belief,' says Zelda. 'Why should I lose everlasting life because of how my brain sees it? Because God let them cover over truth? Whose fault is that, really?'

'How could I have raised such stubbornness?' her mother mutters, peeling the label on a bottle of squash. 'I don't make the rules, my girl.'

Zelda stares at the fridge door. 'We come from darkness and go back to darkness. A few decades of light.' She looks up at the gloomy ceiling. 'I can't lie any more, Mum.'

Her mother's chair creaks as she leans back. 'I don't know anything about darkness.'

Zelda gets up. She presses her palms flat against the chipped melamine and waits. But there is no movement from across the table. Not even a flicker.

Outside, the air is clean. Outside, she can breathe again.

Postcards

Isobel

Isobel goes there straight away.

She stands behind an old phone-box, where she has the advantage of not being seen. The entrance to the office building is cavernous glass, and those exiting half-spin in a hamster wheel before being spewed out in suits on to the pavement. Isobel watches every face.

When her daughter comes out, she is frowning at her phone, and panic seizes Isobel. *She knows. Someone has told her. Look out, your mother's on her way.* But now she slips it into her bag, giving an absent-minded glance at the grey sky, and is about to turn off towards the car park when she hears:

'Cassandra!'

Her daughter stops. She turns, her face stunned.

'What do you want?' says Cassandra, looking around.

'I-I . . .'

'You shouldn't be here.' She walks away.

Isobel watches her go. Everyone says Cassandra is her double. Is this how she looks from behind? She stares at the back of her daughter's head, and, for a split-second, sees herself walking.

'Wait,' she calls, stepping forward. 'Please, Cassandra. We must talk.'

Cassandra stops. She sighs with her whole body – 'Fine' – then gestures to the park across the road. 'In there. But don't walk beside me.'

They go in through the gate and follow the path as it twists and curves. The park is a rectangle of grass surrounded by lush plants and mature trees, with a pencil line of iron railing keeping it contained. Isobel walks a few feet behind. They do not talk until they

321

come to a quiet bench, hidden from the road. Cassandra waits until Isobel has sat down, then takes a seat at the other end.

'How was work?'

Cassandra frowns. 'That can't be your question.'

'I only get one, then?'

She sighs. 'Work was fine. Actually, I've just been offered a promotion.'

'Oh? That's nice.'

'Yes, well, I'm not going to take it.'

'Why not?'

'Because it would mean far more hours and stress. The money would be useful, but I've enough stress already. I don't need to miss meetings and ministry too.'

'You shouldn't be stressed at your age.'

Cassandra stares at her, then looks away. 'Right.'

'Remind me what you do?'

She laughs. 'Same job I've done for eight years, Mum.'

'Well, my memory's not what it was.'

'And I'm not Patrick, of course.'

'Okay. This is where it's going, then.'

'I don't know, Mum,' says Cassandra, bristling. 'I don't even know why you're here.'

Isobel opens and shuts her mouth. Should she move further along and close the chasm between them? Which news to start with? That her father should be in jail? No, perhaps that should be softened. Perhaps sacrifice herself first.

'I'm getting married, Cassandra.'

The words settle, pushing them further apart. Cassandra's face has no expression. Isobel pulls her jacket tight against the breeze.

'But the ink's hardly dry on your divorce,' Cassandra says, her voice flat.

'That's my fault, is it? Nothing to do with your father.'

'Daddy? You're going to blame Daddy for this, this . . . *dalliance* with a worldly man? That's obviously who it is. I hear he's some biker with greasy hair and a beard.'

Isobel looks down at her lap, smiling. 'Yes, that describes him very well.' She feels Cassandra's eyes, and her daughter shakes her head.

'Who *are* you?'

Isobel pauses. 'Is it a problem that I'm finally taking control of my life?'

Cassandra stares at her. 'You don't care about being disfellowshipped. You're revelling in it.'

'No, that's not true.'

'This carrying on . . . Who even is this man?'

'He's wonderful, Cassandra. Yes, he has long hair' – Isobel laughs as she thinks of his face – 'and he rides a motorcycle and he's untidy and he's . . . wonderful.' She remembers her audience. 'Besides, I didn't deserve to get disfellowshipped. Up until then, nothing had actually happened.'

Cassandra gives a triumphant smile. 'Oh, so it has now. Same thing, then. The elders were right to disfellowship, because they knew you'd be deceitful.'

'And that's okay, is it?' asks Isobel, quietly. 'To punish someone before they commit a crime? There's no responsibility on their behalf to avoid being the reason someone makes a false step?'

'They're doing the best they can.'

Isobel looks at her. 'We're all doing the best we can.'

Cassandra shifts on the bench. 'I don't know why you've come here to tell me this. To *gloat*. It's not as if I'd go to your wedding.'

'No, I know. That wasn't the only reason. I . . . Cassandra, did your father ever . . . When you were a child, did . . .' Isobel takes a deep breath. She cannot give life to the words. 'Have you spoken to him?'

Cassandra looks away. 'Of course not.'

'Has he tried getting in touch?'

She bites her lip. 'I ignore him. Like I should you.'

'And you will always ignore him, yes? You won't ever contact him?'

Cassandra's voice is cold. 'Can you stop with these questions? He's disfellowshipped. I won't have anything to do with someone who's disfellowshipped.' She stands.

Isobel's hand flies out to stop her. 'No, Cassandra, don't go.' Her fingers brush her arm.

Cassandra jumps and stares at Isobel's outstretched hand. She steps forward, her eyes moving up and down the path, her body breathing heavily. Then she sits down, turned away from her mother.

Isobel cannot bring herself to ask outright, but she knows the answer already. She sighs with relief, for once pleased to see how much Steven is loved. And then it makes her feel very small, like she is falling.

'Do you remember when you were little,' says Isobel, 'and you would scream about the ends of steel pipes on the back of a van, or scaly fruit at the supermarket?'

Cassandra folds her arms. 'How you would tell me off for making a scene? Yes, I remember.'

'You said they made you feel sick. And honeycomb. Or close-up pictures of cells.'

'And I feel sick just thinking of it now. What of it?'

Isobel turns to her, words tripping as they rush out. 'I read an article recently about how scientists are researching a fear of holes or clusters called Trypophobia. Apparently the sight can cause disgust in people because they resemble diseases. I read it and thought *Cassandra was right!* She was right all along. And I told her she was ridiculous.' Isobel grips her hands. 'I need to tell you that you're not ridiculous.'

There is a long pause. There is just the traffic on the road, and the wind in the trees, and a valley between them.

'I've got one,' says Cassandra. 'A story.'

Isobel waits.

Cassandra's words are slow. 'The parents go away for a week and leave their daughter with grandparents. She's too young to remember. She knows it happened only because when she grew up, she found an album of postcards. The mother had sent one every day. The pictures were the usual sunsets, beaches and flowers. But on the back were the most extraordinary things. Words. *My darling, I miss the scent of your head* and *Only three more days till you're in my arms.* When

324

she got older, the daughter recognized the handwriting, her name and address. But those words were strangers. They taunted her. They still do.'

Isobel pulls her bag on to her lap. She remembers the holiday, somewhere in Greece where the weather was hot and unbearable, but there is nothing in her memory of postcards. 'Your father wanted to play a golf tournament,' she says. 'So I went with him. The dutiful wife.'

Her daughter turns, but Isobel keeps her eyes ahead. 'I know you think your father was the soft one, but he was never around, so he could be. He was also the one who insisted we leave you behind.'

'Were we really that dreadful?'

Isobel thinks of her daughter's birth and those lost months, when she dreamt of disappearing into the walls. 'Cassandra, you have no children of your own, so it's impossible to understand.'

'No, I don't,' she replies. 'Have you never wondered why?'

Isobel puts down her bag. She leans forward, then back again, pushing her hands down hard on her knees. 'You were always fine, though,' she says, her voice harsher than she intends. 'You rarely cried or asked for anything. It was as if you were born not needing me at all.'

'Why cry for someone who wasn't there?'

'Not there? I left the bank so I could be with you night and day.'

Cassandra stares ahead.

'Like I said, you were born independent. And your instinct was always to do the opposite. If I told you something was hot, you touched it deliberately. You'd put a hand over a flame and hold it there. Do you remember? When you burned yourself on the candle? You didn't cry, not even then.'

'I wanted to feel something, Mum.'

Isobel's voice is laced with hysteria, the opposite of how she thought she would be. I'm happy now, she said to herself in the bathroom mirror that morning. I'm a changed person. I'm done with all that was. So why is she now reverting back to how she always dealt with Cassandra? Why is she taking them further apart?

A dog-walker passes by, throwing them a curious glance, and Isobel sees how they look to the outside world. Opposite ends of the bench. Talking in different directions. The bookies' money would be on their arranging a drug deal or hitman. Nobody would guess they were mother and daughter, however the genes appeared.

'Cassie,' she says, and her hand flies to her mouth as her daughter flinches. Only Steven called her that.

Cassandra stands. 'It's too late, Mum. It's too late.'

A Way Out

Jen

She spent many childhood minutes staring at dead flies on window-sills. The house was regularly cleaned, but the flies still built up. Jen would imagine the final moments of their lives, banging their heads against the glass as they searched for a way out. Finally, they stopped.

She looked around and saw the room for what it was. A death chamber. Looking closer, she examined the fly and its bulbous eyes, the paper-thin finery of its wings.

I'm sorry, she whispered. It's the fault of the builder who built this room, or the architect, or the person who wanted a house, or perhaps even the inventor of glass, who made something clear when it wasn't. Her brain searched further and further back through time, its childish logic searching for the source of blame. She was taught that blame always lies somewhere.

It wasn't the fly's fault. She was certain of that. It didn't want to die. She didn't understand why the fly should have to suffer because of the actions of everyone else.

Let Us Pray

Jen

Jen reapplies her lipstick in the car mirror. She picks a flake of mascara from her cheek and smooths her hair. The growing-out stage of her crop is torture. How simple it was when short. And how that seems like years ago.

A car pulls up behind, and, in the mirror, she watches Susanna do the same. Mirror, check, a hand to the hair. Jen opens the door.

'Hey, you,' Susanna says, jumping out. She zips up her parka over her jumper and knee-length skirt.

'Love your shoes,' says Jen, taking out her ministry bag.

'Ah, thanks. Got them from Emma at a clothes party last night.' Susanna does a little twirl in her burgundy Mary Janes.

'Clothes party?'

'Yeah. You bring stuff you don't wear any more to sell or swap with other people. Always a bargain to be had. I'll let you know next time? There're always a ton of sisters there.'

'You've done your hair differently too.'

Susanna laughs. 'You're always so observant.'

Jen smiles and pretends to search through her bag.

'Have you got enough mags?' says Susanna. 'I have spares if not.'

'Think so. I'm finding this month's tough.' Jen holds it up. *Help for Those Who Grieve.*

'Ah, I bet.' Susanna squeezes her arm. 'Not long now.'

They begin walking along the pavement, their arms linked. Jen closes her eyes as she inhales Susanna's scent. No, she says inside. Tear out your eyes, rip out your heart. Do not go there.

They wave at sisters going into a house at the end of the road. Jen and Susanna talk, their heads close together, not noticing the red-headed woman on the other side of the street.

'Jen!'

Susanna turns to look at the woman, then back at Jen, who stares straight ahead. She has to nudge her.

Finally, Jen turns.

Zelda steps off the pavement. She carries a white garment bag, but manages a wave and two small words. 'Hey, you.'

Jen smiles, her face tight and blushing. Time seems to slow down on the street – a car crawls past at a glacial pace – and she knows they are waiting for her to speak. She has the distinct feeling of being found doing something she shouldn't, but it's unclear to her which of the two women has caught her out. She pulls Susanna along.

'Who was that?' Susanna whispers when they're out of earshot.

'Nobody. Just someone I used to know.'

There are seven of them in the dining room, Bibles resting on the polka-dot vinyl tablecloth. They laugh together. Everyone greets Jen and Susanna as they take a seat.

'Ben's running late,' says a woman, looking down at her phone. 'He says to start the group without him. We're doing Northern Road, apparently. He'll meet us there and organize who's working with who.'

'Northern Road. That's the one with the flats, isn't it?' says an older woman with hair too dark for her age. She groans. 'I hate doing flats.'

'Oh, I love them,' says a girl of around nineteen. She has glossy, blonde hair and is admiring her own fingernails. 'You just ring the bell and speak through the intercom. *Hi, would you like to read the magazines?* Done. No messing about.'

'Some of us do enjoy doing presentations, Michelle,' says Susanna, laughing. 'We're not slackers.'

'What can I say?' says Michelle, then turns to the man beside her. 'Looks like you're doing the prayer, Sid.'

Sid is the only man present. In his early seventies, he's a shy, reserved brother who rarely talks. He looks at the women. 'No, no, I can't.'

'Nora, tell him,' Michelle says, still checking her nails.

Nora leans forward. 'You've got to, Sid. You're the only brother here.'

Sid doesn't reply, but continues shaking his head. He looks like he's going to cry.

The women all stare at each other.

Nora sighs. 'Best get a tea-towel, then.' She gets up and goes through the kitchen door.

'Well, I'm not doing it,' Michelle says, touching her hair. 'It took me half an hour to do this braid and I'm not messing it up.'

Nobody speaks.

Jen leans forward. 'Here,' she says, reaching out for the towel. She drapes it over her head and ignores the mirror. Michelle's hand concealing her laughter is all the reflection she needs.

Everyone bows their heads as Jen stands.

'Dear heavenly Father,' she begins, and hopes the holy spirit will take care of the rest.

The Colours of Life
Isobel and Zelda

Zelda walks to the end of the street. With every step, the garment bag weighs more heavily in her arms, and she regrets taking the first parking space she found. She hadn't thought the road would be so long, but here she is, half a mile on, still not there.

Finally, Zelda reaches the house. She checks it's the right place, then climbs the steps to the front door, where she presses the button marked ATTIC FLAT. The door clicks open.

Isobel is at the top of the stairs, leaning over the banister. Her hair is wet and her bare face wears a huge smile. 'What's wrong?' she says, when Zelda reaches the top. She touches Zelda's arm, her expression now worried. 'Is there news?'

Zelda shakes her head. 'It's fine. Let's get you married.'

They have seen each other many times over the past few weeks. When Zelda gave the police a statement, Isobel came too, giving details of Steven's last-known address. The police were kind, listening to Zelda and acknowledging what she said. They promised to do everything to track him down. When the interview ended, Zelda stood on the station steps and cried. She'd been listened to. She'd been heard. A weight had been put down.

Isobel took her for coffee afterwards and didn't push her to talk. She let Zelda be. Zelda was surprised by this. Her reckoning of Isobel Forge was of a woman who had to fill a silence. We're a hundred different faces, she thought, all trying to look out.

Zelda has repaid her with the dress. Just as Isobel has been by her side, she has been by hers. Pinning, fixing, adjusting a hem.

The flat is bathed in sunlight, and Zelda stares open-mouthed at Isobel.

'I know,' says Isobel, her cheeks flushed. 'The light. It's something else.'

Zelda unzips the garment bag, taking out the dress, and now it is Isobel who gasps. 'Oh,' she says, holding her heart. 'And there I was, wondering how it would be.'

Ivory silk tulle. Butterfly-wing arms. Ruched and gathered and flowing. Across the dress are embroidered splashes of colour – hot pinks, reds, golds, all entwined around green branches. The colours of life.

They begin with hair. Isobel sits on a stool near the window as Zelda styles the soft waves. There is none of the morning chaos Zelda usually sees at a wedding. No bridesmaids jostling for a mirror or open suitcases splayed out on the floor. Just the two of them and the occasional line of conversation.

'Butterflies yet?' says Zelda, as she picks up a palette and brush.

'Should I? Because I'm not nervous at all. I'm perfectly calm, as if –'

'It's totally right?'

Isobel smiles as Zelda stands back and studies her face. They have agreed on minimal make-up, to allow – as Zelda calls it – Isobel's glow to shine. She doesn't want to look like a different person, even though she feels transformed.

When Isobel is ready, Zelda leaves to fetch the car. She drives slowly up the road, past the space where Jen had been and where another car now sits. She keeps going until she sees the bride on the steps.

'Smells lovely in here,' says Isobel, getting in.

'Really? Of what?'

Isobel takes a deep inhale. 'Orange blossoms.'

They drive on to the register office, where Victor waits outside to meet them. He wears a smart, checked suit and his hair is freshly trimmed, and when she sees him, Isobel is overwhelmed by the strength of her feeling.

Zelda watches him help Isobel out of the car, and the tenderness between them as he kisses her nose and shakes his head at how she looks.

'Speechless,' he says.

Will is there too. As she walks towards him in her seventies trouser suit, he shakes his head and gives a chef's kiss. She laughs. He leans in to kiss her under her wide-brimmed hat. 'There you are,' he whispers.

After the ceremony, Zelda takes their portrait. There is a group photo on the steps, and Isobel feels a rush of grief as Victor's children stand beside them. She pushes the thought away. Look how much can change in a year, she thinks. And another year is coming.

They go to a local fish-and-chips restaurant, where they've been allowed to bring their own champagne. The napkins are paper, the peas are mushy, the love is real. Zelda watches Isobel's face. How she is lit from inside. Victor clasps her hand and gives it the occasional kiss. The gentleness of it all makes Zelda's heart ache.

'A toast,' she says, and raises her glass. 'To second chances.'

Isobel laughs and clinks every glass with her own.

Everyone gathers afterwards to throw confetti and cheer the happy couple as they ride away. Isobel holds tightly to Victor as the bike speeds off from the waving guests. Zelda is the last to put down her hand. She stands in the final rays of sun and thinks of Isobel, and Jen too.

It was strange, she thought, how a person could behave in a different way than expected, and it wasn't that they'd changed, exactly. We just didn't see them before.

Acknowledgements

Huge thanks to my editor Jillian Taylor and the team at Penguin Michael Joseph who have brought this book to print, as well as my agent Madeleine Milburn, Liv Maidment and everyone at MMA.

I am ever grateful to my friends and family who show up. My one wild and precious life would not be the same without you.

The women in this book go through certain experiences unknown to me, and I pay tribute to the survivors I have known in my life. My fictional words can never sum up your strength.

The talk given by an elder on page 173 is inspired by the real-life talk given by a member of the governing body to an audience that included young children, and can currently be found on YouTube.

The findings of the Australian Royal Commission into the handling of child sexual abuse within the religion I was raised in played an integral role in the creation of this book. The methods and ways in which abuse victims were individually treated by the faith in the novel have been lifted from the court documents and videos, which are freely available online.

Truth should always be tested. How else to know if it's true?